Wapiti regional library

No Good Deed

Also by Manda Scott

Hen's Teeth
Night Mares
Stronger Than Death

Wapiti regional library

Manda Scott

No Good Deed

PAPL
DISCARDED

HEADLINE
FEATURE

Copyright © 2001 Manda Scott

The right of Manda Scott to be identified as the Author of
the Work has been asserted by her in accordance with the
Copyright, Designs and Patents Act 1988.

First published in Great Britain in 2001
by HEADLINE BOOK PUBLISHING

A HEADLINE FEATURE hardback
10 9 8 7 6 5 4 3 2 1

All rights reserved. No part of this publication may be
reproduced, stored in a retrieval system, or transmitted,
in any form or by any means without the prior written
permission of the publisher, nor be otherwise circulated
in any form of binding or cover other than that in which
it is published and without a similar condition being
imposed on the subsequent purchaser.

All characters in this publication are fictitious
and any resemblance to real persons, living or dead,
is purely coincidental.

British Library Cataloguing in Publication Data

Scott, Manda
 No good deed
 1. Suspense fiction
 I. Title
 823.9'14 [F]

ISBN 0 7472 7345 6 (hardback)
ISBN 0 7472 7346 4 (trade paperback)

Typeset by Palimpsest Book Production Limited,
Polmont, Stirlingshire
Printed and bound in Great Britain by
Mackays of Chatham plc, Chatham, Kent

HEADLINE BOOK PUBLISHING
A division of Hodder Headline
338 Euston Road
London NW1 3BH

www.headline.co.uk
www.hodderheadline.com

For my mother and for Naziema, with love

A great many people provided invaluable help and moral support during the process of writing this book. Most will go unmentioned but I am nonetheless grateful. A few of the key ones were: Robin, who helped with the geology, provided a place of peace to escape to and made it possible to climb; Nick, from Jones' online who made astute comments on firearms; Steve, who rescued my hard drive from imminent disaster and Jane Judd, my agent, who acted far beyond the call of duty to make completion possible. To all of these my heartfelt thanks with the usual proviso that any defects, misinterpretations or factual inaccuracies are mine alone. Continued thanks to Chloë and Debs for intelligent, constructive criticism of the various drafts and to Chaz for sanity by e-mail.

One

---◆◆◆---

Summer

In the long list of early prisoner releases, his was one of the least remarked; ostensibly a gift to both sides, in practice, welcomed by neither. He walked out of the gates at nine o'clock on the morning of the thirteenth of June, twenty-one years and three months to the day since they had first locked him up. The world lay in the grip of a heat wave so that the air shimmered above the tarmac and it was cooler by far inside than out. He hung around for a while, as if testing the heat and humidity of the air, an act that did nothing to endear him to those watching. In time, he stooped at the driver's door of the car waiting at the kerbside and then the one inside got out and he took over the wheel. There was a moment when it seemed he might have left his companion standing on the pavement outside the gates but he relented and the younger man, whose face was already on file and who was hardly an easy touch, was invited into the passenger side.

He counted three of them following, in varying rotations, in front or behind, as the car passed east towards the ferry at Larne. Two passengers and a very striking red-headed cabin assistant kept their eyes on him on the crossing to Stranraer. At the terminal, they handed him over to their Scottish counterparts and a different three watched him wave goodbye to his escort and rent a car. They followed in two cars on the road up to Glasgow. He took the tunnel and then the switchback and led them out to the pine forests at the southern tip of Loch Lomond where he let himself into a self-catering cabin on the shores of the loch. The school holidays not yet being underway, half of the remaining six cabins in the group were conveniently empty and the watchers, with some gratitude, took up position in those on either side of the mark.

An hour after the man's arrival, he had a visitor. One of the city's more expensive whores, a woman with known connections in Ulster, drove up to the door, knocked twice and was granted admission. The watchers, all of whom were young and male, rigged up a microphone and directed it at the bedroom window, recording the results for later posterity. It was thus added to the file that the mark was not fluent in gutter Glaswegian but that his appetites were as diverse as might be expected in any man who has spent his third and fourth decades locked in a cell. The woman left in the early evening and the watchers had no more entertainment than the sound of a man breathing heavily in his sleep.

It was a newer, less seasoned watcher who recognised, around five o'clock the following morning, that she had heard the same pattern of breathing repeated three times in the space of two hours. No one likes to be woken before dawn for the sake of it and so she took the time to play the tape into a portable computer and compare the exact shape of the wave forms before she rang through to her superiors and asked for back-up and permission to break in. At six thirty, the combat team found a dead woman lying on the single bed beside a tape recorder that played a continuous loop of a man's breathing. The received wisdom from those on the scene was that the dead woman had been strangled. The pathologist's report later in the day suggested instead that the ring of purpled bruises on the neck occurred at least twenty-four hours ante-mortem and that the cause of death was, in fact, a simple fracture of the vertebral column between the third and fourth cervical vertebrae. Bruising on the left lower chin and the upper right parietal region showed where the heels of both hands had been applied to achieve the twist. Later examination of the records found this to be the cause of death in at least one previous recorded killing by the same target.

A watch was put on all known associates but was called off on the grounds of wasted expense after a month with no result. A full case report was lodged with Interpol to the effect that the suspect was loose, whereabouts and intentions unknown. It is an unfortunate testament to the technological age that all those involved felt a computer flag to be a sufficient warning to the local police forces and no one deemed it necessary, or even useful, to pick up the phone and tell the one person who might really have needed to know that Colm Connaught O'Neil was out and looking for trouble.

Spring
Friday, 14 March

'Jamie?'

The child opened his eyes. It was dark in the room, darker than it had been, and there was snow feathering down the outside of the window. They had promised it for Christmas and it came instead for Easter, a gift from the god to make the world a cleaner, purer place. Large flakes flared orange in the sodium glare of the streetlight and piled in drifts against the lower sill, tinged to yellow by the years of filth and tobacco smoke staining the glass.

'Jamie? Can you hear me?' The child was entranced by the snow. He watched the patterns of it grow before his eyes and let the voice wash over him. 'Jamie? Please? I need your help.' The voice was smooth, like the glass, but warmer. It flowed around him, easing the pain. He curled tighter in his chair and turned his face to the dark. The snow had deadened all the other sounds as the evening gave way to night; the noise of cars in the street, the kick-out from the pubs, the smash of a bottle dropping from the top of a neighbouring tenement down onto the street below, the lacerating give and take of a beating taking place somewhere far away but not quite out of earshot. That pain was not his. In these small things, life was kind.

Inside the room the quality of the quiet was different. His mother and her friend had been silent long since but there was no surprise in that. He had seen the needles and the small ritual of injection. He knew the pattern of this and the time it would last and he knew he was safe, from that quarter at least, for most of the darkness. The other sound, the voice, was new and uncomfortable. Usually nobody spoke and if they did, it was simplest often not to listen. He had a lot of practice in not listening. Watch the things that move beyond the window and don't listen. That way is safe.

'Jamie? Jamie, listen. The men will come back soon and when they do, they will hurt you again. You know that. If you help me, I can stop them.' The voice was soft and low, and the accent strange, like the ones on the news, entirely unlike the flat vowels and guttural glottal stops of his world. He couldn't place the voice and that worried him. He hunched his shoulders, pulling himself smaller, blocking out the noise. It came through all the same. 'Jamie? It's me, Sandra. Trust me. I can get us out of here. But you have to help me first.'

Sandra. He struggled to fit a face to the name. An image came of flashing amber eyes with black stripes flaring outwards, like a tiger. The thought made him smile. He turned into the dark of the room. 'Jamie?' She sounded more hopeful. 'Over here. Under the sofa.' Under the sofa? Now that really was strange. With regret, he watched one last layer of snow build on the sill and then he left the safety of his chair.

The sulphured glow of the streetlights pushed in a semi-circle as far as the television but beyond it the room was as black as the night outside. The stench of stale cigarette smoke, cheap scent and congealing chow mein hung, waiting, in the darkness. By the window, the air was cold and clean and welcoming. He nearly turned back but the voice drew him on. 'Jamie? Not much further now.' So he went on, feeling his way forward, past the bottles and the needles, the remains of the takeaway and the debris of clothing, to the inert bulk of his mother's body. She lay across the sofa, locked in a sleeping embrace with one of the other two women. He searched among the tangle of limbs and heads for the flash of light from the eyes. 'Underneath,' said the voice. He crouched down on the floor. She was right. There was, indeed, a woman lying underneath the sofa. His eyes were adjusting slowly to the absence of light but even in the gloom he could see the pale skin on the undersides of her arms with the flat white planes of the old scars and the fresh patterns around them of handprints and bruises. Her hair was crushed and matted, a scarecrow's nest in bottle blonde with the streaks of scarlet through it that matched the fake suede of her skirt. A glimmer of gold pulsed at her navel, rising and falling with the steady rhythm of her breathing. With difficulty, because the space from the base of the sofa to the floor was not great and the weight of his mother made it less than it might have been, she turned her head to look at him. That wasn't good. Her face was a mess – more of a mess than usual and only partly because her make-up had gone. He had watched her in the mornings as she sat on the edge of the bath, using the only mirror in the house to help her paint her face, and he knew the care she took to hide the things she didn't want the world to see. Now the world could see what it liked, and more. A fresh bruise, bleeding at the centre, ran across one cheekbone and up to the inside corner of her eye. On the other side, the stark white snake-line of an old scar bisected one eyebrow and ran on down the side of her nose to make a notch on the edge of her upper lip. On her temple, a palm's breadth of smooth white burn tissue pulled the skin tight angling up the edge of one eye, so that it seemed as if she were forever doubting what he said. Then she blinked and the eyes gathered him in and he was lost. He was entranced by her eyes. He knelt down and put his head level with hers and peered into them. She smiled for him then and it was a new smile, crooked and conspiratorial and really very warm. He chewed his lip for a moment, thinking, then he lay flat on his stomach and put his head on one side, looked into her eyes and smiled back. She laughed at that, soft and breathless and sliding into something not quite controlled that lasted longer than either of them expected. She caught herself, eventually, and breathed deep so that the navel stud rolled on the wave of it.

'Jamie, sunshine, you're gorgeous and I love you dearly but this is really, really not the right time. I need to get out of here, kiddo. I'm no good to either of us like this. Do you think you could try to untie me? Just one hand, I can do the rest.'

He sat up on his heels for a better look and saw what the dark had hidden before; that each wrist, each ankle, was fixed tight to one leg of the sofa. The hand nearest him twitched, palm out, the fingers waggling like the legs of a dying spider. The voice wove out around it. 'Jamie? Can you see the knots?' He could. He nodded. 'I can't see you anymore, sunshine. You'll have to speak to me.' He thought about that for a while and decided safer not. Instead, he put his hand down to touch the palm then moved to the rope. 'All right, good lad.' There was a new warmth to the voice. 'Now, can you untie it. Please?' Another novelty. 'Please' was not part of his everyday vocabulary by any stretch of the imagination. He felt around the square-sharp edges of the wood to the opposite side where the knots gathered. 'You might need to use your teeth to loosen them.'

He tried. He tried for the novelty of being asked, for her smile and for the memory of the tiger's eyes. He tried until the rope was wet with his spit and his fingers slid across it as he tugged. All the while he listened to her breathing, slow and even, and the steady words of encouragement. And the promises. He listened most to the promises.

'Jamie, if you can get me out of here before they come back, I promise you, I'll take you away from here. There's a cottage in the country, with a mountain at the back of it and you can see the sea from the front door and there's a bedroom you can have all your own. Would you like that, Jamie? But we need to get free, both of us, or none of it will happen and what happens instead will be . . . don't think about that. Think about the cottage. And the snow. Think about the snow, Jamie. With the weather we've been having, the snow will be six feet thick outside. We can take sledges up the mountain and race them down to the back door. We can make snowmen as tall as the house. I can make you an igloo outside the back door and you can sleep in it overnight and still be warm. Would you like that kind of snow, Jamie?'

He did like the idea of such snow and although he had no idea what an igloo was he thought he might like that too. But liking it didn't get the rope untied, in fact, if anything, the wet of his spit was swelling the fibre and making it tighter. He sat back on his heels and bit a nail in frustration and without really thinking about it, he said, 'Can't.'

There was a brief silence and then, 'Can't you? Bugger it. Well, never mind, you can talk. That's something.' The voice was still calm. If he'd said 'can't' to his mother, the screaming would have gone on till his head rang. 'OK. Don't panic. They're not finished downstairs yet.' They weren't, although if you stopped to listen to it, the sounds of pain were different. There was a sense of things accelerating towards a close. He shut his ears and turned back to the snow. It was piling deeper on the sill and the swirls of filth on the glass made new and interesting patterns. He moved back towards his chair.

'Jamie, no! Don't crap out on me now. We're still in with a chance. We need a knife. Can you find a knife for me, Jamie?' There was a grating edge in the voice now. Threads of panic wove through it, dangerously seductive. He knew panic well. It was not a place he wanted to be. The snow drew him closer. It was falling faster so that the world outside the window was more white than black and the flakes were smaller, almost like dust. He reached the chair and curled himself into it.

'Jamie. Listen to me. The snow will melt soon. The rain will come back. What will you have then? Do you really want to go on living like this? Jamie? Are you listening to me? Jamie?'

He wasn't listening. He curled tighter and shut the voice out.

'Shit.'

And then there was nothing. The snow fell dizzyingly fast. He could have slept, hypnotised by the swirling speed of it, but the final word echoed round the inside of his head. *Shit.* Just that. A single sound, more of a breath than a word, full of defeat and fear and the promise of pain and all the things he was used to. But there was a kind of dry, twisting humour with it that he wasn't used to at all. It was a voice to go with the smile and the eyes. He listened to it stir round in his head for a while, feeling the newness of it and then he slid down from the chair and padded out across the hallway to the dark pit of the kitchen. The bread knife was in the washing-up bowl. He found it eventually, fished it out and dried it and took it back to the sofa and knelt down so that she could see it in his hands. He thought she might cry at the sight of him but she didn't. She smiled instead, which was good.

'Jamie, I love you. Can you cut the rope, sweetheart? See if you can slide the knife down behind my hand and the wood . . .' He heard the suck of an indrawn breath, bitten off, and then, 'Yes. Good lad. Now, move it up and down. Good. Push it outwards, it needs to bite on the rope. Like that. More. Good. Don't stop now, kiddo, for God's sake, don't stop now . . . yes.' That last, whispered exultation as the final strand parted and then, 'Thank you.'

She worked her fingers for a moment, gripping and re-gripping the hilt of the knife until the life came back to them. She swore with the heat of that but not for long. When she could trust herself to move, she eased across and freed her other hand on her own. He had to help her with her feet because there wasn't room for her to reach down but they came quicker because he knew what he was doing and he didn't make her bleed. He cut the last piece of rope binding her left ankle and then knelt out of the way as she slithered sideways towards him. 'Jamie, I love you forever.' She hugged him tight, running her fingers in the tangled straw of his hair. The amber eyes flashed for him, pulling in the orange light from the window, spinning it round and throwing it out like a beacon. She kissed him, just lightly, on his forehead and smiled so that, for one long moment, his world filled with colour.

And then, because it was magic, and magic never lasts, the colours faded. The woman was shaking. He realised that when he realised she wasn't smiling anymore. It could have been the cold. He would have liked it to be the cold but her skin was grey, the way his mother's went grey when she was up on the smack and the shakes had that extra tremor that said it was more than the perennial problem of too few clothes in an unheated room. He searched her arms for the signs of the needle and found it – a single exploded vein spreading out on the ghosted flesh of her inner arm. She saw him looking and shook her head. 'It wasn't me, kiddo.' But his mother said that often enough and his mother's teeth chattered in much the same way as she said it. He looked into her eyes and the colours were already less bright. The smile was forced as perhaps it had been forced before. The arms that held him let him go. 'Jamie, trust me. We can talk about it later. Just now we have to get you out of here.' He said nothing. Outside, a man cried out, a desperate, long-drawn sound, rising up the scales to fracture in agony at the top. The silence rang loud in its wake. Her head snapped up at the noise of it. 'Oh, Jesus Christ, *Luke*,' and then, in a voice from which all colour and all tremor had gone, she said, 'Stay here. I won't be long.'

She was taller than his mother and lithe and she moved with a feral, fluid grace and a sense of purpose that his mother lacked. He heard the scuff of her bare feet as she ran up the stairs. The light tread moved across the ceiling above him towards the bedroom and something happened in a cupboard and then she was back, standing beside him, fastening a pack round her waist and staring out of the window with an intensity that all but stopped the shaking. She had changed, he could feel it. Sandra-before was all scarlet plastic and east Glasgow vowels and a laugh that could cut through glass. If she spoke to him, it was to get him to bed, out of the way, and she did it as if he was invisible, which meant that he was. Sandra-under-the-sofa was a friend in the darkness, wide amber eyes and a smile that broke through the silence. Sandra-now was different and not necessarily pleasant. He was setting off down the road to nowhere but she shook her head and nodded forwards and so he stopped and in time he realised that she was listening, not looking, and then, when he let go of the snow and listened with her, he could hear what she could hear, which was nothing. Under all the small, wilderness cries of the night, the sounds of the beating had ended.

In the enclosed space of his world, where all women wear cheap plastic miniskirts and all men mete out violence, the end of it somewhere else means only that it is coming closer. He shrugged deep in the chair and bit his lip and started in earnest back down the track to the other world where he would be invisible in this one.

'No. Not now.' A hand fell light on his shoulder. 'We need to get you out of here while there's still time. Get your shoes and we'll . . . oh, shit, no we won't . . .'

Down at street level, a door slammed shut. Hard boots and harder voices filled the stairwell. '*Fuck.*' The fingers tightened in frustration, digging hard through his T-shirt to the collarbone below. It hurt. He turned round to protest but she had already let go and there was a gun in her hand that had, perhaps, been there all along and a shine in her eyes that was quite the opposite of the magic he had seen before. He might have tried to run from her then but the hand came back to his arm and the voice that went with the eyes said, 'Don't move, Jamie. Just sit here and look out of the window and whatever else happens, don't move a muscle. Stay invisible, kid. You can do it. I won't be far.'

And then she was gone, feather-footed, out across the hallway to the dank pit of the kitchen, and there was time enough for a single oversized flake to spiral down the full length of the window before the front door smashed open and the world caved in.

Three. The redhead with halitosis, the blond with the beard who gave the orders and the obese grunt with the gun and the novel uses for living-room furniture. She stood behind the kitchen door with her eye to the crack at the hinge and she had the silencer tight on the barrel as the first of them reached the top of the stairs. The doing of it helped with the shaking but not as much as she needed. Luke, grinning, spoke in her head. *Keep it still, kiddo. You won't bit a barn door if you wiggle the end of it round like that.* Luke. I don't need to hit a barn door. I need to hit three men, and I need not to hit a boy. Then I can come and find you. Just stay alive for me now. He shook his head, still grinning, and the echo of his last cry looped round and back in her skull.

They crashed in through the front door, all three of them together, loud and drunk with the power of another man's pain. The smell of fresh blood washed past her in giddying waves, a rising tide that pushed ahead of the beer and the sweat and the reek of his fear. She breathed in the mess of it and breathed out his name. In: hell. Out: Luke. *They will pay for this, I promise you.* The first one passed the crack in the hinge and she counted each of them through to the living room opposite; redhead, blondie, fatso. Three . . . two . . . one ˙. . .

Now!

The fat one died first.

Her arms moved with a will of their own and the mouth of her gun hung in the air an inch behind his ear. The round mass of his head was bigger than a barn door. A different voice – Strang's – took over inside her head. *Head shots are best. Hit them once if you have to, twice if you can.* The silencer breathed twice and the man's own momentum carried him two more strides to the far end of the sofa before his knees gave way and he fell face down on the floor.

'Get up, you fat bastard.' The redhead was slow; deaf to the sound of a weapon simply because it was not possible for there to be one there. The bearded blond was faster. He was moving even before the second shot; spinning sideways, going for the shadows, thinking on his feet. 'It's the bitch. Get the kid.' And so he had to go next. *If the target is moving or obscured, go for the upper torso.* He was down in the angle between the wall and the floor, rolling fast towards the fat one. Four rounds hit the mass of his body. It bucked, as Ciaran had bucked, as her father had bucked, once for each shot. At the end, it lay still, the arm outstretched, still reaching out for the gun. He sighed like a slashed tyre, the final exhalation from lungs punctured more than once. She stepped over him into the room.

The redhead may not have been overly smart but he was intimately acquainted with death and its precursors. He turned very slowly towards her, keeping his hands well away from his sides. 'Whit're you after?' he asked. He smiled, brokenly, and the decay of his breath added to the pollution of the room. She said nothing. Possibly she smiled back. The colour drained from his face. 'It wisnae me. It was Tord. Tord did him.'

He whined it, as a child whines for a broken window. 'It wasn't me. It just broke.' Who cares? I do. *Luke.* The shaking was back. The end of the gun wavered in her outstretched hands.

The target was moving, easing himself back, a step at a time, towards the window. *At all costs, keep the angle of fire away from the public.* She stepped out sideways, moving to put herself between the standing man and the boy. The man moved opposite her, a well-drilled partner in the dance. The orange glow of the streetlight marked an arc on the floor that kept them apart. *Take extra care in the dark. Your vision will be compromised. Keep away from the light source.* She was outlined against the window. She felt the light stripping her bare, leaving her naked before hostile eyes. She stepped sideways again so that the boy's chair was behind her. The man was keeping to the shadows, moving with her, still whining. The words had no meaning. 'Tord knows all about yous two. He'll be back in the morning. Better to get out while you can. I'll no' get in your way now. Take the kid and go. He'll be needing someone to take care of him. You go now before he comes back . . .' And then she lost him. He dropped down out of sight somewhere between the bodies and the sofa. The fat one had carried a revolver in his shoulder sling. She heard the slick of metal on leather and then the ratchet of the hammer clicking back before it fell. Her body moved once again of its own volition, spinning her sideways into shadows. White light erupted from the black space near the door. The sound of the shot shattered her hearing. She heard herself scream with the shock of it and then heard an echoing cry from the chair. But she was rolling, still, into the darkness and her arms were outstretched and she was firing and firing and firing into the place where the flash had come from and the spit of the silencer gave way to the solid thud of rounds slamming through flesh and bone and then the louder, more solid sound of metal falling on wood and still she fired until the only sound was the faintest of clicks as she pulled the trigger and there was nothing at all coming out of her gun.

Luke.

The body of the redhead blocked the doorway. She stepped over it into the hall, swapping clips unconsciously, filling up the gun with hands that could barely hold the rounds. The first waves of nausea caught her as she passed the kitchen. She fumbled for the light, gagging against a closed glottis. The kitchen was foul. A bowl of foetid water stood in the sink, a rancid dishcloth hung on the edge, growing life of its own. Unwashed tea towels hung from the door handle. A carton of old milk congealed on top of the fridge because nobody could be bothered to open the door and put it away. In all the hell of the months just gone, she had wanted very badly to set fire to that kitchen. Now it was simply a staging post in purgatory. She threw up into the washing bowl, retching and choking on the stench, on the shock of what she had done and the fear of what she was going to find downstairs. *Luke.* She spat a final time, ran a tap and drank the water straight from the spout then wiped her mouth dry on her sleeve. *Wait for me. Live.*

She was at the front door before she remembered the boy. He was sitting where she had left him, curled tight in the chair, staring out at the whirling white-on-black of the night. She crouched down in front of him, not quite blocking the view to the window. 'Jamie? Are you all right?' He was shaking as much as she was shaking. His lips were blue in the snow-lit white of his face. His teeth made a dented line along his lower lip, holding it in. There was a single tear track running down from the inner corner of each wide-open eye. She saw all of this before she saw the blood. It ran in a wash of sticky black from the lower sleeve of his T-shirt down his arm and onto his thigh. The fingers of his other hand gripped tight to the wound, so that it leaked from between his fingers, and they, too, had gone black in the odd sodium glare of the night. 'Jamie, let me look.' He shook his head, still biting his lip. The tears, such as they were, had stopped. 'Luke,' he said. He whispered it, the way she had whispered it before the shooting started. He barely knew him. He just knew that he mattered to her. It was the second word she had ever heard him say.

'In a minute. When you're safe.' She looked around for something to bind the wound, something not worn by the dead. 'Wait here, I'll be back in a second.' She ran for the kitchen, jumping the body of the redhead as if it wasn't there. A pair of clean tea towels lay in a drawer. She tore one in half as she ran back. 'Here. Let me wrap it up.' His hand was limp and cold to the touch as she moved his fingers away. Fresh blood ran freely from the wound in his upper arm. He was only nine and he was small for his age and he had no spare flesh on him anywhere. A .38 bullet has the power to take off the arm of an adult. God alone knows what it can do to a child. She held his hand in her own.

'Jamie. I have to get help. I'll wrap you up and then we'll call people who can do something to make you better. Is that OK?'

He nodded. Fatigue and pain warred with the fear of strangers. She wrapped one of the tea towels round his arm and made a sling of the other. The simple act of movement dragged a strangled half-cry from his throat. 'You can cry, Jamie, it's all right. There's no one to hear you but me.'

He shook his head and bit deeper so that his lip, too, turned dark. She tied the last knot on the sling. He was wearing nothing but his mother's T-shirt in a room where the last flicker of gas ran out of the meter just after the nine o'clock news. It was as cold inside as out, possibly colder. His feet were as blue as his lips, drawn up underneath him for warmth. His hands were like ice. She tried to smile into his eyes and got nothing back. 'Wait here,' she said again.

She took the stairs at a run, slamming on lights until she reached his bedroom. He had no furniture beyond a bed and not much in the way of clothes but there was a sweatshirt and a pair of jeans and thick socks for playing football. Back downstairs, the sweatshirt slid down over the injured arm and he let her manoeuvre him into the jeans. The socks took longest because she wasn't used to putting socks on someone else. The steady voice of Strang inside her head was counting seconds, explaining to her that Luke was dying and the boy would live. When he was wrapped against the cold and not bleeding, she listened to it. 'Right, I'll go and find him. Are you OK to stay here?'

He nodded. He was shaking less. She reached into the belt pouch that had held her gun and pulled out a black box the size of a small cigarette packet with two buttons on one side. 'This will call the people we need. They'll be faster than an ambulance and they'll know what to do with your arm.' They will know, also, what to do with the mess of bodies in the room but this is not his problem. She held out the box in front of him. 'I want you to hold this, do you think you can?'

His uninjured hand reached out to take it. His eyes stayed on hers. 'Good. Take a look. There are two buttons on top here, one red, one green. OK?' He nodded. 'Good lad. You can press the red button any time now. Then count, very slowly, to a hundred and press the green button. The guys aren't far. That's the signal to come as fast as they can and be ready to deal with the wounded. If they get here before I get back, make sure they sort out your arm before they do anything else.'

Fear shadowed his eyes. She laid a hand on his leg. 'Jamie, please trust me. None of them will hurt you. You have to believe that.' He nodded. There was no way to know if he believed her. Seconds passed. She crouched back by the chair. 'OK, listen. There are three of them. Alec

Strang's in charge. He's solid, like the blond one, but he's clean shaven and he's got wee round glasses, like this.' She made two circles of her fingers and held them in front of her eyes. 'He's fine, but he'll not know how to talk to you. Andy Bennett's lank, like he's been on smack and not eaten for a week. He's going bald, with his hair pushed out over his head, you know?'

He nodded. Bald men, he knew. 'Good lad. Andy's the doctor. He'll sort out your arm. The third one's Murdo Cameron. He's our kind of guy. He's not so broad as Strang but he's taller, about this height,' she held the flat of her palm a hand's length over the top of her head, 'and his hair's black like treacle and wild. If we're lucky, he'll have it bunched back, like this,' she swept her hair back and held it. The action changed the planes on her face. When she let it go, it sprung up round her head. 'If we're not lucky, it'll be hanging down round his shoulders getting in the way. Either way, you'll know him when you see him. Tell Murdo Cameron, when he asks, that I've gone to find Luke. OK? Jamie?' She did her best to smile for him the way she had done under the sofa. 'Jamie? I know it's difficult but they'll not be hard on you for speaking. Just tell them that, you don't have to say anything else. Do you think you can do it?'

He was nine years old and he had a bullet wound in his arm. It was three o'clock in the morning and he was about to sit alone in a house with the bodies of three men, any one of whom, when alive, would have killed him without a second thought. He had more stamina, more courage, than any man she had ever worked with. A smile lit up his face like a candle in the darkness. He blinked once over eyes the colour of night-time snow. 'Tell Murdo Cameron I've gone to find Luke,' he said. If you taped him saying it, you would think it was her.

She took hold of his head, very gently, and pressed her lips to his forehead. 'Jamie, I love you.' He pushed her away. His eyes moved to the door and back.

'OK. I'm going. I won't be long.'

He heard the sound of her feet on the stairs and in the close below. He heard the front door opened and slammed shut against the wind. He waited until he saw the shape of her move round the side of the building and then he put both thumbs on the red button and pushed.

'It's OK, son, you can let go of it now.' The boy sat curled in the chair, his whole body curved round the transmitter, both hands stabbing tight on the buttons. She said to press them. She didn't say to let go. And so he had held tight for twelve and a half minutes, first to the red button, then to the red and the green together and the transmitter sent out its continuous silent scream to the three men waiting on the other side of the city so that they, believing the woman to be dying, if not already dead, had broken all the limits to get there.

Alec Strang was relieved, more than he could have said, not to find her body in the carnage on the floor, but that didn't mean that she was safe. He sent Murdo Cameron upstairs with his gun out, checking for bodies, alive or dead. 'Use your torch. I don't want any more lights on till we know where everyone is.'

'Right.'

Andrew Bennett, the medic, was already in the living room, playing his own torch over the two women on the sofa although there was nothing about either of them to suggest that they were within reach of anything short of a miracle. That left Strang with the child. The file said nine but he could as easily have been six; small and lean, with pale skin and paler hair and the dark shadows of sleeplessness hammered in beneath his eyes. He looked blank, in the way of all children who have seen too much of the things they should never see, but there was a sense of stone in the stare that said if he broke, it would not be here or now. Still, as he picked his way forward over the debris and the dead, Strang caught the pungent smell of fresh urine hanging over the chair and he saw, and chose to ignore, the darker stain blending with all the other dark stains on the bare wood beneath the chair. His experience of children stemmed solely from a childhood too far gone to contemplate but he knew enough of basic human pride not to pass comment. He moved round the chair and leant back against the window frame, putting himself between the eyes and their target.

'Jamie? It is Jamie, isn't it? It's OK, you're safe now.' His accent was English and educated. It rang oddly in the cold of the room, an intruder in a foreign land.

Over by the sofa, Bennett gave the thumbs down on the two women and knelt down to examine the hulking body of the man lying on the floor beside them. Strang nodded acknowledgement and then, looking back to the chair, saw that the exchange had been noted and understood. He smiled. 'No problem, son. Your mum'll be fine. We'll get someone here to take care of her.' He lied, always, with fluent ease and was surprised to see that, too, noted and understood. He ran a tongue round teeth still thick with sleep and redefined the problem. Nine going on ninety, or at least a reasonable average between the two. He swept a hand through his hair. A pair of snow-pale eyes stared up into his. 'OK, forget it,' he said. 'You know what the score is.' The eyes gave nothing away but there was a faint inclination of the head which showed, at least, that the kid could hear.

Murdo Cameron returned from the upper rooms. He shook his head once and joined Bennett in his examination of the bodies. The man had no medical training but he was very good indeed at assessing the patterns of fire. If you know who fired what and when, you can create a reasonable picture of who was left standing at the end. In the absence of witnesses, these things matter. Except that they did have a witness, of sorts. The boy sat, transfixed by the snow, the transmitter still gripped in both hands, the buttons locked in their silent alarm. Strang moved out to take it and changed his mind. He tapped it instead. 'Did Orla give you that?' he asked. The eyes gazed through him to the window beyond. He might have been talking to snow.

'She's in cover. She's not calling herself Orla.' Murdo was standing behind the chair. There was fresh blood on the tips of his fingers and, now, streaks of it down the front of his T-shirt as he wiped them clean. 'If the lad's any sense,' he said, 'he'll have learnt long ago not to talk to strange men who don't know the name of his friends.'

'Very funny.' Strang pushed the heels of both hands into the pits of his eyes. Twenty minutes ago, he was sound asleep. Now, with the first adrenaline rush receding, the pall of unfinished dreams dulled his thinking. Murdo, who had been the one sitting up and was by far the most awake, was still smiling at him when he moved his hands away. Strang sighed and wished for sleep. 'Did you find anything useful?' he asked.

'Maybe.' The tall man folded his arms on the back of the chair. 'The damage in all three came from one gun.'

'Whose?'

'Pass. I don't know. It was a small calibre automatic which would fit with it being McLeod's but there's no saying she was the one firing it. Whoever it was, they started in here with the big one by the sofa,' he nodded back towards the dead man, 'went through the blond one for a short cut and then got into a shooting match with the redhead. The revolver's been fired once. We need to trace the angle of shot and find out if anyone's been hit.' He was doing it as he spoke, swivelling round on one heel, his eyes measuring an arc from the fallen gun to the wall, seeking out the point of impact and tracing the route in between. He reached the end of the arc, paused and did it again. 'Oh, shit.' He said it quietly, sliding it into the conversation between one sentence and the next. His eyes narrowed and he slid round into the space between the chair and the wall, taking care to keep out of the way of the window. He was tall, as she had said, and he did have his hair tied back. With unusual presence of mind he had removed his holster and left it out of sight in the hallway, leaving only his radio hanging from his belt. He signalled to Bennett to join him, found a clean space on the floor then crossed his ankles and sank down in one smooth movement.

'Hey, Jamie. I'm Murdo. This is Andy, he's a doctor. Will you let him look at your arm?' The boy shook his head, pushing himself deeper into the chair. Bennett slid up beside him. 'He's hit?'

'I think so. Entry site in the back of the chair. Round's in the wall up here. Looks like it's grazed along his back and maybe clipped the side of his arm.' The tall man nodded upwards, his eyes still on the chair. The medic glanced up and then back to the boy then he, too, crouched at the side of the chair. He slid out a hand and laid his fingers on one narrow wrist. A pulse threaded through beneath his fingers, like feeling along knots in a piece of string. The key to medicine in children, in anyone, is to find a common link with the patient. He tried to remember the name the woman had used. Scots. Glaswegian. The kind of thing half the girls use when you pick them up and they don't want to be known. Suzi? Sally? Sandra? 'Sandra?' he asked. 'Did Sandra give you that box you're holding?' A nod. 'Did she tell you we'd come if you pressed the buttons?' Another nod. 'So did she say where she was going?' Nothing. The grey eyes wavered and slid off his face. Murdo Cameron looked up and found them drawing him in. He leant forward and put his hand on the chair. 'Are you sure? She's a smart lass. I think she would have left us a message. Did she not say where she was going?'

'Gone to find Luke.' The voice was husked and strained from lack of practice but the tone and the intonation were perfect. Like a parrot, trained in a single speech, he said it again. 'Tell Murdo Cameron, when he asks, that I've gone to find Luke.'

'Where? Where has she . . . ?' Strang was back, behind Cameron, pushing for answers. He got a hand across his mouth from Bennett. 'Shut up, man. Don't go hard on him now. Murdo, go on.'

'Never mind him, he's got no manners.' The man smiled. The skin round his eyes creased like tanned leather. 'Did she say where she'd gone? Did Sandra tell you where it was she'd gone to find Luke?' Nothing. He tried it again, asking in a different way, in case it was the order of words that triggered the answer. Still nothing. Strang turned round to face the window and pressed his forehead to the glass, cursing. The boy looked as if he'd been struck. He shook his head. His mouth opened and shut again like a fish and then, 'Don't know,' he said. 'She never said.' It came out as a whisper, even less practised than the rest and the effort of it was painful to watch.

'OK, lad. You've done your best.' Bennett moved to sit on the arm of the chair. With great care he slid one hand down and over the black box. 'Maybe you'd like to let go of that now we're here? There's no one else waiting to hear it.' The thumbs came off the buttons. The red light on top of the transmitter blinked off, extinguishing as it did so the matching light on Murdo Cameron's receiver.

'Thank you. Now, can we get this sweater up and have a look at what's underneath? Good. That's nice. Did Orla . . . did Sandra put this on for you? Fine. That's very good. She'd make a good nurse, eh? I'll just undo this knot here and have a wee look . . .'

It was a long time since Andrew Bennett had practised medicine on anyone who wasn't a colleague and even then it was first aid and nothing more. There were well-defined limitations to what he could do and they stopped far short of gunshot wounds in a child. He got as far as the bandage and made the same assessment as had been made before him. 'This is more than I can handle.' He turned back to Strang. 'He needs a hospital.'

'Then call the ambulance.' Strang stood with his hands on the window frame, staring out into the night. 'Where the fuck are they?' No one answered. He turned back to the room. 'Murdo, how long since the three in here died?'

'Not long. The blood's barely clotted on the head wounds so we're talking minutes, not hours. I'd say she was out of here around the time the red alarm went off.'

'Wherever she's gone, it's not that far.' Andrew Bennett had his mobile to his ear and was halfway through dialling for an ambulance.

Strang didn't bother to turn round. 'Because?' he asked, wearily.

'Because she's left her shoes.' He nodded over in the direction of the door and they all looked round, even the boy. A pair of red plastic stilettos stood side by side just inside the door of the living room. 'She needed to run,' said the medic, simply, 'she didn't need to run far.' His line connected. He spoke three words into the phone and hung up. 'The others went out on OD opiates,' he said. He kept his eyes away from the boy's. 'Fast and quick. It looks self-injected but there's no saying they knew it was lethal when they put it in.'

'How long ago?'

'A while. They're down to ambient. Five hours, maybe six. Depends if it's been this cold all night.'

'Christ. This is getting out of control. If the shit hit the fan six hours ago, anything could have happened. Right,' Strang pushed himself clear of the window, 'Andy, you stay in here and wait for the ambulance. Don't let them go until we're back. They may have more than the boy to deal with. Murdo, you come with me.' He led them out to the hall, stepping neatly over the bodies, avoiding the loose shells on the floor.

'Where are you going?' Bennett, stepping where Strang stepped, followed him out.

'To find McLeod. We're wasting time. You're right, all we need to look for is bare footprints in the snow. She's looking for Tyler. If we find her, we've found him and then we can—'

'Don't bother, I've found him.'

She was there in the doorway, soft-footed, like a cat, and God, she was a mess. Her hair was wild; white-blonde with coloured highlights, back-combed away from her face like a mane. A bottled tan darkened her legs from ankles to groin, hiding the worst of the scars. Her fingernails were scarlet, matching the plastic of the crotch-ventilating skirt and the abandoned shoes. She had a cheap stud in her navel and if you strained hard to see through the thin lycra of her top, there might well have been one in her left nipple as well. Even so, it was her eyes that grabbed the attention. A pair of mirrored gold contact lenses with radial black lines caught the dim light of the overhead bulb and spun it back, sharper, brighter, more vicious than before. If you didn't know her well you'd never look beyond the eyes. Strang, absorbing this, gave her credit for ingenuity. Murdo Cameron wondered how in the name of God any sane man could ever have believed she was a whore. Andrew Bennett, who had no real interest in what she looked like, was already halfway down the length of the hall.

'Where is he?'

'No.' Her arm was there across the doorway, like a ramrod, blocking his path. 'Forget it, Andy, you don't want to see him.'

'I have to. He needs help.' For a man with a good brain, he wasn't using it well.

'No, he doesn't. Trust me. I'd have been up here before now if he did. He's way beyond help and you really don't want to . . . I said *no*, damn you. Strang, hold him.' The arm that had been across the doorway thrust suddenly forward and Alec Strang found himself catching the taller man and clasping him in the bear hug necessary to stop him throwing himself once again at the exit.

'Andy, give it up. If she says it's too late then believe her.'

'Thank you, Alec.' Her smile was very distant.

Strang locked his hands in front of the struggling Bennett and said, 'So where is he?'

'In the basement. There's no reason for any of you to go down. Let the crime squad do it, that's what they're paid for.' She stepped in over the threshold, pushing the door shut behind her and it was only then, as she stood beneath the naked bulb, that the real mess of her showed: the circular cuts, as of wires pulled tight, at wrist and ankle, the bruises on her legs, on her hands, on her neck, the blue track of the needle on her inner arm. Melting snow leaked from her feet onto the floorboards by the door. Threads of pink spread out across it from a gash on her ankle. Murdo Cameron stepped forward, one hand out. 'Orla, you're—'

'I'm fine.' She fitted her shoulders to the door, one hand on the handle. 'The ambulance is downstairs for Jamie. He'll need someone to go with him and clear the way at the hospital.' She nodded to the medic. 'I'll talk to him first. You go with him when I'm done.'

'Fuck that.' Bennett broke free of the restraining grip and moved forward. 'What about you? You're a walking disaster zone. You need a hospital a sight more than he does.'

She opened her eyes wide. The gold mirrors lied brightly. 'I'm fine,' she said again.

'Right. And I'm your granny.' He had a medic's way of laying his hands on her unasked. He ran a finger up her arm to the blasted vein. Another hand lifted her eyelid and he tried to look past the contacts to the reality hidden beneath. 'Heroin?' he asked.

'I think so. Maybe something else too.' She tried for a smile and abandoned it half done. 'I didn't think to ask for the prescription.'

'Right.' He wasn't listening. He was holding her arm up to the light so he could more properly examine the cord cuts at her wrists. There had been an hour, more or less, between the time the first wash of the drugs wore off and the time she realised the boy was alive and was still in the room. For ten minutes of that hour, she lay in a stupor, listening to what they were doing to Luke and waiting for them to start on her. For the rest of it, she was trying to break free. The result was not pretty although the pain of it was responsible in a large part for keeping her awake. She felt her arm dropped and the other one lifted and thought that perhaps it would be nice to be asked.

Bennett looked past her to Strang. 'This is through to the tendon sheath. It needs looking at or she'll lose the use of her hand. She can go with the kid. They'll do her as an emergency, he'll wait till there's a free theatre.'

'No.' She pulled her hand free. 'Not yet. There are things I still have to do here.'

'You're—'

'*Jesus Christ, just do it, will you?*' Her voice cracked on the rising note. The shaking was visible even to Murdo standing at the far end of the hall. He moved closer, ready to catch her when she fell because it was clear to them all now that she was right on the edge and going over and that the crash, when it came, would be spectacular. She saw him moving and put up a hand to stop him. 'Not yet, OK?' He stopped and sank down with his back to the wall. She smiled dry thanks. 'I'm sorry. It's been a bad night. I'm trying not to make it any worse. Jamie Buchanan may be the only person left alive who has seen Tord Svensen and might be able to identify him. Svensen may know that. The lad needs someone with him who is still capable of acting if the shit hits the fan. That's not me, obviously. We need someone who can handle the medics and knows the inside of a hospital. Andy, that's you. They'll let you places they wouldn't let any of us. I want you there with him even when he's in surgery. Get a round-the-clock watch and make sure it works. Is that clear?'

'Yes.'

'Thank you.' It became necessary to move. She was losing her grip on the door handle and, with it, on the vestiges of self-control that kept her upright. She pushed between Strang and the medic to the living-room doorway. The boy seemed impossibly far away. That she could still walk felt miraculous. That she could also think and feel and remember was very possibly a curse. What she wanted more than anything else was to find a clean way to oblivion, a way out that would switch off the sound of a man stretched beyond endurance and the sight of the things that had taken him there. Because this was not a totally new experience, she had held his hand and promised him she would not give way to the dark. It had never been an easy promise to keep.

She reached the window. The child was still sitting as she had left him. His left side was the one she had bandaged. She sat on the right-hand arm of the chair. His body looked warmer than it had. His soul looked bleaker. She put a hand on his hair. He looked up at her, his eyes asking the questions that the rest of him wouldn't voice. She shook her head. 'He's gone, kiddo. He's where they can't hurt him anymore.' He took that in as he took in everything else, silently and with due thought. The night was warming, at least outside. Sleet replaced the snow on the window. They sat together in the quiet and watched the patterns dissolve. She dragged her fingers through the lank straw of his hair. 'You have to go to the hospital, Jamie. They need to have a look at your arm. There are things I need to do here before I can come and you may be asleep before I can join you but Andy will go with you. If that's all right?'

He shrugged for that, as if it didn't matter who went with him. Neither of them believed it. His gaze flickered back towards the bodies on the sofa. There was no question this time, simply an incorporation of facts into the bigger picture. She spoke that for him too, 'Kirsty's gone with him. Your mum's dead too. You did know that, didn't you?'

He nodded. His good hand sought hers, and lay within it. She looped her fingers through his the way she would have done with Luke. 'I haven't forgotten what I promised,' she said. 'The cottage is there. We can go and look at it when they let us both out of hospital.'

Bennett took him to the ambulance. Murdo Cameron went with him, to help and, because he knew both of them well, so that Orla could be sure that the medic was with the boy and not wandering the basements trying to see things he shouldn't. It didn't take long. When he came back, she was sitting in the boy's chair, her legs drawn in, her chin on her knees. Strang stood off to one side, talking to someone on his mobile phone in the short, structured phrases he used whenever the recipient was of comparable rank. Murdo found a light switch just inside the door and flicked it on. A pink, fly-specked bulb in the centre of the ceiling lit up, casting harsh, roseate shadows on the stiffening dead, on the junk, on the peeling wallpaper and rising damp, on the stinking, sordid squalor of the room. He flicked the switch back off. There is dignity in darkness. He pulled out his pen torch and picked his way across to the window. Downstairs, the ambulance revved up. For a moment, an electric blue pulse merged with the orange of the streetlight. The tall man leant back against the glass and let the colours wash over him onto the woman in the chair. He pulled the band from his hair and shook it free. Hair like steel wool bounced around his shoulders. 'I take it we need to keep Andy away from the pathology reports?' he asked.

'If you can.' Her voice was flat. 'I don't think any of you should see it if you don't absolutely have to,' she said. 'Andy . . .' she shrugged. 'I can't see you keeping him away from the paperwork but for God's sake don't let him see Luke before he's a handful of ashes in a pot.' She was shaking less now. Her face had lost the grey mask of earlier. The unnatural eyes glittered in over-flushed skin, as if she was the one who had just sprinted upstairs and not yet caught her breath. Murdo put out his hand to feel the temperature of her forehead and thought better of it at the last moment. 'Are you running a fever?' he asked.

'Possibly.' The question came from a long way away. She was beginning to hallucinate which was not good. Luke grinned at her from the ruin of his face. Further back, her father shouted her name. A step back from him, Ciaran screamed blue murder at a man in a hand-knitted ski mask. All of the ghosts out on one night. Not good. She kept her eyes on the swirling flow as the sleet washed the snow from the window and did her best to ignore the rest. Murdo Cameron was still watching her in the way a bitch would watch pups straying too far from the nest. She would have told him to fuck off but there had been enough injuries for one day without her causing more. So she shrugged again and reached through the phantoms to touch the cool, hard glass of the window. 'It might just be the drugs,' she said.

Strang hung up his call. 'Laidlaw's on his way. The crime squad will seal the area. I don't think you need to be here when they arrive. Murdo can drive you to the Western. If he drives like he did to get here, you could still get there ahead of the ambulance and have time for a coffee before the kid arrives.'

'No . . .' Thinking was becoming impossible, oblivion harder to resist. 'You need to . . . They need to . . .' She took a breath and tried again. She had a promise to keep. 'Svensen was here. He's coming back in the morning. He won't come if . . .'

'If Laidlaw's got two vanloads of goons taking the place apart. Right.' Strang flipped his phone open again. 'I'll hold them back till the afternoon.'

'No . . .' She gave up trying to keep her eyes open. It was easier looking into the blackness. 'He may not come. We need forensics. He shot him.'

'Who shot whom?' Only Strang would say 'whom' on a night like this. Public school education will out.

'Svensen shot Luke.'

'How do you know it was Svensen?'

'I didn't hear the shot. I would have heard the revolver.'

'Did you hear anything else?'

She smiled at that. Murdo Cameron caught his breath and looked the other way. 'All of it,' she said.

Strang pinched the bridge of his nose. 'Thank you.' He nodded absently. It is not possible to silence a revolver. They all knew that. His eyes drifted to the window. The sleet was melting fast. The wind drove it onto the glass in long, drumming sheets. He found a hole in a back molar and probed it with his tongue. The sharp, electric shock of it ran through him, as if he needed to remember what it was to feel pain.

'How long did they have him?' he asked.

'Long enough. I don't know exactly. I was out of it for most of the time but the shit hit the fan in here before ten and they were still working on him at three.'

'And they shot him at the end of it?'

'Yes.'

'Christ.' Murdo said it quietly, reverentially, profanity transformed to respect. Strang said nothing. He watched as the sleet gave way finally to good, honest rain, his mind cluttered with images he didn't need and didn't want, of other men in other places, trying to hold onto the threads of an unravelling cover. There are the myths of what pain a man can stand and then there is the reality. In neither world do you shoot a man who has anything useful left to tell you. He considered the work, the time, the effort, the basic human misery of three months undercover and saw it consigned, in that one simple fact, to the scrapheap. He sighed.

The woman heard it and closed her eyes. 'I'm sorry,' she said. He hadn't meant it as blame. He didn't believe in a culture of blame. Nevertheless, watching her, he saw it taken as read, saw it turned inwards and hardened into the promise of action. It was what she did best. Later she would act. For now, she was simply fighting to stay conscious. He nodded to Cameron and saw that the tall man was already watching. If she fell, when she fell, he would be there before she hit the floor.

'Come on,' Strang leant over and tapped her arm. 'Bennett's right. You need the medics as much as the lad does. Let's get you out of here while you can still walk.' She was sitting in the chair with her knees drawn up to her chest and she was wearing no underwear. Somewhere in the past half hour he had become aware of that and managed to look elsewhere. Even now, as he reached out to touch her, his gaze was on the window and so he didn't notice that she stood up too fast for the state she was in, he missed the moment when the ghosts and oblivion both staked their claim. She was pitching forward towards the sheet glass of the window before he realised she wasn't upright and then he was back against the wall, nursing a bruised shoulder and swearing roundly and so, for the rest of her life, Orla McLeod owed the lack of further glass scars on her face to her friend and colleague, Murdo Cameron, who was there to catch her when she fell.

Two

———◆———

'Religion?'
  'I have no religion.'
  'What do I put on the chart then, Father?'
  'Ask her again, she didn't understand you.'
  'What's your faith, child? You must have a faith.'
  'I have no faith. I don't believe in your God.'
  'She's confused, Sister. She doesn't know what she's saying. Put down
Catholic. It's what her father would have wanted.'
  'Will I tie her hands again, Father? She will tear at the bandages.'
  'If you must.'

She woke, looking for Father Kavanagh. A nurse she didn't recognise
hovered by the bed checking the drips and the bandages. Her arm hurt
where the grafts were not taking. Her face hurt where the glass had cut it.
She wanted to ask for her mother but the words wouldn't come. The nurse
smiled a plastic smile, her eyes fixed somewhere on the pillow and not on
her face. She wanted a mirror so she could see the damage. She tried to talk
again. The nurse shook her head and reset the rate of the infusion pump.
  'Sleep now. One of the doctors will be round to talk to you in the
morning.'
  She slept, carried out on a chemical tide.

★   ★   ★

'You're going nowhere, McLeod. Feel that?'
'She's out of it. She's not feeling anything.'
'Aye, she'll feel it well enough when she wakes up, but.'
'That'll do. Leave her. Take the bastard downstairs.'
Luke.

She lay still in the silence and she knew she was too late. The space around her was black and impossible to measure. She listened for the rhythm of breathing, for clothes rubbing on clothes, for the creak of a chair, for anything that would tell her who was waiting in the darkness. Nothing. She tested the ties at her wrists, left and then right, a slow tensing of the tendons to find where they would give. The cord was sharp-edged and bit into her skin. Her arm ached coldly where the needle had entered. The memory of a scream rang round in her head. Fear surged in its wake. She bit back on a name. *'Luke.'*

'McLeod?'

A shadow moved in the dark. She turned her head, ready to deny it. *My name is not McLeod. I am Sandra Smith. I am thirty-five years old and I come from Maryhill. I have been on the game since I was nineteen. Luke Tyler picked me up at a bus stop at St Enoch's. I never saw him before in my life.* She fought to find a place inside where she could hold to the reality of the lie. Rising waves of panic made her pull again at the ties on her wrists. A light sparked on, blindingly bright. Cool fingers closed over the crook of her elbow. The voice was closer the second time: 'DI McLeod? Gently now, it's all right. You're in hospital. We're guarding the door. You're safe.'

Safe.

'Luke?'

'He's dead.'

She closed her eyes. The light went out.

Murdo Cameron took over at midnight. The first thing he did was to rip off the Velcro ties fixing her wrists to the sides of the bed. The young officer he was relieving – a mess of chin spots and young arrogance and a simmering resentment for having been made to sit half the night at a bedside – was not impressed. 'You can't do that. She goes wild when she comes round. She's pulled the drip out twice already.'

'I'll bear it in mind.'

'It's policy. The nurses'll have you.'

'Fuck the policy. If she wakes up like this she'll go over the edge.'

'Aye, and you'll know the difference, will you?' The lad had his back turned, shrugging into his jacket. The words came muffled with the weight of it. Murdo spun him round to face the bed.

'What was that?'

'Nothing.'

'Good.' He sat down by the bed and took her hand in his own. The skin was less hot than it had been, her colour less flushed. He tilted the light away from her face. 'I'll stay with her now. You're off. Get lost.'

'See you tomorrow.'

'Maybe.'

Tomorrow, there may be answers. Tonight there were only questions and the waiting did not come easily. Murdo Cameron paced and sat and worked on his laptop, none of which helped noticeably to pass the time. Later, he read the case notes and watched the drips and tried, with no real success, to work out how much longer it would take for the junk and the fever to work their separate ways out of her system. Later still, he simply sat and watched her breathing.

Outside, it was raining. In another part of Glasgow, a long way from the good living of Byres Road and the west end, a woman and a girl of seventeen shared shelter from the rain, one or other of them stepping out if a car slid past slower than the rest. The man who came to join them was lean and mostly bald and in need of a shave. His jeans had gashes across the knees and oil stains on the thighs where he had used them to clean his hands. His suede jacket was too expensive and too big across the shoulders to be legitimately his. His trainers were built for serious running. He leant back against the wall with his hands in his pockets as if he, too, were waiting for a pick-up.

'Nice night,' said the girl, just in case.

'Aye. If you like this kind of thing.'

A Volvo estate with child seats in the back cruised down the road. The girl stepped out unsteadily on heels too high for sanity or comfort. A wash of water sluiced up towards the hem of her skirt. The car stopped and the window slid down and those left in the doorway watched the girl bend to look in. Voices blew back on the rain until the bargain was made and the girl opened the door to slide into the passenger seat. The Volvo indicated and pulled away, slicing up more of the roadside runnels of rain.

'Mirror, signal, manoeuvre. Very good. Very Highway Code. Nice to know he follows the rules.' The man had moved forward. 'Will the lass be OK?' If you had been more than two feet away, you would not have heard him speak. The woman heard and, in a while, she answered.

'Aye, well enough. He's been here before. He has a wife and four kids and he doesn't want more. He pays what he's asked and doesn't push for what he's not going to get.'

'A model client.'

'You could say.'

Another car passed, slowed and accelerated.

'He doesn't want you?' The man was surprised. The woman had an elegance that her younger colleague lacked.

'He saw you.' That he should leave was implicit. The woman had no need to say it aloud. 'Were you after something?'

'Maybe. Luke's dead.' There was no way to soften that, for himself or anyone else. He didn't try.

'Svensen got him?'

'Big time. He may have talked.'

'Fuck.' The woman stared into the wet as she had done before. Now, she saw things other than the rain.

'You didn't know anything was going down?'

'No. I was with Big Drew last night and he said nothing. None of them did.' If she had known, she would have got word to the lean man with the thinning hair; that, too, was implicit. She pulled the nothingness of her jacket around her. 'Say something for me at his funeral.'

'I will. Patsy—' It was not often that he used her name. 'It's not too late to run. We can get you somewhere safe, with money, a new name, new home, new—' he was going to say new career which would have been foolish and was only because it was really very late, '—new job.'

She thought about that. He saw her make up her mind and change it, twice. Whatever pictures she saw in the haze of wet tarmac and litter were more than he could counter. 'No,' she said eventually. 'I'll stay where I am.'

'If he comes for you—'

'Then he comes for me. That's my problem. If he's got a lever into Luke then I'm safer where I am.' She was getting edgy now, wanting him to leave.

A new model Audi slowed to thirty and then to twenty.

'That'll be for you.'

'Likely.'

'Fine.' The lean man took his hand from his pockets. The highest denomination note he could find flipped between his finger and thumb. She took it before she stepped out into the rain. The Audi stopped.

'If you change your mind—'

'I'll know where to find you.' And she was gone.

In a private ward in the Western Infirmary, Orla McLeod woke just after dawn. Her eyes, without the mirrored lenses, were grey, almost black, and dense, like the cape on a jackdaw. The pupils were wider now, free of the micro-dot stricture of heroin. She lay still, staring up at the ceiling, and Murdo Cameron watched her struggle against the returning tide of memories. It was an ugly process; swift and brutal and not meant for an audience. He looked out of the window and waited. Overnight, the rain had dried and the cloud layer thinned enough to let in a bit of the dawn. Pale light glanced off the windowpane, showing up a single set of prints on the glass; two hands had rested side by side, one splayed outwards, pointing up to the radio mast on top of the pathology building. He studied the size of the palms that had made them, the angle of placement, the likely height of the individual involved and realised, later than he might have done, that the prints were his own, that he had, at some point in the long wait, leant on the window and stared out at the stars and the streetlights and the few cars turning in the car park.

'Murdo?'

'Yes. I'm here.'

She moved. Cotton whispered under her hair as her head turned on the pillow. Eyes still busy with the residue of dreams took in the whole length of him and came back to his face. 'What day is it?'

'Sunday. You lost twenty-four hours. It could have been worse.'

It could. 'What's happened with Luke?'

'They finished the postmortem last night.' He said it carefully, balancing clarity with compassion. There had been time enough to think of what she might ask and to pull the necessary answers from the chaos of the day's events. 'Strang was there, Andy wasn't. I have the report in the car if you want to see it but it doesn't say anything you don't already know.' She nodded, not fully listening. He went on. 'Strang wants a meeting as soon as you're up. Forensics have got some things they need to show us and Strang wants to get the debriefing over while there's still some point.'

'Right. Thank you.' Her gaze swung back to the ceiling. She watched the shadow of a cloud pass across the full width of it and down the wall opposite. She frowned. 'I killed Jared and Trent and Cas. I shot them.'

It wasn't a question but it needed an answer. 'Yes.'

'It was too easy, Murdo. Nobody said it would be so easy.'

In all of his life, Murdo Cameron had killed no one. He lifted her hand. Her fingers lay still in his. He squeezed them, feeling the too-sharp knuckles slide past his own. 'You did what you had to do. It wasn't your fault.' And then, because the frown was spreading, making troughs and peaks across the whole of her forehead, he said, 'Orla, none of it was your fault.'

She rolled on one side, dragging the pillow with her, bunching it up under her chin. Her eyes were alert. 'How do you know that?'

He hadn't planned for this, for the sudden change in her. 'I know you,' he said. 'I knew him. We have a file on Svensen an inch thick with nothing in it to suggest that he's ever yet cut anyone up like this before. He's not the type to waste time doing things he doesn't have to

34

and he's not into mindless sadism. If Luke had given him the answers he wanted, he'd have got a bullet at the start. He died the way he did because he was too stubborn to know when to give in.'

'I'd be dead if he wasn't.'

'He didn't hold out for you. If Jamie hadn't cut you loose, you'd be dead anyway. That's not the kind of wild card you plan your life around.'

'Maybe.' She dropped the pillow and sat up. She would have stood if the drip line in her arm hadn't held her and for a moment it looked perfectly possible she might slide off the bed anyway and walk away and let the thing rip out.

Because he did know her well, Murdo Cameron had spent some time talking to her doctors long before there was any chance of her waking. He knew both what they wanted from her and what they thought they could get and he had his own views on their chances of either. Now, he said nothing until she relaxed back onto the bed, then he lifted the pillow back up and plumped it up behind her so that she could sit upright in comfort.

'You've got stitches in the left wrist,' he said, 'the right one's fine with a bandage. They'll be stiff for a while but you'll have full use of both in the long term, as long as you don't push it too hard too soon. The medics are not over-keen on you walking round with a skull full of smack, which means that, in an ideal world, they'd keep you in for the rest of the week and run twelve-hourly tests until they were sure you're clear of chemicals and infection. However,' he held up a hand and she bit back the breath she had taken, 'however, given that we're living in the real world where that's not going to happen, if you can sit up and drink some tea, they'll take the drips down at ward round and if we ask nicely after that, they'll let you leave in time to go to Strang's meeting.'

He reached behind him for the mug on the bedside cabinet and held it out for her. 'It's cold, it's black and it's got two sugars. See it as a test. If you can hold it down, you're fit to walk out of the door.'

'Right.'

She had spent more time in hospitals than he had and she had been awake longer than he knew. The clock on the wall above her head read just short of seven o'clock. The sounds from above and below and both sides were of nurses waking patients and house officers beginning their treatment rounds. The door to her ward was shut and there was every chance it would remain so for at least another thirty minutes. Patients in isolation, whatever the reason, are always treated last. She studied the bandage covering the catheter on her arm and found that the end of the tape holding it in place had been folded in on itself, like the end of a roll of Sellotape, the easier to lift and tug. 'How's Jamie?' she asked.

Murdo Cameron watched her start to take out the drip and silently collected on a bet with the senior registrar. 'All the better for seeing you.'

She looked up. 'I'm sorry?'

He was grinning at her. His hair was hanging loose by his shoulders, flickering round his head like so much wire wool, the black of it so dense it was blue. He said, 'The lad wouldn't go to sleep last night. It took a while to find out what was wrong but in the end we brought him down here to have a look at you. Andy did his doctor bit – he looks good in a white coat and stethoscope – and told the lad that you were still sleeping off the surgery and not to be woken. We all sat around talking in stage whispers until he believed us.'

'And then did he sleep?'

'He did. I've not been in to see him this morning but as far as I know, he's fine. They fixed his arm the night you both came in. He'll have to wear a sling for a while but nothing worse than that. I sat with him so he had a known face when he woke up and there's been someone on the door round the clock ever since, with no sign of Svensen showing an unhealthy interest. He threw a bit of a temperature yesterday which means they won't let him out until they're sure he's responding to the antibiotics but if everything's clear, he'll be free by Tuesday. In the meantime, he's eating and drinking and scaring shit out of the nurses because he won't play games with train sets or fight the other kids for their Pokémon cards.'

'Surprise.' And so she found that she could smile, which was good to know. 'He needs a room with a window, then he's happy.'

'He's got it.'

'Thank you.' The catheter came free with a small leak of blood. She dabbed at it with the corner of a sheet and wound two turns of the bandage round her forearm to cover the hole where it had been. As she leant over, her hair fell forwards into her eyes, shielding the world in a haze of ugly peroxide blonde. Somewhere in the dreams, she had thought they had got rid of that. She dragged her fingers down the length of it, flaring it outwards. The moment she let go, the static grabbed it and stuck it back flat to her head. There was a time when she had believed that the best part of being free of the flat would be having the chance to get rid of the hair. She looked round the room. 'Did you bring my bag?' she asked.

'It's under the bed.' Murdo hooked it clear with his foot and lifted it up onto the chair at the side. Sometime in early January she had packed it, just in case; a collection of clothes and shoes and make-up and jewellery – and scissors and a mirror and something to take care of the blonde. She tugged open the zip and spilled the contents onto the space by her feet and began to sort through for clothes she could wear. On the far side of her, the discarded drip leaked salted water onto the floor where she hadn't quite closed the tap. Murdo leant across and rolled the clip shut. 'I had a bit of a chat with Jamie yesterday afternoon,' he said.

'Did you?' She found jeans that had been ironed and a shirt that would cover her wrists. 'What did he say?'

'Not a great deal. He has a fluent way with silence. "Snow", I think, came up once or twice. And you.' He waited. She stripped off her hospital shift and began to dress. He looked away. When she was decent again, he said, 'He seems to think you promised him a future in return for cutting you free.'

'Ah. I wondered how you knew about that.' She pushed her feet into a pair of shoes and knelt to tie the laces.

Murdo pressed for an answer. 'But was he right?'

'Yes.' She sat on the edge of the bed and began to repack the bag. Of the two promises made to the two separate people, it was by far the more easily kept. It was not, however, the one that had followed her through the fog of the night. In the minutes after waking, it was the impossibility of honouring both that had kept her still. She had given up and opened her eyes only when it became clear that she could not ask the dead to step back and give way to the living. Daylight, at least, was keeping the ghosts at bay. She stared at the wall on the far side of the room and saw only pastel paint and a mirror, reflecting the clock above her. Still, the words rang in her head.

'You're going nowhere, McLeod. Feel that?'

'That'll do. Leave her. Take the bastard downstairs.'

Luke.

She turned on the bed. Murdo was watching her, saying nothing, eloquently. She leant over and took the mug from his hand. The tea was cold and sweet and foul and she drank it all.

'They knew my name, Murdo. My real name, not my cover name. In the flat, just before they took Luke, they called me McLeod.'

He looked up. Things changed in his face. In a while, he asked softly, 'Who told them that?'

'I don't know. But I've promised Luke I'll find out.'

'Ah.' He was not Luke. He would never be Luke. But there were times when that was no bad thing. Luke would have sat her down and teased out the twin, irreconcilable parts of her and made them talk it through in endless circles until one or other side gave way under the pressure. Murdo Cameron simply gazed at her with his brown eyes carefully neutral and the multitude of expressions smoothed clear from his face and said, 'That's not going to be easy.'

'No.' She found a belt and began to thread it through the jeans. It was leather and old and had been her father's. She had rubbed it with neat's-foot oil before she packed it. Now, the soft, animal smell rolled out as she uncoiled the leather. It was the smell of her father and it brought back the other smells of him: pipe smoke and shaving cream and the mix of Scotch and peanuts and Imperial mints. For a small, olfactory moment, the ward became another place and the ghosts took solid form. Luke was not among them.

She finished threading the belt, pulled the buckle tight and found she could pull it in a notch more than she used to, not quite back to when she was thirteen, but certainly a retreat to her early twenties and university.

She tucked the free end into the belt loop and looked up. Murdo Cameron was there as he had been before, still watching, still waiting for an answer. She sighed.

'Murdo, you have to remember that Jamie Buchanan was besotted with Sandra Smith – the whole hair and eyes thing fired him up like cartoons at Christmas. When he sees this – me – who I really am, there's every chance he won't want to have anything to do with me.'

'Really.'

'And that notwithstanding, the lad's never in his life been outside Glasgow. His mother may not be here anymore but his life's here, all his friends are here, everything he's ever known is here. He won't want to leave all of that.'

'I'd check that with Jamie, if I were you.'

'I'm sure you would, but I'm—' She stopped. It wasn't a good time to fight with Murdo. It wasn't a good time to fight with anyone but especially not him. She ran her fingers through the ends of her hair and her skin crawled at the feel of it. 'OK, fine. I'll go and talk to him now but I have to do something to my hair first. I can't live with it much longer and, frankly, if we're going to shake the foundations of his world, we may as well get it all over in one go.'

'Jamie?'

The boy opened his eyes. The room hadn't changed. The ceiling was still turquoise. Balloons in all three primary colours floated through cotton-wool clouds. Somewhere over towards the centre, a family of Teletubbies danced in a circle. Everywhere, there was too much colour. He wanted snow and he couldn't have it. The god had brought rain and the world outside had returned to grey. Waking was a mistake.

'Jamie?' A hand reached out and touched his. He let his gaze drift down the wall to the woman sitting at the side of his bed. She, too, was grey; grey eyes, grey skin, grey soul. She wore a grey cotton shirt tucked into over-washed jeans and the belt was so old the leather had bleached to no colour at all. Her hair was cropped short and black, like a raven, with a sheen to it that said it came out of a bottle. She smelled faintly of shampoo and shower gel, both of them men's. 'Good morning.' Her smile had a professional reticence. 'How are you feeling?'

He shrugged. In this place, the doctors asked questions for the sound of their voices, not because they wanted to hear any answers. His bad arm hurt in spite of the sling and the skin itched where the needle had gone into the vein when they put him to sleep. He wanted to go for a pee but not while there was a stranger sitting at the side of his bed. He shrugged a second time.

The woman was amused and trying not to show it. Her fingers traced the red wheal on the back of his hand. 'Bet it itches,' she said. He nodded for that. Elsewhere in the ward, the morning treatment round was coming to an end. The six-year-old girl in the opposite bed was resisting the needle. At his own bedside, the woman leant over to pick up his glass of water. 'May I?' He shrugged. He wanted her to go away but didn't know how to make her. He had no power to stop her taking his water.

She drank and put the glass back on the bedside table. 'Jamie, I don't want to insult your intelligence, but do you know who I am?' She had her head tipped on one side. His eyes roamed over her face and down to the hand that lay on the bed. Flat planes of scar tissue spread out across the back of it in patterns he had known for three months. Above that, half hidden by the cuffs of her shirt, wide-weave bandages encircled both wrists. He looked back at her face. A sticking plaster covered one cheekbone, hiding most of a bruise. He looked harder. Sunlight filtering in through the window behind him brightened the skin so that the snake-thread of the scar didn't show until he really looked for it, but it was there all the same. He reached out and traced the line all the way down from her eye to her lip. When he came to the end, he smiled for her, tentatively. She smiled back in a way that he knew.

'Good. I told Murdo you'd know.' She kissed the finger that rested on her face. 'Sorry about the eyes.' So was he. He touched her hair. It felt brittle. 'Dyed,' she said. She pushed her head against his hand so that his fingers ran through it. 'I'm afraid I'd had as much of the blonde as I could take. This is closer to the real thing. It's the right colour, if nothing else, and I've always wanted it short. Give it a month or two for the dye to grow out and you'll not know the difference.'

So she was grey and black, not scarlet and gold. He took time to absorb that information.

Orla McLeod shifted back in her chair. The lad looked better than he had done in the flat. Daylight suited him. Morning sun patterned the straw of his hair, warming it, softening the highlights. A series of nurses had washed him and fed him and cared for him so that his bones looked less likely to break if you touched him and his skin was losing the translucent quality she had known before. Even his eyes looked newly done. A faint wash of green coloured the grey and, for a moment, they had life to them, like water caught under ice. Then the smile and the flushed colour of greeting died away, and the frown that had been there on waking came back, carving a groove like a knife cut down the centre of his forehead.

'What's up?' she asked.

He shrugged.

'Is it the hair? I'm sorry, but this is who I am. I was hoping it wouldn't make too much difference.'

He shook his head. It wasn't the hair. There was nothing wrong with black hair. The eyes were a disappointment but nothing he couldn't handle.

'Then what?'

Nothing. He was silent, as he had been silent with his mother. He had been silent with Sandra, but not in the same way. Sandra – most of Sandra – had been safe. Orla McLeod was not necessarily so.

She reached out and took his good hand, the one not in the sling. It was a boy's hand, grown beyond the chubby plasticity of the child but not yet strengthened into the man. She stretched his fingers out and found that it was a musician's hand too, or an artist's; when she put her palm against his, the fingers were almost as long as hers.

She said, 'The day before yesterday, when we were still in the flat, I told you about a cottage in the mountains, and snow. Do you remember?'

He nodded, carefully. He remembered every word. He had repeated them to himself as a litany to help get him through the day and the night and part of a day that he had spent waiting for her to come to him. *Jamie, if you can get me out of here before they come back, I promise you, I'll take you away from here.* Each time, he had tried to believe that the words had been meant. Each time, the voice of his life's experience had told him that they were simply the coinage of the time, convenient bribery paid by an adult to a child to get what she wanted. *The snow will be six feet thick outside on the mountain. We can take sledges up the mountain and race them down to the back door . . .* If he closed his eyes, he could smell the snow. He could feel the crunch of it underfoot and know the dizzying lurch in his stomach as the sledge flew over the crest of the mountain. He could make snowballs and throw them at snowmen and if he worked hard, the snowmen would throw them back. But none of it was real. In a world of uncertainties, only the ward and his mother's death were real. He watched the woman with the grey eyes and the black hair and he was no closer to knowing the truth.

He sucked on his bottom lip, edging his tongue along the fresh line of healing tissue. The woman was looking at his hands and not at him. It was his mother's way, not to look at him when she was about to break a promise. He felt the knowledge of it sink in his stomach like a stone.

Orla McLeod linked her fingers through the boy's. 'The cottage belongs to my mother,' she said. 'We moved there when I was thirteen. I was like you, except that it was my father who had died. And my brother.' She ran her thumb across the palm of his hand. The lines on it were cleanly pink where before they had always been grimed and grey. She said, 'The village was a strange place to grow up. I think I was the only kid older than five and younger than sixteen in the whole of the village. We didn't walk to school, we went by bus. In winter, we went out in the dark and came home in the dark. On days when the snow was bad, we didn't go at all. I left them as soon as I was old enough – the school and the village both – and came to university in Glasgow because it had an underground so I could get from the flat where I lived to the library and back again even if the snowploughs hadn't got in to clear the roads. It wasn't a bad place to study, but it was the worst reason in the world for choosing it.'

She turned to look out of the window and shook her head. Both of them tried to imagine a snowplough working its way down Byres Road. For different reasons, both of them failed. She went on, 'I still go back home, though. I've always gone back and it has always been home. But I don't live there all the time. Not when I'm working on something where I have to be in Glasgow all the time. Like the last three months in the flat.'

She looked at him then. He sat very still. Her voice was very level, very practical, very reasonable. The words flowed past with the same liquid warmth they'd had in the flat and it would have been very easy for her to slip in the final denial without him noticing. He strained to catch every word and make sense of it. She saw him sit up and pay attention and smiled her thanks. 'I promised the other night that I'd get you out of the flat. I wasn't thinking, really, about the practicalities of taking you out to the village. You've lived all your life in the city. It's very different out there. You might not like it.'

There's a cottage in the country, with a mountain at the back of it and you can see the sea from the front door and there's a bedroom you can have all your own. Would you like that, Jamie?

He liked it. He was certain he would have liked it. He saw the chance of it vanish into the stale air of the ward like the aftermath of a dream. He stared past her at the bed opposite and had no way of knowing how much of the loss showed on his face.

'Jamie?' She reached out for him, sliding an arm round his shoulder, taking care for his sling. He sat stiffly, easing forward the fraction of an inch needed to keep her from touching him. She took her hand back. 'Jamie, what's wrong?'

He shrugged. On the far side of the room, the six-year-old had succumbed to the nurses. She was weeping noisily into her pillow and refusing to be comforted. Somewhere else, they were replacing a dressing, sticking it down with adhesive spray. The heady vapour of it spread out through the room so that he could no longer smell the woman beside him, which was good. He found a white cloud on the ceiling with a dark line drawn round it. It wasn't snow, but it was the best substitute he could find. He fixed the point where the white became black and let his mind go free. Her voice came from the far end of a tunnel, moving further away with each word she said.

'Jamie, all I'm saying is that you don't need to feel any sense of obligation . . . Jamie?'

He was gone, absent in a way he had not been absent with her before. She watched his face slacken and his eyes glaze. She slid off the chair onto the bed, folding her legs in so that her knees touched his. She took his one good hand in both of her own. 'Jamie, listen to me.' He didn't listen. She ducked her head so their eyes were level. 'Jamie? Don't leave me now. I wasn't saying you couldn't come. If I make a promise, I keep it. You saved my life, I'm not going to abandon you. If you still want to do it, you can come to the cottage and meet my mother and live there for as long as you want and I'll do my best to be there as much as I can. I can't promise you snow. There might not be snow. But I can promise you the mountain and the woods and the bedroom upstairs that looks over the sea. If there's enough snow, we'll take the sledges up the hill, or build an igloo in the woods and I'll teach you tracking, so you can live out there without getting lost.'

Watching him was like watching a glacier at the end of winter, waiting for the thaw that may never come because who knows when – or how – the ice ages start? She talked mindlessly of snow and the cottage and her mother and, because the ghosts were not really that far away, of her brother and her father and what it was like to live with them *there* without being *here*, and sometime around then, the spring happened and the thaw began. Slowly, and with gathering strength, the patch of skin on his cheekbones flushed as it had when he first knew who she was and the water ran clear again in the deeper layers of his eyes. Finally, to prove that he was back, the knife-cut frown carved itself anew on his forehead as he listened and tried to make sense of her. She reached out and smoothed it clear with the ball of her thumb.

'Jamie, I love you. Did I not tell you that?'

She opened her arms. With a cry like a distant gull he came to her and she held his head tight against her shoulder, ignoring the fire that pulsed in her wrists, running her hands through the mess of his hair and saying his name over and again into the curve of his ear.

'Jamie, Jamie . . . It's OK . . . Did you think I was saying you couldn't go?'

He was only nine. His fingers knotted in her hair and the words choked in his throat so he couldn't have spoken them out loud even if he had wanted to. The great weight in his stomach lifted and filled and spread outwards and he was sobbing; great, dry, silent, gut-wrenching sobs that reached out far beyond the confines of the bed so that the whole ward fell silent, watching. She picked him up then and carried the shell-weight of him through to the small private room next door with the fake stained-glass windows and the planted aquarium along one wall and they sat together on a beanbag in a patch of multicoloured sunlight with him huddled in the hollow of her body and she gave him the time and the space and the holding that he needed.

A long time later, when he came back to her for the second time, she bent and kissed the top of his head.

'Jamie. Beloved. The whole world is yours. All you have to do is tell me what you want from it.'

He looked up sideways and smiled. She smiled back. For the first time since waking, the promise to the living counted for more than the promise to the dead.

Murdo was in the car park. She found him asleep behind the wheel with the car parked on a double yellow line outside the main entrance to the casualty department. A security guard watched from a distance and did nothing to interfere when she opened the boot to get her purse from the bag. Murdo was awake by the time she slipped into the passenger seat. He waved at the guard as they left. The guard, watched by both of them in the rear-view mirrors, gave him the finger in return.

'Tell me you didn't pull rank.'

'I didn't pull rank.'

'You're a terrible bad liar, Murdo Cameron.'

'I know.' He grinned and it brightened the morning.

He had changed in the time since she'd seen him. Sleep, or the lack of it, showed more in the hollows of his cheeks than it had done in the ward. His hair was scraped back from his face, held tight by four turns of a rubber band, the way he kept it when he was expecting to meet authority. More importantly, he had been mainlining nicotine; the ashtray was full and a lit half-stub rested between his fingers. Getting into the car, the smell of smoke was the thing that had hit her hardest. She wound down the window and breathed brisk morning air. Further on, she sat on her hands. Murdo reached the exit onto Byres Road and stopped for the traffic. 'How's Jamie?' he asked.

'All the better for seeing me. He's coming to the cottage.'

'Good. That's very good.' A delivery van in yellow with a screaming orange logo swung in, taking up all of the entrance. Murdo stuck his arm along the back of her seat, cranking himself round to see out of the rear window so he could pull back into a parking slot. The van passed. He let it go and made no move to pull out again. 'I had a chat with Andy and Strang, yesterday,' he said. 'After I'd spoken with Jamie.'

'Why?'

'Because Laidlaw's talking witness protection and social services and—'

'Fuck that.'

'And we thought that you might not like it.'

'What I like has got nothing to do with it. Jamie Buchanan's nine years old, he's just lost his mother to an armload of smack and seen three men shot dead in front of him. The last thing he needs is a bunch of bleeding hearts in cardigans and corduroy. You can't expect—'

His mouth quirked in a half-smile, teasing and not teasing, together. 'I expect our highly trained professionals in the social services would take a very dim view of the woman who did the shooting asking to hold onto a traumatised child.'

'Do you. Fine.' He was being wilfully obtuse and she wasn't in the mood for it. More than anything else, she wanted a cigarette. She turned her head to breathe only the air from the window. Her hands crabbed under her thighs. Murdo leant across her and opened the glove compartment. Inside, on top of the RAC handbook and the service log, lay two packets of Marlboro. A blast of something not unlike smack swiped through her brain until she watched the packets pushed back and saw, on the envelope immediately below them, the blue-on-white crest of the University Pathology Department. The blast dissolved into a liquid, gibbering panic. She grabbed his wrist. 'Murdo, *no!* Please. I don't want to see—'

'I know. Gently. I wouldn't do that to you. Here.' Beneath that envelope was another, smaller, with her name written on it in Andy Bennett's handwriting. He tugged it out of the pile and dropped it on her knee. 'This is a present from Andy. I think you should read it before we go on up the road.'

It took a while to stop the shaking. Murdo closed the glove compartment, shutting away the red and white temptation. He turned off the ignition and leant back in his seat. A cyclist in a bespoke suit and a cycle helmet pushed a fold-away bike into a rack and bent down to pull off his cycle clips. As he stood, Murdo waved. The man peered in at them both, smiled and waved back. When she looked at him, wanting answers, he said, 'Gerard Galbraith. He was Jamie's surgeon.'

'Right.'

The man lifted a suitcase from a pannier. His route into the hospital passed by the car. There seemed some real possibility that he might venture to make conversation. Murdo wound down his window and leant his elbow on the ridge of the glass.

'If he calls you Mrs Tyler, don't tell him to fuck off.'

'What?'

'I really do think you should read what's in there.'

Galbraith waved again in passing but didn't stop. Murdo let his hand drop and drummed his thumb on the car door. Orla McLeod, who was not, never had been and never would be Mrs Luke Tyler, opened the envelope and found her marriage certificate, three years old, to say that she was.

'I don't understand. What good does it do if I'm married to Luke?'

'Keep going. There's more.'

She kept going. There was more. Folded behind the certificate was a will. She read the first line and the last and didn't believe either. 'Give me a break, Murdo. Lisa Buchanan couldn't write a shopping list without help. There's no way she'd ever get her act together to write a will.'

'Women do the strangest things where their children are concerned. She wasn't always flying kites and I would suggest that if the father of the child had provided the solicitor and the money and the transport to and from, she might have put her signature to something that promised to take care of Jamie in the event of her early demise. Anyway –' he was not smiling at her, not with his lips, but it was there in his eyes and in the tilt of his head and all the things that showed he had tried something difficult and had managed it and was feeling pleased. It wasn't clear, then, if it was her that was the hard thing or something else. 'Anyway, it's all on the computer if you go and look for it. Jamie Buchanan is registered as the son of Lisa Buchanan and Luke Tyler. The CSA have Luke down as the father and if you look at his bank account, you'll find that he's been drawing cash each month to pay over to her for maintenance, so they're all well and happy.'

Orla read the things she hadn't read on the sheet of paper that was supposed to be Lisa Buchanan's will. 'It says she wants Jamie to go to Luke if she dies.'

'Yes.'

'But Luke's dead. Even if I was pretending to be his wife, I'd still have to jump through hoops to have any right to look after him.'

'Only in a manner of speaking.' Murdo rubbed the side of his nose. What he was pleased with was not only her. 'There's not that many folk know that he's dead. He went through pathology under a cover name and Strang's been battening down the hatches on the information spreading from anyone who was there on Friday night. If you look on the computer, I think you'll find that he doesn't die, in digital terms, for a couple of weeks yet.'

'In digital terms?'

He smiled at last – because it had been difficult and he had spent most of a day on it when he should have been doing other things and he was very pleased indeed with the result. So he grinned in the way that showed the chip on the corner of his front tooth and made the crow's feet dance at his eyes and said, 'Hey, it's a computer. I can make it do anything.'

He reached for the key and started the car again. By the time they reached the exit, he was serious again, his voice rougher and more his own. 'We thought you'd need time for you and the lad to see if you rub along. If it goes well, we'll have Luke die in a car accident and you, the grieving widow, will have been named in his will as Jamie's legal guardian.'

'And if we don't "rub along"?'

'Then we'll have to think of something else. Maybe by then we'll know him well enough to know what he might want to do.'

'Fine. Thank you.'

'You're very welcome.'

At the next break in the traffic, they turned right into Byres Road and got caught up in the queue for the lights. Murdo reached into the glove compartment for the open packet of Marlboro, tipped one out and lit it. Thin lines of smoke fanned from his nostrils. He held it out. 'Want one?'

'No.'

'That's two of us make bad liars, then.'

'Piss off.'

'If you say so.' He shrugged and blew the smoke out of his own window. As soon as they started moving again, the wind caught it up and blew it back into the car. In a while, when he held the cigarette out for a second time, she took it. A while after that, when she didn't give it back, he lit another one for himself.

'How did you know I was smoking?' she asked.

'We found cigarette ends in the flat. Most of them had traces of saliva that could be sampled. A percentage of them tested positive to your DNA.'

'And Luke's?'

'And Luke's. And all three of the dead men and the two women. Not the boy and not any other unidentified individual so either Svensen wasn't there or he doesn't smoke.'

'Or both.'

'Possibly.'

They crawled in first gear past the entrance to the underground station. The turnstiles spun a steady stream of students, shoppers and general detritus out onto the street. None of them looked into the car. Murdo said, 'How many were you doing?'

'Fags? Twenty a day, thereabouts. Plus whatever I could bum off Luke.'

He sucked in a breath and held it and spent some time watching his wing mirrors when there was nothing of consequence behind him. She said, 'This is the last one. I'm giving up.'

'Right.' He pulled past a cyclist and needn't have bothered. The traffic stopped again and the bike overtook him at the next set of lights. He kept his eyes on the road behind and said, carefully, 'The medics think you should stay on the nicotine until the smack is clear of your system.'

'What? How do they . . . ? Jesus Christ.' She wound down her window and flung the cigarette, half finished and still lit, onto the street. 'And why the fuck would they tell you a thing like that?'

'They didn't.' He shrugged. 'It was on the computer.'

'Right. "Hey, it's a computer." God, you're so fucking smug. Were you just bored with sitting around at the bedside or did Strang ask you to look?'

He said nothing. They reached the last set of lights and turned left onto Great Western Road and still he said nothing. She pushed up her sleeve and ran her fingers over the greening bruise at the angle of her arm. Simply by pressing on it, she could bring back the stab of the needle and the sudden flooding cold of the drug. From there it was a very short step into the darkness of the other world where the pressing weight of the sofa was the only real thing she could remember. The ache in the pit of her guts became, if she concentrated on it, a vast, screaming void. She lit another cigarette and let the smoke scorch her throat and her windpipe and filter, cooler, through the mesh of her lungs. By halfway down the length of it, the ache had dulled to a simple craving for something she didn't want and couldn't have. 'Do they think I might take to buying my next hit?'

'They think that if you smoke you might find it easier not to.'

'Wonderful.' The nicotine made her head buzz. In the beginning, three months ago, she had hated it. She would have given a great deal to be able to hate it again. 'How long is it going to take?' she asked.

'They're not sure. Anything from two days to a couple of weeks. They don't know how fast your metabolism can chew through the crap. Apparently it depends on how much previous experience you've had.'

'Previous experience of what?'

'Recreational pharmaceuticals.'

'What?' When she frowned, the flat burn at the side of her head twisted the rest of her brow out of line. It was the only time he noticed it. She was frowning at him now. 'Get a grip, Murdo. I smoked Benson and Hedges. I drank vodka. If I was pushed, I drank beer. I didn't do drugs. Neither of us did. We were working, for Christ's sake.'

The traffic slowed back to a crawl on Great Western Road. Murdo balanced the car on the clutch and it inched forward as if towed by the bus in front. He leant sideways against the door. 'Art Gould said they found skunk in the flat,' he said.

'Well done, Art. A blind, deaf, de-scented sniffer dog could have found skunk in that flat. You could have squeezed it neat from the curtains.'

'But you weren't doing it?'

'I wasn't, no. Not unless you count being in the same room as Lisa when she was on a roll.' She reached behind the seat for the bottle of water he kept there, twisted off the top and drank. 'Svensen doesn't let his people do drugs,' she said. 'At least not while they're working. No skunk, no smack, no acid, no nothing. I was Luke's and therefore by default I was Svensen's. Kirsty and Lisa were different. They lived with Jared because it suited them, not because they were his. They did whatever they wanted – which was everything – but the rest of us were clean.'

'Until the end.'

'Until the end. I think you could say that by then all bets were off.'

The traffic moved. They turned right at the lights into a residential street of tall, smoke-stained sandstone houses, fronted by moss-free lawns and square, precision-clipped privet hedges. She tipped the seat back and hooked her heels on the dashboard. 'Was there anything in Luke?' she asked.

'Drugs? No. Not that I know of.' He turned right for a second time and parked at the kerb. 'Should there have been?'

'I don't know. I thought maybe they might have used it on him in the beginning too, to get him to talk. I hoped . . .'

He turned off the engine. In the sudden quiet, a blackbird sang. She blew smoke at the gap in the sunroof. The bruise on her cheek itched beneath the plaster. She lifted the edge and peeled it off. The vanity mirror showed a puffed and blackened island that magnified the asymmetry of her face. Three sutures lined up along the ridge of her cheekbone, the free ends rusted with old blood. She pushed the sun visor up against the roof and turned to face Murdo. 'You've not done smack, have you?'

He looked at her and didn't look away. 'No.'

'No. Neither had I. I asked Lisa once, way back, when we were alone, what it was like and why she kept going when it was taking her apart.'

'What did she say?'

'That you don't realise how much pain you're in until it hits your brain – and then you're not – and then it wears off and the pain all comes back, worse than before, only then you know what it's like to be without.' She watched the glowing end of her cigarette as it dulled slowly to ash. 'I thought . . . I thought that if they'd pumped Luke then he'd have had an hour or two of not feeling anything. That would have been good.'

She was looking out of the window. All he could see was the side of her face. It told him nothing. He said, 'Strang doesn't know that I've looked at your records. The doctors told him that they thought you'd be safe to drive in forty-eight hours. They've advised two weeks off work and he's agreed.'

'Fuck that.' She said it quietly, out of the window.

'I don't think it's negotiable,' he said. 'If nothing else, it'll give you time to get Jamie home and settled.'

'Right. And meanwhile some bastard somewhere is singing to Svensen, only now they can give him anything they want and say it was Luke who blew it.' She reached out and touched his wrist and for the first time he saw her clearly, without the blur of drugs or memories or sleep. She said, 'They knew my *name*, Murdo. Right at the start, they knew my name. They hadn't laid a finger on Luke then.'

'I know. I heard you. I think I'd sleep better if I didn't believe it.'

'You might. You might also die in your bed if we don't find out who it is. There's no such thing as an incorruptible policeman and Svensen's made his living buying folk off. He took three entire stables off three different pimps without killing any one of them simply by finding what the girls wanted and seeing that they got it. If he can buy a whore, he can buy a name or a notebook. All he has to do is find the right price.'

'Maybe.' The street was very still. Two blocks away, the traffic purred its way to Anniesland and back. In the douce, expensive cul-de-sac in which Strang had chosen to base his division, a woman in cashmere and fur stood looking the other way while her standard poodle defecated on the pavement, a cat stalked songbirds from the heights of a wall and a gardener knelt on a newspaper and inched along a gravel path, using a small pair of shears to trim the edge of a lawn. Murdo leant forward and lit himself a final cigarette. He considered the possible price of a notebook and decided that, in the scale of things, it was not really very high. 'Svensen got the Afghan consignment,' he said.

'Luke's sting?' She had forgotten that. And she had not thought they would lose it. 'How did they fuck that up?'

'Svensen went for it early on Saturday morning – an hour or so after we got you and Jamie into the hospital.' The smoke hazed the inside of the windscreen. The woman with the poodle looked in and tutted her disapproval. Murdo said, 'Everyone who mattered was in the basement with Luke – or setting up an incident room, or harassing forensics for information. The drop was Luke's baby; he set it up, he reeled it in. As far as they knew then, he hadn't told Svensen the details. They weren't expecting anything to happen with him not there.'

'Fuckwits.'

'Strang reckons the street value at over three million.'

'Oh, Jesus Christ. And we gave it to him on a plate.' She closed her eyes tight until she saw a bright, arterial red flowing freely against the muted black of her lids. In a while, when it had cleared, she raised her head. 'Who did it, Murdo? Who knew we were in there?'

'I don't know. Not too many. Those three, clearly.' He nodded forwards, out through the window, past the woman with the dog to the house and the drive standing opposite. Three cars sat in line abreast on the gravelled path, facing outwards, ready to leave. Morning dew gathered on the bonnets, glittering in the slanting sun. All of them had been there since dawn, if not longer. He matched the names to the number plates and listed them aloud. 'Strang knew you were in there because he sent you. The buck stops with Billie Reid so there's no way he can't have known. Laidlaw had the manpower for the sting so he'll have been in from the time that got off the ground, if not before. Reid and Laidlaw might have told one or two others, but that's as far as it goes.'

A fourth car stood at a distance from the rest, a six-year-old Astra estate with a not quite perfect respray on one front wing. Orla said, 'What about Art? Was he in on anything?'

'No. Forensics won't have had a clue until they were called on Friday night. Nobody who didn't have to heard a whisper of what was happening. Strang was running this tighter than he's ever run anything.'

'Not tight enough.'

'No.'

They sat in silence, turning over and over the cost and rewards of betrayal. Murdo blew a streamer of smoke at the ceiling. 'Strang wouldn't sing,' he said. 'If we're making a list, his name isn't on it.'

'Why? Because the Division's his baby? Forget it, Murdo, you can buy a man's kids if you pay him enough, and after this, Svensen has enough to pay anyone.'

'Not Strang. There isn't enough money in Scotland to pay him off now. He spent four hours yesterday sitting in a white room in the basement of the Western watching the medics do the postmortem on Luke. It took him apart. You wouldn't have recognised him when he walked out. Last week, getting Svensen was a professional challenge, a tick on a sheet, a way of justifying divisional expenses. Now . . .' He shrugged.

'Now it's personal?'

'Very.'

'Good.' She smiled thinly. 'That makes two of us.' She reached for the packet of fags. He laid his hand on top. She looked at him. 'Three?' she asked.

'Three,' he agreed. And then, because he knew who else was inside the big house at the end of the drive, 'And Andy. Which makes it four. It's not bad odds.'

'It's not.'

The cigarettes lay under their fingers. With his thumb, he opened the lid. It was empty. He reached into the glove compartment for the spare and tossed it towards her. 'Present,' he said. 'Greater love hath no man than that he handeth over his last packet of fags to his friend.'

He smiled. She smiled back. 'Thank you.' She leant over and kissed him on the side of the cheek. The stiff ends of the sutures on her cheekbone scratched at his chin. He pulled his lighter from his pocket and passed her that, too. 'Don't waste them.'

'Trust me.' She unbuckled her safety belt and kicked open the door. 'Let's go and see if anyone in there looks like they've bought a new suit recently.'

Three

From the outside, the tall, square, sandstone mansion at the end of the gravel path mirrored the others in the street. If you pay enough, even bullet-proof glass can be made to look antique and Alec Strang had made sure he paid plenty. The interior was different. Where the neighbours spent their money on replica Rennie Mackintosh inlays for the front doors and original Brockies for the walls, Strang directed the remainder of his resources at his people, his equipment and the excavation of his basement, and he left the finer points of interior decoration to the departmental carpenters, electricians and general handymen. Thus, the oak-panelled walls and Axminster carpets left by the previous occupants burned under the glare of fluorescent strip lights hanging from bare wires and the cold, high-ceilinged reception rooms and bedchambers were subdivided into smaller, more functional units by six-foot-high stands of plasterboard painted with two layers of off-white emulsion. For a certain small group of those born and brought up in similar surroundings, the result was sacrilege, which was, perhaps, one of the reasons why Strang did it. The rest were simply glad to be out of the city centre and made the most of the amenities offered.

The meeting room was on the first floor; a long, narrow room, overheated and under-ventilated and filled with second-hand office furniture. A mix of sound and smoke filtered out through the open door and down to the hallway below; cigars and cigarettes and coffee mingled with Strang's public school vowels, Billie Reid's east end Glaswegian and Laidlaw's Edinburgh laced with a touch of the officers' mess. Orla picked out her own name, twice, and Luke's; everything else was lost in a blur of low pitch and poor diction. She slipped the unopened cigarette packet from her pocket and gripped it end on, seeking comfort in the square-edged pressure on her palm, then she tapped Murdo on the shoulder and they walked up the stairs more quietly than was strictly necessary. As they reached the top, one voice rose over the rest, languid and resonant and educated and spiked with acid humour.

'. . . staringly obvious. Whatever else you want to say about Tord Svensen, the man's not stupid. If he left things behind, it's because he was planning to come back for them when he had time and if he left McLeod to the other three, then it's because there was nothing left he needed to know.'

They stood in the shadows of the doorway and watched him. Detective Chief Superintendent Donald Laidlaw was, indeed, wearing a new suit. The nap of it caught the harsh glare of the light, enfolding it in the way that only very new wool can. Murdo pursed his lips wryly. Orla puffed her cheeks and shook her head. Neither took it as a sign of anything other than personal ostentation. Donald Laidlaw was the kind of man to buy new suits on a monthly basis. He would do it for the same reason he went rough shooting in Argyll and fishing on the Tweed and stocked his bar with twenty-year-old Lagavulin – because his mind-set demanded it and the cost was no problem. That wasn't to say he couldn't be bought, just that the price would be higher than that required for anyone else in the room, if not the force, and a new suit wasn't going to be a significant indicator. Orla watched him as he lounged against the wall not far from the table, fitting his shoulders to the oak panelling as if the craftsmen had measured the width of his back before they ever set out to line the walls of the room. He slipped one hand in the pocket of his trousers, leant a foot back on the skirting board and changed the pitch of his voice. Whatever point he was making, it needed the extra bite for emphasis.

'Svensen makes two kinds of kills,' he said, and the consonants ricocheted off the walls, 'and this does not fit into either pattern. The small fry, the punters, the pushers, the thugs who get in the way, the men who won't or can't be bought off, get the single shot to the head but there's no damage beforehand and he is very, very careful to leave us no forensic evidence. The only way we know it was him is word on the street. Until now, the only one to break this mould was Pyotr Terveyev, also known as Kodiak, who may or may not have had connections to the Russian mob.'

'He had connections, Donald, there's no question of that.' That was Billie Reid, Assistant Chief Constable of Strathclyde, a broad-shouldered, balding individual who fought his way out of Glasgow's east end and up the promotional ladder on willpower and gut feeling and a ferocious intelligence masquerading as working-class wit. The Russian problem was his and he nursed it with the devotion of a family feud. He said, 'That man was the toehold for half of the Eastern Bloc to walk into Glasgow.'

'If you say so. In which case perhaps we can count on the Russians to come in for a spot of revenge in their own right but I wouldn't want to hold my breath. Either way, it is still the case that we have never seen the body although half of Glasgow has apparently been shown the photographs of what he looked like before, and immediately after, he died. I haven't had the pleasure myself but I understand they're not pretty—'

'I have and they're not.' Murdo didn't move. He was leaning against the doorpost with his hands in the pockets of his leather jacket and his hair, which had been caught back when they reached the top of the stairs, was hanging loose around his shoulders. For those familiar with the complex lexicon of his body language, it said quite clearly that he was not in the right frame of mind to make allowances for rank. 'Is this going somewhere useful?' he asked quietly. 'We have a lot of ground to cover on other things if it's not.'

Three men answered him together.

'DCS Laidlaw has a theory—'

'We were discussing the likely compromise to the unit in the wake of—'

'We've got three million quid's worth of smack floating round Glasgow and we need to—'

And then a fourth voice, less weighted than the rest, said, 'Orla. It's good to see you.'

For that, there was silence. Art Gould stepped forward from his seat at the table. He was a lean, pale, bronze-haired lad with freckles and wire-rimmed glasses. They shook hands. His grip was dry, almost parched, and it sent all kinds of comfort. They shared a smile. 'How are you?' he asked and it sounded as if he meant it.

'I'm fine.' Orla sat down. 'Very glad to be able to join you.' If there was irony there, nobody responded. 'Everyone who works for Svensen has seen those photographs. It kept the rest of us in line.'

She waited. None of them responded to that either which made it likely that they had all been allowed to read her first report from the flat. Laidlaw raised his brows politely which was never a good sign. Once, a long time ago, he had been her superior officer and she had learned very early not to trust him.

'Terveyev was spectacular,' she said, 'but nothing like Luke. They cut his femoral arteries and held him down while he died. There was blood everywhere and they enhanced it postmortem but he will have been dead inside three minutes. Luke was in there for six hours. I don't think we can draw too many comparisons.'

Billie Reid, oddly, had the poorest stomach for that. He grasped at other things. 'Terveyev tried to rip off Svensen's first run of smack, aye?'

Orla looked at Strang. He raised one brow and lifted one shoulder in a shrug that seemed, on balance, to be closer to a nod than a shake.

'No,' she said. 'Terveyev topped Leah Harris.'

'What?' Assistant Chief Constable Reid was a big man and very little of it was fat. His forearms rested on the table top, leaking greasy sweat on either side. He kept his hair cropped short so that, as it thinned with age, he looked harder, not older. Liver spots the size of match heads ran in a perforating line along his brow. Orla watched them ripple through a question to its unpalatable answer. Reid had four men working full time on Leah Harris and everyone present was aware of that fact. He was not a happy man. 'Why were we not told about this?'

'Security,' said Strang, calmly. 'If it wasn't on the street, we couldn't be seen to know about it. Luke had this straight from the horse's mouth. We weren't about to compromise his position.'

Reid swore vividly, opened a notebook and made a single note in a hand that scored through the top dozen pages. Orla said, 'Terveyev hit Leah after she left him to work for Svensen. Until then, Svensen's strongest card was to guarantee protection to any of the girls who switch stables and go over to him. If the Bear had been allowed to get away with it, Svensen would have lost the whole basis of his operation.'

'Then why didn't he plaster it all over Glasgow after he cut him up?'

'Because he wants to be seen as infallible. He put it out that the man tried to rip off his drugs – which is enough to show people not to mess with him without letting it be known that he'd blown it with Leah. And I suspect it amuses him to have you throwing time and men at a case when there's no chance of a conviction.'

'Do you? How very droll.' *Droll.* The kind of word that Strang would use, or Laidlaw, in parody. It came oddly from Reid, as if he swore in foreign when all other avenues were closed to him. 'So do I have to continue to "throw time and men at it" or can I pull them off and put them to something more useful?'

Strang would have answered, but he gave her space first and she took it. 'No. Of the people who knew, Luke was the only one at risk.'

'So who's left that knows now?'

'Svensen, clearly, and Drew Doherty. Jared Grant knew because he told Luke – but he died in the flat.' A thought struck her. 'Doherty's probably the only man Svensen's got left that he trusts enough with that much detail.'

'So we need to watch for him recruiting more.'

'Maybe. But he may not need to for a while now. Terveyev died at the start of December which was when Svensen moved up into top gear with his recruitment drive. Since then, most folk have either been prepared to be bought or they've moved out. As of last week, there's only Jake Turner and the Malaysians left in competition and even Svensen isn't going to touch the gooks.'

There was a brief and colourful pause. Reid was making more notes. Laidlaw had made a steeple of his fingers and was tapping it to his lips in a way that made him look like a priest. It was not a helpful image.

She said, 'If we're going to refocus our attention somewhere new, then we want to put a twenty-four/seven on Turner and see what he does. If you put some of Laidlaw's people on him, we may be able to goad him into doing something stupid. It's the only decent angle we have left.'

She had thought of this in the flat, but not with any clarity. In the more lucid patches of the night, she had constructed a single, succinct train of action that would appeal to the hierarchy and get them moving.

Laidlaw was watching her, still tapping his lips. She smiled at him archly. 'Is that what you were going to suggest?'

'No.' He ran his tongue round the outer rim of his teeth. 'But it's very interesting nonetheless.' The man should have been a lawyer. He had the mind for it; the ceaseless unravelling of words and their meanings, the careful twisting of sentences to make them say what he wanted. It made him dangerous in ways that Billie Reid was not. He said, 'I was suggesting – and it was not being well-received – that Luke Tyler had *not* given Svensen accurate details of the Afghan shipment in advance of its arrival—'

'He hadn't. He was running it tight on a need to know and they trusted him to do it. They were gearing up to go out when the shit hit the fan. He hadn't time to tell anyone anything.'

'Thank you. In which case, I would suggest that Svensen left the basement as soon as he realised that it was still possible for him to gain access to the goods, which means, essentially, as soon as he had got that information from Luke.' He paused and when she said nothing, went on, 'This means that the loss of the shipment, while unfortunate in itself—'

'It's a catastrophe, Donald,' said Billie Reid, but then, keeping hold of it hadn't been his responsibility.

'—while regrettable, is not the key issue. We have to accept that if Svensen knew the arrangements in sufficient detail to lift the stuff as cleanly as he did, then everything else that Luke Tyler knew can no longer be considered his intellectual copyright, so to speak.'

No longer his intellectual copyright. This from a man who had spent most of the weekend in the basement where Luke had died and who must, at least once, have seen the body. Jesus Christ.

Orla McLeod swallowed on a mouth gone dry. The void in her diaphragm swelled, like a bubble blown from a pipe, constricting her breath. She looked up again and found that Strang was watching her, that they were all watching her – except Murdo who had his chair tipped back against the wall and his heels up on the table the better to study the intricacies of the plaster rose on the ceiling. Of all of them, she had expected better from Murdo, for Luke, if not for her. He deserved more from his friends. She had taken a breath to say so when, from the far side of the table, without lowering his chair, Murdo said, 'I thought Art had got us some useful forensics. Would this be a good time to see it, perhaps?'

There was a gap and a small sound as she shut her mouth. It was artless and entirely unsubtle – and they let him do it.

Laidlaw examined his fingernails, nodding. Billie Reid took out a tin of tobacco and began to roll his own. Strang said simply, 'Thank you, Murdo.' And then, 'Art?'

The young man sat up. 'From the top?'

'If you don't mind.'

'No problem.' Art Gould was in his mid-twenties and carried himself with the competence of a man twice his age. He reached back from his chair and pushed a button on the wall. Moments later, a series of electric blinds slid silently down the windows and the room lights dimmed. He moved his laptop to the centre of the table and stroked his thumb across the touch pad. A screen on the wall opposite glowed briefly silver and then dissolved to show a small mass of distorted metal photographed against a matt blue background.

'It's early days yet but we have two items of significance in the Tyler case so far.' He spoke with a lilting Galloway accent that made no attempt to soften the facts. 'You both know that, whatever else happened first, Luke Tyler was killed by the single shot to the head which is the trademark – the alleged trademark – of the individual known at Tord Svensen. The pathologist has identified a nine-millimetre projectile entry wound to the left temporal region with an angle of fire estimated at five degrees dorso-ventral, eight degrees caudo-rostral. This,' he used a laser pointer to indicate the mass of lead, 'is the bullet that killed him. We picked it out of the brickwork to the right of where he was sitting in a position consistent with the angle of fire. So far, so much routine. On this evidence alone we couldn't say for certain that it was Svensen, but it matches several previous killings attributed to him and this time we have Orla's evidence to place him in the basement at the time of death. Having got the projectile – and that's a first in this particular series – we organised a fingertip search of the wasteland opposite the flat.' He smiled thinly. 'At the cost of seventy-two hours' total overtime and a dozen of Strathclyde's youngest who now hate my guts, we found this.' He moved his thumb and the screen split in two. A 9mm shell casing occupied the second half. 'It was halfway across the ground in a direct line from the door of the basement to the multistorey car park. It may not look like it from here but you'll have to take my word for it that the two fit together. The bit that's keeping us up nights is here,' he touched the pad again and the screen dissolved and re-formed to show the shell casing magnified, side lit and dusted. A clear pattern of whorls showed at the open mouth. The screen split again and the right side showed two partial prints laid flat in standard format – black streaks pressed onto a white ground. 'It's a thumb and forefinger.' He circled each with the pointer. 'They're not complete, clearly, and they may not be his. Any number of people touch a shell between the time it's made and the time it goes into the gun. But these are the only prints anywhere on the casing or on the round, which makes me think the whole lot was wiped clean at some point and that this is a late arrival. Simply going on the evidence, it looks as if whoever shot Luke picked the thing up in a hurry and didn't mean to drop it.' He turned to look at Orla and then at Murdo.

'If this is not a plant – and that's the big question – then it looks as if Svensen has made his first real mistake. It's not enough to convict on, but it may be enough for us to get a handle on who he is. It's certainly more concrete than anything else we've had in the past six months.' He touched the pad again and the wall dissolved to darkness. The button on the wall brought the lights up in the room. The blinds stayed in place covering the windows. He twisted round to face Strang.

'If DCS Laidlaw is right, this is gold dust,' he said. 'If not, then I've just wasted a scarily big chunk of your annual forensic budget on a worldwide trawl of the data bases.'

'Right.' Strang smiled without humour. 'If it comes up with the Queen Mother, I'll believe it's a fake. In the meantime, spend what it takes.'

'Do the prints match any of the ones you found in the flat?' It was Reid. He held the unlit roll-up in the centre of his mouth and the question came out round it in undiluted Gorbals Glaswegian. The flame of his lighter flickered an inch beyond the end.

Gould shook his head. 'They don't match anything we've picked up so far but we're not finished going through it all yet. It could still come up.'

'Unless he was never there, in which case you're wasting your time.' Laidlaw had moved to sit on the edge of the desk. He toyed idly with the touch pad on the computer, splintering the graphics on the screen. 'We don't have DI McLeod's final report yet,' he said. 'In fact, it would appear that we have only been given a selected reading of all her reports so perhaps DCS Strang has the answer.' He tilted the screen so that pale green light washed over Art and then onto Strang. 'Alec?' he asked. 'Was he ever there?'

'I don't know. He hadn't been up to last time we had a report. Luke was the only one who had seen him face to face. You've seen everything I've seen on that one: we have a Caucasian male of medium height with Nordic colouring and a dental anomaly. That narrows us down to roughly five per cent of the male population of Glasgow, assuming the hair, the eyes and the teeth were real, which they may well not have been. If Orla knows any different, she hasn't had time to pass it on to me.'

Billie Reid was lighting his roll-up and he was using real tobacco, dark, black, tarry stuff, as different from the insipid pallor of Murdo's factory-made tabs as instant coffee is from the real thing. The match touched the frayed and juicy ends, shrivelling them to ash. He sucked in, drawing the flame deeper, and the sweet, woody smell of it crashed into her, lighting her up from the inside out. She closed her eyes and let it flow in all the ways that it could – through the fine membranes of her nose, her eyes, her mouth and, further down, the finer filaments of her lungs. Her blood bucked and fizzed and spun up to her head. Reid grinned and blew her a second hit. 'Well?' he asked. 'Seems you're all we've got left. Was he there, lass?'

She thought afterwards that, without the smoke, she might have had the sense to let it pass. Instead she said, 'Yes. He came up about nine o'clock on Friday morning and left again just after ten.'

'Did you see him? I mean, could you do us an e-fit?'

Orla shook her head. 'No. I'm sorry, I didn't see him.'

And of course Laidlaw was there, worming in for the details. He had always been good at finding the weak spots in her reports. He said, 'Why not, if he was in the flat? That's what you were there for, wasn't it – to get an ID?'

She had been in that flat for many reasons; to support Luke in his cover, to find out the things about Svensen's network that only a woman could find, to make contacts and, yes, to get an ID. Some things are less possible than others. She considered a lie and told him the truth. 'I was in bed. The bedroom is upstairs. He didn't come up, I didn't go down, so, no, I didn't see him.'

'In bed? At ten o'clock in the morning?' He was laughing at her and he wasn't thinking.

'In bed. With Luke. I was his whore, remember?'

There was silence. Around the table, four different men remembered and each one of them failed to keep it from his face. Only Murdo didn't change but then it was likely that Murdo had never forgotten.

'Really?' Laidlaw was never off balance for long. 'I was under the impression that DI Tyler didn't—'

Alec Strang cleared his throat. His glasses caught the reflection of the overhead lights, making it difficult to see his eyes. 'Fine.' He reached out and tapped his fag end on the ashtray. 'I don't think we need the details now, do we, people?' More than Reid's his accent had a way of drawing them back into line. Laidlaw smiled benignly. She stared past him to a point on the wall. Neither of them spoke and whatever might have been said was put away for later. The worst of the tension passed.

Murdo reached over and took the packet of cigarettes from under her hand, opened it and lit one. When he offered it across the table, she shook her head.

'Art,' Strang stood up and reached out his hand to the young man on the other side of the desk. 'Thank you for coming. I'll expect updates by fax unless you come up with anything significant, in which case call my pager.'

'No problem.' The lad stood up, gathering his equipment.

'Hold on.' Orla leant forward, turning the laptop to face her and pressed a key. The two partial prints showed again on the screen, black on white, a few whorls from the tip of the finger and thumb. She ran her hand down the screen, feeling the texture of it, thinking. 'Art, Murdo, is there any way we can map out the rest of these digitally?'

'Maybe.' Murdo.

'I think so.' Art.

'Which?'

It was Art who answered. 'We can give it a go but the technology's new and it's not very sound.'

'It never is. How do you do it?'

'We extrapolate from known partial prints to their final full equivalent and then map the algorithms for that onto the unknown print. It's not definitive and it works better if we've got twenty-five per cent or more of the original. Anything less than that and we generate too many different alternatives.'

'How much do we have of these?'

'Fifteen per cent, thereabouts.'

'Is it expensive?'

'Mapping the prints costs nothing. Running anywhere between fifty to eighty potential red herrings through the data bases will cost an arm and a leg.' He looked pointedly at Strang. '*Another* arm and a leg.'

'So we hop on back to the baseline if it fails. We're not going to get anything on a fifteen per cent print.' She looked across the table. 'Alec?'

He drew in a breath and held it. The part of him that managed the budget balanced a waning income against the chances of finding an answer. At a different time, or in a different case, he would have saved his money for something with better odds of success. Now, he let the breath out through flattened lips. 'Go for it,' he said.

The gloves came off as soon as Art Gould left. In many ways it was simpler like that. Laidlaw stopped trying to modify his smile. Strang stopped pretending that everything was fine. Murdo Cameron still found it useful to study the detail of the plasterwork on the ceiling but he made no effort to hide what he thought from the rest of them. Billie Reid skinned up for the second time. The smell of fresh smoke made her giddy. Orla got up and poured coffee from the filter pot bubbling near the doorway. On the way back to the table, she pressed the button on the wall. The blinds eased up, letting in slanting strands of sunlight.

'So?' she said as she sat down. 'Do I gather Svensen didn't come back to the flat on Saturday morning?'

No one answered.

'Wonderful.' She closed Murdo's packet of fags and sat her mug, with care, on top. 'So much for the subtle approach.'

Strang said, 'Subtlety didn't come into it. There was never any chance he would come.' He pulled a photograph from his file, spun it and pushed it across the table towards her. 'Art took these on the far side of the wasteland opposite the tenement.'

The print slid to a stop against her finger. She looked down at a patch of trampled snow, flecked here and there with a scattering of greyed-out fag ash. It could have been a black and white, but for the sodium orange cast on the white that gave it away as colour. She closed her eyes. For the rest of her life, that orange was going to be linked to the sound of a man's voice, screaming. She opened her eyes. Nobody, this time, was watching her. She spun the print back to Strang's file. The healing cuts at her wrists ached as if they were new. 'Svensen?' she asked.

'We believe so. There's a corner by the multistorey where you can stand and watch and not be seen. Did he have a four-wheel drive, do you know?'

'I've no idea.'

'Never mind, it doesn't matter. We were too late anyway. The tracks we've got aren't good enough to get any kind of meaningful forensic.' He filed the print, in order, amongst the papers in front of him. 'So we have partial fingerprints and a mess of footprints in the snow and that's it. The chances are that he heard the shot that hit the kid. Even if he didn't, he must have seen the three of us going in. There's no way he was going to show from the moment we walked in the front door. I'm sorry.'

'Don't be.' He had no need to be sorry. She was the one who had called for help. They both knew that. She drank her coffee and tried to get a feel for the things she was missing. There were a lot of those. Strang, for instance, was avoiding something. He had been avoiding it since she had walked in. Slowly, she worked it out. 'Where's Andy?' she asked.

The silence changed. Strang hadn't been the only one avoiding that. She looked at Billie Reid who looked away. Beside him, Strang took off his glasses and tapped the curved arm ends to his lips. His eyes were thinly brown, like old tea, with a lacework of vessels crossing the sclera so that the whites were almost as dark as the rest. He was badly in need of sleep. 'He's downstairs,' he said, eventually. 'I sent him to bed. There was no point in him—'

Laidlaw was less patient. 'He's off the case,' he said.

'What?'

The room echoed and twitched around her. Strang sighed and laid his glasses on his file. At the other end of the table, she saw Murdo Cameron finally bring his eyes down from the ceiling and saw Billie Reid, beside him, lay a restraining hand on his arm.

It was Reid, in the end, who answered her. 'This is what DCS Laidlaw was discussing when you came in,' he said carefully. 'Your unit's blown out the water. There's no question of that. We can't have someone working on an investigation of this magnitude when their integrity may have been compromised. I'm sorry.'

They stared each other out. For all his size and the sound of his vowels and the odd mismatch of slang and official idiom, he was not stupid, nor did he speak without reason. He was also, of the three of them, the one most neutral when it came to the welfare of the

Division. He was not, however, her immediate superior. She turned back to Strang.

'That's crap and you know it. You can't let them do this. We've just lost one man out of four. If you take Andy off, that leaves no one but me and Murdo on the ground who know what's going on. It's not enough.'

'No. You're off the case with him. You're here because we need to know what went wrong the other night. When you've made your report, you're free to go.'

'Just me? Or Murdo too?'

'Both of you.'

'Are you going to tell me why?'

'Christ, Orla, do you need it spelling out?' He had picked up his glasses and was twisting them inwards, bending the arms on the desk. 'Luke's dead. You saw him. You saw how he died. We know he gave them the Afghan drop. How much else of what he knew is safe?'

'But—'

'But nothing. You're compromised, all of you – your names, your homes, your covers, your contacts. All of them could be Svensen's and if he feels like it he can sell them to the highest bidder. Half of Glasgow could have your name and number by now.' He was leaning across the table, close enough to touch, trying to tell her things with his eyes and the angle of his head and the relentless pattern of logic that wasn't logical at all. There were times when she would have listened between the lines and tried to understand what he was saying but this was not one of them, it was too much of a relief to be angry.

'No.' She stood, because thinking was easier when she was vertical. 'The heroin was a throw-away, the one thing he could give under pressure that wouldn't start to unravel everything else. You *know* that. You organised the lectures, you brought in the grey units from Ulster, the SAS major they dragged out of Iraq, that bastard who put us through it in Finland. They all spun the same line, every day, every night till we could say it again in our sleep. Do you think he would have forgotten it? Really? Do you think he *could*?'

It had been her prayer for every night in the flat. A litany etched so deep on her soul that she could rely on it to be there when everything else had gone. She said it for him now, for all of them, because Reid and Laidlaw were watching her as if this was new and maybe, for them, it was: '"Hold to your first cover as long as you can, it's always the strongest. If you have to let go, have a second that can't easily be checked. If that goes then give the things for free that can be verified and give lies for the things that can't and if they break through all of that and you're down to the truth then it's the people that count, not the crack or the money."' Strang, at least, could see where she was going. His face was a mask. She leant forward on the desk, both hands flat on the cool wood. 'It's the *people* you protect, the ones with their lives on the line and even then there's a hierarchy, a system to go through, and as far as Luke was concerned, Murdo and Andy and I would be last on the list to go. If he'd broken the way you're thinking, we'd have woken up this morning with a morgue full of . . . Oh, Jesus Christ.'

The words died in her throat. Understanding broke over her like a wave and in its wake came sudden nausea and the need for fresh air. She looked round the table. Of the three who had known and could have warned her, only Alec Strang was prepared to meet her gaze. Murdo, who clearly had not and could not, brought his hand to his face, pressing his fingertips to his eyes. His skin was grey. 'How many?' he asked hoarsely.

'Three,' said Strang. The postmortem prints were in an envelope in his pocket. For the moment, he left them there. 'Adie Mearns went into the river just after midnight last night. Early pathology suggests he was dead before he hit the water. Lal Harris was found early this morning in the doorway of the Ancient Mariner with his skull bashed in and his wallet gone. Kimberley-Anne Fitzpatrick died of an overdose some time last night. They brought her in an hour before you got here.' He lifted the prints out of his pocket and let them lie on the table. 'None of them died in a way that was obviously linked to Svensen. I'd say he's doing what he can not to draw attention to the fact that he had informers on the inside. In this, if nothing else, we have the same agenda. Andy knows, I told him before you got here. Beyond that, this information does not leave this room.'

'Right.' She nodded, her eyes unfocused.

'I'm sorry. I was going to tell you later. When it was quieter.'

Quieter. More private. Without Laidlaw's eyes stripping her soul.

'Thank you.' She walked to the window and opened it. Outside, the gardener had moved and was trimming rose bushes that had been well pruned in the autumn. The woman with the poodle had been replaced by a window-cleaner who worked exclusively on the front-facing windows of the houses opposite. Strang's units worked in pairs or in the full group of four, never in a three. She looked around and found a white BMW parked on the opposite side of the road. The driver sat inside, talking on a mobile phone. 'He won't have given them this address,' she said quietly. 'Whatever they did to him, he will have held onto this. If you're going to put a unit on watch, you want to put them onto the offices in Maryhill. That's where the rest of the world thinks we are.'

'It's a precaution,' said Strang. 'I sleep better if I don't think I'm taking unnecessary risks.'

'Fine.' She watched the unit across the street. The window-cleaner, too, had a mobile. He and the driver of the BMW hung up together. Orla moved sideways and saw the gardener move to keep her in view. 'What are you going to do now?' she asked.

Strang said, 'It's not up to me. DCS Laidlaw is taking charge of the investigation.'

There was a deadness in his tone that begged her not to push that one too far. This time, she listened. Mimicking his formality, she asked, 'In that case, what's DCS Laidlaw going to do?'

The man answered for himself. 'He's going to wait for you to tell him what went wrong in the flat to make them turn on you when you'd been safe in there for so long,' he said. 'He'll work out what else to do once he knows that.'

'And if I don't have an answer?'

'Then I'll consider your advice about putting some of my people onto Jake Turner and see if we can turn the screw that way.'

'Right.' She turned into the room. Her shadow fell straight ahead of her in a long, thin streak that ran like a path to the doorway. 'Put the team onto Turner now. I'll go down and write a report so you have it in black and white but I can tell you now that nothing happened out of the ordinary from the day we walked in until the moment they picked Luke up. Friday was the big pay-off, the culmination of everything we'd worked for. They believed we were about to lift the biggest consignment of smack to come out of Kabul since the trade routes reopened and Luke was the one who gave it to them. He was king of the dung pile. He could do no wrong. They kissed the ground he walked on.'

'Even Svensen?'

'He let him run the drop. He wouldn't have done that if he didn't trust him.'

She was surrounded by eyes and she read doubt in all of them. She said, 'I'll write you a report. Maybe you can see things I didn't.'

'Thank you.'

They watched her leave. Murdo Cameron went with her, picking up her jacket and the open packet of fags as he passed.

'We'll be in the basement if you need us,' he said.

'Thanks.'

The basement was the heart and soul of Alec Strang's operation. When he first bought it, the great, Gothic mansion had nothing below the ground floor but earth and stone. During the conversion, the real money had gone into digging out the extra, subterranean floor in such a way that the world at large had no idea what was happening. Very few individuals beyond Special Branch were aware of its existence and none beyond the operations and surveillance division were welcome inside. Within the wider police force, only two men were regular visitors and both of those had just left the meeting room upstairs. In Strang's world, confidentiality was everything. He believed, because he had reason to do so, that of all the things Luke Tyler might have revealed in the last hours of his life, the existence of the rooms beneath the ground in Kelvingrove Gardens would not have been on the list. He believed it. He was not certain. It was this uncertainty that had kept him awake through all the hours since the man had died.

Now, he stood midway down the stairs, listening to the sounds from the room below. A printer sighed, drawing in fresh paper, and the hammer of the print-head echoed off the walls. In the gaps, more quietly, a single voice murmured dictation and a keyboard stuttered in response. He took a step or two down until he could see past the roof beams into the space below. In the original design, he had specified offices to be built all along the left-hand side with air conditioning and natural lighting that the designers had assured him would reduce the claustrophobia of working underground. It may have achieved exactly that but still, nobody used them. Like the kitchen in a farmhouse, the common room had evolved into a multi-functional space encompassing all the needs and wants of the Division; a pair of computers and a printer had been moved out of the offices onto desks on the back wall, the coffee machine stood beside them. Other corners housed weights benches and the digital television. The pool table took up space not far from the computers and around it were enough chairs to take all five units on the rare occasions they met as a full division.

On this particular morning, the three remaining members of Luke Tyler's unit had gathered in a group near the larger of the two PCs. Murdo was typing. Orla McLeod sat on the padded arm of an easy chair to one side, leaning over, pointing out errors in the text. Andy Bennett sat in the seat beside her. Orla's arm was draped across his shoulders. Closer, it could be seen that his arm curled round her waist. The medic had showered and shaved and looked better than he had done although it was not clear if he had slept.

Strang took the rest of the stairs and crossed the floor in silence. He poured himself a coffee and listened to the murmur of three different voices. Following other, more military models, his units worked in fours – two pairs interchanging in a dynamic, internally stable structure. He considered a three and how they would survive and whether the instability of it was better than bringing in someone new to make up the numbers. He watched the three heads bent together, not acknowledging his presence when they must have known he was there and realised that they had asked themselves the same question and had made their own answer, which was interesting, if not unexpected. He drank coffee and waited. In a while, without turning, Orla said, 'Why are you here?'

He took a step closer. 'I'll leave if you want me to.'

'No.' She looked up. Her eyes were tired. The aftermath of the drugs showed more than it had upstairs. In the time since he last saw her, she had rolled up her sleeves. Fresh white bandages showed at her wrists. 'Are we sorted with Jamie?' she asked.

'More or less. I gave them Murdo's proposal.' He pulled his glasses from his pocket. The arms had not broken but they were not the shape they had been when he last wore them. He straightened them out and hooked them over his ears. 'Assistant Chief Constable Reid is concerned that we don't leave ourselves open to possible prosecution at a later date.'

'Prosecution on what grounds?' Murdo had his back to the room, still typing.

'Falsifying legal documents? Forgery? Illegal alteration of computer records? Take your pick.' Strang found a chair and sat down. 'He wants to be sure he has all the possible loopholes covered.'

'They're covered.'

'Thank you. I rather assumed that was the case. I have told Reid that they *will* be covered. I would prefer he didn't know we were discussing a *fait accompli*.'

'Fair enough.' Murdo finished his final sentence, spun his seat sideways and back. The printer sighed and chattered and was still. 'And Laidlaw?' he asked.

'DCS Laidlaw has agreed that if you take the child out of the way and two out of the three of you are with him at all times until this blows over, that will constitute a reasonable compromise between safety and the child's emotional welfare.' He quoted verbatim. Only Laidlaw spoke like that.

They stared at him. Murdo laughed. Orla picked at the bandage on her wrist. A fine red stain made a trail on the white. 'What happens if it doesn't blow over?' she asked.

'I said we'd reassess at the end of the month.'

'You think it will be over by then?'

'I would like to believe so. If it isn't, we're in for a long haul and we'll have to re-think our approach.' Strang leant forward and lifted the newly printed pages from the printer tray. They followed the format of all her reports, written or verbal: a formal and highly detailed log of events in date and priority order. He read the final page and met himself and his own actions presented in clear, clinical, textbook phrases. No hesitations, no second thoughts, no misgivings; a seamless succession of acts and actions laid out in a way that made them seem, if not inevitable, then at least entirely logical. She had learned that from Billie Reid when she was a new graduate speeding up the fast track out of uniform: the skill of writing so many facts in such good order, that the reader forgets to ask for the things that are not written, the things that really matter. He read backwards, page on page to the start of the week, and found little that he did not know already. The questions that mattered had not been answered. He squared the paper and laid it flat on his knee. 'Is this as much as I get?' he asked.

He had not been sure. Upstairs, she had been closed to him, but there were good reasons for that and he had not wanted to press for answers in the wrong company. Now, there was nothing wrong with the company except that he was part of it. In this place, he was not used to being excluded. He riffled through the report. The pages whispered under his fingers. So many words, so little said. Four pages from the end, he stopped and looked up. Her eyes glanced from his. He said, 'Svensen phoned the flat just before they took you and Luke?'

'Yes.'

'What did he say?'

There was a pause. Beside him, Murdo made to stand up and thought better of it. Orla freed herself from Bennett's embrace and stood up. The pool table had been set up for snooker and the game abandoned, leaving three reds bunched down at the far end behind the black. She took a cue and sighted the length of the table.

'Orla? What did he say?'

'My name.' The cue connected with the white ball. A red on the outer edge of the group spun back into the pocket. It hit the channel underneath and bounced down to the end stop with a noise that was far louder than the printer had been. In the quiet of afterwards, the hiss of their breathing made more noise than the air conditioning. She turned to look at him. 'Svensen told them my name.'

'Are you sure?'

'As far as I can be. I didn't take the call. Luke took it and passed it over to Jared—'

'Jared Grant, who died in the flat?'

'Who was killed by me in the flat, yes. Jared could think, which made him dangerous. He wasn't as sharp as Drew Doherty, but he was switched on enough to be difficult to read.' She bent and measured the angle on the black. 'It was the shortest call I've heard. At the time, I thought they were getting a yes or no for the drop. Now . . .' She paused to take the shot and missed. Strang, who was closest, saw that she had made no attempt to hit. She laid the cue down and leant forward, her weight on her hands. There were stains at both wrists now, blooming outwards like ink blots on paper. 'It might not have been my name. It might simply have been the order to pick me up. Whatever it was, the others were waiting for it. Jared nodded and the others moved before the phone was down. There was no warning, no talking, nothing. Just a nod. I didn't have time to get out of the chair.'

He looked at her, seeking clarity. 'They came for you, not for Luke?'

'Yes.'

'And they knew your name?'

'I heard them say it.'

'But not Luke's?'

'No.'

She sat down. Her eyes were on Bennett. The man sat very still, taking care with his breathing and it occurred to Strang, late, that he was not the only one hearing this for the first time. He laid the report back on the printer. 'Did Luke follow procedure?' he asked quietly.

Her eyes flickered to his and back. Established procedure in this instance was entirely unambiguous: under no circumstances does one member of a pair reveal their identity unless the other's life is threatened. Even then, it is only permissible to break if there is a good chance of recovering the situation safely for both parties. He waited. She was white now, a sick, chalky colour that made more of the bruise on her face. Just when he thought she was not going to answer – which would have been answer enough – she said, 'What do you think?'

Strang nodded. 'Was he armed?'

'No. His gun was in the hallway. Trent was the only one carrying.' She moved, finding a chair by the table and sitting blindly, feeling her way down. 'For as long as I've known him, Luke was always the one reminding me to stop and think before I jumped in. He could have remembered it this one time. All they did was wave the gun at me, get out the needles, throw a few hits. They weren't going to kill me. They wouldn't have dared. Svensen would have shot them all if he'd turned up and found me dead. We all knew that.'

Murdo did move then. He picked up her coffee and took it to where she was sitting. 'None of us would have done any different.'

'But you should have.'

'I don't think so.' Andy Bennett, too, chose to move. He sat on the floor with his back to the leg of the table, his feet stretched across the floor to touch hers. The medic was not a religious man. Nevertheless, had it been possible for the living to give absolution for the dead, he would have given it. Because he did not know it was impossible, he tried anyway. 'Orla, rules are there to be broken. If he'd played procedure and you'd been killed or raped or cut up, he would have spent the rest of his life wishing he'd moved sooner.'

'And is it better this way round?'

'It's not better. It's just the way it is. We can't go back and change it now.' He said it as if he meant it and the words had a rhythm that said they were not newly thought. 'He wouldn't want you to waste the rest of your life grieving over something that can't be changed.'

'Maybe not.' She looked across to Strang. The move had made him a part of the circle. The relief he felt at that surprised him. 'But I think we owe it to him to spend some of it finding out who dropped us in it.'

'You think that's a possibility?'

'I think it's a certainty.'

'Right.' Strang took off his glasses and laid them on the edge of the table. Several metres overhead, a bin lorry rumbled into the cul-de-sac and men ran out across the pavements. They sat still, saying nothing, as if running men might hear what the rest of the world could not. In the space of their moving, Strang tapped the pages of the report, squaring them up, and laid them back on the printer. He had waited in excess of thirty-six hours for Orla McLeod to reach consciousness, to be able to talk to him, to tell him that something had gone wrong; that one of them had lost their grip and blown cover, that they had been recognised in the street, anything at all but that there was somebody placed on the inside feeding names and lives to the highest bidder. If it had been possible to switch off his ears and not hear, or switch off his mind and not think, he would have done it. Instead, he leant forward with his knees on his elbows and his thumbs pinching up at the corners of his eyes and he had no idea how tired he looked. When the room was quiet again, he said, 'Outside of this room, only Laidlaw and Billie Reid knew you were in there. Are you asking me to believe that one of them has sold out to Svensen?'

'Unless you can tell me how else he got my name, yes.'

'Right.' He stood, moving away from them. He needed time and space to think and had neither. 'If we're going to start asking questions at that level, we need more corroboration than a word that wasn't heard on a phone.' He turned and found Orla close behind him, reaching to switch the kettle back on. 'Who have we got on the inside who will talk to us? Is there anyone left?'

'There's Patsy Kerr. Unless she's joined the bodies in the morgue.'

He shrugged. The name rang no bells. 'Should I know her?'

'No. She was a friend of Lisa Buchanan's – my route into the flat. She worked for Jake Turner until November and then moved over to Svensen because Luke asked her to. Luke's been running her for years. She was our first link into what was happening on the inside.'

Strang said, 'She's not in any of his reports.'

'I know. Which may be why she's still alive.'

He didn't need to hear that. She didn't need to say it. The kettle rose to a boil. She offered him coffee. He refused. She poured for herself and the others. In a while, when they had settled, he said, 'Patsy Kerr. How much does she know?'

'About Luke? Nothing more than she had to. About Svensen? I don't know. More than most folk. She hangs out with Drew Doherty and he's the closest thing the man's got to a second-in-command.'

'Fine.' Strang picked a sheet of blank paper from the printer tray and hunted round for a pen. 'Give me her details. If she's still alive, I'll get someone in to talk to her – see what she knows, see if she wants to come out.'

'No.' Orla was up, tossing the remains of her coffee down the sink, looking for a reason to move. 'She won't talk to someone she doesn't know. If you give me half an hour to look different, I can—'

'I've been. I went last night.'

Bennett, sometimes, was the most surprising. They stared at him. Orla sat down, suddenly.

'What did she know?' asked Strang.

'Nothing. She spent Friday night with Doherty, God help her, and he didn't tell her anything was planned.'

Orla said, 'She's a good woman. She's put her neck on the line often enough for Luke. We should get her out while she's still safe.'

Bennett shook his head. 'I tried. She won't come.' He smiled thinly. 'We're tainted goods. She thinks she's safer where she is.'

Orla was up again. 'That's nonsense. Let me go and see her. If she's still alive, I can talk her out. They only know me as Orla McLeod or Sandra Smith. I can go in as—'

'No. Absolutely under no circumstances. Don't even consider it.' Very rarely did Alec Strang throw his rank around. He did so now and the change in him was striking. 'Orla, we've just lost Luke. I am not losing you to some convoluted honey trap on the off chance that a tout wants to walk.'

'Andy went. He came out in one piece.'

'I didn't know he was going or I'd have stopped him, too, and there's no way he's going back. If Patsy Kerr contacts us and wants out, I'll send in one of the other units. It will surprise you to learn that they are entirely capable of bringing a willing woman out of the east end of Glasgow. But if you – if any of you – so much as puts a foot heading east, I'll have you arrested and held for obstruction. You are off this case, all aspects of this case, and I will not have you playing semantic games with your orders. Is that clear?'

Once in a while he was serious. And he was not known for making empty threats. They nodded.

'Good.' He relaxed back into his seat. 'So then why don't you get some money from the funds and go out and buy some decent winter clothes for Jamie Buchanan. If the forecast is right, he's going to need them.'

Four

—•—

The screen flickered, changing resolution. The technician typed new commands, watching for the right response. When it came, the screen flickered again. She picked up the phone and punched a number into the handset. It was answered at the first ring.

'Are you through?' The voice was rolling and smooth and warm and it raised the hairs on her spine. She had tried, once, to place the accent. She had not tried a second time. Now, she simply worked on until she could give the answer that was required.

'On the way.' She dropped lightly into the still water at the heart of the system, weaving through passwords and traps as so much weed. The fire wall took exactly seventeen seconds to breach. 'Name?' she asked.

'Two names. Orla McLeod. James – or Jamie – Buchanan.' She typed them into the waiting prompt. She retyped them in a variety of different places. Nothing came back. In the world she had entered, no such people existed.

'They're not here.'

'Really?' He could put a lot of meaning into one word. Part question, part accusation, part threat. A man of some subtlety cloaking the violence. His reputation had not quite got the balance of that. 'Perhaps you are not as good as I was told,' he said. The threat in that was overt.

'No.' Her fingers moved across the keyboard. 'I am every bit as good as you were told. Someone who knows what they're doing has been through here and taken away what you want.'

'So look deeper.'

'There is nowhere deeper to look.'

'It will be in there somewhere. They don't destroy their files.'

'No. But they do move them to other sites. If the information you want is held anywhere, it's on another system. Either we find where that is or we try someone else. Give me another name.'

He gave her two more names. She tried both of them and failed. 'Maybe we are expected,' she offered. 'Your information may not be fully up to date.'

'Maybe not.' The client was not impressed. He was not a man happy with failure. His reputation was very precise in that regard. She heard a pen tap twice on wood at the other end and then, 'Try Luke Tyler,' he said.

She tried. 'That's better.' Luke Tyler existed in a great many places. She felt the relief as a tangible thing. 'What do you want to know?' she asked.

'Where is he now? What is he doing?'

And that was very interesting indeed. 'There are two files.' She brought them both up on the screen, reading as she did so. 'In the older one, he's dead. His body is in the pathology suite at the Western Infirmary. I could read you the results of the postmortem.' She ran her eye partway down the screen and stopped. 'Or maybe not. It goes on at some length.'

'I'm sure it does.' He was amused at that. 'I'll live without, thank you. I'm rather more interested in what the live version is doing.'

'He's on leave. He's going to visit his mother.'

'He has no mother. She died when he was twenty-seven.'

'True.' She narrowed her eyes, studying the syntax. 'I take that back. He's going to visit *her* mother. So we need a "her".' She scanned a separate file. 'It could be his wife?'

'He has a wife?'

'The dead version doesn't. The living version was married in ninety-seven ... wife not named, which is odd unless ...' The technician stopped and tapped one further key. A tingle of something new and electric spanned the space between her hands. She smiled. She, too, had a reputation. 'It's not odd at all. The living Luke Tyler is married to a Mrs O. Tyler. Is it conceivable that the O stands for Orla?'

He was smiling, too. She could hear it in his voice. 'It is.'

'Good.' She didn't crow. She had more finesse than that. 'Anything else?' she asked.

'No. That will do nicely. Thank you.' He broke the line.

'Fine.' She took as much care in leaving the system as she had in entering it. Some time later, she received the agreed, very large, sum of money. It was not the first she had ever earned, but it was the first she had earned in recent years and it represented a passing of boundaries she had promised herself never again to cross. She found, on reflection, that the experience was not as bad as she had expected.

'Jamie?'

The boy woke to bright lights and piped music, to the sound of traffic and a voice saying his name. 'Jamie?' A hand nudged his good shoulder. He opened his eyes. Bands of green and yellow light crossed his face. The patterns of it fitted the tatters of the dream. He closed his eyes and tried to remember. Sleep, warm and welcoming, gathered him back. The hand tapped again. 'Jamie, are you awake?' He shook his head. 'OK. No problem. We're nearly there but I have to get petrol before we start the last bit. Will you be all right on your own?' Of course. He nodded. 'Fine. Murdo's in the car behind. He'll keep an eye out for you.' Of course. Because he hadn't been alone since he left the flat. The implications of that, when he chose to think about it, were disturbing. On the whole, he chose not to think. For now, he wanted only to sleep. He shifted the pillow to a new place and drew the folds of the duvet up tighter round his shoulders. The voice drifted out over his head. 'Sleep tight. I'll not be long.'

The car door opened and closed, letting in a gust of freezing air and he remembered that the dream had been of snow, not of light, and it had a basis in reality. He opened his eyes and sat up. They were in a service station, parked under the canopy. All around, dazzling electric lights reflected off bonnets and windscreens and patches of oil on the forecourt. Out beyond that, the world was entirely black. In his dream, the snow had been falling through a night sky. Slowly, taking care for the bad arm in its sling, he struggled loose from the duvet and slipped over into the front seat. The door was unlocked. He stepped out, round a parked lorry and over towards the place without light. The chill of the air bit hard on his skin. The cold of it burned the inside of his nose as he breathed in and turned to steam as he breathed out. If he took a deep enough breath, he could make long, spiralling plumes, like the trail of a jet plane. He spread one imaginary wing and reached a lopsided Mach 1 as he loped past the second row of pumps, pausing in his acceleration, as his mother had taught him, to check for the cars. At the edge of the road, he stopped. It was late and the traffic sparse but he was well aware of the dangers of roads. Playing too close to the traffic led, inevitably, to not playing at all. A small crash barrier one foot high ran along the dividing line between the edge of the forecourt and the grit at the side of the road. He put one foot on the top rail and kept one on the ground so that it was clear he had not crossed the boundary and then he turned his eyes to the sky.

Out here, beyond the shelter of the canopy, the false light cut off as if carved by a knife and was replaced by the lights of the night. High overhead, a nearly full moon dominated the dark, out-shining the stars for a wide circle around it. As he watched, a pair of blinking lights, one red, one green, appeared from nowhere, angling down towards the land as a plane made its own attempt at Mach 1. He was too far away to see the vapour trail but he watched it anyway, turning on his heel to follow the slow descent of the flight path as it dropped out of the dark that was the sky towards the odd, wavering brilliance that was the land. And so it was in watching the sky that Jamie Buchanan first saw the mountains. The shock of it hit him the way the bullet had done, but deeper and closer to the heart. He stopped in mid-turn, forgetting the plane, forgetting the road, forgetting to breathe or to think, forgetting, for this one space of time, to grieve. The mountains exploded in the core of his soul and pushed everything else away. Nothing in his entire life's experience had prepared him for the vast, jagged, heart-stopping mass of land that ranged across his horizon. He had wanted a world in black and white and he was given it. Tall fingers of light reflected upwards from the waters of a loch hidden behind the scattered pines, marking the place where the mountain ended and the land began. The light reached no further than the treetops before rock and earth and other trees gathered it in and snuffed it out. In this, least perfect of all worlds, some things are reliable. He was north of Fort William, midway through March and there was snow on the peaks of the hills of Lochaber, an astonishing band of crystalline silver that ran along the top, reflecting the moon. At the end of everything else, Jamie Buchanan looked at the snow and remembered a promise and was lost.

'Spectacular, isn't it?'

And so he was not alone. The mountains were not his alone. The understanding of that was a new pain. He looked round. A dozen yards further down the barrier, the tall man with the long hair stood with one foot on the railing, his hands deep in the pockets of a sheepskin jacket. Half of his face was in shadow, half caught the light of the moon. His back reflected the sulphured green and yellow of the forecourt. He lifted a hand in greeting. 'How's the arm?'

There was no answer for that. It hurt less than it did. With his good shoulder, he shrugged.

'Fine.' Murdo Cameron's smile was dry and knowing. He pursed his lips and sucked air through his teeth and said, 'Orla's gone back inside for a cup of tea. We thought you'd maybe like the chance to eat. You don't have to come in if you don't want to. I can bring you out a plate of chips or a burger or something out here and you can eat it with the mountain.'

He was midway through shaking his head when the real possibility of food grabbed at his stomach and the shake became a nod. He got a smile for that. 'Good lad. Are you staying out here or did you want to come in?' He was already turning, abandoning the joy and the snow for the heat and the offer of chips. They fell into step, pausing together in a way that would have made his mother happy, as a car pulled out from the pumps and drove past them out onto the road.

Murdo spoke the way he walked, with a rhythm that flowed like running water. 'I'm sorry about this. It must go hard having a leech at your back day and night but I'm afraid it goes with the territory. If you want the snow, you get the abominable snowmen to go with it.'

Jamie looked up carefully in the wake of that, saw the flash of teeth and recognised a joke if not all of the meaning.

'You do want snow, don't you?'

He nodded for that. Murdo smiled again and raised a thumb. 'Good. I think we've got you that, at least. Orla called ahead before we set off,' he said. 'It snowed at the cottage this morning apparently, and there's more forecast. When you wake up tomorrow, all you'll be able to see will be white.'

And so in the wonderland of the new magic, where grey merged with black and white, they could organise snow. He took that in and stored it and followed the sheepskin jacket through the door into the heat and the noise and the multi-flavoured assortment of food.

The chips were what you'd expect from a service station in the hours before dawn, which is to say they were hot and crisp and the tea that went with them had sugar and milk and had not been reboiled in the microwave. Both of these were novelties in themselves. He ate and drank and felt the warmth burrow into his fingers and toes and was glad of the thickness of the socks and the weight of the fleece that had been bought for him on his release from the hospital and wondered if the oversight of gloves was perhaps not an oversight at all but a deliberate inducement to spend less time in the cold.

He rode in the front for the rest of the journey. The torpor of travel had evaporated, replaced by hot tea, cold air and the tingling sense of anticipation that had flowed from the woman to the man and spilled over into him as they walked back to the car. 'How long?' was the question. 'Two hours, maybe a bit less if the road in is good,' was the answer and with it a smile that brought back memories of scarlet in gold and the eyes of a tiger. On the strength of this, he had abandoned the duvet and the pillow in the back and taken to the passenger seat. With something close to real joy, he sat, wide awake, and watched the miracle of the mountains grow and recede on either side of the car as the road cut through between them.

They were idling at a junction when he noticed the radio. In the tenement flat, barring the few hours at the end, there had always been music. From the moment of his birth, from long before his conception, the radio or the stereo had filled the gaps between the words with an indiscriminate medley of digital sound. Its absence pushed the world out of balance, like a rainbow with one of the colours missing, and it was a natural, unthinking reflex for him to lean forward and press the button and wait as the receiver hunted for the signal between the peaks of the mountains and then for his mind to fill in the gaps between the notes as the fragments were caught and woven into a language that he knew and understood. He had listened for a good seven bars while Dusty Springfield told the world of her need for the son of a preacher man before a hand reached down from the wheel and cut her off.

The quiet that followed was not what had gone before. The boy sat fiddling with the fraying edge of his sling and counted the conifers on either side of the road, afraid to look up at the mountains as much as he was afraid to look at the woman beside him. She negotiated the left turn at the junction and drove on for another half mile before she spoke. Her voice was dry and light. 'Jamie? I'm sorry, sweetheart. There are one or two things I can't handle just yet and music is one of them. Later, maybe, but not now. We can compromise with the fishing forecast if you want, then the news after that. Or we could talk?'

He looked at her and frowned, trying to match the tone, which was easy, with the words which were not.

The side of her face changed in a way he was coming to recognise as the suppression of a smile. 'OK, daft idea. Forget that. How about if *I* talk and you listen? We'll be at the cottage soon and there are some things you need to know before we get there. Will that do?'

He looked out through the windscreen. A new mountain, just one, grew out of the ground ahead of him. The road aimed straight for its heart. He could die in the sight of such a mountain and be happy. The woman was watching him, waiting for an answer, so he nodded and reached back for the pillow and slid it between his head and the window as a barrier to the cold and the noise of the road and waited for her to tell him all the things she thought he needed to know.

*   *   *

She had exaggerated a little. Even had the road been clear, they had another hour to drive. As it was, the road was not clear and she was driving with more than usual care so the remainder of the journey took them twice that, if not longer. For most of that time, Orla McLeod talked and Jamie Buchanan listened and slept and listened again and the words flowed over him as they always did and he tried to catch hold of the important bits for afterwards.

'We'll start with my mother, you'll like my mother. She was a doctor once – one of the ones you'd go to see at the doctor's surgery, not one of the ones you see in the hospital . . .

'. . . I had a brother when I was your age; Ciaran. He was a bit older than me, two years, or three, depending on who had just had a birthday. I was born in January, his birthday was in June so for half of the year I was only two years younger than he was. It's the kind of thing that really matters when you're young . . .

'. . . time stops when you die. For the rest of your life, your mother will always be thirty-six. It's not a bad age. I enjoyed thirty-six. You want to make the most of it when you get there. It doesn't last long. Thirty-seven isn't turning out quite so well, although I do appear to have got married somewhere along the way which ought to make somebody happy . . .

'. . . they were shot on my thirteenth birthday, Ciaran and my father. I've not been good with birthdays since . . .

'. . . do you want to come out and look? I always stop here. It's the start of being home. Jamie? You'll like it, really, the sun's coming up. You can see the mountains and the sea both from here,' and she was shaking his shoulder again and he was shaking off sleep and the duvet and she was right, there was light. The bulk of Sgurr a Chaoracain blocked the rising sun but the dawn seeped in round the edges, filtering in through the mist, taking away the black of the night and giving grey and white to the mountain behind him and grey and green to the sea before him and a washed-out blue to the sky. The air was damp and it smelled of sheep dung and diesel exhaust and of snow churned to slush. The smash of the sea on the stones far down below rose up and mixed with the mist to make white noise in the white air and he realised, later than perhaps he should have done, that the real magic happened only at night and that his days were destined to be many shades of grey.

In a while, they heard and then smelled the following car as it pulled up at the side of the road a dozen yards back and Murdo Cameron pointedly left them in peace. The boy used his teeth to pull the cuff of the fleece down round the fingers of his good hand and looked down at the spread of a dozen crofts and cottages that was going to be home and then across to the woman who was, to all intents and purposes, going to be his mother. She stood in front of the car with her hands in the pockets of her jeans and one foot cocked up on the bumper behind her. The wind blew her hair flat to her cheek, smearing it in her eyes. She put a hand up to hook it back over her ear as she had done when it was longer and then stopped, remembering. The boy understood then, why she had cut her hair. He moved across to sit on the bumper beside her. She put an arm round him, with care for his sore shoulder.

'Do you see the cottages at the end of the road?' He looked down, following her gaze. Far down at the foot of the mountain, the dark line of a road snaked along parallel to the sea and then angled inland, heading back up the shallow slope at the foot of the mountain. At the end of it, three cottages spread out like the leaves of a trefoil. In the furthest from the sea, a door was open, flooding light out onto snow, throwing the shadow of a figure out across it.

'That's home,' said Orla McLeod. 'I think you'll like it.' They stood together for a while watching the colours change with the morning before she led him back to the car and they set off down the hill towards the sea.

It was always difficult in the first moments when they came together. Time does not stop only with death, but with shock and irreparable damage. Her daughter was younger than Morag had been on the day when time stood still and she was, in her mother's eyes, immensely beautiful. Nevertheless, neither of them was blind to the unhealed scars her daughter carried, nor to the things that opened them afresh. It was one of the great sorrows of Morag McLeod's life that Orla, whom she loved more than anyone else, alive or dead, still carried in her heart the pain of her own survival – and that she herself, on each occasion of meeting, renewed whatever small measure of it might otherwise have been discarded.

Once, a long time ago, she considered making the trip south to the one surgeon who might have had the necessary skills to reverse the handiwork of the past. She spoke at length to her ex-colleague and had photographs and radiographs sent. If the prognosis sent back had been hopeful, she might have gone to see him in person although the prospect of yet another anaesthetic pushed her into an unnameable terror that was as bad as the memory of the blast. Still, for her daughter, she would have done it. As it happened the prognosis for a return to full function was guarded and the consultant advised against further surgery and she had laid the matter to rest until the day she came home from the shops and found the letter and the photographs on the kitchen table and the girl waiting when she should have been at school. In the afternoon that followed they had one of the few serious arguments of their lives and when it was over, it was understood between them that each of them carried scars and that the inner ones that you couldn't see hurt far more than the outer ones that you could and that each would willingly take on the burden of the other if they could but find a way to do it. Theirs was never an easy relationship, there was too much pain in the past for that, but they remembered the letter at each parting and each reunion and if it wasn't easy, there was a great deal of understanding.

She was standing in her kitchen doorway, watching the dawn rise up over the mountain when a car pulled into a lay-by high up at the bend in the road and she knew, without the double flash of the headlights as it drew back onto the road again, that her daughter was nearly home. She had time during the long descent to change into something other than the jeans she had worn the day before to mend the chicken coop, to brush her hair and damp down the wilder strands, to find the dog and brush him too and to put on a collar in case the child was not keen on dogs and needed some way to get hold of him. She put on the kettle and heated the pot for the tea. She took the butter from the fridge and the bag of scones from the bread bin and sliced three and laid them on the griddle to heat up. She put the bacon onto fry and thought about putting the eggs onto boil and realised she was overdoing it and decided to wait. The second set of headlights had turned left onto the track that doubled back for half a mile uphill from the shore when her nerve broke and she went back up to the bedroom for the gloves that she wore whenever she was in new company. Morag McLeod was not proud. Life would not have been bearable had she been proud. But her daughter had few true friends and brought fewer of them home and she had no wish to let her down.

It was not easy, watching them come together. Murdo Cameron had been warned about that as he had been warned about a number of things as they walked together down the length of Buchanan Street, absorbed in the almost normal activity of shopping for two adults and a child. *'It was a petrol bomb, the kind of thing they used to throw at the squaddies on a Friday night in South Armagh; a milk bottle full of petrol with half a shirt sleeve in it lit at one end. They gave themselves a long fuse to get away. If you believe the priests, it was the hand of God that made this one as long as it was and the direct intervention of His Son that kept my mother's surgery clear that night so that she finished early and came home just before the flame reached the top of the bottle.'*

'What did she do?'

'What would you do? She tried to throw it out of the window. The back blast shattered the whole pane – there wasn't one bit of glass bigger than a ten-penny piece. And it burned all the flesh off her hands. That was the end of her career. You can't be a doctor if your hands don't work.'

'I don't expect she was thinking of that at the time.'

'I'm sure she wasn't.'

He believed he knew what was coming. He walked with the boy down the path from the cars towards the small woman with the silvered black hair, feeling the grit underfoot where she'd spread it after she cleared the new snow, tasting the first wash of the sea breeze and the smell of more snow on the way and the smoke from the fire and the billow of cooking bacon from the back door as it opened. Murdo Cameron was not the average man in the street. He had worked all of his adult life in the world of human damage. He should have played with the black tangle of a dog and introduced it to the boy and not stood there and stared as Orla took the breath she needed to pass through the gate and then left him to walk on ahead and meet her mother.

'Mum.'

'Orla.'

They stood facing each other on either side of an invisible barrier. Orla looked straight over the head of her mother, staring past her to the cottage beyond. Morag McLeod was much smaller than he had expected, given the height of her daughter. She, too, looked straight ahead, as if anything more would be an unacceptable intrusion. The greeting continued with the stiff formality of ritual.

'Welcome home.'

'Thank you. It's good to be back.'

He would have wept but it was not his place to do it. Instead he did, at last, bend down to meet the dog, to run his fingers through the rough mess of a coat and accept the splash of a tongue in the ear.

The boy handled it better. He didn't stare. He watched without looking. He knelt, rapt, for the dog's embrace and when they both stood upright together, the boy hoisted one paw on his good shoulder and, for a moment, they were of a height, grey eyes level with brown. So the boy found a soul mate when he had never known that such a thing was possible and he could watch two things at once without looking, which was good.

'What happened?' The older woman had let her eyes wander. It would have been impossible not to. She lifted her fingers to the short row of sutures running beneath her daughter's eye.

The plaster had come off on the walk back to the car as soon as they left the public gaze of the service station. It could have come off sooner for all the difference it made. Everywhere they stopped, curious eyes assessed the small group of man, woman and child and then focused on the flesh-coloured oblong with the greening black sunburst of a bruise that spread out around it. *'You realise they think you did it, don't you?'* *'Of course. Who else would dare land one on you?'* They had joked as they got in their separate cars and he didn't think forward to the morning. He couldn't have made it different if he had.

'I got hit.' Orla shrugged and it was like a wave piling up at the sea front. 'Defence of Queen and country. All that kind of thing.'

'Was it worth it?'

'Is it ever?' She smiled and the wave broke on the shore. 'Hey,' she stepped forward and stooped down for a hug that had been waiting for over four months. 'It really is good to be back.'

It was. In spite of, or possibly because of, everything else, it was incredibly good to be back. Orla stooped for the embrace with her mother and breathed in the mixture of wood smoke and bacon and chickens and wet dog that had been the essence of home for all but the first thirteen years of her life. She ran her hands through her mother's hair and felt the damp ends where it had been combed into line. She let her mother do the same for her and weathered the brief ascerbic glance and the question that went with the harsh feel of the dye and the sharp edges of the cut. 'Queen and country too?'

Morag was still wearing her gloves. Gently, her daughter lifted one hand from her head and slipped it free. 'You wouldn't believe the things Her Majesty expects of her subjects these days.' She squeezed the hand and let go.

'And you a good republican too.' Her mother took the second glove off herself.

'Don't mention that in front of Murdo. He still thinks I'm a royalist.' She stepped back and said it loud over her shoulder and felt him push his way between the gate stone and the dog and she felt her mother's naked hand lift a lock of wrecked hair and heard her mother say, 'Are you responsible for this?' and Murdo grinned his big, wide grin and held both hands up as if he were fending off a football crowd and said, 'You're kidding me. I wouldn't dare go near this one with a sharp object in my hand. That's all her own work. I just held the mirror,' and he hugged her mother as she had done and turned round and called the boy up to be introduced and you couldn't tell from either of them that this was the first time she had taken him anywhere personal or that he was the first man she had ever brought home.

'I'll leave you here for a while and you can make yourself at home.'

The boy stood at the window of the bedroom he had been given. In the flat, he had shared his bedroom with his mother. In Morag McLeod's cottage, he shared it with Bran, a black, rough-coated, long-nosed hound. There was a degree of discussion about that, most of which went on above his head and was irrelevant. He knew and the dog knew, it just took the rest of them a while to get used to it.

He had been shown round the house not long after the clash of greetings at the front door. Between the five of them, they unpacked the car in one trip. His suitcase, which was full of new clothes still with the tags on, was carried upstairs for him by the small woman with the sharp brown eyes and the black and silver hair who didn't look at all like Orla but was, nevertheless, her mother.

'This is your room,' she said. 'Orla said she thought you might like to be able to see the mountains so we've put you up in the attic where you've got good views. If you find you don't like it, you can always swap with one of the others. Your towel's here and the bathroom's down the stairs on the left by Orla's room.' Morag McLeod laid the suitcase on the bed and watched the dog lie down beside it and went downstairs to her daughter with the news that the boy might not be sleeping on his own after all.

Upstairs, Jamie Buchanan pressed his face to the glass of the longest window he had ever seen and looked up at the mountain on one side and then out to the sea on the other and tried to imagine what it would be like with a night sky and the moon up and the snow turning silver.

Footsteps creaked on the stairs and a knuckle knocked on his door.

'I'm not sure it's quite six feet thick yet,' said a voice. 'But it might get there by tomorrow.' Orla was there, standing in the doorway with her hands in the pockets of her jeans. 'May I come in?'

He made her welcome and she came into the room to sit with the dog on the edge of the bed.

'If you look out over the bay you'll see the clouds,' she said. 'They're coming this way which means there'll be more snow soon.'

He looked. The clouds were thickly white and the water underneath them was dull and flat, like the back side of silver paper. He moved to the other window so he could see them better.

She said, 'Your consultant will kill me if I take you sledgeing while you've still got your arm in the sling, but there's nothing to say we can't at least go for a walk.'

A fishing boat motored round the house-sized rock that marked the southern end of the bay. Seagulls swooped and plunged and rose again around it, carving white holes in the water that looked like snow. The boy remembered the dreams of snowmen and sledges and realised that he no longer cared if they were never fulfilled. He wondered if he should say something and decided that doing so would spoil the gift of it, so he didn't and went instead to sit on the bed with Orla. She lay flat on her back with her head hanging over the edge so that her face, disconcertingly, looked like it had done when she was under the sofa in the flat. She widened her eyes and her brows moved downwards in a way that made his stomach lurch. He rolled onto his front and turned his head round so that her face was the right way up.

'Is that a yes?' she asked.

He nodded to let her know that it was.

'Fine.' She stood up and the dog went with her, loyally devoted to the most likely source of entertainment. 'We'll have breakfast first. Then we can change downstairs in the kitchen while the lid's still up on the stove and it's warm enough to take your clothes off without getting frostbite in your toes.'

It had never occurred to Jamie Buchanan that dressing could be a complicated process, even with only one arm working, but then it had never occurred to him, either, that snow could kill. Orla broke him in gently as he stood, almost naked, just inside the boundary of the warm zone by the stove. 'It may look like a Christmas card from the window but there are one or two folk lost on the mountain each year and they don't always find the bodies in the spring when the thaw comes. It's the weather that gets you – if the snow comes in, you want to be very sure you know exactly how to get home again even if you can't see any of the landmarks.'

He stood warming his back at the range, trying to imagine the snow as an enemy and not really succeeding. In the meantime, Orla cut the tags off the things that he needed and helped him into the layers of clothes that were designed to keep him alive in the face of the snow. First, closest to the skin, he wore a soft and not quite white vest that was, apparently, made of silk. 'It keeps you warm like nothing else and this has got a waterproof layer sprayed on so that if something goes wrong and you have to chuck everything else, it'll keep you alive a bit longer than the average T-shirt.'

Next was a black woollen sweater, thick and scratchy and smelling of sheep. 'You want always to wear alternate colours in the snow; white on top with something dark underneath. That way, if you need to be seen, you take your jacket off and the black shows up well against the snow. It would be better in red, maybe, but I couldn't see you in red.' His mother would have put him in red, or possibly purple, with yellow writing across it. He liked the black.

Last came a padded jacket and trousers; puffed, quilted and water-resistant in marbled white with fine zigzags in grey and cream that broke up the outline. 'Snow camouflage,' said Orla. 'It's not ideal but it's the best we could get in the ski shops. Apparently this is the in colour this year. If we'd tried last year, you'd have been in fluorescent pink and blue which would have been a disaster.' It would. He did his best not to let the image of that grow too real, it made his eyes hurt. Orla said, 'It doesn't look much in here but if you need to hide in snow, all you have to do is to lie still with your face down and no one will see you.'

He tried to imagine that, too, as he watched her strip down to the almost-nakedness he knew from the flat and then start on the light-dark alternating layers of her snow-proofing, what it would feel like to be lying flat in snow, desperate not to be seen but not able to look, listening amongst all the other sounds of the snow for the one sound of feet coming closer. Then, as he looked at her clothes and realised that they were not new as his were – that the camouflage was professionally done and that there was wear on them, and creases that came from real use in real snow – he began to imagine instead that it was Orla who was lying face down in the snow, with someone coming too close, carrying a gun and her not having one to shoot back with. It was not a good thought.

A hand brushed along his arm. Morag was there, putting away the new eggs from the chickens but she had stopped near the table and she was smiling for him in a way that took the edge from the thought. When he thought to smile back, she nodded and then reached out to touch the well-creased arm of her daughter's jacket. 'You're scaring the lad,' she said. 'He thinks you've been playing soldiers in your outfit.' Her voice was warm and friendly and it thawed out the images of snow and immanent death.

'He's right.' Orla knelt on the floor, threading the laces on her boots. 'Only playing, though. We went on a month's winter exercises in Finland the year after the unit first started up, courtesy of Strang. He thought snow work would be good for our souls.'

'Was it?'

'I doubt it. I think simply agreeing to work with the man puts us way beyond redemption.'

There was a joke there, or something close to it. Jamie saw the nod and the look and the blink-rapid sharing of memory and he was just beginning to feel the warmth of it swell in his chest and push out the fear when it stopped, harshly, at the onset of something new. Orla had finished with her boots and, while they spoke, she began to rummage through the pile of discarded clothes on the floor at her feet. Now she stood, holding a waist pack that he recognised in one hand and then, moments later, a gun that he recognised too in the other. Morag did not recognise either, or did not want to.

'What's that?' Her voice was not soft any more.

99

'It's what you think it is.' Orla slid the thing, too glibly, into the side pocket of her jacket. 'I'm sorry. I did tell you.'

'You did.'

'Would you prefer that I hide it?'

'Not from me.' There was a space for other things implied. The child held his breath.

In a while, Orla said, 'Jamie's not only seen it, he's seen it in use. I don't think there's any need to hide it from him.'

'And is that good, do you think?'

'It was unavoidable.' There was a spare magazine and a silencer in the waist pack. They slid into other, inner, pockets, slotting into loops and fixtures made to hold them. That, as much as anything, made it all real. Orla, with her hands free now, came to crouch down at the table so that her eyes were level with her mother's. She tilted forward and kissed her brow. 'I've said I'm sorry and I meant it. But it's still unavoidable. And I *did* tell you.'

'You did.' Morag sighed and stood. 'And we're going in circles and there's Murdo trying not to get involved.' She looked past her daughter and she was right, Murdo was there, midway down the stairs, standing still with his boots in one hand and a waist pack like Orla's in the other. Morag gestured in a way that made him part of it without taking sides. 'Come on down. Have you got one too?'

'I have.' He took the last four steps with as little sound as he had the ones before. 'I'm afraid it goes with the territory. If we want to take care of Jamie, we have to do it properly.' He said it gently, with respect and real regret and it was the first time Jamie Buchanan had ever seen him serious. He came across to sit on the floor by the stove and lace up his boots, laying the pack unobtrusively at the side. 'And I did think you'd been told,' he said.

'I had. I am learning the difference between hypothesis and reality. You'd have thought I might have managed to work that one out a while ago.' Morag was leaning with her back to the sink. She reached down and picked up his pack and opened it. 'May I?'

'Be my guest.'

'Is it safe?'

'You could break a toe if you dropped it right.' He twitched a lopsided smile in a way that made him look a lot like Orla and then took it back again and was serious. 'Yes,' he said. 'It's absolutely safe.'

She held it out awkwardly, not wanting to hold it like a gun with her palm on the grip and her finger on the trigger but not wanting, either, to hold it with the barrel facing inwards towards her and there were not too many options apart from that. In the end, she settled for holding it flat across her palms. The oiled matt of gunmetal made an awkward contrast to the wrongness of her hands.

'It's lighter than I thought.'

'It's mostly alloy,' said her daughter. 'They're easier to use if they're not too heavy.'

'Thanks. I'm sure I'll rest easier knowing that.'

'If you don't want to know, you don't have to ask.'

'Thank you. I'll try to remember. Has anyone ever told you that you use logic like your father?'

There was no answer for that, just a silence in which other things and other people were remembered and in which the gun was only a peripheral part. In time, Orla said, 'It won't be for long,' and her mother frowned doubt and acceptance and a depth of humour that eased over the raw hurt of the new shape on old things. She said, 'It'll be for as long as it needs to be and I'll expect to be told when that time is past. In the meanwhile, if you want to go out, you better get going before the new snow comes in. It would be a shame to be all dressed up in your fancy snow gear and spend the next three days playing cards at the kitchen table.'

Five

Four of them went out into the field above the cottage: two adults, a child and a dog. They followed one of the three freshly gritted paths up through the garden, past the wood shed and the chicken run, through a second, smaller gate, and out into a rising expanse of unblemished snow which was, apparently, the place where Jamie could go sledgeing if it hadn't all thawed away by the time his arm had healed. For now, walking was enough The snow was not six feet deep but it was, nevertheless, up past his knees and he could see, as soon as they stepped out onto the hillside proper, why Murdo had made him pull his trousers down over the tops of his boots as they stopped to open the second gate. The first step was a surprise. The second was fun. The third and those that came after it were hard work so that they went slowly and stopped often with Murdo and Orla staying on either side, pointing out the things in the world around them that were new and that they thought he should know. Orla named the mountains in a language he had never heard before, full of soft consonants and flat vowels. Murdo showed him the tracks of a fox and then a hare, the one following the other across the line of the hill. The dog followed them both for a while, quartering the snow for a fresh line, and then came back to the group, circling them all like a collie with an errant flock.

Halfway up the hillside, Orla had them turn to look out over the cottage and the rock of the beach to the sea and the green-grey island that spread like lichen on the fuzzed line of the horizon. The clouds had stretched down to touch the sea by then and the water was more steel than silver. In one of the odd anomalies of West Highland weather, the line of the front matched the line of the shore so that, above the mountain, the sky was a clear, crystalline blue and the sun was too bright to look at. The snow was clean enough to crimp into fistfuls and when you sucked at it to get water, it tasted of wood and of peat. He had his breath back by the time they moved but the hill was steeper after that and there were pockets of powder snow that didn't take weight so that he found himself waist-deep and floundering and began to think that fluorescent pink and blue might not have been so bad because at least then they'd have a chance of finding his body before the thaw.

At the top of the slope they stopped for a proper break. The hill flattened out to a gently rising plateau that spread for a few dozen yards before the trees started. Beyond that, a broad seam of mixed forest stretched forward and gently up before the last, stupendous rise of the mountain soared up to meet the sky.

Jamie sat in the snow as soon as they stopped. He was hot and his arm hurt and the waistband of his trousers was itching and snow *had* got down inside his boots in spite of Murdo's best efforts to stop it. At first, he had been glad of the cool round his ankles but now the damp places were as hot as the rest of him and it made his socks stick between his toes and that was not good at all. The dog bounced up to play and knocked against his bad shoulder so that he cried out and shoved it away moodily and didn't feel sorry when it collapsed back to the snow and lay there panting apologies.

'Here,' Orla reached over and tugged off his hat. 'The wind's less up here, you can take this off for a while. You'll get cooler quicker if your head's not covered. Just remember to put it back on again if you start to get cold.'

He took the hat and folded it to fit in a pocket. It was a nice hat, knitted in cables of dense cream wool and there had been a sense of security in having it press tight to his ears. He shook his head, feeling the sudden release of pressure and found it was true, that the wind was less and what little there was lifted his hair, light-fingered, and teased the heat away.

There was a tree trunk lying at an angle that poked it clear of the snow. He went over and brushed it clear and sat down on the end and looked round. The dog had found a hole in the snow and was digging hard in the certain hope of finding life at the bottom of it. Further along the wood's edge, Orla and Murdo, both bareheaded now, were working together, rolling a snowball that was more of a snow-cube and then a snow-egg, big enough to have come from the biggest of the dinosaurs. They rolled it along the line of trees, leaving a swathe in the snow like a mower leaves in long grass. At the end, they turned it and rolled it back again and when it reached Jamie for the second time, the thing that had been the size of his head reached now past his shoulder and was definitely an egg. He watched with interest as they made a base to hold it in place and Murdo used his fingers to sculpt the edges so that it became an egg with the legs of a table.

'It's a bear,' said Murdo. 'We've made one before, once or twice. If you make the shape right, it looks just like a feeding grizzly from a distance.'

'We need a head, though,' said Orla. 'It doesn't work without the head. Come on,' she stretched out a hand, 'you and me can do that while Murdo gets the body right.'

It was harder than it looked, especially with only one hand. The snow was either too dry and crumbled to powder, or packed up too evenly and made a cube or a ball. 'You need to push it in, like this,' she said, and showed him and he had a go and, on the second or third try, he got the trick of pushing and rolling on a slight tilt to make an egg that could have come from an ostrich, perhaps, or a small velociraptor.

'Good. Well done.' Orla had made her own snow-square, which was in fact a snow-seat and she was sitting on it, watching him. 'Push it up against the body and see how it looks.'

He did so. It looked like a small egg beside a big egg, which was only fair.

'Don't look at it like that. It's a good bear.' Murdo was offended. 'The child's a cynic. No sense of perspective.'

'He's too close,' said Orla. 'It works better from further away. See,' she backed him off to a distance, 'if we look at it from between the trees, it looks just like a bear.'

Jamie squinted and screwed up his face and tried to remember if he had ever seen a bear to know what one looked like. It would have been easier, of course, simply to nod, but that wasn't the game.

'Luke does it better. We're just the amateurs.' Orla left him and went back to the head again, pressing packed handfuls of snow into the palm of one gloved hand to make the first of a pair of rounded, half-shell ears. 'Years ago, he made one for us as a way to keep some people occupied. We were right up in the north of Finland, stuck in trees at the edge of a god-awful half-frozen lake pretending to learn how to move in the snow. They put us into groups and half of us had to hunt and the other half be hunted and God help you if you got caught before the end of the day. Luke made us this snow-bear right next to the trail, and all the time Andy and Murdo were going wild at the time he was taking to get the shape right—'

She stopped, abruptly, as if someone inside had slammed her sideways and then stamped on the brakes. In a moment or two, she started again, speaking with a new attention to detail. 'Luke *would have done* it better,' she said. And then, more carefully, 'It worked, anyway, the bastards trailing us spent nearly an hour stalking a feeding bear before they realised it wasn't real and we were well away by then.' She looked up. Jamie had found two pine cones and was making the eyes. Murdo was carving a stump of a tail. 'It was night, mind you,' she said, to neither of them in particular. 'I think it helped with the illusion.'

'I think it made them scared of their own shadows,' said Murdo, and it was harder to tell what he was feeling. 'That was why they sent us up to Finland. Russia was just across the border and there could have been anybody out there. Myself, I think Strang was trying to get rid of us, he just didn't believe we'd come back alive.'

'But we did.'

'All of us.'

'Yes.'

You couldn't tell what either of them was thinking, then.

They finished all together and stood back to inspect the result. It looked much more like a bear with the ears on and the pine-cone eyes. In the right light, from the right angle, you could maybe be afraid of it, especially if you were near Russia and already scared. Jamie let them know it would do.

'Want to go up?' Murdo was beside him, offering linked hands as a hoist. He nodded and was lifted high onto the humped back to sit astride it, like a jockey on a horse. Orla followed and wrapped her arms round his waist so that he felt the warmth of her on his back and the solid outline of her gun against his side. Then Bran stood up with his front feet high on the beast's shoulder, barking at them both to come down until Murdo got fed up of the noise and slid one arm under the dog's chest and another round his hindquarters and hoisted him up too, so he was wedged between them with his back to Orla and his nose on Jamie's shoulder and he was quiet, suddenly, so that the silence echoed off the snow.

It wasn't as warm as it had been. The wind was cutting in from the sea, shaving the heat away in layers. Jamie reached into his pocket for his hat and pulled it down over his ears. When he looked round, he saw that Orla and Murdo had done the same and then, before he could think whether it might be time to come down, Murdo had reached in his jacket and found a bar of chocolate and split it between the three of them.

'Like it?' asked Orla.

Jamie nodded, working his tongue round a square of something hard and cold that still only hinted the taste of chocolate.

'Do you want to go back home now?'

He thought about that and decided not yet. He craned round to look at Orla and decided that she didn't really want to go yet either. He shook his head.

'Thought not.' Over the top of the boy's head, she said to Murdo, 'What do you remember of winter survival?'

'As little as possible.' Murdo's grin was all chocolate. A smear of it trailed down from the corner of one lip. He scrubbed it away with his glove. 'Why? You think we should practise?'

'It wouldn't hurt.' She shrugged. 'I could take Jamie into the wood for a walk. You could come with Bran later and find us.'

Murdo looked at her sideways. The smile was still there, but was not entirely the same. 'You're still thinking of Kajaani?' he asked and then, when she nodded, 'Is that wise?'

'It's not unwise,' she said. 'At the moment, I'd rather think about there than anywhere else.'

'Is it safe?'

'It's safer than most places. I've lived here since I was thirteen years old. I'm more likely to get lost walking down Byres Road.'

'I didn't mean that kind of safe. You're still half cut and you're not dressed for real snow work.' He fingered his jacket. 'This is hardly forestry gear.'

'Murdo, we're going for a walk in the woods. This is Scotland, not Finland, and I wasn't planning to take a nine-year-old with one arm in a sling on a crawl through the undergrowth. We're as fit as each other. We'll be fine.'

'That's what you always say.'

'And I'm always right.'

'Usually.'

'Pedant.'

They traded insults, lightly, while all the not light things were being said in other ways. Jamie, watching, saw a question and its answer and a decision, not easily taken.

'Fine, then. If you say so.' Murdo reached up and helped Jamie down. Then he folded the silver paper across the remaining chocolate and handed it over. 'Hang on to this, youth, it's your afternoon ration. You can only eat it if she gets you so badly lost you miss lunch.'

He was joking, clearly. Jamie weathered a snort and a sour look from Orla to unzip his jacket and put the wrapped square into an inside pocket where it would be safe from harm but not so warm it would melt.

'How long do you want?'

'An hour? Maybe a bit less. The tree line thins out higher up. We'll go up there and wait for you.' Orla looked out at the darkening sky over the bay. 'If the weather comes in, we'll turn round and come back.'

'Right. See you later.'

Murdo whistled the dog who had launched itself from the snow-bear and made a four-point landing halfway to the trees. A second whistle brought it back to heel and they walked together, man and dog, to the edge of the plateau. The hill was steeper than it had seemed coming up. In a dozen paces, maybe less, he was out of sight. In a few more, he was out of earshot as well, the scatter and crunch of four feet and two lost to the muffling snow. Jamie turned in to face the trees and found that Orla was crouched down beside him, straightening his jacket and his scarf and checking his sling. She was brisk and organised, as she had been in the packing and sorting before they left Glasgow.

'OK, sweetheart, did you understand all that? When we went on the course in Finland, we learned how to walk in the snow without being seen. If you want to, I can teach you. We can try to walk through to the other side of the woods without leaving too many tracks and then Murdo will bring Bran up in a while and try to find us. Does that sound good?'

It did sound good. He let her know. She smiled. 'Good. It'll be fun.' She stood up. 'Right, the basic rule is not to do anything that's expected, not to leave footprints if you can help it and to make sure that any you do leave are confusing. Like this.'

The snow was thinner than it had been in the open field. She waited while he put his glove back on then took his good hand and showed him where to step on the tree roots that poked above the snow so that his footprints didn't show. They walked three times in a circle round a small thicket so that he could get the feel of it and then set off through the woods.

It was an old forest and the trees grew haphazardly, more so than the Nordic forests Orla McLeod had learned in. She took the child's hand and led him on a twisting, turning route between oak and beech and mountain ash that had seen centuries of Highland weather and lived to tell of it. She talked to him as they went, showing him how the slope of the land meant they always knew which direction to go in and how the light changed with the density of the undergrowth so that there were places where it was always so dim, it didn't matter if they left marks because it would be almost impossible to see them. In a while, when it really did begin to look difficult, she made marks on the bark as signposts for Murdo to follow if he remembered to look for them, or for her to return by if she had to. Soon after that, she showed the boy what she was doing and let him pick which trunks to mark and how to do it.

She was moving by then, inevitably, to the rhythm of another voice, thin and sour and unfriendly. *Get up off the ground. Break the track. Keep the bastards thinking. Every minute they waste looking in the wrong direction is a minute longer you live free.* The memory of it went with the bite of the cold through her jacket that was very different to the chill of the flat without heating. It came with the smell of sodden pinewood and the murmur of falling snow as it slid off the branches, with the crackle of breaking ice beneath her feet and the burn of the air on the back of her throat as she breathed.

It was four years since Strang had sent his teams on the Air Force jet to Finland They had complained about that, all of them; sixteen highly intelligent individuals had each pointed out in their own way that a division designed for urban criminal surveillance did not need to know how to fend for itself in the snow. He had listened to each of them, as he always did, and sent them anyway and they had spent thirty days and nights, singly or in pairs, and, once, in full teams of four, living rough in a climate that could and did kill. Whatever Murdo Cameron said, it was not an experience any of them was likely to forget.

For three weeks of their month, they had learned to move silently and unseen; in daylight and at night, in good weather and in driving snow, through an alien, inimical land, full of dark and savage trees and slick with lakes that bred mosquitoes big enough to suck heart blood that left puncture wounds bigger than cat bites. The one who taught them had seen service inside Russia when it was still the Soviet Union and where death came very slowly to the careless, the cold or the chilled-to-the-soul exhausted who left tracks that could be followed in the snow. He was efficient in his teaching, but not kind. Three weeks were not enough to become perfect, or even good, he was very clear about that. In the fourth week they were tested and Orla McLeod was deemed adequate at hiding her tracks. Watching Jamie Buchanan as he balanced, one-armed, on a root, stretching up with focused concentration to make his mark on a rotting pine stump, she thought that, with the use of both arms and a few more weeks of practice, he might be very much better than adequate. She was uncommonly pleased at the thought.

'Nice one. Well done. We'll make a tracker of you yet. OK, if we're going to get to the edge of the trees we have to head more up the line of the slope and – *what the fuck?*'

The shot came suddenly and without warning. She moved on a reflex, 'Jamie, get *down!*' and they fell together in a rolling heap, pushing deep into the shelter of the thicket, tasting snow and mud and feeling the cold shock of it smash over their faces as the echo of the blast passed over them and was quiet . . .

'Fuck.' She lay still for a moment, holding him, until the fast, nasal whistle of his breathing brought her back to who he was and she remembered his arm.

'Jesus, Jamie, I'm sorry.' She whispered it hoarsely, rolling back to take her weight off him. 'Are you all right?'

He wasn't, of course, but he wasn't going to say so. He bit his lip and said nothing and pushed her off when she tried to look. His eyes were perfectly circular with white showing all round the rim and the pupils had flared out to the edges. For a moment, she thought he might be fevered again and cursed herself for not seeing it. Then, bending, she kissed his forehead and felt heat, but not too much. When she looked at him again, his eyes were less stark. He gazed at her warily, wanting it to be part of the game. 'It's OK,' she said. 'It was a shotgun. If it was anyone who knew what they were doing, they'd have a rifle.' They could, of course, have both, or there could be more than one, but there was little point in saying so. She pushed clear of the snagging branches and crouched at the edge of the clearing.

The aftermath of the shot sounded loud in her ears. The rest of the wood had fallen silent. Where before there had been crows, coughing hoarse, ribald commentary on their progress, now the silence sucked the air from her ears. Turning round on the spot, she looked for signs of movement and saw nothing. Everywhere, all the way round the circle, ancient, black-barked, unthreatening trees cast shadows on the snow. None of them glinted with the barrel of a gun. She breathed out and her breath made a column of steam. She sat still, watching for other rising columns of steam. Nothing lived within sight, except for the small huff beside her that was Jamie as he crawled out from the thicket. She put a hand to his lips. 'Sweetheart, I think I should go and see what that was. It's probably just someone shooting at crows, but better to be safe, huh?'

He nodded, because that was his part in the fiction, if no longer part of the game, and she chose not to tell him that Angus Shearer, who managed the land on the mountain, was an ardent, almost fanatical, conservationist and had banned shooting in all its forms long ago. There was no point in burdening the lad with unnecessary facts. She looked round. The place from which he had come was more sheltered than she had thought. The thorns were old and there were good spaces between the trunks. She touched his shoulder and then pointed back in.

'Do you think you can go back into the middle of that? Go in as deep as you can.'

He was small and he knew all about hiding in inaccessible places. He eased himself into the core of the space and turned round to check if he had done it right. She smiled for him and, remembering what Murdo had called him, said, 'Well done, youth. You'll be safe in there.'

Murdo had said other things too, and most of them were proving right. She was not dressed for real woodland work, that much was certain. If nothing else, the jacket was too bulky to move with any speed and it was forever catching on the brambles. She slipped the gun and magazines from the pockets, shrugged it off, folded it up and passed it in to Jamie.

'Here. Put it round your shoulders. You'll get cold if you're sitting still.' He looked at her sideways and did as he was told.

The sweater she wore underneath it was as heavy and black as the boy's. It made sense, in Finland, in the safety of the cottage, in the exercises on the moors, to have a second layer that could be seen from the air, or by others with field glasses, searching. She took that off, too.

'See if you can keep it dry, can you? And warm. I'm going to need it when I get back.' He looked even less impressed about that. For a moment, he might have said something but she crouched down and pushed it into his hands. 'I don't want to be seen, sweetheart. Just in case,' and he remembered the shot and was still. The third layer was double-knitted silk with its water-resistant spray that was so much better in theory than in practice. It was the right colour, there was that much to be said for it. The thin breeze of the forest pressed it flat to her skin, drawing the heat from her flesh. She pushed her gloves into the thicket, rolled up the sleeves of the vest to keep them out of the way and stripped the bandages from her wrists. When she checked the gun and screwed on the silencer and slipped it into the pocket of her trousers, the boy's eyes followed the movement. His skin, which had been a healthy, open-air, new-to-the-country pink, was turning grey-white and translucent.

She reached in for his good hand. 'Do you still have the chocolate Murdo gave you?' He nodded, tightly. 'Good. Now might be a good time to eat it. I want you to wait here until Murdo or I come and get you. If it's Murdo, you'll have to tell him what's happened so that he can get you back to the cottage and then come and find me. Can you do that?'

It mattered to her that he understand. He looked out through the trunks and said, 'Yes.'

'Thank you.' She squeezed his fingers. 'I'll try not to be too long.'

She moved faster alone than she had with the child. For twenty-five yards, she kept off the ground in case the gunman should have occasion to follow her tracks back. After that, she simply chose the fastest route she could find between the trees in the direction from which the shot had come. It wasn't hard but it was wet and very cold and she cursed, with passion, the necessary loss of her sweater.

The second shot came five minutes after the first. She splayed herself flat in a snow-filled hollow between an oak and a moss-covered stone and waited out the long seconds of the echo and fade, chewing on ice and feeling the meltwater beneath her body soak through the feeble resistance of the hydrophobic spray on her vest as it would have soaked through a sponge.

'Fuck it.' She sat up. The shot had been closer, without question, but it was still a shotgun and not a rifle, for which she continued to be grateful. She listened for the scatter of lead shot falling through leaves and heard nothing, which meant that it had been fired away from the wood or the trajectory was too low to hit foliage.

'Fuck you. Bastard. What are you playing at?'

She pushed herself to her feet and tugged the vest from her skin. In the beginning, the cold had a bite to it that burned and she could pretend it was warm. Now it sucked like a leech, leaving her leaden and dull. She was shivering violently which was good if you were worried about hypothermia and very bad indeed if you were thinking of aiming and then firing a gun. She flexed her fingers and found them plastic and white with no feeling at all.

'Shit. This isn't clever.'

I should think not. The voice in her head was changing, becoming less nasal, more painfully familiar. Still, it was not happy with what she was doing. *Snow kills*, said Luke Tyler, and he should know. They had both seen, and had no wish to experience, the full sequence of hypothermia. *Get yourself warm.*

Sure. Right.

She put her fingers in her mouth, one at a time and sucked. When she could feel the pressure of her teeth on all of them, she folded her arms tight to her body and pushed on. The training in Finland had been all about extremes. It occurred to her, four years too late, that Strang had sent them for just that reason; to push them up to and past their limits rather than because he had ever believed that they needed to know about snow. Later, and more slowly, came the understanding that she should not be *in extremis* on a mountain she knew backwards within an hour's walk of her mother's home, that Murdo had been right in this as in everything else and it was not only the cold that was dragging her down. Still, what had once been learned had not been unlearned. Her body responded to the nerveless pull of her mind, crouching low to reduce her exposed surface area, moving more slowly to reduce the noise, taking more care with the placement of her feet. The trees folded in around her, offering support. And Luke was beside her, more tangible than usual. Luke and everything he brought with him.

Where are you going?

To find the gun.

Is that useful?

It's essential. I haven't forgotten what I promised.

Still a long way from Glasgow though, aren't you? What will you do when you find the gun?

Stop it from firing. We don't know that Svensen's still in Glasgow. If he's here, then I need to be here too.

If you thought there was the slightest chance he would come here, you would not have brought Jamie. Anyway, Svensen's never yet used a shotgun. Why has the snow got lighter?

Because I'm nearly at the edge of the wood.

So . . . ?

'Shit.' She made herself stop. 'Thanks a bunch, Tyler. Next time I want some warning before I walk out in the open.' Luke grinned and stepped back. She was right at the margin of the wood. Windblown snow drifted against the outermost rank of trees; the branches facing out to the mountain were heavy with unstable slabs of it, the undergrowth gathered smaller flurries and held them aloft on webs of leafless stems. Luke was no help. He shrugged and faded in and out of existence. She moved along just inside the tree line, walking more slowly, working harder for silence. Round the bole of an ageing birch, she found what she was looking for: a patch of trampled snow and a scattering of ash. Given an orange cast and a concrete backdrop, it could have been a photograph taken from the wasteland opposite the flat – except that the ash had been knocked from the bowl of a pipe, not dropped from a cigarette, and forensics ought to have noticed that. A small part of her stored that to tell Strang when she saw him. The rest of her turned, sweeping her gaze in a circle. Half a stride away, a single bootprint stood out, shadowed by the light from the edge of the wood. A stride beyond that, the heel of the pair showed on the root of an oak. Both were heading south-west, deeper into the trees. She would have followed but the breeze backed round and the scent of pipe smoke was swamped, suddenly, by the denser, more metallic reek of a shotgun, recently fired. *Fuck.* She stopped still, bracing her shoulder on the tree for support and tried to reach into her pocket for her own gun. She failed.

'Shit. *Shitshitshitshitshit.*' Her hands were still folded tight to her biceps and would not unfold. With an appalling amount of effort, she unclawed her fingers and brought them round to where she could see them. They were yellow, mottled with white and completely insensate. 'Fuck it. Not now.' She drew back deeper into the sheltering undergrowth and knelt down, burrowing her hands down inside her trousers until she could see them poking in on either side of her groin. The cold of them burned through the fine silk of the long johns. 'Come on, damn you. Move.' She cursed silently, castigating her fingers until she could see them open and close and feel the sweep and curl of absolute cold against the flesh of her groin. Her fingers themselves felt nothing and nothing and nothing until, with excruciating slowness, the first red coals of recovering circulation prised into her joints and the pain began. 'Fuck. This is going to be bad.'

It was. The pain built slowly, like the banking of a fire. Red coal became yellow coal became white-hot, fire-acid needles machine-stitching her knuckles, her flesh, her skin, her whole body because it wasn't only her hands that were cold but it was only her hands that were warming and in her new state of sensory overload those parts that were yet numb took on the screaming, searing pain of those parts that were not. *'Jesus Christ Almighty.'* She pressed her face flat to the birch and bit hard on her lip to keep the noise in to herself. For the most part, she succeeded.

A slab of snow slid from the tree beside her. The hollow impact of its landing dragged her head up. He was a stride away, standing on the patch of trampled snow. The broken barrel of the gun hung over the crook of one arm. The stem of a pipe poked from one pocket. He was smiling.

Her gun was still in her pocket. She tried to move her hands and the pain split her apart. She sank back against the tree.

'Are you all right there?'

The voice was dry and little used. The run of it grated like a boat on sand, rasping the accent to nothing. She said nothing.

'Orla? It is Orla? Orla McLeod?' He took the last step forward and knelt beside her. 'There now, don't move. You're fine where you are. Let's see what's happening here.'

He was not a young man; closer to sixty than forty. His hair was white and strong, like her father's. His breath smelled of pipe tobacco and, more faintly, of Scotch and when he smiled, there was a gap between his four front teeth and the others that made him look like an overly intelligent, faintly carnivorous horse. He was smiling now as his big, warm hands took hers and levered them into the open, smoothing the palms flat, exposing the blotched and tortured flesh. The smile faded. 'Christ, you're halfway to frostbite, woman. What are you doing out here half-dressed on your own?'

Every movement was undiluted pain, in her feet now as much as her hands. She hugged her arms to her chest, digging her fingernails into the soft parts of her biceps to keep from screaming. 'Guns,' she said, breathlessly. 'Shooting.' She looked to Luke so that he could help but couldn't find him. 'Guns,' she said again.

'Is that right? There's some strange folk on the hillside, right enough, but I never expected it from you. It was one gun and two pheasants and I wouldn't have thought that was worth all this cold for.' The white hair moved out of line. 'Here, we'll not have you dying yet.'

Warmth and the smell of tweed enveloped her. Calloused hands eased her own away from her arms and into the arms of the jacket. 'Can you stand?' She tried. It is possible that she succeeded. Her world descended into a succession of smells, each with a texture and colour and pain all their own; tweed roughened and sank into the smooth stab of birch bark which folded in turn into the pressure of skin on skin; human, age-worn, smoked and pickled, moving her with a courteous insistence. 'And then if you can manage a step or two, we'll go this way.' She felt the trunk of the tree press into her spine and then the lightness of its leaving as she was helped forward. Like the mermaid sculpted in flesh, she walked on knives that sliced her feet. Light came in bands between the trees and hurt her eyes. Big, solid hands held her shoulders, the weight of an arm on her back pushed her on against the need to sit and be still and sink into the cold. 'I can take you back to your mother's or we can go to the Manse. It's closer, but if you want to go home, I can get you there, the Land Rover's just up the . . . no, maybe not . . . maybe if you just stay here for a bit and wait until your hands have come back and then we can go on.'

Blood came back slowly to places it had not been for some time. In the time of waiting, instinct and training rolled in to fill the gap. There were other things she had been taught, not all of them in Finland. When she had enough sense to feel it, she dug her fingers into her palms and counted and when she reached ten, she made herself remember her name and her date of birth and her mother's maiden name and Strang's mother's maiden name and what it was she was supposed to be doing and why. With more pressure and more counting and at the cost of blood on her palm, she found speech and a pool of lucid thinking.

'Nobody shoots on the mountain,' she said. 'Angus won't have it.'

'That's better now.' He held out a hand and she felt the warmth of it in her own. 'Hugh Carlaw,' he said. 'I would say I was a friend of your mother's but that might be presuming too much. I am an acquaintance, at least, and, strange though it sounds, I own this bit of the hill so what Angus Shearer will or will not have is largely academic. I have, however, come to an arrangement with him that between May and September when he has the mountain stocked full of his twitchers and ringers and his hotel packed with his lunatic runners and his bloody gawping tourists, I won't shoot a thing, but the rest of the year I can take the occasional bird for personal use on land that stretches beyond my own.' He lifted his hand. Iridescent feathers in green and gold and red glittered in a stray slice of sun. Two heads peeked together from the clench of his fist, both with their eyes tight shut. Drying blood collected in the trough of one wing. 'Pheasant,' he said.

'Yes, I can see.' Thought was coming in small packages, wrapped round with memories. 'You live in the Manse?'

'I do. And it is, as I was saying, within a reasonable walk of where we are now.'

'Duncan MacGregor lives in the Manse.'

'No. He did when you were a child. He died nearly twenty years ago.'

Of course. She knew that, if she had not left her memory along with her mind out there in the snow. Long-ago images pushed into view: of herself as a teenager, dressed in black, taking afternoon tea in a tall room that smelled of leather and mildew and sickness; of her mother, expressing shared sorrow on the telephone; of an elderly cat, sleeping on the knee of an even more elderly woman who didn't stand. She fought for more and couldn't find it. 'Dorothy?' she asked. 'What happened to Dorothy?'

'She died not long after Duncan. Some Americans bought the place after that and made a dreadful hash of renovating it. They left a year or two back and I bought it from their lawyers and I like to think that I'm making a mite less of a hash of renovating it back to what it was before they got to it.' His smile was genuine and his teeth were not so disturbing now that she could focus on him properly. 'I may be a blow-in but at least I was born on the right landmass and I speak the right language so if you give it another ten years or so, I could be a local almost.'

He was laughing at her. She tried to return it, feeling the creases tighten in her face. 'Angus said that, did he?'

'Of course. Who else has the nerve? And me the new Laird, too.' He was up, brushing the snow from his knees. 'Now do you think you can walk? And if you can, do you know where you want to go to? I don't have a cottage like your mother's, but the kitchen at the Manse has taken half of my pension to fix and there's just me knocking about in it like a pill in a pot. Somebody should see it sometime.'

It was a kind offer and well meant and if it wasn't for the memory of Strang's mother's maiden name and what she was there for, she might have let him usher her, one knife-step at a time, to his new-old kitchen, just to see what it was like. Instead, she pulled herself upright, using his wrist as a fulcrum, and stood, swaying back and forth between his grip and the tree. Standing was hard. Her whole body begged to be allowed to sit back in the snow. She screwed up her eyes and forced her index finger onto the ball of her thumb. 'Jamie,' she said, between breaths, 'still in the wood . . . I need to find . . .'

'Jamie's the dog, aye?'

'No. A boy. He's nine, he—'

'You left a nine-year-old child out in this with the weather coming in?' He was not feigning the cut to his voice as he had been before. 'Orla McLeod, what were you thinking of? Would your father be proud of you now?'

The shock of it hit her like water after sun. She turned, stumbling on a root. 'My *father*?'

'Your father. I knew him once. He was a fine man. I doubt he brought up his only daughter to leave a boy alone in the woods.' His face was too close to hers and his hands too tight on her wrists and he was, in too many ways, like her father. She was twelve again and not being understood. Her eyes pricked. 'He's fine. He's got my jacket. And my sweater, and—'

His face moved away, suddenly. He spoke very carefully. 'And so would that be him, then? With a friend?'

It was the way he said it that made her look. Jamie was indeed there, half kneeling with the dog in the shelter of a hawthorn, flushed again with the sight of her and the achievement of having followed her and the knowing that he had done everything she had asked of him. She smiled for him across the space between them and the look that came back to her lit the snow to full summer. But it was not for him that Hugh Carlaw was standing so still, and Jamie Buchanan could not – no, *would* not – have followed her alone. So she looked again with greater care and found that Murdo was there, three trees away, leaning over-casually on the trunk with his left hand steady in his pocket because he was ambidextrous and although he might write with his right, he shot with his left and he looked now the way he had looked in Finland the night Rory Donaldson died, which was little short of lethal. Beside her, Hugh Carlaw let go of his shotgun and they all heard it topple forward onto the snow.

'Murdo!' She stepped away from the tree, which was necessary, if not altogether wise. Information condensed into manageably small units in ordered priority. 'I'm fine. This is Hugh Carlaw. He owns the Manse. It's not far from here. We could go there and get warm before we go back. He has a phone. We can call Morag . . .' and she saw his hand ease from the pocket, which was all she needed to see and then he was at her side, holding her elbow, and he was back to the safe, sane, exasperated Murdo she felt comfortable with, holding onto what he thought and making daft conversation and moving her steadily, nearly gracefully, through the snow on a path cut in front of them by a man, a boy and a dog, walking easily, three abreast. The world, it seemed, was going to be all right.

'What happened to you?'

'I went for a swim in the snow.'

'And you found Hugh Carlaw's jacket riding in on the surf?'

'It's a life belt. He gave it me to keep me afloat.'

'Right. Well, you just see it keeps your head above water until we can get you somewhere closer to dry land.'

'It's OK, there's no rush. I'm fine. And I don't want to spoil things for Jamie.'

'Do me a favour. The lad's in heaven. The only way you'll spoil anything now is by making yourself too ill to play any more cowboys and indians in the woods.'

'I'm not ill.'

'Of course not. Anyone can see that. And pigs can fly and the earth is flat and there was nothing at all in your medical reports about compromised immunity secondary to a near-fatal heroin overdose and the resulting increased risk of infection. Get a grip, woman. I know exactly how ill you are.'

'That report was a private document, Murdo Cameron.'

'So? It was on the computer . . . Would you like a cigarette?'

'No. I don't smoke.'

'Really? Amazing how neatly the sows can dive when you're this far up the mountain . . . But you were right, we seem to be going to the

Manse after all. I'll call Morag as soon as we've got you warmed up. How about if I carry you the last hundred metres, will that offend the fragile McLeod sense of propriety? No, I thought not . . . Right, let's get you inside before you manage for yourself all the things that bastard didn't do in the flat.'

'. . . I was an engineer. I did some work for Harland and Wolff, the shipbuilders in Belfast, importing turbines. Hardly earth-shaking stuff although I'm sure I thought it was at the time . . .'

She came to, slowly. Smell came first, as it always did, although this was different: tweed and pipe tobacco and burning peat, none of which she expected. Somewhere nearby there was coffee, and Murdo and, further away, a dense, primeval musk.

'. . . everyone in Ulster knew of John McLeod. He was one of the best lawyers the Republican movement had ever had. If you were a Catholic, he was the avenging angel of the law, come to earth to right all the wrongs of the Protestant ruling order. If you were a loyalist, he was the anti-Christ . . .'

The voice oiled through her with the smell and it was just as wrong; almost and not quite her father, talking of him without being him, talking of him without getting him right. Forget Ulster, everyone in the whole world knew of John McLeod. He was the world. It surprised her that Murdo had to ask. But he was asking, she could hear the burr and rise of his voice even if the words were too far away to be clear.

'The Brits? They hated his guts. It wasn't that long after Bloody Sunday. You'd have to have been there to understand, but as far as the British establishment was concerned, the only good Catholic was a dead one. They'll not have been sorry when – Jamie, my child, she's not that fond of people yet. If you lose a finger, I'll lose a good friend in the village and, myself, I don't think it's a fair swap – ah, look, here she is, lights on and maybe somebody home. Are you back with us now, Orla McLeod?'

Hugh Carlaw was not as overwhelming as he had seemed on the mountain. Age sat on him more obviously than it had done, bending his shoulders inwards, twisting one hip when he stepped forward to touch her. The rub of his palm scratched the too-sensitive skin of her hand.

When she flinched, he drew it back sharply, aware of what he had done. 'I'm sorry. It'll hurt for a while yet. Can I get you a coffee? We were just discussing your father.'

'I know. I heard.' Her voice sounded strange, as it does with a cold. She cupped the curve of her palm to her ear and popped it and tried again. 'Yes. Please. Coffee would be good.'

He moved out of her way. Murdo was there behind him, keeping a good layer of humour over whatever was going on underneath. He moved his chair forward and she found, looking down, that she was in two chairs pushed face to face, sitting in one, stretching her legs on the other, that a blanket smothered her from armpits to ankles, that a range poured heat at her from one side and there was a fire in a hearth somewhere close on the other side and that she should have been too hot, but was not. Behind her, Hugh Carlaw was making coffee the old way, grinding beans that he must have bought in from Glasgow, or maybe Fort William if they sold coffee beans there now. A swan-spouted kettle sat on the range spewing steam up to a cumulus near the ceiling, filling the valleys between some very tasteful reclaimed oak beams. Somewhere closer, one of the two dead pheasants hung from a meat hook. A single congealing lens eyed her up, too wrinkled now to be of any use as a mirror but enough to shame her thinking into shape. She remembered her mother's maiden name and everything that went with it. She sat up. 'Where's Jamie?'

'Over there.' Murdo pushed his chair an inch or two sideways and she followed the line of his gaze. The child, warm in his black sweater, without his hat or his jacket or his gloves, was sitting in front of a pen in the far corner of the room, watching its occupant with the rapt attention he had previously reserved only for windows on the days that it snowed. The dog sat behind him, very pointedly not taking notice, all the hairs along its back quivering with the effort not to turn.

'What's in there?'

'Go and look.'

She shoved the blankets off her legs and found, belatedly, that she was still wearing her trousers and that her gun was no longer in her pocket.

She glanced at Murdo who tapped his side and nodded. 'You're fine,' he said. 'Go on. You're the one who's going to have to prise him away. I wouldn't know how to begin.'

The smell invaded her head and loosened her tenuous hold on reality. *Bear.* Not bear. The pen is not big enough for a bear and Hugh Carlaw is not terminally insane. *Skunk.* Don't be bloody ridiculous, woman, this is Scotland. *Stoat.* Possibly. Would Jamie Buchanan be enthralled by a stoat? An otter, maybe, or a badger or – a fox. Naturally. Common things are common. It was a fox, an excruciatingly thin, nervy, wild-eyed, prick-eared, white-fanged, pheasant-gorging vixen, half hidden in a thicket of cut conifer boughs that failed entirely to cover the harsh rise of her pelt or the pencil-sharp edge to her ribs, standing out like furrows straight after the plough. She fed like a starving cat, hunched possessively over the body, ripping flesh from feathers in a gale of blond and rust and glimmerings of gold that rose and fell as she whipped her jaw sideways and took the head from the neck.

'God, she looks—'

Jamie shushed her with a silent intake of breath, panic brushing his face and away again as the beast paused and then resumed its meal. Still, he tugged Orla's hand and pulled her down to his side, putting his finger to his lips in urgent reproof. The vixen looked up at the movement, shook her teeth clear of feathers, and started on the second wing.

'It's all right, you can talk. She's not that easily put off now.' Hugh Carlaw stood beside her with a small glass in one hand. This close, the fox musk outbid the steam and the coffee. He held it tight to his chest, not quite ready to hand it over. 'This is the real reason Angus Shearer lets me shoot,' he said. 'If it was just me wanting pheasant for the pot, you could forget it, but he found a wildcat last year that had lost a fight with a car and between us we put it back together and fed it up and now he takes his visitors to see where it hunts. Of course, the thing had to be fed and I was the one with the gun so I got special dispensation. I found this one a week or so back. She's a young one from last year and she hasn't quite got the hang of hunting in the snow yet. The last big fall finished her off. She was near enough dead to let me pick her up and bring her in here, which is enough, really, to get something done. I thought I'd feed her up and wait till the thaw and let her out. I maybe shouldn't keep her in the kitchen but I was afraid I'd forget to feed her if I put her anywhere else in the house.'

He was talking in a steady, rhythmic monotone and the vixen eased at the sound of it, becoming less flighty in her feeding. Near the end, he remembered the coffee and passed it over; sweet and scalding and spiked with Scotch. He watched Orla taste it and taste it again and not refuse and nodded approval and gratitude, mixed. In the pen, the fox moved down the carcass to the abdomen and sharpened the air with the acid of split guts. Jamie sighed happily as if this were expected and right, as if he were entirely at ease watching entrails sucked in like overcooked spaghetti with the gizzard snicked off and discarded at the end. He was leaning forward now, with his brow pressing up against the front of the pen and his hair plastered down on his head where his hat had crushed it and he hadn't taken the time to brush it out. She reached down, ruffling it with the tips of her fingers until it looked more like straw and less like wet silk, then she stood still with her hand on his head and felt the wonder and the awe slipping through him, grasped at and let go because if he held one thing, it didn't leave room for the next. She had never in her life watched a child falling in love. She had never, if she thought about it, watched any human being fall in love. It was not in any way as she had imagined.

'Orla.' Hugh Carlaw had gone and come back again. He stood beside her with one hand held stiffly in his pocket. When he was sure she was listening, he said, 'Murdo and I have discussed the potential problem of your imminent departure.' He nodded in a roundabout way, taking in Murdo and the door and the window all in one movement. Outside, the light was failing in a way that meant the cloud cover was lower than it had been all day. 'There really is going to be snow soon and I think it would be best to have you home before it hits. In view of the obvious attractions of here, would *we*,' he looked down at Jamie, 'accept, ah, how could we say it, *un petit cadeau* in consolation, do you think?'

He had been a father once, or perhaps an uncle, in a family where children were eased sideways out of adult conversations. Orla McLeod had not.

'I don't know,' she said. 'You could ask him.' She knelt down with her back to the crate. 'Jamie?' He knew he was being discussed. He sat still, waiting for permission to turn. Even without the fox there, he would have done the same. She found the thin edge of his shoulder and squeezed it. 'Jamie, beloved, Hugh thinks we should go home soon before the snow comes in. He's wondering if you'd like a present to take with you. Sadly – no, actually, not sadly at all – I suspect he doesn't mean the fox.'

Up above them, Carlaw shook his head, his tongue lodged in the gap between his teeth. 'No, he doesn't. He isn't entirely irresponsible. And he apologises for patronising the lad.' He crouched down to join them and, like a magician with a rabbit, he brought his gift up to eye level, holding it cupped and hidden between his palms. 'Last winter a friend and I found a wildcat,' he said. 'It was injured and then it couldn't hunt, so it was hungry, like the fox. I had to shoot things for it to eat. It was a very hard winter, harder than this one, and almost everything had died or was hiding away but the cat wouldn't eat anything not freshly shot so I had to get *something*.' He stopped and pursed his lips and age came and went from his face. 'The first thing I got was a hare, a snow hare, with pure white fur. I felt very bad shooting it because it was so beautiful but it was all there was. I wanted to keep something to remember it by so I fed the body to the wildcat but I kept the head and cleaned it out. I think maybe I was keeping it for you.' He opened his hand. The gift lay revealed on his palm; a thing both alive and not alive, a coupling of eggshell fragility and bone-hard strength, of arches and domes and tunnelled eye sockets and long, chiselled teeth that had been glued precisely into place. Jamie stared at it as if the snow had spoken and promised to be his forever. 'This is the skull of the hare,' said Hugh Carlaw. 'If you want it, it's yours.'

The new snow came as they reached the cottage. Jamie borrowed a tea towel to make a nest for his treasure and then took to the windows, moving around from east to west, from kitchen to living room and back again, watching the hard, granular flakes fall on the mountain and melt in the sea. During dinner the snow stopped and the sky cleared and, soon after that, the grey of the day passed to night and he watched the magic happen.

The moon rose not long after dusk. For a while, it was obscured by high, thin cloud but by bedtime it shone clear through the attic roof so that a square of liquid silver spilled onto the counterpane, splashing over the dog and up onto the pillow. He slid across so that the light shone full on his face and lay watching the mountain and listening to the wind and the sea and the lilt of voices in the room two floors below. The dog tired of licking fingers that tasted of toothpaste and squirmed up the bed the better to reach an ear and a nose. In time, the boy pushed him away and rolled on his side and slept far sooner than he had meant to.

Later, Morag McLeod sat on her own side of the fire and watched her daughter lean back on the hearthstone, drawing in heat as if the cold still ate at the core of her in the way it had when Hugh Carlaw and Murdo brought her back in from the Manse. Morag's hands worked of their own accord, putting rows on the new piece of knitting she had started as the night drew in. She was not, and never had been, the kind of woman to sit of a night in her rocking chair turning socks for the children. In the years before the assault on her home she had had a career of her own and had given it every spare minute that she didn't give to her family. In the years afterwards she learned to live in a world where, for a while, even the washing-up was a minefield of unseen disasters. The nuns in the first convalescent home after the hospital had persuaded her that knitting was a way to keep her hands mobile and she had tried it at first to keep them happy and found that they were right and that it kept the stiffness at bay and she had practised nightly through the years so that it happened now without her thinking.

She had spent the early part of this particular evening watching Jamie and had found that he was entranced by the mountain and the moonlight as much as he was by her daughter. Because she had lived a great deal of her life as a mother, she waited until he had gone to bed before she took the balls of black and white wool from her box and set about knitting a replica of her daughter's black rollneck sweater but with a moon on the front and a silver-peaked mountain on the back. It gave her something to do and if she was seen to be counting stitches or reading the pattern then it gave the others space to talk and to work on the mobile computer and to make whatever plans they needed to make in the light of the things that had changed on the hill.

Many things had changed on the hill. That much was clear from the moment when the three of them came back from Hugh Carlaw's, stamping in ahead of the snow with Orla grey around the lips and having trouble framing her sentences but nevertheless denying that there was anything wrong. It said a lot for Murdo Cameron that he didn't waste energy arguing with something so plainly untrue, he simply took her upstairs and ran her a hot bath and when she was in it and safe, he came down to Morag and Jamie and made tea and put logs on the fire so that she could warm herself inside and out when she came down to join them.

'How are her hands?'

'There's no frostbite that I can see. They'll be sore for a while longer and then she'll be fine. Hugh Carlaw was a godsend.'

'What was she doing?'

'Carlaw was shooting on the hill. She heard the shots and went to check that Jamie wasn't in danger.'

'I suppose that is what you're here for – in a manner of speaking.'

'In a manner of speaking. Yes.'

They settled themselves down to wait. The world outside changed from a few falling flakes to a blizzard, enclosing the cottage in a world of whirling white. Jamie retrieved his treasure from the mantelpiece, called the dog and curled up to immerse himself in his watching of snow. On the far side of the table, Murdo Cameron opened his laptop, connected it up to the phone line and, to all intents and purposes, left the room. Morag McLeod, finding herself alone when she least expected it, picked up her old knitting – a sweater for Tam Gillespie who ran the fishing boat, commissioned by his wife as a birthday present – and let her hands do the thinking.

She was a good four inches further up the back towards the neck when Murdo stretched and rubbed his temples and smiled at her across the table.

Morag nodded companionably. 'Your tea's cold.'

'Yes. Thank you.' He made no effort to touch it.

'Are you all right?'

'Fine. Absolutely.' He frowned and bit the edge of his thumb, still lost in the guts of his machine. 'He knew your husband, did you know?'

'Who?'

'Hugh Carlaw.' He looked up, more present than he had been. 'I'm sorry, I should have given warning of that. Carlaw had business in Ulster at the time you were living there, has he not told you?'

'He hasn't, no. But then there's maybe not been the right occasion.'

'Do you talk to him?'

'Of course. We talk all the time – about the weather and the fishing, about his garage full of smart cars and why he doesn't have time to drive them, about the state of the paths and the roads and whether the gritting lorries have been, about the frighteningly big number of tourists we get in the summer and the absolute lack of them in the winter – and the perennial question of whatever on earth possesses Angus Shearer to make him spend his days running up mountains half naked, to which nobody has an answer. I'd say that's about as personal as we've ever got about anything.'

Her needles tapped out a string of soft syllabic Morse. Murdo tapped less regularly at his keyboard, making new notes, or transcribing what she had said, nodding to himself at the new input. 'What cars?' he asked.

'I don't know. More than enough for one man. A fast one, a very fast one and one of the new fancy Land Rovers. That's as much as I know, I'm afraid. I'm not into cars.'

'No problem.' Still, he typed in something and hit a question mark and went on to type something more. In a while, he raised his head again. 'What's your impression of him as a human being?'

'I don't know.' He still had not touched his tea. She took the excuse to stand and fill the kettle and put it back on to boil. His mug had a rim where the milk had settled. She rinsed it clear under the tap and reached for a tea towel to dry it and leant back against the sink, thinking back through a year of chance encounters in the post office, of evening dinners with mutual friends, not often spent sitting together, of the infrequent, but pleasant, shared walks down the fields to the shore. In a while, with him watching, she put the mug down on the side and tidied the tea towel away and said, 'He's a good man,' she said, 'but then you could say that about a lot of folk and it wouldn't tell you anything.'

'You could indeed.' His hand hovered over the keyboard, ready to type what she said. It stayed there, frozen in space. His eyes teased. 'Come on, you're better than that, Morag. You may not know about cars but you know all about people. You didn't raise Orla to look at folk and see nothing deeper than "a good man".'

'Did I not? All right then, I'd say on the surface he's quiet, reserved, meticulously courteous – every part the Laird.'

'And underneath?'

'He's brighter than average. He watches, he sees what happens, he asks questions, he considers the answers. He thinks before he speaks.'

'Hell. God defend us from those who think before they speak.' His teeth showed very white as he grinned. 'All right, let me ask it a different way. Would you trust him with your daughter?'

'I would so. I think the pair of them would get on well together.' She followed his tone into nonsense, finding a good Galway lilt for her voice. 'Does your computer say I should not?'

'Not at all. My computer doesn't say much of anything, but then I only have access to the police files so this is either good or bad depending on the depth of your cynicism.' He worked his fingers at his temples, easing the dents of half an hour's concentration. His voice was languid and lazy and richly full and he squandered it without due regard to its value. He said, 'As far as I can tell from here, Hugh Carlaw hasn't so much as picked up a speeding ticket which means, from my position of extreme jaundice, that either the man's incredibly lucky or he's unnaturally well-behaved and, he's not the right sort to be trusted in the care of the next generation.'

'Is that right?' She turned on him, eyes afire with proper indignation. 'I'll have you know I've never had a speeding ticket in my life either, Murdo Cameron. Does that mean I'm not the right sort to be trusted with the next generation too?'

'Christ, no,' he wasn't thinking, still half in the machine, and neither of them was taking it seriously, 'but then you have a daughter who's killed enough men in the last week to make up for all the speeding fines in the—'

He crashed to a halt, biting down on his lip. One hand moved across to cover his eyes. In the breathless pause that followed he said the only thing he could think of: 'Morag – I'm sorry.'

'Don't be. You should never apologise for speaking the truth.' It had been there for a while now, humming along in tune with the laughter and it was only time before it broke through to the surface. With care, she put the cup down on the counter beside the draining board. 'She said as much this morning and I chose not to listen. Perhaps now would be a better time.' She sat down with him at the table. Behind her, the kettle rolled towards the boil and they both ignored it. 'How many lives does it take to make up for a speeding fine, Murdo?'

'I don't think it's my place to . . .' He spread his fingers so that he could see her, and sucked a breath through his teeth. 'Three.'

'Thank you.' She looked past him to Jamie who was listening and not listening, as if this were a skill he had practised all his life. She said, loudly enough for him to hear and know he was meant to, 'And Jamie was with her?'

'He saved her life.' With the humour gone, he looked tired and tense and she could, for the first time, believe he could kill. He snapped shut the lid of his computer and reached back to rip the power cord from the wall. 'There was no way round it, Morag. They had already killed Luke and they would have gone on to kill her and Jamie if she hadn't acted as she did. As it was, she did well to control the crossfire so he only got hit in the arm.'

'Did she? I must be getting old. I had never thought controlling the crossfire to be a particularly useful life skill for a woman – for anyone

– in our brave new world of harmony and peace.' She paused, tilting her head back and up. Above them, water choked and spat down the plughole and bare feet scuffed on the lino of the bathroom floor. They both stopped for a while and did other things. Murdo coiled the power cord of his laptop and nested it safely in its carrying case. Morag found her knitting and began to work her way into the shoulders and the neck. At the window, Jamie sat curled with the dog, half of his mind on the snow, half on the new treasure he held cupped in the palm of his hand. The dome of it glimmered softly matt in the wash from the window, like porcelain, or breath-dulled ice, the twin-tunnel eyes sparked occasionally with a reflected flake of snow in a loose, haphazard set of signals. After a while, the knitting happened on its own and the skull of a hare asked unanswerable questions in a code only Morag could read. Some time after that the bathroom door closed at the top of the stairs and a bedroom door opened and the sounds of waking became sounds of sleeping, or its closest approximation. Downstairs, the tensions eased.

'She'll do better with sleep,' said Morag.

'She will. Sleep and antibiotics and new dressings on her wrists and not going out in the cold for a day or two, very little of which will be allowed to happen.' Murdo had found his humour again, dryer than before but there all the same.

'You might get the bandages,' said Morag. 'You won't get much else. For the daughter of a medic, she has a shocking lack of faith in the benefits of science and the broader reaches of pharmacology . . .'

She let the sentence fade to a natural silence, very carefully not asking the question that it was not her business to ask. Still, when he said nothing and she looked up, she realised she may as well have written it on a postcard and passed it across the table. Too many decades had passed since she had spoken to a man who listened through the words to the meaning behind them in quite the way that this one did. Even then, the eyes had never laid her quite so bare. She sighed and spiked her needles through the remaining ball of wool. In her own defence she said, 'I was a doctor before I was ever a mother, Murdo, and I know a blown vein when I see one.' Then, when he was still silent, 'She and Jamie changed down here by the stove before you all went out. I would have to be blind not to have seen it.'

He nodded, giving nothing. 'If you're a doctor, then you will know the difference between a needle inserted voluntarily and one driven in by force.'

'Maybe, but if we're talking hypotheticals, then I can also tell you that habitual users have an accuracy that is sometimes lacking in the novice and folk sticking themselves for the first time often end up with bruises far worse than hers.' She caught his eyes and watched him flinch. 'Forget dancing round the houses, Murdo, we're both too old for that. I am asking you to tell me that she didn't inject herself, or, failing that, to tell me the truth. I am aware, however, that I have no right to ask this and you're under no obligation to answer and if you say you don't want to, we will forget this conversation ever happened. Is that fair?'

'Totally.' The kettle was screaming, had been doing so for some time. He stood up to pull it off the hob and busied himself with the minutiae of making tea. With his back to her, he said, 'She's very like you, did you know?'

'She's very like her father. It's what made him a good lawyer and would have made Orla the same if she'd stuck with it after she'd done her degree. With her, it comes naturally. I'm the one who's had to learn it to survive.'

'That must have been fun.' He reached into the fridge and found the milk and then leant back on the range, cradling his mug in both hands. He was smiling again, gently, just enough to crease the skin at the corners of his eyes, enough to make them co-conspirators rather than opponents, to unstring the humming lines that ran from her hands to her shoulders and on down her back. It was, she realised, something that he did naturally, like her daughter's forensic conversation, and it was no more accurate a barometer of the pressures moving inside. She was on the verge of apologising, of calling it all back and unsaid, when he reached a hand to her arm.

'She may not agree – she almost certainly won't – but if we are going to be here under these circumstances for any length of time then I think there are some things you have a right to know.' She nodded. They had already passed beyond the line to which her daughter would readily agree, they both knew that. He went on, 'Orla did not inject herself. She never has done and, as far as I am aware, she never will do. In the flat, there were three of them to one of her although one or more of them may have been holding Luke with a gun at his head which is probably the only reason she stood still enough to let them get near her. They used what passes for heroin in the current cesspit that is Glasgow, which means it was roughly fifty per cent pure. The medics haven't worked out what made up the remainder but we can take it as read that it wasn't picked for its beneficial effects on her system. As far as anyone knows, it's only luck that the initial dose didn't kill her. Even so, if Jamie hadn't been there, she'd have been dead within hours and it would have been very much worse than an overdose. If you think about it, that explains quite a lot of what has happened since.'

'Thank you, it does.' He offered tea with a nod and she accepted and when it came and he was quiet again, she said, 'Is Luke the one she has married?'

'Yes.' He had found the biscuits she had bought for Jamie and was playing with one, holding it in the tea, watching the darkening edge creep upwards from the fluid line and lifting it clear just before the weight became more than the structure could carry. It was a small boy's game, from the time when small boys were all going to be engineers and small girls were going to be – not people who controlled the crossfire to stop a dead woman's child from following her to an early grave. She looked up and found he was simply watching, not searching. He said, 'How much has she told you?'

'That a man is dead, that she married him posthumously and only on paper and with the blessing of the man who was his partner and who is still alive. I was to understand that it was done for Jamie, so that he had at least one living parent, not for the memory of the man. She didn't tell me his name. Or perhaps she did and I wasn't listening. It was one of our busier phone calls.'

'Luke Tyler,' he said. 'Technically speaking, she is now Mrs Luke Tyler.'

'Thank you.'

His free hand lay still on the table. The skin was as brown and worn as the rest of him, but less smooth. The middle knuckle on his ring finger was swollen, as if it had once been broken, and he ran the edge of his thumb across it, as if the asymmetry could be rubbed back into line. She watched for a while until he noticed and stopped, then she said, 'I have found with Orla, more than most folk, that what she does is often more revealing than what she says.'

He nodded and let it sink in and sorted through it for the meanings that lay beneath the obvious. In a while, he said, carefully, 'For some of us, loving the dead can be a great deal easier than loving the living.'

'Particularly if you have had a lifetime of practice.'

'And if the men you have loved most have both died.'

'Yes.' She would have changed the subject then, but he leant across the table and took her hand in his own. The broken knuckle finger threaded more stiffly through hers than the rest.

'Morag?' The burr of his speech moved down his arm and into hers. 'I don't believe that's any reflection on you.'

'No. Possibly not.' She had not expected it so baldly said. It caught the thought in her and drew it out. Without pausing to consider, she said, 'All the same, it's not an easy thing, living life for three other people as well as yourself. Especially when one of them is still living to see you do it.'

He said nothing but she felt a change in the grip of his fingers. Searching his eyes, she saw the same thing reflected there; a slower current that ran under the irony and the reflex warmth. Understanding came slowly, like waking from sleep. 'Or maybe not just three other lives, Murdo? Have we just seen it go up to four?'

'I don't know. I think we might have done. It would seem very likely.' His hand turned over so that hers was on top. She let it lie still while he took in the shape of it and the marbled whites of the grafted skin. He, too, was not used to this level of exposure. In time, he said, 'On the other hand, your daughter wasn't living for anyone else when she lifted a nine-year-old boy from a tenement in Glasgow and brought him home to the only place she knows is safe, to live and grow in the company of the only person she knows she can trust. When things get bad, you may want to remember that.'

There was a gift in that if she chose to take it. She accepted with what grace she could find. 'Thank you,' she said. 'She chooses well in her friends.'

'Maybe.' He stood, gathering the debris of the mugs and the biscuits and she realised she didn't know him well enough yet to read everything that went on in his eyes. 'But then again, I will never be Luke Tyler. Or her father.'

At the back door, he turned. 'I'll go out and take a look round before we close everything for the night. Give me a shout if she wakes up before I'm back.'

She woke sooner than she should have done and refused to stay in bed. For the rest of the evening she walked like a grey shadow, her lips tight, her body shaking as she failed to melt the wedge of ice at the core. Murdo said nothing with his mouth and a lot with everything else and there was a friction between them that grew worse for the lack of words. After dinner, with Jamie in bed, Morag took out her knitting and counted new stitches onto the needle and let the two of them sit by the fire with the computer open on the chair in front of them, working out their plans for the coming days. The conversation was spare and did nothing to release the pressure. The row, when it finally came, focused on a packet of cigarettes that lay on the hearth.

'I don't want one.'

'I don't care what you want. You *need* one. You can't come off everything overnight.'

'Watch me.'

'I'm watching. You should take a look in a mirror sometime, it's not a pretty sight. If Svensen springs something now, are you going to be fit to deal with it? I don't think so.'

He opened the pack and leant forward to the fire. When he leant back, a thin wire of smoke curled up from his fingers. He fanned it across under her nose. 'Take it,' he said. 'This isn't a challenge, Orla. You're not losing anything but pride.' And then, when her hand stopped halfway to his, 'Would you rather I got out the methadone?'

'You have it here?'

'Of course. Andy Bennett packed my medical kit. He wouldn't have let me come without it.' His hand moved to lie over hers, the lit cigarette sliding between her clenched fingers. 'Please? For me? Tomorrow, you can be a non-smoker. Tonight, you're allowed to let go.' At which, to her mother's very great astonishment, she did.

Murdo went to bed not long after that. Orla sat on the hearthstone with a second, unlit cigarette held between her fingers. She watched her mother and felt her mother watch her. The toilet flushed above their heads. The plumbing rattled to rest. A log fell in the fire, crumbling the ones beneath it to red ash. Outside, the sea moved stones on the shore. So much was the same each time she came home, so much was different. She looked across at her mother and her mother looked back. 'What are you knitting?' she asked.

'A sweater for Jamie.' Morag held the needles aloft. The first curve of the moon showed white in a flag of black. 'Will he like it?'

'I expect he will. He might not show it quite as you're used to but it doesn't mean he isn't pleased.'

The brown eyes were watchful. 'Maybe he's learnt his ways of showing gratitude from you.'

'Thank you.' And so it was not going to be easy, being home. She turned sideways and laid a new log on the pile of the others. The fire grew round it, catching the resin. A brief, blue flame reached up to the sky. She leant forward to light the second cigarette and looked up to find that her mother was watching that, too. 'Is this all right?'

'Of course.' A smile. 'I understand it's not becoming a habit.'

'No.'

The knitting went back in the box it had come from. Her mother drew her armchair closer to the fire. A flicker of flame reflected from the surface of her eyes. 'Can he talk?' she asked. As if Jamie Buchanan were the centre of their universe.

'He can. He chooses not to. Where he comes from, it was safer for a child to stay quiet.'

'But you didn't stay quiet?'

'I'm not a child.'

'No.'

And that was it; as much of a question as would ever be asked. The fire was scorching her ankles. Orla moved round, letting her hand dangle down in front of the fire. The updraught caught the smoke from the cigarette and drew it up the chimney with the rest. She was tired and it clouded her thinking, like fog obscuring the moon. The nicotine helped. Murdo was right in that as in everything else. She was doing her best not to hate him for being so. She closed her eyes and let that one settle. All of the anger, traced back, came round in a circle and none of it belonged to Murdo Cameron. She planned an apology for the morning and the fog began to clear in her mind. She stared into the dark and Luke Tyler stared back. She opened her eyes.

'Tord Svensen,' she said. 'His name was Tord Svensen.' Even saying his name was hard. The wind soughed in the chimney. Her mother could have been asleep but wasn't. Morag McLeod watched the changes in her daughter as a painter watches the changes in the light. She saw the struggle with the name and sought a reason. 'Is he the man who killed Luke?' she asked.

Her head came up sharply. 'Murdo told you?'

'He only gave me the name. Beyond that, he didn't tell me anything else about him that you hadn't already said on the phone. The man is dead. He mattered to you. I don't need to know more.'

'They all matter. Luke, Murdo, Andy Bennett. We were a team.'

'And now he's gone, is the team broken?'

'I don't know. It's never happened before. Not to us.'

She moved round to sit with her back to her mother's chair, hugging herself close to the knees as she had as a child. So much had changed. So much stays the same.

'There's only been one other death since we started. A man called Rory Donaldson died on the training exercise in Finland. He got wet, he stayed out in the cold, he was found too late.' Her face moved in a smile that went no further. 'There wasn't a hot bath and a mug of tea within easy reach when it happened.'

'What happened to his team when he was gone?'

'They fell apart. They tried them with three different substitutes. They didn't work. None of them is working for Strang any more.'

'And it's important to keep working for Strang?'

'It's the only thing I've found that makes life worth living.'

The second cigarette was a mistake. The fog, in its way, was a blessing, clarity a curse. In the clear space that was the past, she lay in a snow hole under a fallen log with a dead man sharing her sleeping bag. His hair was red. A three-day growth of beard pushed into her cheek. His frostbitten fingers lay like iced stones in the hollows of her armpits and his wide-open eyes stared straight into hers. In the catalogue of ghosts, he was small fry, but the minnows ever precede the bigger fish.

She put her hands over her eyes and knew that if she slept, she would dream and that if she didn't sleep, she would not be fit to face the morning and that either way she couldn't face it. *Please, not now.* It was only when she saw the flames flicker in the fire that she realised she had given it sound.

She felt her mother's fingers stroking through the harshness of her hair and heard her mother's voice asking. 'Were you there when the man died?'

'Yes.'

'Were you responsible?'

'He was alive when I got there.'

'Did you set up the exercise? Did you lay down the rules?'

'No.'

'If you asked Jamie to take Bran for a walk and didn't tell him about the marsh at the back of the hill and the dog went in and couldn't get out, and the boy stayed on the bank talking to him while he died, would it be Jamie's fault?'

'We've been through this already. Jamie Buchanan is a child. I'm not. What we do is different.'

'Is it?' Her mother's voice was still soft. Her hands were still gentle at her neck. Somewhere in the rest of her was the steel with which she faced the world. 'It's a normal part of childhood to feel responsible for every bad thing that happens in the world,' she said. 'But Orla, when we grow up, we are supposed to stop believing in our own omniscience.'

The hands left her shoulders. She felt her mother rise and heard her move back to the kitchen. She heard the top come off the bottle and two glasses poured and her mother returned. The whisky was dark, almost black, and she could smell the peat in it from halfway across the room. A tumbler slid into her hand as if it was moulded to fit. 'Drink,' said her mother. 'It was your father's. It works for me when I start to hear the voices in the fire.'

Six

It was raining. God, was it raining. Water ran in spate from a broken downpipe to the street. A wet newspaper disintegrated slowly at the edge of the kerb, spinning sodden fragments into the gutter. A bus driven too close to the edge hurled a gout of spray at the pale blue Escort parked at the kerb. Inside, DI Gordon McRae rocked with the impact of it and turned on the wipers. A semi-circle of Glasgow filth smeared across his windscreen, drizzling downwards with the rain. He swore and stared forward and made every effort not to consider what better things he might be doing with his evening.

A radio fizzed static in his ear. Voices overran each other as two men and a woman threw soundbites at each other.

'. . . gone to ground. Third floor, flat six . . .'

'That's Patsy Kerr's place . . .'

'Thank you, smart-arse. Home and business address for every whore in Glasgow . . .'

'Subject has his own key. Lights going on . . .' McRae leant over to look upwards. A square of yellow lit up in the rain-dulled concrete above him. '. . . and off again. No movement inside. Fuck, it stinks here . . .'

'. . . can't handle it, get a transfer back to traffic . . .'

'You come up here and I'll sit in the fucking car . . .'

He reached for his mouthpiece. 'Cut the crap, children. Stainton, how close are you?'

'As close as it gets without camping on the doorstep.'

'Well, go camping. I want to know what he's doing.'

'If he comes out, he'll see me.'

'Let him, it doesn't— Fuck, hold on.' The second of his two mobile phones rang. Very few individuals had that particular number and none of them appreciated a slow response. He spoke into the radio. 'See what you can do without getting yourself killed.' The connection died under his finger. He keyed the mobile. The line was exceptionally good.

'McRae?'

'Yes.' He sat straighter in his seat.

'Your people are on target?'

'They are, yes.'

'Good. Call them off. All of them. Terminate surveillance with immediate effect. Send the others home. You go back to Maryhill. You'll be needed in the next hour.' There was a pause during which a number of obvious questions presented themselves and were discarded. The voice said, 'Is that clear?'

'If you say so.'

'I do.' The line died.

He stared out through the rain. A taxi pulled in ahead of him, dumping another gallon of water on his windscreen. An elegant brunette stepped out and paid the driver before making her way up the steps to the main entrance of the flats. McRae reached again for his radio. 'Everybody happy out there?'

'Do you want to swap places?'

'I'm happy as long as you're doing my laundry. Subject is stationary. If you want an educated guess, I'd say he's in for the night.'

'That's cool. Patsy's just got home. She'll be on her way up any minute now. You can listen in to the happy hour.'

'Not unless you're sadder than you're letting on.' McRae smiled tightly. 'Anyone who wants to hang around from now on is doing so on their own time as personal recreation. That means no overtime, children. Anyone who doesn't want to stay is free to go home. Surveillance is cancelled with effect from now. If you want a lift back, I'll be here for the next five minutes. Is that clear?'

He received no answer but then he expected none. They were a good team and none of them had been selected for their tendency to sit out in the rain for the fun of it. The static hissed without interruption until he snapped it to silence. Within thirty seconds, a knuckle rapped on his passenger window and Ben Wiseman bailed into the back seat.

'You smell fresh.'

'This is nothing. You wait till you get close to Jules.'

'I can wait.'

Tim Hughes was next, wet but fragrant. Julie Stainton did, indeed, have a legitimate claim for laundry expenses. The other two opened the windows and bickered over who should sit next to her while McRae keyed the engine and set the wipers on full and drew out to join the desultory flow of traffic. As they reached the red light at the head of the road, he checked his watch and wrote the time in his log book. It was twenty-one seventeen and forty-four seconds.

At the same time in another part of town, a drunk sitting in a doorway drew his feet in and hugged his brown paper bag to his chest. A cardboard box sat at his side with 'HOMELESS AND HUNGRY' written in fading Biro. Three coins flashed silver in the reflected light of the passing cars but they were the same three that he had put there when he first sat down. An hour ago, the last of the evening shoppers walked past, hands in pockets, heads down against the rain. Since then, the only human life he had seen was a middle-aged woman with two children who steered them past at a speed that suggested poverty and alcoholism were highly infectious. The drunk pulled his woollen hat further down round his ears, lit another cigarette, took another drink from his bottle and tried not to think about the cold. Two more cars passed and then a small, slight redhead with a skirt that defined her upper thighs walked past and lounged against the plate glass of the shop window. The mannequins inside had manifestly more flesh on them than she did.

A chilly five minutes later, the woman, who was known to her contact as Maria Kilbride, flicked a glance at the drunk. 'Quiet, eh?' she said. The man offered her a cigarette. She leant towards him for a light. The flame flickered back and forth between them. She said, 'Jake Turner's lost his stable.'

'*Christ.*' That woke him up. 'Who to?'

'Who do you think?'

'Shit.' The drunk hawked and spat. The lighter flame between them went out. He dragged on his cigarette and wrote nonsense in the air with the glowing end as he considered her news. His eyes had more life to them than you might have expected. 'Would he come in to us, do you think?' he asked. '"The enemy of my enemy is my friend"?'

She laughed. 'No chance. He wants blood. He'll not get that from you.' Her smile mocked more gently. 'Not the right colour blood, anyway – *fuck*.' She stepped smartly back. The bow wave of a delivery van dashed the glass where she had been. The drunk shuffled after her, tugging his cardboard box to safety. The move took them both into the shadows of an alley. The drunk stood without swaying. 'What colour blood is he after?'

'Patsy's. He's going after her this evening. He thinks she set it up with Tord Svensen.'

'What? That's daft. Svensen doesn't need the likes of Patsy Kerr. If she was dog meat, he'd have got the rest of them just the same.'

'Tell that to a cretin with his brains in his balls. Turner wants his pound of flesh and his long day of pain. If he can't get it off the ringmaster, he'll have the ice-cream girl instead.' Students hovered round the end of the alley, contemplating its use as a short cut. The woman stepped in close to the drunk and slipped off his overcoat. Underneath, he wore oil-stained jeans and a black leather jacket. She slipped her arms round his waist and drew him in. The students laughed, too high and too short to be real, and chose another route. The man bent his head, touching his brow to her hair. She breathed in his ear. 'Get her out, man. She was good to you when you needed her.'

He made every man's promise. 'I'll do what I can.'

'And don't come back here. Things are different since Luke's gone.'

The name twisted through him. Briefly, he stepped out of persona and the woman found that the man she was holding was neither drunk nor needy john. 'Luke didn't know about you,' said Andy Bennett. 'If you're having trouble, it's not down to him.'

'Is that right?' She let him go. 'I hope someone's told Big Drew that. He's another one after blood and if Tord lets him off the leash I don't want to be the one he goes after.'

'We could get you out. There are safe houses.'

'You think so? Your man didn't know about them either, did he not?' She was not unkind, but it needed to be said and he was more able to hear it than he had been a moment before. She stepped back, moving her hands at his waist, fastening flies that had never been open. 'Thanks, but no thanks. I'll make my own way. I'll do fine as long as you're not dropping me in it.' She looked up at him. Her eyes were as dark as the rain. 'Tell me you aren't going to drop me in it?'

'We won't drop you in it. I promise.'

'Good.' She lifted his coat from the gutter. In the passing from her hand to his, she felt an inner pocket and retrieved the selection of folded bills secreted therein. Strumming them past the edge of her thumb, she found a sum higher than she had been paid in all the other times of their meeting. He had known, then, that this would be the last.

'Thanks.'

'No problem.' Andy Bennett smiled thinly and with real regret. 'Go safely.'

'That's the plan. You see to Patsy.' She turned left at the end of the alley and was gone.

Patsy Kerr's was half an hour's convoluted drive away. From the outside, her home was not unlike the tenement in which Jamie Buchanan had lived and Luke Tyler had died although the pavement was largely free of debris and most of the windows were intact. By then, half of them were also dark. Once in a while the lights of the lift rose up through the floors and then transferred, briefly, sideways. On the far left-hand corner of the third floor, the place of Patsy's bedroom, a single light shone continuously, if dimly, through thin curtains.

It was just after ten when Colin Thomas came home from his regular wind-down at the Anchor, maudlin and peevish and unhappy with the weather and not at all looking forward to an evening of domestic disharmony. His collar was pulled up to meet his cap at his ears, leaving a narrow wedge of eyes and brows exposed to the rain as he hunched his way to the double glass doors of the main entrance. Later, he would remember the lean, balding man with the coat draped over his arm who pushed open the door ahead of him, chiefly – and this was written carefully in the report – because, although the trainers he wore on his feet were worth a fortune, the man smelled like a drunk. Colin Thomas spent his life selling sportswear and knew the value of footwear. He was almost as closely acquainted with the tones and undertones of cheap whisky but he had spent a good hour perfecting his illusion of genteel sobriety and he was in no mood to have it destroyed by a man quite so clearly under the influence. He suffered a moment's minor panic as the lift blinked its imminent arrival and he faced the prospect of a journey shared in a confined space, but the deity of small drunks smiled on him this once and the stranger proved himself stranger than anything by turning left as the lift doors opened and making a good show of running up the stairs.

Andy Bennett, who had paid good money for good shoes for good reasons, worked his way up two floors on air-cushioned soles in something close to silence. On the landing just below the third floor, he stopped, shrugged into his drunk-coat and, cursing softly in language that would have surprised even Colin Thomas, settled down on the concrete. The stairwell was foul, if not noticeably worse than any of those below it. He wasn't the first to give up on his legs at that particular point, but he was, in his opinion, probably the first in a long time to do so while still conscious. Layered stains all around him gave up a bouquet of urine and vomit and other things best not considered. His coat was waterproof and probably sick-proof and had been tested against most other excreta of human and non-human origin, but it never quite kept out the aura of rotting piss. He drew his hands deep inside the sleeves and rolled his eyes and muttered oaths to the listening walls about hospitals and bodily fluids and all the reasons he had given up being a doctor in favour of a cleaner, less olfactorily challenging career. Shortly, when he had used up his vocabulary of invective and his senses had dulled to the stench, he shifted the focus of his attention from his nose to his ears and did what he could to find out what was happening around him.

It was a busy street at a busy time of night and it took a second or two for the sounds to resolve into recognisable layers. Outside, cars passed by, moving as fast as the road and the rain would allow. None of them crawled, it wasn't that kind of street, and the noises followed the continuous red-blue shift of approach and retreat, varying only with the size of each engine. Downstairs, someone much larger than Colin Thomas pushed open one half of the double main door and stepped in from the rain. Bennett pushed himself back into a corner and poured a dribble of young, sour Scotch onto the steps around him, enhancing the general aura of inebriation. He needn't have bothered. The incomer rode the lift to the second floor and came no further. Flat, male feet trod concrete and then carpet and then stopped as a door closed behind them. Closer, behind one of the doors next to Patsy's, two women finished a fight and made up. Upstairs, on the fourth and final floor, a child girned and was settled to sleep. He sat still for a full sixty seconds and the pattern remained much the same; all the way through the building, people ate and drank and fucked and fought and snored and wept and laughed – except in the flat on the left at the top of the stairs, from which no sounds of life came at all. Bennett listened as a four-wheel drive diesel and a small automatic passed each other on the street below and then, in a window of relative quiet, sloughed off the coat and the jacket beneath it and eased himself up the last eight steps to the landing.

The quiet followed him up. Ahead and to the right, two doors stood blankly solid, protecting whatever or whoever lay inside. To his left, Patsy Kerr's door, clean, newly painted, with good locks and no signs of forced entry, stood half an inch open.

Shit.

He wiped his palms dry on his jeans and drew his gun. The door swung inwards at a push, catching halfway on the carpet, giving him an angled view into a wide, airy living room, bright with the glow of streetlights flooding in through full-height windows past curtains that had never been drawn. For a moment, with everything still, there was a chance she had merely gone out in a hurry, forgetting to pull the door shut behind her. Cool air eddied past him, washing away the ancient piss and shit and sick of the stairwell, bringing in their place the clean wool of a new carpet, Opium perfume, laundry; all that was safe in the home of a woman living alone. Then the currents billowed with the sway of the door and the back-draught delivered to Bennett the stuff of his most recent nightmares: the charnel house cocktail of a basement he had never visited but had nevertheless repainted nightly on the naked canvas of his mind, flavouring it from memory with exactly this mix of all the human fluids bar one, cut and squeezed and strained and shaken into the thick, curdled scent of fresh blood.

Jesus . . . Patsy?

She was in the far corner near the kitchen, fresh from the shower with damp hair and a towelling dressing gown, sitting curled up like a child in the embrace of an armchair too big and too old for the room; a family heirloom saved for better times, wide-winged and solid and darkened with age. From the doorway, she could have been smiling, with perhaps an excess of lipstick in a shade that didn't suit her, except that the smile was three inches lower than it should have been and her face was turned sideways, hiding in the wings of the chair while the smile faced him head on, complete with a pink tongue of tracheal foam and a beard of drying blood. *Oh, Christ.* Closer, the cut gave up more detail: a right-handed slice from behind, with the deepest part at the start and the prints of the left hand, the hand that had held her still, splayed across her jaw. Whoever held the knife had been going for silence, not subtlety; a quick, quiet kill with a spectacular amount of blood that would look good on the photographs afterwards. That much, at least, Turner had gleaned from Tord Svensen; that lessons are learned more quickly if they are backed up by graphics and few things are more graphic than a good spray of scarlet.

There was a very great deal of that. Four vessels had pulsed in the beginning; a fountain from each carotid spattered the waiting wings of the chair in a mosaic of arterial red. Slow rivers had leaked from each of the jugulars beside them, flowing in wider channels that wicked down her sleeves to the arms of the chair and from there, in fat, black-cherry drops, onto the carpet. The plaque of pink-stained foam corking the cut surface of her trachea said that there had been time to breathe in and out, maybe twice, in the small sleep before the end.

Bastard.

She looked very calm. Andy Bennett could believe if he wanted to – and he found that he did – that she had not known what was coming when Jake Turner took his walk round the back of her chair. She showed none of the signs of a long death, or even of a long time spent awaiting its arrival. Half kneeling in front of her, Bennett searched without success for signs of void urine, or faeces, or vomit, all of which he had smelled as he walked in the door. *Fuck.* He dragged his fingers through the thinning edge of his hair, careless of the diminishing follicles. *You're cracking up, man. Strang's right, you need time away.* Except that time away was time to think and to dream and neither had proven a good idea. This was his reason, had he needed one, for being there alone in defiance of explicit orders, sanity and protocol. *Take your time. Check it out again.* He backed away to the entrance and tasted the air. It was there, definitely; hovering under the copper-rust of her blood, the reek of a bedpan, used and not yet cleaned away – or of a toilet, not yet flushed.

He spun in a circle. It was not a big flat. The bathroom door was open to his right. Inside, a collation of mirrored tiles took his reflection and bent the edges, adding silhouettes and shadows and twisting it round. Old streaks of condensation hung drying in the corners and a nest of grey-brown hair gathered foam at the plug. The last of the bubbles collapsed to slime as he passed. The lid was down on the toilet in the corner but when he lifted it, the water was clean with the bleached scent of fresh chemicals and a wavering rim of green above the waterline.

Not the bathroom. The kitchen?

The kitchen stood opposite; a clean, uncluttered place of white fitted surfaces and knives kept in blocks. The place was more sterile, if that were possible, than the bathroom.

The bedroom, then.

The bedroom was on the right, next to the bathroom, and if he bothered to think, the light had been on since he first cruised past in his car at half the speed of the other traffic. It was still on now. A line of bright yellow light showed under the door and, as he went closer, the pressing, florid, sewer stench gathered, humming, at the hinges. *Fucking hell.* He fought for breath and clear thought and for a name to put with the source. Only one made any sense . . . *Not Maria. Please God, not Maria as well* . . . With his gun leading, and keeping low to the carpet, he punched open the door, counted five and came upright at the foot of the bed where he found, as he had expected, a dead body. Only the identity was a surprise.

Jesus Christ Almighty.

Not Maria.

Not Maria at all.

The sirens screamed on the echo of the door, as if a particularly assiduous neighbour had dialled the last of three nines as the wood hit the hinges and the squad car had been waiting round the corner with the blue light spinning, waiting to go. Both squad cars. All three of the bastards. And Billie Reid with them which meant they weren't coming simply for the sake of a woman with her throat cut; an assistant chief constable has better things to do with his nights than pace out the lounge of a dead whore. *Fuck.* Bennett backed away from the carnage in the bedroom, from the lesser bloodshed in the living room and stepped out onto the landing. In the darkness, he pulled the door almost shut, leaving the half-inch open as he had found it and then skipped down the eight steps to the half-landing to pick up his jacket and drunk-coat – which were no longer there. *Fuck. Fuck. Fuck.* The pen torch from his pocket stabbed a narrow beam at the flight below and the landing below that and showed no signs of anything beyond the empty lager can that had been there as he ran up. *This is getting silly.* Noises below indicated that the occupants of at least two squad cars had reached the front door and that most, but not all, had elected to wait for the lift. A single set of footsteps sounded on the stairs, coming at them hard, three steps at a time. *There's always one. Fuckwit.* The steps became hollow and then solid again as they passed the first landing and came on up to the first floor. This close, they were not simply steps, they were stamped in leather, hard and sharp with no need, ever, for silence. *Laidlaw. Christ, we've got the whole bloody circus. How do they know?* The steps reached the first floor and came on up. Between them and him, doors began to open, heads to jut out, asking questions that received no answer. With no other option, Andy Bennett turned on his heel, took the half-flight in two steps, spun on the landing outside Patsy Kerr's door and carried on up to the top.

Because he was trained to notice detail and because he was expecting trouble, Bennett was still in the dark of the stairwell when he caught the signature whiff of his drunk-coat. Nothing else in Glasgow carried quite the same essence of excrement and alcohol. He hugged the wall as a close friend and drew his gun. Up on the landing, all he could see was a square of barred glass in the roof. Diffractions of starlight and moonlight leaked in, casting graphite shadows into pitch darkness and etching the ghost of a square on the landing at the top of the stairs, a light trap for the unwary. *Bugger. Think, man.* He still had his gloves. He peeled the left one off with his teeth and rolled it up in his hand. Somewhere, up in the no-light of the landing, someone took in a breath of the kind that goes before firing. With a prayer for the silence of his running shoes, Bennett stepped up another three stairs, tossing his glove away from him, to the far right-hand side of the patched pallor on the concrete. It worked. Back in the darkness, a shadow moved in other shadows. Bennett's gun came up and his finger took in the first slack of the trigger. A second, less driven part of his brain took note of contour and colour, of the dull sheen of a ghost light on gunmetal and, above it, a muted blink of glass. On a different level again, he heard a voice that he recognised hiss out a warning: 'Christ. Bennett, *no!*'

Two men trained to kill as a reflex altered their aim in the last moment of firing. Two weapons whispered in the dark, their hollow-nosed bullets flattened harmlessly on the walls, scattering flakes of dusted concrete to the floor. Andy Bennett lowered his arm. His pulse rushed in his ears. His tongue stuck to the floor of his mouth and he swallowed green bile. He began to shake; not violently, but enough to make it difficult to think. Because action was better than no action and standing still was a sure way to collapse, he slid his gun back where it came from and took the last step up onto the landing.

'What the fuck are you doing here?' he asked.

'Waiting for you.' Alec Strang bent to pick up the spent rounds from the floor. His voice echoed up from the concrete. 'We had a three-nines call half an hour ago to say that Jake Turner was dead in Patsy Kerr's flat. Under the circumstances, I thought you might need some back-up.' He stood up. Old smears of rain had obscured his glasses making it difficult to see his eyes. He jerked a nod towards the lower floor. 'Is she dead?'

'Patsy? Yes.'

'And Turner?'

'Very much so. Drew Doherty's been let off the leash again. Same as Pyotr Terveyev with a couple of graphic variations. They think he's talked to us. Or they want everyone else to think so—' He stopped. Downstairs on the third floor, the lift doors hissed apart. A voice weathered by several centuries of breeding called from the flat for the dozy bastards to get a fucking move on. Strang stepped sideways. The moonlight cast him in shades of grey, giving him a distinction that age had not yet achieved. He nodded back towards another short flight of stairs. 'Let's go. There's a fire escape leading down off the roof. I have a car in the back alley. We can drive back in the front way and they'll never know—'

'Wait.' Bennett took his arm. 'How did you know I was here?'

'How do you think? I put a trace on your car.' Strang shrugged off his hand and backed up the steps, his voice a hum in the moonlight. 'Come on, man. Neither of us should be here.'

Bennett followed him up. 'I'm on leave,' he said flatly.

'Exactly.'

'So why the fuck are you running a trace on my car?'

'Why did you set up a meeting with Maria Kilbride?'

There was no acceptable answer to that. They faced each other in silence. Strang stood with his back to the fire-escape door. Four floors below, an ambulance howled round the corner and slewed at an angle across the road. Under cover of the sirens, Strang pressed down on the exit bar. 'Your choice,' he said. 'You can go back down the stairs and face Laidlaw alone if you want to. You never know, he might be feeling reasonable.'

'There's always a first time. Or?'

'Or you can come down here with me and we'll go in the front way with you there on my orders and we'll see if two of us together can find out who the fuck pulled off the round-the-clock watch on Jake Turner.'

The door scraped open. A wall of wind took its place, bringing cold and the after-spray of rain. Strang pulled his collar up and thrust his hands in his pockets. He turned, pushing his head back to where he stood a chance of being heard. 'It's entirely your decision,' he said. 'But if I were you, I'd at least be curious as to how Svensen got to know the operational details of a tail that wasn't set up until two days after Luke Tyler was killed.'

Patsy Kerr's bedroom was not big and there were too many people in it with too many different agendas for any of them to be comfortable.

Laidlaw was there, languid, like a cat, with his shoulders propped against one of the few clean patches of wall and his hands loose in his pockets. It had been one of Luke's basic tenets that Laidlaw was at his most dangerous when he looked most relaxed. He was, in Andy Bennett's opinion, the most relaxed he had ever seen him. Billie Reid was not relaxed. He stood like a bull in a pen, a foot inside in the doorway, blocking the entrance and exit so that everyone else had to breathe in to get round him. The photographer, who was young and new and scared of authority, gulped like a diver going through fire and squeezed his way past only to discover that he had left the batteries for his flash in the living room and would have to go back out and get them. If he had been younger, he would have wept. Instead he held his breath and squeezed out again. He took time to throw up in the toilet before he came back.

If Reid noticed these signs of frailty in his lay staff, he gave no sign. Other people noticed and added them to the grinding frustrations of the night – Art Gould who had a job to do and couldn't begin it while the management was standing all over his floor space; the pathologist, who needed the photographs to be taken so she could turn the body and begin an inventory of the injuries on the hidden side; Gordon McRae who had explained and explained again that the orders to pull off the tail had unquestionably come from his superior – and had been informed as many times that they had not; Alec Strang, who had too many new questions and was staring at the remains of his last real chance of finding the answers; and Andy Bennett who had been expressly forbidden to be there and whose presence, so far, no one had chosen to acknowledge.

The photographer squeezed his way back in again and began a serviceably methodical recording of the scene on the bed. The naked body of Jake Turner burned and flared under the flash. The initials carved on his inner thighs blackened in the flooding light, smearing into the pools of lifeblood soaking the bed. Smashed bruises on his knuckles, the edge of his right hand, his shin, his forearms, and in the centre of his forehead stood out as highlights in the pallor of his flesh, graphic evidence of a man who knew all of the rules and the un-rules of Glasgow street fighting and had inflicted serious damage to person or persons unknown before he succumbed. The Russian, Terveyev, under similar circumstances, had not fought back. Possibly he had not had the chance, or he had not known what was coming and had given up quietly. Jake Turner, who knew exactly what was coming and who was not known for his fear of physical violence, had fought hard and had paid for it later. Sweating, the photographer changed lenses and then leaned forward over the bed for a close-up of the head, focusing on the macerated testicles clamped between the teeth. You'd have to hate a man very badly to gag him with his own balls – or have a very perverse set of orders. Three flashes later, the photographer stepped back and nodded to Gould and to the pathologist. 'Turn him over?'

'The grass, man.' Reid was growling which was never a good sign. 'Get a decent shot of the grass.' Which showed, at least, that he was watching. The photographer crouched down chest high to the body and focused on the neatly cut sod of turf that had been placed on Jake Turner's chest. The camera flashed eight times in succession and whined on the end of the film. The photographer stepped back into places he shouldn't. Billie Reid jerked his head back over his shoulder. 'Get out of the way. We'll call you back in when we need you.' The man left, faster than one would have thought possible. Reid took a step forward. 'Right, Bennett. Since you're apparently more acquainted with this end of town than the rest of us, give me your version of what happened. Gould, you keep your mouth shut.'

Several of those present drew breath. Bennett felt Strang force himself not to be one of them. He looked around the room. He was not as good as Murdo at working out the sequence of things but he was good enough to make a coherent, plausible story. 'Word on the street is that Turner lost his stable to Svensen,' he said. Reid nodded as if this were not news. 'The rest of the word is that Turner held Patsy Kerr responsible and he wanted blood. I'd say he let one too many folk know what he was after. He came here, he killed Patsy with that,' he jutted an elbow at the domestic blade lying on the pillow at Jake Turner's head. 'It looks like one of hers.'

'It is. And then?'

'Then they caught up with him before he could leave. Svensen's hot on looking after his own. Terveyev may have killed Leah but he kept quiet about it – and they still took him apart. Turner told half of Glasgow where he was going and why, there was no way they could let him live and keep any kind of credibility.'

'Who got him and how?'

'I don't know. This has Drew Doherty written all over it but he'll have needed help. That could have been Svensen but all we know of him suggests he doesn't mess with the pond life. He gives the orders and lets the others get on with the details. This,' he poked a finger at the square of bloodied turf, 'will have been his idea. Grass for a grass. Very graphic.' He looked at Laidlaw. 'Had Turner shown any signs of talking to us?'

'What do you think?'

'I think it doesn't matter either way. Even if we swear that he didn't, nobody who's seen the pictures of this will believe it.'

'"Never believe anything until it's officially denied."' Strang, astonishingly, sounded amused. 'There's no point even trying. The more we say we'd never set eyes on him, the more they'll be sure he was singing like a bloody canary.' Strang, too, had found a clean patch of wall to lean against. He used it less ostentatiously than Laidlaw. He looked round at his colleagues. 'Has anyone checked out their lawn recently?'

'Is that meant to be funny?' Laidlaw sounded mildly intrigued. Gordon McRae, who was standing beside him, quite suddenly found it useful to sit on a chair.

'Not particularly, but given the amount of forethought that's gone into this, I doubt he just went down the local park and picked a wee bit grass for the photo shoot. Svensen is sending messages all round. This is for us as much as the streets. Nobody in Glasgow is going to talk to us this side of Armageddon. We can forget even asking.' Strang turned to his left. 'Art? Would you go with what Andy said?'

'Yes. The only real question is whether Turner killed the girl or whether he's been set up to look as if he did. We have two things that suggest the former: first, two different weapons were used. The knife that killed Patsy Kerr came from the kitchen, which would fit with Turner coming here on impulse and finding the blade when he arrived. Whoever did for Turner himself used a Stanley knife and took it with them. That would be a big pointer to Drew Doherty. The second mitigating factor is Turner's clothes. I haven't looked at them in detail yet but I'd be prepared to bet big money that we find the girl's blood on his clothes when we sample the DNA. It would be impossible for him to do a job like that and not end up covered.'

'Do we have them? His clothes?'

'There.' Gould nodded to the head of the bed. 'Folded up on the pillow.'

'Very considerate. Right, that'll do for now.' Reid spun to face the door. A pair of uniformed sergeants stepped rapidly out of his way. 'Gentlemen, I would suggest we leave Art and the good doctor to get on with their respective jobs. I'm sure we each have plenty of other things to sort out before the night's over and we don't need to be here to do it.' He was smiling and the effect was a great deal more intimidating than Laidlaw's half-raised brow had ever been. The room emptied in his wake.

At the door he turned back, raising his voice to carry. 'Donald? I'd appreciate it if your people could keep their eye on the dead Mr Turner even if they couldn't quite manage it with the live one.'

'One of them is lying.'

'Who?'

'Laidlaw or McRae. Either Laidlaw called off the surveillance and is lying when he says he didn't, or McRae got his call from someone else and is lying when he says it came from Laidlaw.'

'Or McRae got his call from someone else who sounded enough like Laidlaw for him not to ask questions. It wouldn't be hard. If you listen in on the radio, you could hear him any night of the week.'

'True.'

'Or Svensen owns them both in which case it doesn't matter which of them is lying because they both knew what was coming.'

'Thank you. That makes my night.' Bennett lay full length on a single bed in the front bedroom on the second floor of the unit's headquarters in Kelvinside. Four feet away, Strang lay on its twin. A half-empty bottle of red wine stood on the table between them. Outside, the woman who walked a standard poodle for longer than was strictly necessary every morning sat in a car and listened to Travis on CD. Her partner leant on the bonnet to smoke his cigarette. The last time round, Bennett had stood and watched the glow of it from the window. Now, he was too close to sleep to watch anyone. It occurred to him that he should get up and brush his teeth. Later, maybe, when the moon had moved round and no longer laid its pattern on the bed-head. He watched the slow slide of the shadows and considered the implications of multiple betrayal. 'Who called in the three-nines?' he asked.

'Anonymous.' Strang sounded less close to sleep. He lay fully clothed on top of the duvet. It had taken two glasses of wine before he had kicked off his shoes. He had still not removed his glasses.

'Male or female?' asked Bennett.

'Definitely.' A pause. 'I'm sorry, it's late in the day for that. Female. Glaswegian. East end.'

'What did she say that got them to call in the circus so fast?'

'Exactly what she was told to. She was reading it off a script. Hold on.' The bed shuddered. Bare feet scuffed on the carpet. The door opened and swung back. The stairs squeaked on the way down and the way back up and he was there, standing at the foot of the bed. 'Here,' he held out a slim square of technology, 'have a listen.'

It was a mini-disc recorder. In the dark and by touch, Bennett unrolled the earphones, pushed them into his ears, located the controls and switched on. The disc lifted and whirred. Silence gave way to not quite silence that gave way, suddenly, to white noise. The original conversation had been taped and the hiss had transferred perfectly to digital sound. A voice cut in mid-sentence, male and dull, trying for calm and finding only trite. The woman on the other end was in a phone box, or a booth perhaps, and was not noticeably agitated. Other, more distant, voices reverberated in the background. A car – or not quite a car, but something else mechanical – passed by. In its wake, she spoke. *'There's been a murder.'*

'Christ.' Bennett sat up fast enough to rock the bed. The woman let another vehicle pass and said, *'Tell DCS Laidlaw that Jake Turner's at Patsy Kerr's.'* There was a pause and a search and a whisper of unfolding paper. *'Tell him that Mr Turner won't be using up his valuable resources any longer.'* The paper was folded again. The telephonist asked a question that was never going to be answered. Other things happened in the background, things that may have been important but were not as important as the woman's voice. *'Bye.'* The line died leaving the tape hiss to fill the space. Bennett's fingers fumbled over the player, seeking the Braille of the stop and rewind.

Strang was watching him in the darkness, lying on his side with his head propped on his fist. 'It must be better than I remembered.'

'It's Maria Kilbride.'

'Ah.' A hand reached out for the light. They both blinked in the sudden brightness. 'That's interesting. Not better, necessarily, but definitely interesting. Are you sure?'

'Completely. What time did this come in?'

'Twenty-two oh four.'

'Shit.' Bennett played the sequence again, listening more to the hollow echo of the background. The second vehicle was electric. As it passed, another voice boomed faintly in the distance and a man coughed. Right at the end, just before she hung up, he heard what he thought he had imagined before. 'She's at a railway station, a big one. Queen Street maybe, or Central?'

Strang said, 'Those in the know say it's Central. Apparently, if you play with the acoustics enough, you can hear the Inner Circle being announced just before she starts. When did you leave her?'

'Half nine, thereabouts.'

'It's a fair run over to Central from where you were. Could she do it in forty-five minutes?'

'She could if Big Drew was waiting for her with his car.' He played the track again, listening this time for any of the usual indicators of stress; for the sound of drink or drugs, for unnecessary precision, or the lack of it, for bitten-off consonants or slurred vowels. He heard none of these. She sounded exactly as she had when she waved goodbye to him in the alley.

'Are we listening to a woman with a Stanley knife at her throat?' Strang was sitting up now, one leg crossed over the other. He reached for the wine and thought better of it and reached back across the bed for a glass of water instead.

'I don't know. I don't think so.' Bennett lay back and paid attention, briefly, to the process required to wind the earpieces in a neat coil round the player. 'Why her?' he asked. 'They could have got any grunt in Glasgow to make that call. Any one of two hundred whores could have read two sentences off a piece of paper – probably better than she did. Why Maria? Why take her to Central?'

'Because they knew you would hear it, I suspect. Or rather, Svensen knew you would hear it. Drew Doherty might, just, have the brains to lay a sod of turf on a dead man's body but he absolutely hasn't got what it takes to fuck with your head like this.' Strang flopped back on the pillows and hissed a sigh at the ceiling. 'What I hate more than anything is being read like an open book.' He reached out again and the light flickered off. Some minutes later, he took off his glasses and laid them beside the bottle on the bedside table.

They lay in silence. In time, Bennett said, 'Patsy introduced me to Maria. Luke didn't know about her.'

'I know.'

'And he can't have known who was running Jake Turner's surveillance. He was dead before it ever started.'

'Correct. If you think back, you'll find I mentioned that.'

'So Orla may be right that Svensen's getting his information from someone else.'

'Also correct. Which takes us back to square one. One or both of Laidlaw and McRae may be lying. Or they may both be telling the truth and someone else entirely is dropping us in it. Half the force could be working for the other side by now and we'd be the last to know.'

The bed rattled in the darkness as he stood. His shadow and his silhouette merged at the window. He leaned forward until his forehead touched the window, letting the cold of the glass reach through to his brain. 'We need to get someone back on the inside,' he said. 'Someone no one else knows about.' He turned back into the room. His voice came thickly through muffling palms and slowly, as thoughts spoken aloud. 'Maria Kilbride,' he said. 'No one outside your unit knows her. If I call Murdo back in from the coast, you and he could watch her, see who she meets, where they take—'

'No.'

'I'm sorry?' His hands fell away from his face.

'We can't use her. We broke contact this evening. I promised that we'd leave her alone.'

'I don't think you—'

'I do. Patsy Kerr's dead because I couldn't persuade her to come away to a safe house. Maria Kilbride is not going the same way.'

'Then bring her out.'

'I tried. She's another one that won't come. Every move that bastard makes cuts our credibility. As far as she's concerned, we have no safe houses left to put her in and I'm not in a position to tell her she's wrong. If we can't keep her safe, we don't mess with her. That's the bottom line.'

'Andy . . .' Strang sucked in a long, flat breath. In the wake of that, he began to pace, very softly, measuring the distance from the window to the bed, two steps forward, two back without ever turning round. Three times he touched his knees to the edge of the bed and retreated until he realised what he was doing and forced himself to stillness. His outline truncated as he bent over, resting the heels of his hands on the sill. A thumb drummed lightly on the wood. When he spoke, the words came in short phrases, feeling their way. 'I hear what you say. I respect it. But this is bigger than the life of one woman. A week ago, Svensen was one more rising turd in the pan. He floated a bit higher than the rest but he wasn't a real problem because we had him where we wanted him. Luke and Orla were in the thick of it – not right in the heat, but close enough to set up a sting – and they were about to pull the chain. On Friday night, Luke died and the rest of us fell into the sewer. Tonight, we started sinking. If we can't find a way right into the core – a way in Svensen and Drew Doherty aren't going to carve to pieces as an object lesson for the cannon fodder – we're finished. Everything Luke lived for, every day in that flat, every moment of keeping his mouth shut at the end will have been a complete and utter waste of time.'

He stopped. The beat of his thumb carried on in the silence and then faded away. Bennett lay in the dark twisting his fingers ever deeper into the pillowcase. Strang said, 'You never read the postmortem?'

'No.'

'Don't.' He made himself lie on the bed, listening to the ragged edge of the other man's breathing. 'Just be glad that you didn't have to. You can have your moral crisis, that's your prerogative and nobody's going to deny you the privilege. I have a division to run and a man's death on my conscience. Some things weigh heavier than others. If Maria Kilbride's still alive – and I'd give heavy odds that we're going to fish her out of the Clyde in the morning – then I have no choice but to use her. There is nobody else.'

They lay very still, neither sleeping, both aware of the other's presence; the proximity, the pressing silence, the weight of things said that should, perhaps, not have been said, or should not have needed saying.

Bennett rolled over to face the wall. Memories he didn't want rose up to meet him, one more clearly than the others. In time, when it refused to go away, he rolled back again. 'There's Orla,' he said, and heard the catch in the other's breathing that told him Strang had got there ahead of him.

'I can't do that. *We* can't do that.'

'We can't, no. She might when she finds out what's happened here. Maria Kilbride is a pigeon at best, she might lead us back to Drew Doherty but she isn't going to give us a name in time for it to be useful. We need someone intelligent right there in the centre, asking questions, listening to the answers.'

'Orla has no cover. Sandra Smith was blown out of the water when Luke died.'

'Faith Maguire wasn't. And even Murdo doesn't know about that one.'

There was a gap, a long moment's thought. Then Strang said simply, 'No.'

'No, she wasn't blown or no, you won't send her in?'

'Just no. Go to sleep.'

Seven

Wednesday, 19 March

Orla McLeod opened her eyes. The world was dark, but not as dark as it had been. She lay on her side and breathed in beeswax and bed linen, old wood and stone. In a morning ritual that had been twenty-odd years in the making, she reached up past her head until her hand met cold granite, splayed her palms flat and pushed up until her joints cracked. The stone remained reassuringly stable. The cottage was old and the walls were two feet thick, built in the days when a good layer of rock made all the difference between living through the winter and freezing to death. Now, with a range downstairs and an unlimited supply of fuel and a radiator on the far wall that would toast the room if she ever chose to turn it on, it was simply pleasant to feel the weight of the stone all around, like the square sides of a cave – and to know that it could not burn.

She let go of the wall and rolled onto her back. The bed was too small; her hair brushed the headboard, her feet pressed flat to the wooden panel at the base. Long ago, when she'd grown faster and further than expected, her mother had offered her a new bed. She had refused and would go on refusing. As a child, her bed had been an ocean of space; a gift made by her father for one of the early birthdays just at the age when she was old enough to go to the workshop in the garden and watch the black-haired giant who worked all day with important men in town and came home at night to run a plane along wood so that his daughter could sail smoothly to her sleep. Later, he had taught her what to do with the beeswax to keep the surface perfect and she had followed his instructions over the years so that, here, the first breath in the morning was of wax and of wood and the second of linen and stone and with both she knew she was home.

She sat up, pulling her duvet up around her shoulders and drawing her feet in. The curtains hung open because she didn't like sleeping with them shut. In the flat, this meant that she had woken to the looming presence of the tenement opposite, to raised voices competing with Breakfast TV, to fried bacon and last night's chips and alcohol and skunk weed. Now, kneeling on the bed with her elbows on the sill, she watched the mist make waves against the background of the sky and listened to the wash of the sea and the distant avarice of the gulls and tried to remember that this was the world in which she belonged and that the other was the delusion. She failed, but then she regularly failed and the first morning was always the hardest. Of the two parts of her, the half that was of the cottage looked out on a landscape that had not changed since her teens and never wanted to leave, while the half that was of Glasgow screamed frustration at the lack of action and wanted desperately to return. Had she woken in the city, it would have been the other way round.

And then, this morning, of all mornings, new lives weighed in the balance. Beyond the window, half a mile of snow-covered land led down to the sea. The tide had been in and gone out again since the blizzard, washing clean the stones of the shore so that they lay now as a greying band between the cast iron of the water and the salt lick of the land. Out across the sea, dim in the dawn, the Cuillin stood swaddled in cloud the colour of coal smoke. Between them both, Tam Gillespie's fishing boat churned phosphorescence in its wake, trailing gulls like screaming mosquitoes as it headed out of the bay in search of deeper water. All of this, the snow, the water, the gulls, the people, were promised to Jamie as his future. The pulse and the acid, the drive and the violence of Glasgow were pledged to Luke, to Strang, to the assorted ghosts of her past and their hold on her future. '*And it's important to keep working for Strang?*' her mother had asked and, because she was her mother and because it mattered, she had answered with the truth: '*It's the only thing I've found that makes life worth living.*' Now, perhaps, warmer and more rested and with time to watch the patience of the sea she could modify that: 'It buys me peace.' And Morag, because she was her mother and she lived with her own ghosts, would have understood and might, perhaps, have helped her find other ways to the silence.

Orla sat for a while, not thinking, and watched the dawn come up. The sea shunted pebbles on the shore, grinding them over millennia to sand. All across the world people rose and went to work and were faced with bigger or smaller choices and made decisions and lived with them and still the sea ground pebbles into sand. In a small village on the west coast of Scotland, the sun nudged over the shoulder of the ben and the sea caught fire, quenching the ghost phosphor of the night and lighting it again with the brilliance of the day. When the entire bay was ablaze and the beauty of it was too painful to watch any longer she opened the middle drawer of her dressing table, pulled on a T-shirt and underwear and took herself down to the kitchen to face the morning.

Downstairs was darker than upstairs. The curtains were drawn and most of the light came from the rhythmic blink of the digital clock on the cooker. Shadows of shapes overlaid each other in a three-dimensional mosaic that came and went with the seconds. She let go of the bottom rail of the banister and felt her way towards the range and the kettle.

'It's just boiled. The tea's in the pot.'

She turned. Murdo Cameron sat on the floor with his back to the big hearthside chair. Her mother had banked slag on the fire before she went to bed and the mound of it glowed dimly red in the hearth, lighting the side of his face. He was watching her with unusual intensity.

'What's up?' she asked.

'Nothing.' He nodded down towards the floor at his feet. 'Jamie is teaching me to play chess.'

'I thought I taught you to play chess years ago.'

'So you did. Jamie is teaching me the Buchanan variation. Come and see.'

She poured herself tea and went to look. Jamie Buchanan sat cross-legged on the floor in front of the chequered board that was the last thing her father had made for her. The dog lay in the scoop of the other chair behind him, beating the air in silent, grinning greeting at her arrival. To Jamie's right, the hare skull nested on the black felt that lined the lid of the chess box. At his feet lay the dead ranks of his conquest, all of them bleeding red in the wash from the fire.

'Hi.' Orla crouched at the side of him, with care for where she put her feet. 'How's it going?'

Murdo answered. 'He lost the first two games. He hasn't lost anything since.'

The boy glanced up a brief half-greeting. For now, his heart and his soul belonged to the board. Orla studied the layout. Seven pieces remained upright; four of them white, for the boy, three red, for the man. She looked up at Murdo who was losing and must know it.

'I'd give up now, if I were you.'

Jamie raised his eyes from the board to stare at her in horror. The concept of resignation had not been explained to him.

Murdo shook his head. 'I don't think so. We're at two all. This is the decider.'

'Suit yourself. Whose move is it?'

'Mine. And you're not allowed to help.'

'I wouldn't dream of it. Jamie doesn't need any help. You're beyond it.' That won her a smile, a quick flash of pleasure that sparked in the firelight. She moved up to sit on the arm of the chair beside Murdo and drank her tea in silence. He smelled of shower gel and shaving foam which meant that he had both washed and shaved and she had heard nothing, and that in its turn meant he had been up far longer than she had. She bent forward and sniffed the sleeve of his T-shirt. It smelled of fresh gun oil and, underneath that, of cigarettes. 'Have you been up all night?' she asked quietly.

'Since five. It was quiet and no one else was around. I thought I'd go out and have a look around.' His hair was damp from the shower and he had left it loose so that it hung free past his shoulders, collecting and reflecting the glow from the fire. He moved his bishop three spaces diagonally and put pressure on the boy's knight.

'Did you find anything?' she asked.

'Our fox-loving friend gets up early and goes out for a walk on the hill before dawn, which would suggest that he knows his way around better than most folk.'

'It would suggest he's prone to insomnia as well. Anything else?'

'Kind of. I had an email from Andy.'

So that was the bad news. She should have known. His face should have told her, or the edge in his voice, or the fact that he was losing at chess to a nine-year-old boy when honour and basic integrity would not have allowed him to throw the game. The morning's peace shrivelled and died inside her.

'What is it?' she asked.

'Art's drawn a blank on the partial fingerprints. He put through as many variations as he could create and came up with nothing.' His voice was light, falsely so. He didn't expect her to believe it.

'And? Come on, Murdo. There was more than that. What's up?'

He reached for her hand and held it. In that, more than anything else, there was a warning. *What?* became suddenly, sickeningly, *who?*

'Who, Murdo?' Waves of nausea clenched her stomach. She brought her fist to her mouth. 'Not Strang? Murdo? Not Strang?'

'No. He's fine. Not Strang. Not Andy. Not any of us. It's Patsy Kerr,' he said. 'Jake Turner got her,' and then, still holding her hand, he talked her through the sparse details of the night before, truncated for Jamie's sake so that Patsy died of a 'fatal haemorrhage from a linear incision just above the larynx' and Jake Turner had 'our Nordic friend's initials engraved on his femoral arteries with a surgical excision of the gonads first' and the betrayal of Laidlaw's surveillance was reduced to its functional parts.

Afterwards, he summarised the decisions that had been made on waking. 'Andy's on his way over. He doesn't know the way to the cottage but he'll be at the hotel around lunchtime and call us when he gets there. Given the chain of events with Jake Turner, we're cutting back to sealed-unit operating – we have no contact with any of the other units, they have no contact with us. We're to consider anyone and everyone outside the unit as potentially compromised, including Strang. Our priority is to take care of Jamie.'

She heard him in disconnected snatches, some clearer than others. 'We're to work as a unit? Just the three of us?'

'I think so. Yes.'

'Right. Good.' Her eyes began to find focus again. Murdo's hand lay on top of hers. His thumb moved unconsciously along the back of her wrist. Across the chessboard, Jamie was watching them, his hair russet in the glow from the fire, his eyes cautious.

'Hi.' She smiled for him, as real as she could make it. 'Did you ever meet Patsy? She was a friend of your mother's once. She might have been to see you when you lived at the other house.'

He thought about that, dredging memories from half a lifetime away. His eyes searched her face for clues and didn't find them. In a while, he shook his head.

'Never mind. She was a good person. I'm sure Lisa would have liked her. I liked her a lot. I think she liked me – or at least the person she knew who didn't look like me. I should have gone to see her before we came away. That way maybe—'

Jamie leant forward. Still with his eyes on her face, he moved the threatened white knight two squares forward and one to the side, putting Murdo's king in check. He made it clear that the challenge was for her and not for the king or for Murdo. He held his breath, waiting for her to respond.

'Ah.' She stopped and ran her tongue round the edge of her teeth. Something of the morning came back to her. After a while, she said, 'Maybe not,' and then, as Murdo saw the check and put his fingertips to his temples to consider his next move, 'Tell me you saw that coming.'

He heard the change in her tone and mirrored it. 'I didn't, actually. But do feel free to point out that I should have done.' He moved his king one space closer to the corner and glanced up. 'All yours.'

Jamie watched Orla for a moment or two longer and then turned his attention to the board. His lips moved in a silent whisper as he worked out his strategy, talking himself through the possibilities. The knife-edge groove etched itself between his eyes, but only faintly, as if the pressure of thought did not run too deep. When he reached for the board, the bishop died, as it had clearly been going to, courtesy of the white knight.

His rook moved after that and then his queen and suddenly there was nowhere left for the red king to go. He said nothing. He didn't have to. It was all in his eyes.

'Nice one, youth.' Murdo leant over and toppled the king. The piece was red cherry, carved in absolute simplicity. It bled in the light from the fire. The white queen, cut from apple wood, glimmered like white gold, casting long shadows across the board. Jamie started to move the pieces back into line.

'Hey.' Murdo leant over and stopped him. 'Best out of five,' he said. 'We did agree that.'

They had. The boy tightened his lips for a moment, then nodded and moved the piece he had been holding and stood it upright in the box with the same absorbed concentration with which he had moved it across the board.

Murdo's jacket hung over the back of the chair. He reached over and flipped it round so that the inner pocket was facing outwards. A rectangular shape stood out in the fall of the lining.

'Do you want one?' he asked. It was a straightforward offer, with no hint of coercion.

'Later. I'll let you know when. Thank you.' She stood, collected the mugs and took them to the sink. 'Did you have plans for the day?'

'Not yet. You?'

'I was thinking we could go to the Sgurr Alasdair for lunch.'

'Andy's coming in there around midday.'

'I know. So we can be there ahead of him as a distraction. It wouldn't hurt to give the locals something else to talk about.'

Andy Bennett arrived, as expected, in time for lunch and his appearance created only a small ruck of interest amongst the regulars in the lounge bar that evening, the advent of a stranger being swamped almost entirely by the greater fascination with the new family group that was Morag McLeod and her daughter and her daughter's new man and the boy who came along with them.

The bar was divided as to the parentage of the child. The Connolly brothers, all three of them, backed the man as father, with Orla a late arrival. As evidence, they cited extensively the obvious care the man showed for the child. Had they not all seen him walk through the lobby with the lad sheltered under his arm like a hen with a new-hatched chick? And they had. Even Angus Shearer, who by that point had been catching up on six months' worth of gossip with Orla McLeod herself, had seen the way the man looked after the child. But Angus had seen also the way the lad looked after Orla and if you went by looks, then his eyes were Orla McLeod's eyes and Hugh Carlaw was there to testify that her father had them in the generation just gone and that was as good as a DNA test to prove that the child was hers. That, in turn, meant that the man was the newcomer and taking care of the child to get in good sort with the girl. It was left to Tam Gillespie, who was quiet and not prone to gossip, to suck in a long breath and, at the end of it, point out that neither the lass nor her man had behaved like newlyweds, nor even like newly found lovers, and that maybe the lad belonged to both of them, in which case, knowing Morag McLeod, there would be some good reason why neither the boy nor the man had ever been home to visit her before now.

They considered this option for most of the way through the next round. It wasn't how any one of them would have done it, but it made sense of the empirical observations and Donald Connelly was very keen on use of empirical observations and so they accepted Tam's judgement as proven under the rigours of scientific testing and set about instead to apply the same rigours to the origins of the balding man with the new car who had walked back along the beach to the cottage with Orla McLeod as if it was him, and not the tall one with the long hair, that she really wanted to talk to.

The jellyfish floated in the water at the edge of the rock pool. Five violet circles shimmered in the moon of its body. When the child had first settled down to look, it had been clear, like glass, so he could see through it easily to the knurls and furrows of the rock below. Now, after nearly an hour of direct sunlight, the thing had acquired more shape and texture as if someone had poured milk in through one of the rings and it had settled, showing up the tiny fracture lines and striations in the clear material. It was possible, of course, that this phenomenon was a good thing from a jellyfish's point of view but he thought probably not. The problem was how to be certain. The beast had no eyes that he could see, no mouth, no heart, beating or otherwise. He had studied it periodically throughout its transformation, trying to work out how to tell if it lived but he had not yet found an answer.

He transferred his attention to the other things that had been caught in the rock pool – things that definitely lived. Along the line of one cleft, a handful of mussels had clammed shut with the retreat of the tide. Below the violet rings, deeper in the limpid water, a trio of orange sea anemones had unfurled, loosing their tentacles in the small currents of their world. He picked up the gull feather he had found and trailed a V on the surface, watching the patterns of it displace downwards. He was making an S when a shadow fell across the pool, changing the water from sky-blue to a dark marine green. The jelly fish darkened with it. He looked up, shading his eyes with the flat of his hand.

'Jamie?' It was Orla. He had expected that it would be. Andy Bennett, who had been sitting with her on the driftwood at the edge of the foreshore, was too shy to come and talk to him alone. She looked down into his rock pool, watching her reflection vibrate in the troubled surface. 'May I join you?'

He moved back to make space. She sat neatly, like a cat, with her feet tucked in and her bulky lilac jacket folded beneath her for a cushion. The jacket was a new face of Orla, one created for the locals and, possibly, for her mother; an uncommonly *ordinary* Orla, casual in jeans and checked shirt with her hair moussed back from her face and pearl earrings making soft lights at her ears. Murdo had not needed to change. Simply by being Murdo, with his hair hanging free and his sheepskin jacket hanging over one finger, he fitted in. Still, the chemistry between them was different so that, by the time they reached the hotel, the small strains and frictions of the morning had been laid aside in favour of a togetherness that went with *ordinary* and made them a family.

It had pleased Morag. He had seen that. He hoped, although he could not be certain, that it made up for the moment in the morning when the older woman had walked past her daughter's bedroom and found her sitting on the bed showing him how to reload the gun, explaining the need for soft-nosed, low-velocity rounds because they would be indoors where the risk of a ricochet was greater. The conversation had stopped, abruptly, with Morag's arrival. He was never sure, in this, if it was the gun itself that was the problem or the fact that he was being shown it. All he knew was that the stillness and frigid silence that followed were uncomfortable and that the quiet question, 'You really think you can "control the crossfire" in a crowded bar?' and its equally quiet answer, 'Yes, if we have to,' went so much deeper than the words themselves would allow.

Now, looking at Orla perch on an arm's width of rock, with her feet inches away from the jellyfish, he realised that she had changed again, that without touching her hair or removing her earrings she had ceased in any way to be *ordinary* or to behave like family. There was a sharpness to her that reminded him of a moment in the flat before the shooting started. He found that he would have liked the company of the dog, or his hare skull. In the absence of either, he sat back on his rock and chewed on his scabbed lip and waited.

She was looking at him, trying to see into his thinking. He considered asking about the jellyfish and decided it was not the right time. Orla leant over and borrowed his gull feather and made furrows in a smaller pool higher up the rock, more a splash than a real pool, with old seaweed in the bottom. The feather lifted denser tones of brackish water, deepening the salt-sharp of the sea. Orla said, 'You should let Andy see your hare skull. He's good at drawing. He might be able to draw you a picture of what it looked like when it was alive. If you'd like that?'

That sounded good. It was also not what she had come to say to him. He gave a short nod and waited. Out in the bay, a long, black bird dived off a rock as big as the cottage and came up with a fish in its mouth. 'Cormorant,' said Orla, although he hadn't asked. He stored the word and they both watched the bird dive a second time.

She started again, hesitantly, as if the words were dragged out in spite of her. 'Jamie . . . do you remember when we were talking in the hospital,

I said I might not always be at the cottage, that I might have to go back to Glasgow sometime?'

He remembered. It had been with him since they had driven out of the city and he had seen the snow on the mountain. He was careful only to nod, to show nothing else of what he was thinking.

'Thank you.' She had her elbows balanced on her knees, her fingers arced over her face, making her voice hollow. 'And you remember this morning what Murdo said about Patsy Kerr being dead?'

That was not easy to forget. For Murdo, Patsy Kerr was a name. For Orla, she was a friend. The difference had been distinct. He nodded once more, cautiously.

'Good. I think . . . no, never mind.' She put the feather down and came to sit behind him with her legs outside his legs. Her arms wrapped round his waist, holding his hand, slipping her fingers through his fingers so that, as she opened and closed her fist, his went with it. Her chin rested on his head, her breath pushed down on his hair. When she tipped forward, her lips came together on the very top of his skull.

Jamie relaxed into the embrace, moulding his back to her chest, feeling the warmth of her press through her jacket. It was good to be held this closely. It would have been better to be able to see her eyes. Together they watched as a second cormorant came to join the first and the pair dived in synchrony, leaving small whirlpools on the surface as markers of their passing.

'Jamie.' Her voice breathed through him, thrumming through from her lungs to his, spiralling down from her chin through the top of his head to his throat. 'You know I love you?' It was not a question that needed an answer. He let more of his weight fall onto her. 'And you know I loved Luke.' That was not even a question. 'I didn't love Patsy Kerr but she was a very brave woman and she helped me at a time when I needed it badly. I should have gone in and brought her out.' He was not in a position to move a chess piece and bring her away from this. He waited more. Her breaths were slow and deep, as if she counted each one. He could feel the things shearing inside her, tearing her in two. The breathing helped her to stay together. 'The man who killed Patsy is dead. The man who killed Luke is not dead yet and if we leave him, he will kill more people. There is a way that we might be able to catch him – or if not him, then to find out who's helping him. He couldn't do what he does without help. I suppose that's obvious, none of us could do what we do without help.' She smiled, but she was not happy. He felt the tightness in her voice. 'In this case, it seems likely that someone is telling him things we don't want him to know; things about Luke, about the man who killed Patsy, about other people who might help us to find him. If we're going to stop him, we have to find out who is giving him the information.' She was talking in circles, going nowhere. He made a small, impatient gesture. 'Sorry.' She pressed her lips to his head and huffed into his hair. 'I'll stop.'

They sat for a long time. Up at the cottage, he could hear the dog greeting someone new which meant that Andy Bennett had made the five-minute walk up the field and they were alone with the sea. The cormorants hunted their fill and left, two black scribbles jerking along the skyline, growing ever smaller until they rounded the head of the bay and were gone.

A new rock appeared in the bay. Orla pushed on his hand and pointed. 'Seal,' she said. 'It's come to watch us,' and indeed it seemed as if it had. As they sat, it bobbed closer until Jamie could see the detail on the marbled sleekness of its head. Its eyes were round and black, like coal, and had no white anywhere. Speaking to the seal as much as to him, Orla said, 'If we're going to get anywhere, I have to go back to Glasgow for a while. Andy will take me in and leave me and then come back as soon as he can to help Murdo take care of you. I'm sorry. It's not that I don't want to be here, but there is no one else who can do this and it has to be done. It's not safe for any of us if we leave things as they are.'

It was what he had expected. It wasn't good, but he could live with it. He squeezed his fingers, still looped through hers, and pushed his head up against her chin. 'Thank you.' She sneaked a kiss down past his ear. 'I do love you.'

He believed her. He twisted round so he could see her properly and reached up to return the kiss and they rocked together, arms in a knot, her hair mixing with his. She grinned at him, awash with relief. 'You are

a constant source of surprises, Jamie Buchanan. Did I ever tell you that?'
He grinned back and let her lift him up to standing. The seal snorted
water, shut its nostrils and sank. Waves washed the place it had been.
A breeze twisted round them, binding them close. In the rock pool, the
sea anemones ruffled slowly, like well-gelled hair. Orla knelt to retrieve
her jacket. Even with it on, she still looked different. She held out her
hand for him. She asked, 'Did you want to know about the jellyfish?' It
was dead. He knew that really. He shook his head.

They walked back up towards the cottage. Patches of snow melted
slowly, dribbling water onto the stones and the harsh, cutting grass. Out
on the left, a dry-stone wall kept the sheep from the foreshore. An early
lamb lay in the lee of it, basking in a small focus of sunshine. The ewe
grabbed at grass a few feet further into the field, turning her head between
mouthfuls to check that her child was still there. They stopped to watch.
Jamie climbed up to sit on the wall. Orla put her elbows on a flat place
and rested her chin on the hammock of her fingers. The sheep blethered
urgently. The lamb raised its head, assessed the trouble as nothing and
dreamed on.

'Jamie?' Orla was thinking aloud, he could hear the tentative push of
thought in her voice. 'You know that we made Luke to be your father?
So that I could be your mother and make it all right for you to come
here?' He did know that, she had explained it to him one evening in the
hospital, before they came away. Now she said, 'Supposing we changed
that? Suppose we made Murdo your father? How would that be? Would
you like it?'

He was watching the lamb, absorbed in the thrill of its heartbeat, the
wrinkling of the skin round the elbows and armpits, the ruffled curl of
its coat, so blazingly white against the greyed-out greens of the grass
and the lichen. The words came through to him as through syrup and it
took him a moment to hear each one and string them together to make a
sentence, several sentences, and then sort through each of those to make
sense. Then the world slammed into a wall so hard it made his head spin.
He looked at Orla who was waiting for an answer. He tried to think, to
understand, to make sense of what she had said. He had liked Luke. To

have been offered a father of any kind, even one newly dead, had been yet another part of the magic. To be offered a live father, to be offered *Murdo*, was something else entirely. He wanted to grab at the moment, to hold it and not let it go.

Orla was saying, 'Not if you don't want to. I was just thinking that you seemed to get on well with Murdo and it would be good for you to have at least one of us around.'

He clutched at the first half of the sentence, hearing the doubt in her voice, feeling the offer retracted, taken away. In something close to panic, he took her wrist and held it. 'You do want it?' He did. Absolutely he did. He wanted it more badly than he could imagine wanting anything else. He would have said that out loud if he could have found the words to do it.

'OK, relax.' She moved his hand from her arm. 'Slowly now. We need to get this straight. Is it a good idea for Murdo to be your father? Nod for yes, shake for no. Nothing hard.' He nodded, with emphasis. She smiled a small and complicated smile. 'That's good. I'm sorry, I wasn't understanding. OK. Let's go in and talk to Murdo and see how he feels. And check if he can do it. I can't see it'll be a problem, mind you, it's all on the computer system. All we have to do is ask him right.'

'No.'

'It's a computer, Murdo, you can do anything.'

'That has nothing to do with it. No, I'm not going to do it because no, you are not going to go back to Glasgow so there is no point. Are you out of your mind? You can't go in now. You have no back-up, no groundwork, no safe house, no lines of supply, no one to lift you off the street and make it look like a job. You have nothing and no one and the moment they see you and know who you are, they will take you apart in small pieces. Dying the way Luke died is not going to bring him back. Can you not see that?'

'Leave Luke out of this.'

'Why? Are you still trying to pretend this has nothing to do with him?'

'This has nothing to do with him.'

'Fuck that.'

Tension ached in the room; the kind of bitter, twisting, frustrated tension that came from one person wanting what another could not give. It had been like that for the entire afternoon and evening since she had brought Jamie back from the walk down to the sea and given him into the care of Andy Bennett who had sat at the kitchen table and drawn him a hare in charcoal on white paper, and then another one, painted in watercolours on a pale green background.

Jamie was upstairs now, and for all the force in the words, Murdo was still speaking softly and there was a chance it wouldn't carry to the attic. Not that it made any difference. The child was better than most at sensing the strains in the air and he had spent the evening not meeting her eye, not wanting to know that she had asked Murdo and he had refused her. She hadn't asked him. She hadn't said anything. He had simply worked his way through the same set of facts and reached the same conclusion. The difference between them lay in how they viewed the inevitable. In his place, she would have done no different.

She left the chair and stood with her back to the fire. Her mother was showing Andy Bennett the spare bed they had made up in Murdo's room. They were taking an inordinately long time over it.

'All right, so maybe it has to do with Luke. He died because he believed in what we were doing. We have a chance now, probably the only chance, to get in and get the answers we need. If we leave it, then he died for nothing. I think that counts.'

'Living counts. Staying alive for Jamie counts.'

'I'm not planning to die.'

'Then why are you asking me to change Jamie's heritage if it's not so that he has one parent left alive at the end of this?'

'It's a precaution. I am doing my best, with no practice, to be a responsible mother. If I come back, we can change it back again. If you want to leave it until we know which way it's gone, then that's a possible option, but I talked to Jamie about it this afternoon and he's gone to bed broken tonight because he thinks you don't want to be his father. I don't want him to wake like that tomorrow morning.'

'It didn't occur to you to speak to me first?'

'So we could go through this in the middle of the afternoon with everyone watching? No, it didn't. And Jamie is the one I promised to look after, not you.'

He was silent for a long time, watching her. The flaring light of the fire pressed the shadow of his nose into hard relief on his face. In the end, he said, 'So the promise to Luke matters more than the promise to Jamie?'

She closed her eyes, shutting him out. Luke would not have asked that. Luke, perhaps, would not have had the understanding to ask it. She said, 'Maria Kilbride is still alive. I would like her to stay that way.' He took a breath to reply. She cut across him. 'I'm not breaking the promise. I said I'd keep him safe. While he's with you, he's as safe as he can get, short of locking him up and putting guards on all the doors and windows.'

He said, almost gently, 'You can't do this, Orla. You can't keep juggling them both. Luke is dead.'

'So is Patsy Kerr.'

'And *she* counts for more than Jamie? Really? Or is it simply that the dead count for more than the living?'

'Or guilt counts for more than . . . whatever I feel for a child? It's ten o'clock, Murdo. Is this the right time to start psychoanalysis?'

'Will there ever be a better one?' He might have pushed further on that but she turned away to light her cigarette in the fire. Murdo bent his head on clasped hands, pushing the knuckles of his thumbs into his eye sockets. From that position, without looking at her, he said, 'Did Strang authorise this?'

'Don't be ridiculous. He can't go back on a direct order from Billie Reid.'

'But he knows it's happening?'

'He'd be stupid not to.'

'And he let Andy come here?'

'What else could he do? Murdo . . .' She was sitting on the floor by his chair now, holding his hands. Blue smoke curled up from the cigarette, fanning sideways towards the fire. 'We have to do something, it's what we're here for. If we throw it away now, then everything – not just Luke, everything – has been a complete waste of time.'

He straightened his head. His hands stayed in hers. 'What do you want to do?'

'I want Andy to drive me in tonight – now – so we can set up before morning. I'll go in as deep as I can as fast as I can. We'll keep it neat and quiet and if it's not going to work, we come out. This isn't a sting. I'm not doing another three months in a shit-hole waiting for one or more of Laidlaw, McRae or Billie Reid to find out and blow the whistle. Either I can get in and hear the right name in the right place or I can't, in which case I'll pull out.'

'And Jamie? What do you want to do with him?'

'In an ideal world? I want you to go up now and talk to him and tell him that you're happy to be his father in principle at least. What you do with the computer is up to you.'

'Jamie?'

The child woke. Orla sat on the edge of his bed. The dog, always a lighter sleeper, had shuffled over to lay its head on her knee. Its teeth showed white as it grinned. Jamie sat up. She was black this time; black and silver with eyes of dazzling electric blue. Her hair was silver with a blue-black streak in the centre. Her nails were long and black with a silver sheen, her make-up was heavy round her eyes, contrasting with chalk-white cheeks. Her lips were dark blue. He could see very little of her clothes under the falling sweep of her coat but the boots were black and pointed and there was a lot of leg above them. The stud at her navel, this time, was silver.

She shrugged a half-smile and pulled her coat shut. 'Has Murdo been up to talk to you?'

He had. He had sat on the edge of the bed for almost an hour and between them they had sorted the tangled web of family-that-was and family-that-might-be and family-as-Jamie-would-like-it. There were distinctions between these last two that he and Murdo understood, if Orla did not. He nodded, smiling at the memory.

'Good. I thought he had. As long as you're happy with it.' She pushed the dog over to make more room. Even her voice was changing, as if the old Orla didn't quite work when she was black and blue. She slid a hand round his shoulder, taking care for a wound he barely remembered. 'I have to go now, so we can be ready by morning. Murdo will look after you and then Andy will come back and maybe show you how to draw a hare. I'll come home as soon as I can.'

It hurt her more to say this than it did him to hear it. He wanted her to have something to remember the old Orla. Slipping free of her arm, he slid out of bed and crossed to where the hare skull lay in its nest of linen on the window ledge. Trying to imagine Sandra with a hare skull defeated him. The black Orla would be no better. He reached instead for the charcoal drawing. It was small and, when folded, was smaller still. He held it out.

'Are you sure?' She was kneeling beside him. There was really very little clothing underneath her coat.

He was entirely sure. He nodded, solemnly.

'Thank you.' The picture vanished into the depths of the coat. Her eyes were bright. She bent forward and kissed the top of his head. 'Have fun while I'm gone.'

Eight

'There now.'

The sound was a breath, not even a whisper. The boy strained to see. At the foot of a pine tree, a circle of trampled snow stood out as a grey scar on perfect white. Within it, scatterings of corn gleamed like gold on velvet. Still, he could not see what he was supposed to see. Then a patch of snow moved and there was a flicker of red at the core. The boy nodded once and looked across at the tree beside him. The man drooped one lid in a wink. 'Ptarmigan,' he mouthed. 'We'll leave it.'

The waiting continued. Wrapped as he was in four layers of wool and a down jacket, with his hat well on his head and his gloved hands in his pockets, Jamie Buchanan was not cold, simply stiff and sore from the waiting. His breath made clouds in front of him and he made a game of it, breathing twin gouts of smoke from his nostrils, seeing how far he could make them go. If he held his breath long enough and breathed out hard, he could reach almost to the trunk of the next tree in the line ahead where the third of their party waited. He curled his toes in his boots and considered how they would feel when he was back in the warm with his feet by the range. The memory made his eyes water.

'Yes.' And that was a hiss. It could have been ice sliding on ice. He looked out to the corn circle and saw what he was meant to see. The faded brown of a hen pheasant stood out well against the ruined snow. Slowly, he lifted his hands to his ears and pushed his head against the

181

tree. Still, the sound of the shot carried through him and into the ground below and his bones ached with the impact. When he looked again, the ptarmigan had gone and the pheasant lay twitching at the foot of the tree. Hugh Carlaw lowered his gun.

'Breakfast, lunch and dinner,' he said. 'If she doesn't eat that, your furry friend can come out and hunt for herself.' He smiled, his lips moving with numbed slowness. Over the tea-brown eyes, his brows were thick with frost. 'Shall we take it back while it's hot?'

They walked back down the hill far faster than they had walked up it. Murdo led the way, his bound hair sticking out from the back of his head like the steering oar on a ship. Jamie jogged to keep up with him as he had been jogging to keep up for the half week since he had stood at the attic window and watched Orla McLeod kiss her mother goodbye and get into the passenger seat of Andy Bennett's sleek, low-slung car and let the man himself drive her away up the mountain. The whole world had changed then, although he had not understood the full measure of it until the next morning. Even then, it had taken him a full day to realise that the Murdo who took him out to walk the trackways of the mountain was not the same one that had lifted him up onto the back of a snow-bear and given him chocolate to keep him from starving.

He had not expected Murdo to change although perhaps he should have done. Because there was no make-up and no new set of clothes, the metamorphosis was harder to see. Over the past three days, he had followed the course of it, had seen the progressive hardening of the lines around the eyes and the increasing rarity of the smile. He felt it in the way they walked through the woods and over the moors. Before, it had been a game, he was leading and leaving no marks or else they were following Orla and it was up to Jamie-the-tracker to find the clues she had left on the trees or to read the lie in the way she had placed her feet. Now, there was no Orla and the days out in the woodland were as much for the man as the boy. Between them, they walked, crawled, or ran all of the paths and the half-paths through the trees. They stalked rabbit and deer, lying still in snow-covered bracken, watching them feed. They lay high up on an outcrop above the source of a river and watched the back of a buzzard riding the thermals in the valley below. They sat stone still on the shore and lured the seals in to bask on the rocks so close they could touch them.

In four days, Jamie Buchanan learned how to test the wind and know which way his scent was flowing, how to read the clouds to know when the wind would change, how to see the dampness around freshly nibbled bark to know that the deer had fed recently because their spit had not frozen and so they must still be close at hand. He learned to listen to the soft grunts of them talking, to hear the thudded warning of the rabbit, to recognise when the scolding of a blackbird was directed at him and when it meant that the single, solitary eagle that hunted the mountain was flying overhead.

He did not need to learn how to sit still for long periods because that was something he knew from the life that was gone, but here, he learned what else there is to see beyond the patterns of falling snow for a boy with the patience to wait and the tenacity to out-sit the cold. On the Sunday morning, with the church bells filling the shoreline and the high reaches of the mountain with a brazen wall of sound, he had lain perfectly still in the bracken with a light breeze in his face and watched a brown buck hare cross the open snow and stop still four feet from his face. He made his breath slow and shallow and let his eyelids droop. A single black eye stared at him out of the side of its face. An ear twitched, the better to hear the noise of the bells. The hare stood up on its hind legs and the boy saw the russet tinge to the fur of the underbelly as it raised its nose and tasted the wind. It turned round on its haunches to face him and both eyes stared into his. In that moment, if someone had told him he was freezing to death, Jamie Buchanan would still not have moved.

Later, back at the farm, he sat by the fire. Murdo sat with him. They had played chess, both of them badly, and put the board away. Now, Jamie sat with the skull in one hand and Andy Bennett's painting in the other, matching the dead thing to life.

'It's difficult, isn't it?' Murdo had a glass in his hand and he was making it last. That, alone, was the same as before. If Murdo Cameron ever got drunk, it was not in the company of Jamie Buchanan. In all of his life, the child had never seen any man stay so sober for so long. He looked up. The lines round the man's mouth were less deeply etched than they had been. His computer lay open on his lap. He had been working on it, quietly, since the chess. He tapped one more key and let it rest.

'Everything dies, Jamie. You know that.' He leant forward and took the skull in his hand. The size of it shrunk, moving from one palm to the other. 'Do you know what a wildcat looks like?'

He did not. He shook his head.

'Here,' the computer swivelled round, so that he could see the screen, 'I found you a picture. We can print it out if you like.' This was what Murdo was good at, thinking of things you would need before you knew that you wanted them. Together, they made the picture the right size and sent the image to the printer. A sheet of paper rolled out from the machine at the far side of the hearth.

The cat held the same kind of magic as the fox, the same kind of wildness, but better, because the eyes, from some angles, were amber and shone like a tiger, or a woman he had thought that he knew. They enlarged the head, with emphasis on the eyes, and printed that out as well. Murdo reached sideways to lay the skull on the mantelpiece. Matt grey granite showed cold through the empty sockets. He said, 'The hare died so that Hugh Carlaw's wildcat could live. If the cat hadn't been hit by a car, it would have been hunting for itself. This hare might have lived but something else would have died in its place. That's the way things go. Some things are born just to be hunters, some just to be hunted. Most are caught in the middle being both.'

'That'll be people we're talking of, is it? Or one person in particular?' Morag could walk more quietly even than Murdo. She was standing behind the chair with an armful of wood and the cold of outside clinging round her like a cloak. She smiled and nudged the man on the shoulder so he would realise she wasn't cross with him. Not that she was usually cross with him.

He shrugged and said, 'We were discussing the nature of the food chain.'

'Is that right? Not people at all, then. That's good.'

It was very hard to tell when Morag was being serious, particularly when she wouldn't meet his eyes. She laid the logs, one at a time, in the box at the side of the hearth. The fire was Jamie's responsibility, had been so since the day after Orla left. He was learning, slowly, how to keep it going steadily all night. Only once had he had one die on him before the end of the evening. Tonight's was going well under the circumstances although he should probably have gone out to get the logs before Morag thought of it. Still, she didn't seem to mind. She sat down in her chair opposite Murdo with her knitting box at her feet. The sweater for Tam Gillespie was complete and delivered and she was working on something similar for her daughter, in black with scarlet flecks running through it like arrowheads. She lifted the balls of wool to her knee and put a couple of stitches on the needle and concentrated on that for a while. Murdo took himself through to the kitchen to find a glass and poured her a finger of whisky. The spirit was dark, almost black, and smelled strongly of peat. Without asking, he poured apple juice for the child.

Back at the fireside, he settled in his chair, hooking one ankle over his knee. 'Can I talk to you?' he asked quietly. He wasn't talking to Jamie. The boy kept his head down and his attention on the print-out. It was close enough to bedtime for them to decide that he should leave and he didn't want to. There was a deepening burr to Murdo's voice that said he was not planning to talk of the weather.

Morag heard it too. She cast a glance at the boy and away again. 'If you like.' The needles moved of their own accord, making soft, musical squeaks.

It took him some time to think how to phrase his question. In time, with some delicacy, he said, 'If I believed the circumstances required it, would you let me teach you to shoot?'

Of all things, she had not expected that. She laughed, which surprised all three of them. 'No,' she said, 'I would not.'

'It would be for self-defence. And . . . protection. In the last resort. In case I'm not here.'

'Murdo, it doesn't matter what it's for. I'm not ever in my life going to shoot someone, whoever they are, whatever they might have done or may be going to do. Not for me, not for anybody else. I'm sorry. On this, there is no negotiation.'

He had not expected such a solid rebuttal. He asked, 'Because of the way her father died?'

'No. Because of the way he lived.'

He took time to consider that. She watched his face grow still in the damped glow from the fire. In four nights of talking, they had touched on everything else but her husband, her life in Ireland, the way it had ended. At length, because he was Murdo and it was Orla who worried him most, he said, 'If it is not from you that she gets her anger, and not from her father, then from whom?'

Over and again, he had this way of finding her weak places, the unmortared joint in the dam that needed only a questing knife blade slipped through to bring everything down. She watched her hands put a whole row along the back of the sweater and chose not to think. Around her, the room was at peace. Inside, the dam broke, as she had known it would. Surprisingly, because this happened rarely in public and she had little experience of how she might cope, the shell that was her exterior held the ensuing cataract confined. Two more rows were added to the sweater. She became aware of Jamie sitting like carved stone on the floor at her feet, taking small, shallow breaths as if anything deeper might break her or him. Murdo knew he was there. When she dared to look at him, he flicked his eyes upwards. She shook her head. If life was ever going to come out the way her daughter intended, the child would need to know his history. It was not ground she would willingly cover twice. She dropped a hand to the boy's shoulder to let him know she had remembered he was there and took a steadying breath.

'I didn't say I carried no anger, Murdo. I particularly never said that of John. He was an immensely angry man. If you grew up a Catholic – even a lapsed Catholic who has rejected for all time the faith of his fathers – in Ulster, you were faced daily with a form of apartheid that was no less invidious for not being named. He came home some evenings weeping with the frustration of it.'

'But he didn't fight?'

'Not with guns. Not by killing. There is a lot of him in Orla. He was a wilful, driven, passionate, obstinate individual but he waged his war with words and laws and he wouldn't give the time of day to the men with the guns and the Semtex. And he would never, ever have walked into a hotel bar with a gun in his pocket.' Her mouth had tightened without her wishing it. She puffed her cheeks to make it relax.

Murdo said, 'Does Orla know that?'

'Of course. How could she not? All the rest of her world believed that if they were ever going to win, it would be with the ballot box in one hand and the Armalite in the other; it was told them at school, it was painted on the walls in the streets, it was sung in the playground and the bars. Then she came home after school and there was her father telling her that it was the ballot box and the rule of law that would win in the end and nobody needed to die in the process. It wasn't just her he said it to. He stood up at public meetings and said it there too and the hard men with their guns came to stand at the back and listen because he was the only one of his calibre who was talking the right language about what was being done to us and what else could be done to change it.'

'But they still went out and killed people.'

'They did. He wasn't making his changes fast enough.' The whisky was gone and she had no memory of having drunk it. She laid her glass on the hearth and tucked her feet up underneath her for warmth. When she had settled again, she said, 'That was always the way. He wasn't making changes fast enough for one side but he was making them far too fast for the other.'

He raised a brow. 'The English?' he asked.

'Them and their friends in Ulster. They hated him in Stormont. There they were, the big men in suits with their two sets of rules, the ones they wrote down because they sounded good and the ones they believed in and lived by which sounded good only to them. Then they had this man they couldn't control who stood up in open court, showing them the gulf between the two and pushing them to change it.'

She stopped for a while. Murdo left her in peace. Jamie was breathing more easily now it was clear he wasn't going to be sent to bed. All three of them watched a filament of ash free itself from a burning log and spiral up the chimney. In time she said, 'We always thought it would be the men in suits who would have him killed. You've been on the other side, you'll know how it goes; they don't give orders, they don't do anything on paper, but someone "finds" an address and a name and they pass it to someone they know who passes it on and on down the line and later, when the bullet comes out of the blue and someone anonymous claims the kill, they can wring their hands and cry pity and make statements in the House about bandit country and the lawlessness of it and it gives them an excuse to pass a new rule that keeps the Papists under the thumb and everyone else knows that the idea for it came from the top.'

'Is that how it was?'

She smiled, like her daughter, in a way that failed to warm her eyes. 'No. That was the strange thing. It wasn't anonymous at all. He was prosecuting a man for the murder of a visiting US senator with nationalist sympathies. His name was Patrick Colquhoun. They said he was collecting for Noraid. They could have been right but even if he wasn't, just being there gave the republicans a boost so he had to go.' She was lost now, miles away in another season and another country. 'He died the way they all die, with a bullet in the back of the neck. Would you believe he was standing outside a pub, using the wall for a urinal? His minders were giving him privacy to get rid of his beer. It was so easy for a man to walk up behind him, pull a trigger and walk on. They would never have got him if someone up top in the loyalists hadn't given his name away.'

'Why would they do that?'

'I don't know. The killer was a Catholic and maybe they'd rather he went down than keep their own name out of court. It didn't matter. The American was dead. The man who killed him was disposable.'

'So what happened to your husband?'

'John? He was counsel for the prosecution. He had a good case but it wasn't watertight, he had fingerprints and forensic evidence from the gun but the defence was screaming a stitch-up and if you looked at it from their angle, it could have been that way. Their man was from the mainland, he'd come on holiday, there was nothing to suggest he had paramilitary leanings of any sort. He could easily just have been in the wrong place at the wrong time. He wouldn't be the first, by any means.'

'Did your husband think that?'

'No. He was sure that he did it. The papers were on our side for once so the nearer it came to the deliberation, the more it looked as if we might get a conviction.'

There was a tightness in her throat. The child had heard it growing all the time they were talking of Ireland and it seemed as if Murdo, too, had heard it at last. He put out a hand. 'Morag. You don't have to do this.'

'No. But I want to. Do you know I haven't told anyone about this? Not ever. Everyone around us knew it all when it happened and there's been no one to talk to over here. It's good for me, I'm sure.' She took a breath. 'Colin Gaskill and Brian Mayhew. They were two lads off a council estate a mile or two from where we lived. They were so far down the ranks of whatever organisation they were in that they didn't even merit a military funeral afterwards. They were just young men – unemployed, nothing to do, no real idealism – looking for a way to prove themselves. They barely knew how to hold a gun but it didn't matter then. All you had to do was know where to get one, which was easy, and how to wave it about and shout, which was easier still. They got it into their heads that John was going to win but that they wanted their man – their Catholic man, mind you – to get off with it. They didn't have the wit to run a bath between them but they picked up their guns and their petrol and they got drunk and came to push their legal position. I don't think they meant to kill anyone. I think they were just too scared to know how to back down when they knew it had gone wrong.'

'Did their man walk?'

'Don't be daft. Of course he didn't. What jury's going to let a man walk when two of his friends have just murdered the chief prosecuting counsel and put his daughter in hospital with half her face cut to pieces? He went down for life. They locked him up and threw away the key.'

'What about the two who did it? You knew their names, you knew where they lived. Did they go down?'

'No. There wasn't time. They were dead within the day. The loyalist "high command" put out that they'd acted without authorisation and had paid the price. The first visitor I had when I woke up in the hospital was Father Kavanagh with his scrapbook of newspaper cuttings and right on top was a picture of the two of them dead in a ditch, each with a bullet through the back of his neck.'

'Poetic justice.'

'Don't you start.' She shook her head. 'Donal Kavanagh has a lot to answer for. They let Orla have visitors without telling me and he was up there all hours breathing fire and brimstone and God's holy vengeance.' She smiled, tightly. 'I wasn't there when the shooting happened. That Orla was there has always been between us. And then there was Father Kavanagh's version of justice straight out of the Old Testament with an eye for an eye and a death for a death and a good dose of old-fashioned Catholic guilt to go with it. She may have had the strength to deny his religion, but she couldn't shake off the poison that cloaked it.'

She looked up. The fire was nearly out. She should have put the slag on to hold it till morning and it was too late. She said, 'I think when you have all that inside you, she probably does better than either of us would give her credit for. But I still look back on what her father died for and what I have lived for and I know I have failed.'

He was a compassionate man and he knew her daughter very well. He thought for a long time before he spoke. 'It's not over yet,' he said. 'You haven't failed while there's still time to keep trying.'

'I know that.' The fire died. The last of the logs fell to white ash and dust. The dark of the room closed around her. 'I think I'd sleep better if I believed there was still time.'

No Good Deed

Wednesday, 26 March

They waited two more days and each of them dealt with it privately, in much the way that they had done before. On the afternoon of the Wednesday, Jamie Buchanan walked up from the shore with Murdo on one side and the dog on the other. The day was overcast but warmer than it had been. The wind came from the south, laden with salt and water. Even the deepest snow on the flanks of the hill was melting to muddied slush, running in narrow streaks to the shoreline so that the whole lower half of the mountain looked like the dirt on a window after rain. A week ago, the child would have hated the loss of the magic. Now, he looked for the beginnings of growth beneath the snow. He was thinking of that, considering the changes as he walked behind Murdo up the back path towards the cottage. Morag was there making lunch. He could see her through the open door, rolling pastry on the table. She had her hair tied back behind her head in a way that made her look like a miniature version of Murdo and she was humming something he had heard from her before, a boat song where the fisher boy drowns trying to rescue his boat at the height of a storm and the love of his life is left bereft in the company of her family. The dog ran along the path to greet her as it always did. A scattering of house sparrows flew up from the bird table onto the roof. Jamie caught the smell of shaving foam and was looking up to see if the wind had changed when he walked straight into Murdo Cameron's back. It was solid, like concrete. Then he heard a voice he barely recognised say, '*Where is she?*' and knew that the waiting was over.

'In town,' said Andrew Bennett. He had come out to meet them and stood leaning against the doorpost, both hands holding his coffee. 'She's in as deep as she can get and still stand any chance of coming out again.'

'And you *left* her?'

Jamie moved away. For nearly a week now, he had felt the pressure building in Murdo Cameron. He had no wish to be near him when the volcano erupted.

'She told me to go.' Bennett had shaved since he had arrived. He had done nothing, because there was nothing he could do, about the look in his eyes. 'I can't get near her without blowing her wide open. She doesn't want any more help. If she gets something useful, she'll call us here. If she doesn't . . .' He shrugged. His eyes flicked to Jamie and away again. 'She said to remind you about changing the lad's parentage.'

'I'm not doing it now.'

'No. But later, maybe.'

'Just wait and see.'

'*Faith?*'

The ghosts crowded close. Father Kavanagh held her hand. '*You must have faith, child. It is your armour against the forces of evil, the sword in your hand, the gun at your shoulder. With faith, your enemies are as corn before the Reaper.*'

Her father took his place; the big man with black hair and the smile she would have died for if she could. '*There is no God but yourself. Have faith in the things that drive you. Integrity, self-knowledge and compassion are what sets us apart from the apes.*'

'*Bollocks to that.*' Ciaran was never subtle. He had died too young to understand either subtlety or compassion. He stood at her other shoulder, red-headed like none of the rest of them, alive in ways the others were not and giving voice to the rage as her father had never done. '*Kill the fuckers. What else can you do?*'

She lay still and tried to give room to them both. It was always the problem, finding the balance. Her father, the voice of reason, ranged against his son, her brother; the boy who had been raised to believe in compassion in a society where the Papists killed the Prods and King Billie fucked the Pope and ordinary people cheered on the sidelines. Ciaran he had come early to understand, because it had been beaten into him by his peers, that whereas it was fine to be on one side or the other and to have your tribe around you, to be neither was to be a pariah and as good as dead. He had learned that attack was the best form of defence and it had worked for him in the schoolyard. He had not seen the difference when the opposition was adult and masked and the guns they held were real.

She never saw his eyes as he died. She never had done, even at the first. But she saw over and again the back of his chest as the line of shots ripped up from waistline to clavicle, each one punching him backwards like a fist. She heard, over and again, the sound of her father screaming his name and then, later, her mother, screaming for her father, and herself simply screaming.

'Faith?'

The noise echoed and was lost. Her vision blurred and refocused. Luke was there, but then Luke was never really gone. He sat at the end of the bed with his elbows on the bed frame and his chin balanced on the upturned heel of his hand. His eyes were ice-grey with a touch of green which was wrong although she couldn't say what they should have been. He smiled his slow, lazy, knowing smile and pointed a finger. *'You promised me, kiddo. I won't let you forget.'*

'I haven't forgotten.'

'That's not what it looks like from here.'

'Faith? Faith? Christ, woman, will you wake up?'

'I'm awake. I think I'm awake. Oh, Jesus and Holy Mary.'

The room was too big. She rolled over and stretched her hands above the headboard but there was no wall to touch. Her feet stretched down and there was no end to the bed. She breathed in and gagged on the smell of stale sweat, tobacco and beer. Her arm ached. Her groin burned. Her mouth tasted of cigarettes and latex and semen. She remembered why.

She had time to roll over to the edge of the bed before she was sick.

'Faith? Will you sit up and drink some tea?'

'Fuck off.'

'Christ, give me strength.'

The blow to her face stung more than it hurt. She made to strike back and felt her arm twisted back to the wall. The pain in her elbow spread up to her shoulder. 'What the . . . ?'

'Get up.' It was not a voice she could ignore.

She opened her eyes. Maria Kilbride was five foot one and slim-built and her hair was a brilliant, cornelian red. She sat in Luke's place on the end of the bed with a mug in one hand and a packet of cigarettes in the other.

The woman who called herself Faith rolled over in bed and reached for the mug. Her head hurt. 'Mother of . . . Do you want to tell me what I drank last night?'

'Pernod, vodka, Bacardi and Coke. Anything else you could get your throat round.' The voice cut like a knife dragged down glass. 'It's not what you drank that matters.'

'Tell that to my head. Have you got any Nurofen?'

'Not enough to do any good. Here.' The smaller woman lit a cigarette and passed it across. Her eyes were hazel and clashed with the hair. There was an intelligence to them that had not been there before, and a scathing pity. 'You've not done smack before, have you?' she asked.

'What?' She sat up too fast and turned her forearms to the light. On the inside of her left elbow, a new bruise spread out where the old one had been. 'Oh, fuck.' She let her head fall back on the wall behind her. The thud of it knocked her brains about. It made very little difference to the pain.

You don't know how much pain you're in until you're not. And then it wears off . . .

'Once,' she said. 'I tried it once before.'

'Right.' Something changed in the searching eyes. 'You don't want to do it too often. You talk. Did anyone tell you?'

There was a boy who could have done, had she thought to ask. Her hand was shaking. She took a long drag on the cigarette and blew the smoke at the ceiling. She smiled as if this might be amusing. 'God forgive us. Was it exciting?'

'You could say.' Maria Kilbride had an empty bag by her feet. She moved to a small chest of drawers and started to fill it. 'Who's Luke?' she asked.

A chasm gaped at her feet. 'A friend,' she said lightly. 'He's dead.'

'Aye. Isn't he just? But word is, his woman got away.' The bag landed heavily at the foot of the bed. 'The main man's got every grunt in town looking out for a blonde whore with gold eyes and a scar who killed Jared Grant and his friends.' A finger swept down the side of her cheek leaving a clear track behind it. 'He wants to talk to her, mind – that's important. Anyone who kills her will not die as soon as they might like. What happens after he's had his wee chat is anybody's guess. Me, I wouldn't want to spend too long thinking about it, it gets in the way of my sleep.' She sat back, wiping the end of her finger clean on the bedspread. Her smile was as acid as her eyes.

The taller woman dragged on the cigarette. She had no gun. At the time she had made the decision not to bring one, it had seemed like a good idea. She watched the curl of smoke hit the ceiling and move sideways. 'How long have you known?' she asked.

'Long enough. It's not me you have to worry about.'

'Who then?'

'You screwed Drew Doherty last night. Do you remember?'

She closed her eyes. The wash of vomit returned to her throat. She reached for the tea and found it made no difference. 'Bits.'

'Aye, well, remember this. You were doing fine – for an amateur. He liked you. He wanted you again. You can thank God he wasn't working which means he matched you score for score. He's gone off this morning with a head worse than yours and he's got enough trouble remembering the name his mother gave him, never mind the ones you were calling him last night.' She stood up and took back the empty mug. 'That was luck, not judgement. If there'd been anyone else here with their head screwed on straight, you'd be in a chair by now with your feet bolted to the floor praying for a bullet. Do I make myself clear?'

'Very.'

'Good.' Her coat hung on the back of the door. That, too, came to lie on her bed. 'You're a liability,' said Maria Kilbride. 'I'll cover for you once, I won't do it again. I like my blood on the inside where it belongs, not on the outside painting the walls. So you get the fuck out of here before I decide to make myself popular, right?'

'Right.'

The nicotine made the difference. Nicotine and danger and the nauseating return of memory. The ghosts skirted the fringes of the room, fastidiously avoiding the heaving, sweating, slamming images of life. She reached over to a chair and felt for the underwear she had discarded the night before. Her skirt and sweater were in the bag. Maria pulled them out and passed them over without comment. Orla McLeod dressed herself in clothes that she could wear on the street in broad daylight. The stud in her navel had long ago fallen out. She bent down to tie the shoes on her feet. The part of her that could still think was acting independently, feeding her thoughts in small doses. Two questions still had no answers. As she stood, she asked, 'Why have you not told them already?'

The smile faded to nothing. 'I liked Patsy. She didn't need to die like that.'

'Svensen didn't do it.'

'No. But he knew it was going to happen. He should have got there sooner and stopped it.'

'Right.' She was ready to go. She pulled her bag to her shoulder and considered the sequence of moves needed to walk a straight line. She sat still on the bed. An older memory knocked at her head. 'It's our fault as much as his,' she said. 'We could have got her out. *I* could have got her out.'

'She didn't want out.'

'She didn't believe she was going to die.' She stood and walked to the door. The handle bore the weight of her without breaking. 'Maria, I think you—'

'No.'

'You don't know what I was going to say.'

'Yes I do. You were going to ask me to come with you. The answer's no. Believe me, I'm safer where I am.'

'No you're not. You're blown. Svensen knows you were talking to Andy Bennett. That's why he got you to phone in the message about Turner.'

The smile was not as warm as it might have been. 'Svensen's known I was talking to Andy Bennett since Luke died. If he wanted me dead, I'd be dead. He doesn't, so I'm not. I'm fine as long as I stay where I am and nobody else knows I talked to you.'

'He told you that?'

'Of course. He's way ahead of you, woman. The only thing he doesn't know about is this and if you hang around much longer, there won't even be that.' The redhead rose and moved across the room. Cold hands unhooked her fingers from the door handle and turned her carefully to face the stairs. A voice that had known too many late nights said, 'Get yourself up the road and get a coffee then get back to where you came from and when you're sobered up, get out of this game and do something useful with your life. And don't worry yourself about me. I know what I'm at. All I need's a good reason to give them why you're gone.'

'Right.' Orla stood at the top of the stairs and considered the long fall to the bottom. 'What day is it?'

'Friday.'

'Good.' Some things were still as they should be. 'Then tell them I've gone to sign on.'

The phone box had no glass and it had been used as a urinal in the recent past, but it worked. She dialled the operator and gave the number to reverse the charges. Her head ached and she had been sick twice, spitting phlegm and bile at a gutter already full of second-hand curries and recycled beer. She leant back on the steel frame of the box, keeping the phone away from her ear because the ring of it upset her sense of balance. After three rings, Murdo answered, which was not what she had expected but was better, under the circumstances, than speaking to her mother. She had trouble forming intelligent sentences. She had trouble, if she were honest, forming any kind of sentence at all. She had spent ten minutes planning a message that she could give to her mother to give to Murdo and she could remember it, word for word, plus a sentence or two that would not have been suitable for relay. He had the sense not to ask questions, which was good. They agreed a place to meet and she hung up while she could still hold the phone.

In the kitchen of the cottage, Murdo Cameron realised he was talking to a dead line and he, too, hung up. He stood still. The others were all there, waiting for him to say something. Their eyes held the same question. None of them spoke. He reached for Morag's hand and held it. 'She's alive,' he said, and felt the smashing relief crest and tumble and pour through her and out the other side.

For Andy Bennett, he had more. 'Maria Kilbride is also alive. Her last meeting with you was by arrangement, apparently, which makes it more likely she will stay that way. Orla thinks she has a handle on the conduit to the other side. It may be that the details of our current location are more widely known than we would like.'

There were too many implications in that to deal with now. He watched Bennett close his eyes and swear. He turned to Jamie, kneeling. 'Youth, that was Orla. She sends you her love. I have to go into town now to meet her and check out some stuff. While I'm gone, I think it might be better if you stayed in here and didn't go out too often. Andy will have his work cut out watching all sides of the circle on his own without us taking unnecessary risks with you.' The boy was smiling, just a little, with that luminous, far-off look he kept for hare skulls and seals. The prospect of house arrest either didn't reach him or didn't matter.

It reached Andy Bennett and mattered to him, but then it was supposed to. He said, 'Hugh Carlaw invited us all up to the Manse tonight.'

'I know. So you'll have to cancel. If you're feeling keen, we could invite him here instead.' Murdo turned back to Morag. She was flushed and her lips were not entirely steady. 'How do you feel about entertaining your Laird for the evening?' he asked. 'Would he come, do you think?'

Her return to composure was good but he expected no less. 'He's versatile enough. I'm sure he'd come. And yes, I'll cook for him if that's what we have to do. I'll be sorry not to see the fox before he lets her go but there might be time yet after you come back.' She let her eyes search his. 'If I'm right in thinking you are coming back sometime soon?'

'You are. I am.'

'Alone?'

'Not if I can help it.'

Nine

Angus Shearer was a hill runner. He lived for it and he had built his life around it. For the duration of a run, he was free and the world existed for him alone, narrowed down to the intertwining rhythms of breath and legs and heartbeat, the grinding pain of the climb and the freewheeling gallop down the other side. Coming back down from the mountain afterwards was like returning to earth from a moon walk or rising from the depths of a deep-sea dive; he needed half an hour to himself simply to readjust to the normality of things. Anyone who cared for him, indeed anyone who knew him at all, did him the favour of leaving him in peace to enjoy it.

Clearly, then, the man standing foursquare on the path did not know him. He stepped forward and held out a hand. 'Angus Shearer?'

'Could be.'

'You own the hotel, the Sgurr Alasdair?'

'I do.' At his best, Shearer was a good landlord and he could hold an hour's talk with any one of his guests. At worst, he was monosyllabic. He ignored the outstretched hand. An answer at all was doing the man a service. The incomer shrugged and stepped back. Shearer jogged on as he had been doing before. The man matched pace beside him. He was not an imposing man; an accountant, maybe, with brown hair and muddied grey eyes that you would look past and never notice and an accent that would have fitted in with the crowd anywhere north of Carlisle without ever belonging anywhere specific. Still, he was dressed, as Shearer was dressed, in shorts and a singlet and both were damp with sweat so that it seemed, looking at him a second time, as if he, too, might have been up the hill and back again.

He said, 'Your barman told me that you might be here. I watched you come down off the scree slope. Is it not a bit soon after the snow to be trying that?'

So the man knew running. Shearer slowed to a walk and then stopped and bent over, his hands pressing flat above his knees while he caught his breath.

The man said, 'I read Colin Loughlin's article on the race you set up over the mountain there last autumn. He said it was his test piece in Scotland and it had the best bit of scree he'd ever met in the world. I was wondering if you might be able to show me the route sometime?'

The man was a connoisseur. Shearer stood up, breathing deeply. Maybe not an accountant. Maybe a television producer, or an engineer, or something else more worthwhile. 'There's a better slope than any of those if you can get yourself far enough up the hill.' He looked at his companion. 'You're here to stay for a while, aye?'

'I don't know. I was thinking maybe a week or so – if you have a spare room.' The man smiled then and it made all the difference. The two eyeteeth on the upper row were crooked, angling inwards just a bit, enough to overlap the teeth beside them and change completely the smile and the nature of the man that went with it. Walking with him back along the gravelled path to the Alasdair, Angus Shearer could think of at least three women of his acquiantance who would buy his new guest a drink on the strength of that smile alone. One or two more would climb on the bandwagon for his body as soon as they saw he could run. And then they got back to the hotel and it seemed that they wouldn't be waiting for his body or his smile because he had an Aston Martin DB7 sitting in the car park and his credit card, when he brought it out to pay for the week's booking of his room, was platinum. Shearer tested the feel of fit as he swiped it through the machine. Even in high season, a platinum card was a rarity. He made an adjustment to the room allocations and gave the man the suite on the northern corner that had views of the mountain from one side and across the bay to Skye on the other. It seemed politic, under the circumstances.

It was dark by the time Murdo Cameron reached Glasgow. He parked the car in the blackest, most shadowed space he could find beside the underground station at Kelvinbridge and rode one stop round to Hillhead. She was waiting for him in the entrance although he had walked past her twice before he realised that the blue-eyed girl-child with the overdone make-up sitting huddled on the pavement with an army surplus trench coat pulled round her shoulders was someone he should recognise. He bought two tickets, dropped both and picked one up. Her foot stayed on the other. When, later, she bent to retrieve it, she found that 'Kelvinbridge' had been written on the back, together with a sketched diagram of the car park and his place beneath the bridge.

Murdo Cameron rode the underground one stop back and then sat behind the wheel of the car, watching the late evening commuters and counting the minutes. Half an hour, exactly, from contact, Orla McLeod opened the door and slid into the passenger seat.

He had disconnected the interior lights so as not to advertise their presence. In the darkness, she was a shapeless, faceless mass. He could smell the cigarettes and the sex and the drink. In that moment, he had no wish to know more. They sat in silence and the questions he might have asked were left unuttered. He took a cigarette and passed the packet to her and she accepted it without comment. They used the cigarette lighter to avoid a naked flame and kept their palms cupped round the glowing ends. Orla lit her second from the stub of her first. She leant back in the seat and blew smoke at the ceiling 'Were you followed?' she asked.

'No.' About some things in life he was certain. His ability to see and lose a tail was one of them. No one, on foot or on wheels, had followed him since he left the cottage. 'You?'

'I don't think so.' She sounded more hoarse than she had on the phone. 'I'm not absolutely certain.'

'Fair enough.' He started the car. 'Let's find out.' They eased up the hill to the bridge and turned right, drove over the bridge and turned right again. In five minutes, they had completed a full circle. No headlights had followed any of the four turns. They crossed the bridge for a second time and drove up towards University Avenue. Murdo said, 'I've a room booked at a hotel in Bearsden. There's a phone line, a shower and a bed. If you think we need anything else, let me know.'

'Right. Thank you.' He felt her eyes searching his face. In time, she said, 'Did you change Jamie's details on the computer?'

He slowed for a group of drunken students blocking the road opposite the library. 'More or less.'

'What does that mean?'

'It means I talked to him about it and we came to a compromise. I can't be his biological father because it's too easy to prove that I'm not. Also, he would prefer that you stayed as his stepmother. If I were to replace Luke directly, you would no longer have any legitimate reason to act as his mother.'

'So?'

The lights on Byres Road were turning as he drove up. He considered jumping the red and thought better of it. He pulled into neutral and sat still, tapping his thumb on the steering wheel. 'So we reached a compromise. You and I are married. In digital terms only. I am Luke's successor both with you and with Jamie. That way we both become step-parents.'

There was absolute silence. She lit a third cigarette. He counted the students as they filed past both sides of the car. Twenty-three of them passed before the lights changed. The last few dallied in the middle of the road. He pushed the car forward, herding the crowd ahead of him.

Orla had turned sideways, with her back to the door. Her eyes were the only part of her with any real animation. They raked the side of his face. 'Does my mother know about this?' she asked.

'Nobody knows except me and Jamie. I've explained to him that once everything's settled, we'll divorce, also in digital terms. And I'm not going to fight you for custody. We do whatever turns out best for the lad.'

'Right.' She lapsed back into silence. Twice she seemed about to speak and both times changed at the last moment to take another draw on the cigarette. Her eyes burned less on his face. When he chose to look, he found that it was because they had closed, her mouth slackened in sleep. He reached across and lifted the dying stub of the cigarette from between her fingers. Her eyes fluttered open. 'Put the seat back,' he said gently. 'Go to sleep. We've twenty minutes more at least. I'll wake you up when we get there.'

Hugh Carlaw was big. In his own home, with the furniture big around him, it didn't show. In the cottage, he dwarfed everything. He treated it as a joke and, after the first time he had walked into it and banged his forehead, he made a show of ducking under the beam that marked the boundary between the kitchen and the living room. At dinner, he sat next to Morag McLeod and she looked like a teenager although in other ways the match was even. They were both articulate, intelligent individuals of similar years who watched the world they lived in, formed their own opinions and were not afraid to state them. The dialogue was lively, turning to heated and only occasionally did it find room for Andy Bennett or – more rarely still – for Jamie Buchanan. Towards the end of the main course, the conversation turned to Ireland and her husband and became more exclusive still. As it turned out, what Carlaw knew of John McLeod came mostly from the newspapers after his death. Before that, he was a man with a reputation and he had provided a professional service which was not enough to make a personal connection or to hold the conversation for long. Carlaw had personal experience, though, of Ulster in the seventies, of Bloody Sunday and the Troubles, of the problems of living in a divided country without being part of either faction, of the terror and the tension and the way that it was changing.

In time, they exhausted Ireland. With coffee, they returned to Scotland and the village and thus a wider participation. Andy Bennett asked about the fox and the dead specimen that Jamie had brought home and they found that he, too, had common ground and could talk as if to a friend. The boy listened and, once, ran upstairs to find the various pictures that had been drawn and brought them down to show their guest. The skull was already there on the window ledge to provide a ready comparison. After that, they talked art and artists and what it is to draw a wild thing from life instead of from death or other people's photographs.

They finished and cleared and left the washing up for later and each of them took a drink by the fire, the boy with his apple juice and the others with their whisky. As if it were part of a normal evening routine, Morag brought the portable phone to sit by her knitting basket. Jamie sat down to play single-handed chess, himself against himself. Andy Bennett sat in the armchair nearest Carlaw and stretched his legs to the fire. 'I think I may have known your son,' he said.

The face that turned towards him was quite blank. 'What makes you think I have a son?'

Bennett shrugged. 'All right, I knew a man called Douglas Carlaw. He had a father who lived in Glasgow and whose name was Hugh. It seems a reasonable assumption.'

'Does it?' Carlaw stared into the fire. His lips twitched towards a smile that fixed and became real. 'Elementary for a man of your calibre, doctor. How did you know him?'

Discomfort shrugged in the air. Bennett bit on a nail. He thought for a moment and said, 'The usual. Edinburgh's not that big a place and you couldn't have somebody famous on the scene without the rest of us knowing it.' And then, when there was no response, 'I was in the stands when he won the medal at the Edinburgh Games.'

Jamie Buchanan looked up from his chessboard. In his eyes, you could see Hugh Carlaw rise to a new plane of estimation. Bennett said, 'Douglas Carlaw ran the five hundred metres in a personal best time to win a bronze at the Commonwealth Games in eighty-six.'

For the child's sake more than anything, Carlaw said, 'What were you doing there?'

'Trying to decide what kind of a doctor I wanted to be. I took time out after my houseman's year and spent most of it serving in bars in the back streets of Edinburgh.'

'And what kind of a doctor did you become?'

'I didn't. I never went back. I left Edinburgh at the end of the year and lost touch with most of the folk there.' He held up his glass so that he could look through it to the fire. 'What happened to Doug?' he asked.

'What do you think?' The pale eyes were distant. 'He was on the scene in Edinburgh in the eighties. He's dead.'

And that was probably no bad time for the phone to ring. Morag took it and listened and nodded and said nothing until the end when she finished with, 'That's fine, thank you, Angus. That's very good news. I'll pass it on to Dr Bennett.' When she hung up, she looked at Andy, smiling brightly. 'If you were still wanting to go fishing, Angus Shearer down at the hotel will sort it for you. The boat's fine and he can get you a man to take it out but maybe not for a day or two.'

'Thank you.'

For a woman who had spent most of the last two decades alone, she had a very good grasp of dissemblance. The things she said with her eyes were quite different to what she said with her voice. Andy Bennett nodded and leant further back in his chair. Hugh Carlaw was still staring into the fire. The boy was looking at both of them, frowning. He opened his mouth and closed it again and there was a clear chance he might be about to ask a question. Morag cocked her head and looked down at the board.

'I think that was the call you were waiting for, sweetheart. Would it be time for bed?'

He wasn't bad at covering either. He smiled and nodded and hugged her and kissed her on the ear and took himself and his dog upstairs to get dog hairs and water all over the bathroom and then just the dog hairs all over the bed.

Hugh Carlaw, quite rightly, took it as his cue to depart. In leaving he kissed Morag warmly on the cheek, and then, surprisingly, offered a hand to Bennett. 'I'm glad you knew him,' he said shortly. 'It's good that there's someone living who has the right memories.' With that, he left.

'Did you know that his son was dead?'

'Yes.'

'So why did you ask?'

'To see what he would say.'

'Was there bad blood between them? Hugh and his son?'

'No more than usual.'

'But he wasn't there to watch the lad collect his medal?'

'If he was, I didn't see him.'

'He's not the kind of man you'd miss in a crowd.'

'No.'

There were just two of them, drinking dark malt by the light of a dying fire. There was no accusation in her questions and no defence in his answers. She said nothing more and they let the matter lie.

In a while, Bennett said, 'Do I gather Orla's all right?'

Morag swirled the spirit in her glass. 'As far as Murdo can tell. He hadn't long picked her up when he called. She's asleep and they've not had much of a chance to talk yet but he thinks she'll be ready to come home in the morning.'

'That would be good.'

'Maybe. If she's feeling better in herself.'

His brows came together. He looked at the fire through his glass, watching the way the flame changed the colour of the spirit. 'I think maybe it would be enough to ask that she's not feeling any worse,' he said quietly.

'We can hope.'

'Indeed we can.'

The silence stretched without doing any harm. The fire glowed lower in the grate. Morag picked up the bucket and tipped on the last of the slag. Tarred yellow smoke filled the chimney and then settled to something finer. Two floors up, the dog jumped off the bed and the boy giggled.

She sat down again and picked up her glass. 'Can I ask you something?'

He moved his gaze across to her. 'Go on.'

'Do you miss medicine?'

'No. But then I gave it up by choice, not force of circumstance.'

'Can you tell me why?'

The answer came very easily, as if it had been given before. 'Because I went in thinking that being a doctor was about helping people and came out realising it was about beating the system – and that patients were part of that system.' He slipped off his shoes and lifted his feet to the top of a log on the hearth. 'I think if you'll find,' he said, 'that Orla left law for much the same reasons. The difference between us is that my father was still alive to hear my explanations.'

'Your father was a doctor?'

'He was an orthopaedic surgeon. They don't come much more wedded to the system than that.'

'How did he take it?'

He smiled slowly, with uncharacteristic irony. 'I think you could say that under the circumstances, it was the least of his problems.'

'But he took it better than Hugh Carlaw might have done?'

'Just about. We're still speaking.'

'Good. I'm glad.' She stopped. He left her in peace. Both of them watched the smoke spin up the chimney. She said, 'It seems to me your loyalty is to Orla before Jamie and that if the phone call had been to say that they needed you, you would have been on your way to Glasgow tonight. Am I right?'

He nodded. There was quiet, then he said, 'And if I had to go, would you be happy to be left with Jamie?'

'If you were happy to leave him. And as long as you didn't try to leave me with a gun.'

He finished the last of his drink. 'I was never keen on pointless gestures.'

'No. I didn't think you were the type.'

The bottle stood at her side. She poured them both another finger. Later, with the fire still glowing, they went their separate ways to bed.

Orla McLeod woke in another strange room. She was warm and clean with her hair free of gel and her wrists had been bandaged again. The bed was soft and the sheets were fresh. Her skin smelled of someone else's soap. Her mouth tasted of toothpaste and sleep and nothing ached beyond the usual. A forty-watt bulb glowed by the bed, the poor light barely reaching beyond the end of the blankets. On the other side of the room, a brighter light shone on a desk. She pushed her head free of the covers and heard the erratic rattle of fingers on keys, punctuated here and there by a curse or a muttered, unanswerable question or the sound of a coffee cup placed quietly on a mat. She lay still and listened. He stopped every so often and the hard drive ground out some data. Once, he got up and walked through to the bathroom and she heard him urinate, but not flush. She expected him to come back and talk to her then but he didn't. She could have got up and gone over to see him but she didn't do that either. She drifted in and out of sleep, in and out of dreams, in and out of memory. When she woke properly for the second time, he was sitting on the edge of the bed.

'What did you call yourself this time round?' he asked.

'Faith Maguire. Why?'

'We had a raider at six and again just now, searching under that name.'

'What time is it?'

'Two.' He was tired. It showed in the way his eyes scanned her face. When he was awake, he would do it more with more subtlety. He smiled and it did nothing to clear the shadows under his eyes. 'Well done, that woman.'

She slid a hand out from under the covers and touched his wrist. 'Was I right?'

His fingers curled over hers. 'Of course.'

'Did you get a trace?'

'I didn't.' He shook his head. 'But I have an idea who it might be. We can check it in the morning.'

'Not now?'

'Not now. We both need sleep.'

'Right.' She lay still, feeling the press of the pillow on the back of her head and the cool edge of the sheet at the far side of the bed where her warmth had not touched it. Murdo sat beside her. He was wearing only a towelling bathrobe, initialled with the name of the guest house. He shrugged it off. His gaze was open and direct. 'If you can bear company in there,' he said, 'I'll join you. If not, I have a sleeping bag in the car.'

A memory touched her. She smiled. 'In case I didn't want to be married?'

He stood quite still. His face was hidden beyond reach of the light. He said, 'I can fire up the computer and annul it now if it's going to be a problem.'

'No. It's all right. As long as it's only on paper.' She moved sideways on the bed. He laid his gun on the bedside table. The silencer was on, the safety was off. When she turned to look, hers was the same on the other side.

'Do you want the light on?' she asked. Luke had slept with the lights on; Andy Bennett, apparently, did the same. The knowledge that no one can sneak up on you in the dark is as necessary sometimes to the adult as the child. Murdo Cameron hadn't considered switching it off. 'If you don't mind,' he said.

He lay on his chest with his head turned away and the pillow pulled down under his shoulder. He was warm and clean and he wanted comfort and sleep and nothing else. She rolled in towards him and pushed a hand under his arm so that her fingers linked with his and squeezed. 'I'm sorry,' she said, quietly.

'For what?'

'The things I said at the cottage before I left.'

She felt him grin in the half light. 'You mean when I called you a paranoid cow with a suicide complex and you told me to fuck off?'

'More or less.'

'Don't be. You were right.' He rolled over. He had bathed her and washed her hair and it was the second time he had carried her to a bed and bandaged her wrists. He had seen and catalogued the bruises and the semi-circle of bite marks on her breasts and shoulder. She was less of a mess than before, but not by a significant margin. He ran his hand down a scratch on her arm. 'Can I ask who it was?'

She was silent a while. It is difficult, lying naked in bed, to keep the darker things hidden. 'Drew Doherty,' she said.

He was Murdo. He said nothing. He closed his eyes. In a while, without opening them, he said, 'Why?'

'Because I'm a paranoid cow with a suicide complex.'

One brow rose up. One eye opened and stared into hers. 'And?'

'And he's the only one Svensen has left to talk to. All the others are dead. It was him or the main man and however much I might want to get away from this, I don't want to go like that.'

He took note of that and let it pass. 'Doherty's bad enough,' he said. 'If he'd had the slightest idea who you were, he'd have skinned you alive.'

'I don't think so. Not unless he was bored with life. Word is that I'm Svensen's private property – as and when they find me.'

'Jesus Christ.' He rolled over to lie on his back with both hands under his head. 'Who told you that?'

'Maria Kilbride. Shortly after she told me I didn't do badly for an amateur.'

That did what she meant it to. His laugh was more of a bark, but it was real nonetheless. He opened both eyes wide. 'I hope you hit her where it hurt.'

'Not at all. She's right. And she kept her mouth shut when it mattered.' Orla reached up and pulled one of his hands down to lie across his chest. 'Did you find her on the data base?'

'No. I wouldn't expect to.' He was warm and his skin touched dryly on hers. He rolled the ball of his thumb across the palm of her hand in the way he would have stroked the dog. She eased closer to sleep. His voice reached her from the other side of a dream. 'She's one of Andy's,' he said. 'He doesn't believe in paperwork and he certainly doesn't believe in putting anything in the machine. As far as the central server's concerned, no such person exists.' He was barely there, as real only as Luke who sat on the edge of the bed and held her other hand. Between them, they tugged her apart. She curled into herself, drawing her knees up to her chest. Neither let go. A question pushed at the edge of her thinking. It mattered to both that she have an answer. 'Luke,' she said. 'He didn't know about Maria.'

'No.'

'Then how did Svensen get to her?'

'The same way he knew you were in the flat, I imagine.' He kissed the palm of her hand where his thumb had been and rolled over to lie on his front.

'What do you mean?'

His voice came thickly, muffled by the pillow. 'I mean Luke might have given him the access codes to the server but he didn't start the ball rolling. We still have a leak. You weren't on the machine. Neither of you. Not until after Luke was dead.'

He slept. She could have woken him but it would have made no difference. She lay still for a long time, looking out through a crack in the curtains at the shifting patterns of clouds and stars and trying to think. The ghosts kept watch at the door and the windows and did not intrude on her sleep.

Thursday, 27 March

The Land Rover was cold and not keen to start. Morag, wrapped tight in a man's coat, leant on the window and peered into the cab. 'Not so much choke,' she said. 'A flat battery won't get you there any faster.'

Andy Bennett pushed in the throttle, let the thing settle and tried again. The starter motor screamed in the quiet of the morning. Blue diesel fumes filled the barn; light and heady at first and then with the denser aftertaste of smoked oil. The engine coughed three times in succession and stalled as he took his hand from the key. He cursed in the sudden silence and apologised on the same breath. Beside him, Morag McLeod smiled for the first time since she heard the phone ring and heard Murdo's voice, rasped and faint through the crackle of a mobile, asking for Andy. She said, 'Shall I have a go?'

'Please do.' Bennett slid across to the passenger side. Morag hoisted herself into the driver's seat, played on the choke and the gas and spoke Irish to the engine. When she turned the key, it started. When she let go, the long coughing fit settled slowly to a roar that sounded as if it might last beyond the end of the lane.

'She takes a bit of practice.' She shouted to him over the noise of it.

'Keep her revving until the engine's warm. She'll be fine by the time you hit the top of the hill.' Her voice was lost in the rattle. He made out the words by the shape of her lips.

'Thank you.'

'Put your foot on the gas.' She pushed open the door and swung herself out of the cab, keeping her left foot on the pedal until he had moved back to take over. 'Call me when you get there,' she shouted. 'Give my love to both of them. And tell them not to worry about Jamie.'

There was no point in talking. He waved and nodded and stuck up a thumb. She ran forward to haul open the front door of the barn and then he was out, bumping on hard suspension, jerking forward on kangaroo fuel, destroying the peace and calm of the morning. He kept an eye on the rear-view mirror until he could no longer see the woman who stood alone in the gateway watching him leave. After that, he turned both his eyes to the road and the largest part of his mind to the destination and what he would find there. With the small part that was left, he enjoyed the drive.

Dawn came up slowly. The air was cold and clear and smelled of salt and drying seaweed. High, thin cloud lifted over the roof of the mountain. By the time he reached the end of the track, the sun had begun to bleed colour into the day. The sea paled from charcoal to pewter and grew an edging of rose. Peach-breasted oyster-catchers peeled away from the shoreline in singles and twos, their high, fluting cries ringing him like fingers circled on glass. A seal cow shuffled forward and slid without sound into the liquid glass of the bay.

At the junction with the main road, the Land Rover turned right and changed down a gear, coughing into the still air. Angus Shearer, hearing it, paused in his descent of the path, turned sideways to come out near the road and thus saw the smaller of the two men Morag McLeod had at her cottage wrestling to keep the front wheels clear of a pothole. He made a mental note to call in on the woman in the next day or two and find out who was what and how long they were staying and whether they were in need of a hand. Morag McLeod herself, watching from her back doorstep, saw the blue cloud blossom over the road, bit back on a smile and ducked into the kitchen to look out the number of the garage so that she could book the thing in for a service as soon as she got it back. The watcher high on the hillside smiled more tightly than the woman had done and exchanged his binoculars for a telescopic sight, panning round until the cross hairs focused on the balding head of the man at the wheel. He held it in view for the long minute of straight road and then, when a bend took it round behind a hillock, he reached down into the bag beside him and carefully, with precision, he began to assemble his rifle. The scope was last. He was screwing the front wheel nut tight to the mounting when the cough came again, closer this time, as the Land Rover changed down for the sharp-angled bend just below him. He lay flat on his stomach with his coat beneath him for warmth and set up the gun so that the front of the barrel sat on two short legs and the stock rested on the ground beside his elbow. As the cough drew nearer, he shuffled forward and lifted the stock to his shoulder. A wave of diesel flooded over him as the target rounded the last but one bend before the crest in the mountain. The watcher let the worst of it pass and then breathed in, held the breath and put his eye to the scope. A haze of blue smoke dirtied the air and was gone.

The Land Rover changed down and down again for the second and tighter of the two bends. The cross hairs met on the black band of the outermost front tyre. At the apex of the turn, on the final point of a held breath, the watcher fired and the tyre exploded. The Land Rover slewed sideways into a skid, the naked hub striking sparks from the loose stones at the edge of the tarmac. There was a second or two when it seemed as if that might be enough to send it over but Andy Bennett had spent many hours in a skid pan and knew better than most how to handle a blow-out, albeit in a strange vehicle on a Highland road with a hundred-metre drop down the mountainside if he got it wrong. If nothing else, he had the advantage of four-wheel drive and he knew how to use it. He slammed his right foot to the floor and threw his weight on the wheel. The rear tyres smoked. The engine screamed. For a long, howling moment, the momentum driving him towards the edge was balanced by one hundred and eleven horsepower pulling away from it. The wheels bit in the dirt and the Land Rover jolted forward. Bennett angled the wheel for the road. The watcher breathed in, refocused and fired twice more. Both rear tyres evaporated in a scorch of burning rubber and the Land Rover slewed sideways off the road.

Angus Shearer had not lied. The scree slope high up on the southern side of his mountain was excellent; torridonian sandstone combined with the bed of shale to form a loose rusted gravel that fell smoothly down the steep incline below the road. After a winter of wild weather with thick snow and a fast thaw, the surface was fresh and new; the deeper scores had filled out, the contours had remoulded to the lie of the land, the layers of gravel had sorted themselves by weight, the lightest and finest rising to the top to leave a smooth, unblemished finish. It was a hill runner's dream and the Sgurr Alasdair's latest guest had spent quite a large part of the night looking forward to it. The Land Rover currently careering down the longest stretch had not been part of the dream. It tumbled, roof over wheels, bouncing from rocks and hidden angles, spewing dust and noise and torn metal and – once – a human body onto the mountainside, scouring the top layer of scree down in front of it with all the pitiless efficiency of a bulldozer clearing rubble.

The man sat back on his heels and watched the shattered hulk roll to rest in the gully below. Behind it, the scar in the scree showed red like a wound. Fragments of blue metal bled from its edges. The driver's side door was closest to the top, ripped off in the first spin of the fall. The back door with the spare tyre fixed to it was closest to the bottom. Somewhere in between, a human form lay face up across the line of the slope, arms outstretched, one leg bent underneath at an angle that promised at least one long bone broken. As the sounds of the crash folded in on themselves, the body rolled one full revolution further down towards the gully and was still.

Still the runner didn't move. Dust rose in spiralling eddies from the wreck and the scar on the slope. The smell of fuel filtered up on the cool air and a tarry stain spread out from the ruptured tank, soaking in through the layers of shale. It was the leaking diesel as much as the physical disruption that would destroy the scree's running potential for years, if not decades, if nothing was done quickly to contain it. Still the runner waited and watched. The figure lying like a flung doll on the slope showed no signs of movement but then neither did anyone else. It was coming up for seven o'clock in the morning and if anyone was awake and working, they were not listening and nor were they looking up towards the mountain. The man watched the cottages, the hotel, the Manse and the jetty, looking for someone to see the rising column of dust and raise the alarm; waiting for the time when Angus Shearer and his team would take on the role of Mountain Rescue in the same way they would have lifeboatmen if the accident had happened at sea. In a small community where everyone looks after everyone else whether they like it or not, they would know exactly who had just driven past the hotel and up the mountain and they would drop anything to help if they believed that individual to be in trouble.

Nobody did.

When ten minutes had passed with no signs of life either from the hillside or the bay, the man with the crooked teeth stepped down off his rock, stretched his cramped calves, tightened the straps of his backpack and began his first scree run of the season. It was not what it could have been and it was certainly not what he had dreamt, but it was hard enough to be taxing and there was a precision to it that his planned run would have lacked. He angled down and across, aiming for a point higher than the body, relying on the collapse of the newly ploughed surface to bring him skidding and sliding in his own right to the place he needed to go. Red grit spattered over the inert form as he slid to a halt beside the head but there was still no movement. A casual observer watching from a distance would have seen him crouch by the body and test eyelid reflexes, feel for a pulse, make a quick search of the pockets for identification and then bend down and press his ear to the chest to listen for a heartbeat. It would have taken someone standing a great deal closer than that to see him find and read the one name he needed together with a telephone number and then to remove from the body the waist holster and the 9mm automatic contained therein and transfer both to the hidden pocket at the back of his rucksack. After that, anybody could have seen him pull his mobile phone from his pack and make two consecutive phone calls.

Morag McLeod was cutting wood at the bottom of the garden when her telephone rang. The bell sounded in time with the fall of her axe; once, twice and into the third, before she remembered that there was no one in the house likely to answer it. In so little time she had forgotten what it was to live alone. She split the last log on a poor angle and the axe head ran skittering across the top of the chopping block to fall with splintering weight on the kindling stacked at the side. There was time to curse at that and to imagine the mess before she reached the back door and then she was wrestling with the latch and fighting with her boots and praying that whoever it was wouldn't ring off.

They did.

'Bastard.' She stood on the doorstep with her hand on the latch and one boot flipping off the end of her foot. 'That was five rings. Five. What kind of a chance do you call that?'

The dog came to greet her, all black hair and enthusiasm and no answers at all. She was fending him off and wrestling with the other boot when she heard the child's voice, more breath than anything, say, 'She's here,' and then, 'Wait.'

She took the last step over the threshold. Jamie Buchanan was standing barefoot by the range holding the phone in his hand like a thing alive. He looked shocked, caught in that half space between daylight and dreams with his hair and his T-shirt crumpled with sleep and flecks of green matter crusting his upper lashes and the corners of his eyes. She stood very still, watching him, and then said, 'Jamie? Are you all right?'

He thrust the handset towards her. She kicked off the second boot, losing a sock with it, and reached for the receiver and the child together. 'It's OK. I would have got there in time. Who is it?'

'Luke's friend,' he said, and there was no point in asking him how he knew that. 'He's hurt.' His eyes were very bright. Her daughter would have recognised the look in them. Morag did not.

'Andy?' She grabbed the phone and said it again where there was more chance he would hear her, but then it wasn't Andy Bennett at all, it was Angus Shearer who'd had a call from his new guest and he needed to tell her that the Land Rover had gone off the road and was likely beyond repair and that 'hurt' was a euphemism rendered safe for the ears of a child.

Morag McLeod stood in the warmth of her kitchen with one arm still on the child's shoulder and looked up to the horizon as she was directed. The haze of red dust drifted high over the crest of the mountain, becoming paler by the second as the thermals spun it out in the morning air. Jamie twisted free and ran for the door. On the phone, Angus Shearer was offering a space in his van so that she could be one of the rescue team. She would have taken it without a second thought, but for Andy Bennett's last words before they went out to the barn: 'That was Murdo. They're in trouble in Glasgow and I have to go. Jamie's all yours now. Look after him, he means a lot to your daughter.'

She had held his gaze across the width of her kitchen table. 'And not to you?'

He had smiled for her, dryly, which was how he always smiled and said, 'And to me. Both of you. Take care, won't you?' Then he leant across and kissed her on the cheek, dry-lipped, and she followed him out to the barn to do battle with the stubborn beast that was her Land Rover. He had not expected, neither of them had expected, that it might conceivably be a battle the beast could win.

She stared up at the dust and the road. The phone crackled close to her ear. 'Morag?' Shearer's voice was a tone higher than usual, fuelled by need and a sudden awareness of time. 'Gareth Liddell and Tam Gillespie just came in the door,' he said. 'I'm waiting on the man Carlaw and the Connolly brothers. If you can get here before they do, there'll be room for you and the lad in the winch truck. Otherwise, we'll head off up and bring you back what we can. There'll be the man at least, however he is. I don't think there's any point in bringing you back your van.' He left a pause which she chose not to fill. 'I'm sorry,' he said and it sounded as if he meant it.

'Thank you.' Her eyes dropped to the child. Jamie sat on the doorstep with the dog's chin on his knee. His T-shirt was riding up round his waist.

Beneath it, his legs were blotched pink and blue with the cold. He had seen the dust and heard enough to know what was happening. Viewed from the side, with the angle of the light on his face, it was possible that he might be crying. Morag turned back to the phone. 'Angus? I'll have to talk to Jamie and see does he want to stay here. We'll be there in five minutes if we're coming.'

'Fine. We'll be out the back by the oil tank.' The phone cut off in her hand and she stood still, staring blindly out of the window, one foot bare on the wood of the floor, one foot with its sock working down round her ankle, and wondered if perhaps she might weep. Not in front of the child.

'Jamie? Can I join you?'

He said nothing but she sat down beside him on the doorstep. He was taller than he had been when she first saw him and there was muscle where before there had been none. Still, when she put an arm round his shoulder, she could feel the sharp edge of his bones under her hand, and the planes of his face, turned towards her, seemed thinner. He was not crying after all. She licked the ball of her thumb and swept the sleep from the corners of his eyes. He frowned, but didn't shy away. 'Andy might be badly hurt,' she said. 'They'll bring him down here before the ambulance comes. But if you want, Angus says we can go up with the rescue and help them to find him. Would you like that?'

The frown deepened at that and she saw his mouth moving, as if he was rehearsing something or reading a text without saying the words.

'You don't have to say anything, sweetheart. A nod will do.'

He shook his head, like a horse shaking flies and grabbed her arm. His eyes flicked to the mountain and back as if he needed it to give him permission or strength or to free up the words. She took his hand in her own and kissed the fingers. 'Jamie, love, if you don't want—'

'Is he dead?' It came out in a rush, like the breaking of a dam, and it wasn't at all what she had been expecting.

Honesty. With children, it is all that really matters. She let go of his hand. 'I don't know,' she said, carefully. 'Angus doesn't know. His friend on the mountain thinks he might still be alive but he isn't sure.'

The grey eyes took that in and rejected it for the non-answer that it was. He bit his lip in frustration but the flow of words had dried up. In itself, that made the decision. She stood, lifting him to his feet. 'Come on, let's go and see. If he is dead, waiting here won't make him any deader. If he's not, then maybe we can do something useful to help. Go.' She took him by the shoulder and spun him round to point in the direction of the stairs. 'Get your clothes on and be ready to leave in three minutes. You can brush your teeth in the car.'

Angus Shearer was an organised man who functioned best in an emergency. He had a good system for lifting injured parties off his mountain and although he didn't generally want an audience there to get in the way, he had no objections to a fellow sportsman taking part, particularly if the man in question had potential connections in the running world. For a number of reasons, therefore, he was happy to see Neil Jamieson waiting for him, sitting on his backpack down on the scree beside the body, or the injured man, whichever it turned out to be.

Shearer swung down from his cab and walked round the second bend in the road. It was easy enough to read what had happened – the black rubber and scored tarmac wrote their own script – but it was always worth having a proper look. He spent a good minute eyeing up the tracks and their tale and then waved down to the runner and made his own neat, precise descent to the victim. 'Blow-out, aye?' he said as he came to a halt.

The man eyed him thoughtfully. 'Three blow-outs,' he said, distinctly. 'Like Earnest's aunt, I'd say one is unfortunate, two is bad luck. Three is downright careless on somebody's part.'

'Whisht, man—' Shearer spun on his heel. Up on the road, Morag McLeod was being handed down from the front seat of Hugh Carlaw's Discovery, the lad behind her. Shearer said, 'The lassie there's Morag McLeod. She's—'

'The owner of the Land Rover? And sound carries, doesn't it. How unfortunate.' He said it more quietly and he was shielded by the innkeeper's shoulder but the woman had heard him. At least, she was looking down at the pair of them and she had heard something. Shearer turned back. The runner smiled.

'In that case, maybe we should have some introductions before I offend anyone else,' he said and, bending to scoop up his bag, he began the harder, reverse route back up the hill.

Morag was talking to Hugh Carlaw and both of them were studying the tyre tracks on the road, trying to think how Andy Bennett, driving uphill with a cold engine, could ever have got the Land Rover to a speed where it would skid hard enough to go over the edge. Hugh was down on one knee, examining the tracks, and he was just coming to the same conclusion about the burst tyres when the runner reached them. Neither of the adults was paying attention to the shape coming over the edge. It was left to Jamie Buchanan to see the man, coated lightly in red as if rinsed in blood, emerging from the depths of the earth to take him. The sight of it froze him as nothing else had done, withering all the patient weeks of work. He stopped still and stared and the part of him that was alive and awake screamed aloud in the silence of his mind while the part that understood survival made the only choice it knew how to make. His hand, which had been reaching for Morag's, fell to his side. His eyes searched the higher peak of the mountain for snow and found it where he knew it would be. His face settled in a semblance of peace and was still by the time the nightmare reached him.

'Hello. I'm Neil.' The runner crouched down and put a hand to the child's arm. Eye to eye he said, 'You must be Jamie,' and smiled in the way that had opened the bar for him in the Alasdair. There was a pause while three adults waited for a response. When it was clear none would be forthcoming, Morag dropped her own arm round the child's shoulder and drew him close. 'Yes, this is Jamie.' She held out her free hand. 'I'm Morag and this,' she half turned, 'is Hugh Carlaw from the Manse. He's come to give Angus a hand with the rescue. Hugh, this is Neil.'

'So I heard.' Hugh Carlaw turned and stood. The runner was not a big man, taller than Morag but not a match for Hugh Carlaw. The older man looked down and it was clear he didn't like what he saw. His eyes bored into the bland, smiling face. 'Neil what?' he asked.

'Jamieson.'

There was a longer pause this time and a tension that Shearer, arriving late, sensed but did not understand. 'Neil Jamieson.' Carlaw rolled the name in his mouth, testing the taste of it. He did not offer to shake hands. 'And you found the crash?'

'Just so. I was down on the path there checking out the start of the scree run when it happened.' Jamieson nodded in the general direction. The head of the path was hidden behind an outcrop. All of them craned to see it. The man waited until he had their attention again. 'No doubt if I hadn't been here, someone else would have found it in due course but this way, God willing, we'll be in time to keep Mr Bennett alive.'

His accent was Scots but there was a cadence to the rhythms that was not West Highland, nor even Glaswegian. The white brows peaked and fell. 'Are you not a little far from home?' asked Carlaw.

'Possibly, but then I am here for a reason.' The runner smiled, winningly. 'When it's done, I will leave.'

'Providing you are still able to do so.'

'There is always that.'

'Gentlemen, perhaps we could continue this conversation some other time?' Angus Shearer was not a man to lose control of his team, however exalted its members. The three Connolly brothers were already working their winch, hauling out the wire hawser, feeding it down the scarred line of the scree. They knew about motors and how to repair them but they knew nothing of men and he would ask for their help only if he had no choice. Gareth Liddell, the GP, had his doctor's bag in his hand but he was manifestly not a man to go scrabbling around on a hillside when there were others to do the work for him. Tam Gillespie, the fisherman, who had come up in the Discovery with Carlaw, Morag and Jamie, was the one who knew the mountain and wasn't afraid of it. He had the stretcher laid out on the side of the road with the neck brace fixed and the straps looped across it for binding the victim. When it was clear that he had the attention of his team, it was to Gillespie that Shearer turned. 'Tam? Are you ready to go?'

'Aye.'

'Hugh?'

'Of course.'

Shearer turned last to his guest. The man was crouching down by the child, his eyes following the boy's gaze to the snow. He was asking him a question although the sound of it didn't carry any further than the two of them and Jamie, as far as anyone could tell, wasn't listening.

'Neil, we need four men on the stretcher,' said Shearer. 'Dr Liddell's not that keen on the mountain. I was hoping you'd be able to help.'

The man nodded blithely and smiled, showing his white, uneven teeth. 'Of course,' he said. 'Why else did I wait?'

Andy Bennett was alive, if barely. He had a jagged break in his left thigh, with the two ends of the bone angled inwards so they poked through a gash in the skin a hand's length above his knee. His left shoulder was similarly broken and there was a possibility of a crack or two in his wrist. He had lost a lot of blood from the wound on his leg although prompt and effective action on the part of the man Jamieson had stemmed the flow sufficiently to keep him alive. Now, with him lying in the living room at the cottage, still strapped to the stretcher with a drip in his arm and a great, wide dressing on his leg, it was the damage to his head that was the unknown quantity and which meant that, when the helicopter came, he would be flown to Glasgow, where they had a scanner and people to use it, and not one of the closer, less well-equipped casualty units where they did not. In the meantime, all that Liddell, in his capacity as a family doctor, could say was that the man was unconscious, which was obvious, and they should make no effort to wake him.

Morag McLeod, who was also a doctor and had formed her own opinions, stood in her kitchen where she could see both Andy and Jamie and made tea and coffee in that order for the doctor and the remains of Angus Shearer's stretcher party. There were only two of them left. Shearer himself had retired to his hotel to organise a midday meal to which all those involved were invited as guests. Tam Gillespie, quiet, diffident, competent and a superb mountaineer, had jumped free of the cab as the Land Rover passed his cottage and was almost certainly in the process of launching his boat for a late day's catch. That left her with Gareth Liddell who had no concept of conversation beyond the medical, Hugh Carlaw and Neil Jamieson who sat in silence on either side of the fire – and Jamie. From the moment he first laid eyes on Bennett's body, the child had changed. She had held him on her knee all the way back down the hill in Hugh Carlaw's Discovery and it was like holding a stiff-jointed doll. At the cottage, he had walked ahead of her across the kitchen and squeezed himself into the corner with his back to the range and the table in front of him. It was the one place with a clear view out of the window to the mountain they had left behind. His eyes rested on it, transfixed. In the time it took to boil the kettle, she saw him blink only once. She made him a mug of tea and cut a slice of cake before she took the rest through to the living room. When she came back to the kitchen, he had touched neither. His face was translucent, like pearl, with a faint sheen of sweat. His eyes were not unlike those of the man on the stretcher, except that she didn't have to lift up the lids to see the void inside.

'You don't have to stay down here,' she said, carefully. 'If you want to take Bran and go upstairs, I'm sure no one will mind.'

He heard her. The grey eyes darted up to hers and then down to the dog lying at his feet. He nodded, once, and slid down from the table, taking the long way round to the foot of the stairs so that he kept as much distance as possible from the stretcher.

Hugh Carlaw, watching him go, said, 'I knew he was fond of Orla. I hadn't realised he felt the same about the men.'

Morag shook her head. 'I don't think it's the depth of feeling that matters. He lost his mother less than a month ago. I'd say he's afraid of another death in the family, it doesn't matter whose it is.' She leant back on the wall, staring up the stairs. 'It's my fault, I should have realised. I forget, when he acts so adult, that he's still only nine.'

'He's coping well, though,' said the runner. His eyes followed the soft pad of footsteps across the ceiling and up the second flight of stairs. 'I knew a child like him once. They live in their own world and you think there's nothing going in and nothing coming out and then, just once in a while, they say something completely surprising and you know they're all there and watching.' He looked at her along the full length of the stretcher and for the first time he wasn't laughing. 'Would you let me go up and talk to him?'

'What?' She was standing under the dividing beam that separated the kitchen from the living room. The man was kneeling by the hearth. In the time she had taken to pour the tea and cut the cake, he had found her supply of old newspaper, rolled the sheets neatly into spills and laid the fire. He was looking up at her now with a piece of her kindling in one hand and an unstruck match in the other. She stepped forward to stand at the foot of the stairs. Up above, the latch fell shut on the attic door. 'Why?' she said.

'I don't know,' he shrugged. 'Because he reminds me of me, possibly. Because he's hurt and one of us should do something.'

'And of course it should be you?' Hugh Carlaw was sitting where he had sat the night before, in the big chair opposite the unlit fire. He was not the man she had come to know but he spoke with a bitterness that echoed the tone he had used when he had spoken of his son. It occurred to Morag, rather later than it might have done, that there might be things about the runner that he could recognise and dislike. She thought of Andy Bennett and the man Luke whom she had never met and took a step into the room to look at him better.

Jamieson took it as refusal. 'Of course not. Forget it, I was being selfish. I apologise.' He struck the match. 'Perhaps I can offer to light your fire?'

The flame flared in his fingers. The brief light carved out new hollows in his face. Alert grey eyes rested on hers, lit from below so that the fine veins showed in black and she saw for the first time the circling hairline just beyond the iris. On the basis of this, she made a decision.

'No.' She said it too sharply. The flame died, unfed. Morag McLeod stood at the head of the stretcher and felt the wash of its light fall away from the scars on her hands. 'You're right,' she said. 'Jamie shouldn't be left to sit up there on his own. We'll both go.'

'A delegation?' The eyes mocked less than his voice. He inclined his head. 'If you like. It might be better that way.'

Hugh Carlaw didn't like it but there was little she could do about that if he was not prepared to talk to her. Morag left him in the company of the doctor and led the way up the first flight of stairs and along the landing to the base of the second. Her bedroom door stood open. She led the way inside. The runner turned and looked at the second set of stairs. 'I thought the lad went all the way up.'

'He did. Do I look daft? We're not going near him.'

'Ah.' He moved past her to stand by the foot of the bed. He had his backpack in his hand.

'Ah, indeed. And you can put that thing down before we go any further. If you move a hair the wrong way, I'll scream fit to bring the house down. I think Hugh Carlaw would love me forever if I gave him a good reason to kick your head in.'

'I'm sure he would.' He laid the pack on the floor at his feet and stepped sideways, his hands held wide. 'Then again, if I was going to hurt you, I'd have done it before now.'

'I know that. I may look completely stupid but . . . oh, stand up, man.' He had sat down on the edge of her bed and put his hands on his head which was just ridiculous. He stood and dropped his hands. She leant her back to the door. 'Why did you want to talk to Jamie?' she asked.

'I had something to give him. It needed to be done in private and I had not expected to have the opportunity to give it to you instead.' He nodded down to the pack. 'It's in there. If I bring it out, you *will* scream and with good reason. You do it.' He nudged the thing towards her with his foot. 'If you feel down in the space between the spine and the main compartment, you'll find a Velcro fastening. Undo it and lift out what's inside.'

She did. It was a gun. As with so much else, she would not have known one from another before her daughter changed the course of her life. Now, she knelt by the pack with it lying across her hands and looked up at the man standing opposite. If there was recognition in her eyes, he didn't acknowledge it.

'So?' she said.

'I'm sorry.' He looked unsure of himself – the way the child had looked when he was trying to speak, as if the words were not coming in their right order. He sighed and pushed a hand through his hair. 'There's so little time,' he said. 'I don't know how much you . . . Do you know whose gun that is?'

'Would I tell you if I did?'

He smiled wryly. 'I am beginning to see where your daughter learns from. Fine. Forget I asked. I will tell you that I took it from Dr Andrew Bennett when I first found him. If you go a little deeper, you will find his holster.' She did that, too. He nodded as she fitted the pair together as if this were a normal act for a woman in her sixties. 'It seemed to me that the local worthies did not need to know that your house guest carried a gun. Your daughter, however, must know as a matter of urgency both that the crash has happened and that it was not an accident. The implications, as I'm sure you'll understand, are immense.'

'What makes you think it wasn't an accident?'

'The tyres were shot out. There are bullet marks on the wheel rims. Orla will find them when she examines the Land Rover. Don't let any of the locals try to mend it before she gets here.' He moved to the door. 'For now, I suggest you put the gun away somewhere in here where it will be safe. When we go downstairs, I will leave. Hugh Carlaw may try to follow me, but that's my problem and I will deal with it. You should call your daughter as soon as is humanly possible and tell her everything I've said.'

'I had a call this morning. She's in trouble in Glasgow. Andy was going out to meet her.'

'Try it. I may be wrong but I suspect she's as well as a good night's sleep can make her. I think you'll find that the call did not come from her or her friends.'

'Is that so?' She would have liked to be angry but she had no heart for it. 'And what do I tell her about you?'

'Whatever you like.' He smiled, briefly. His eyes carried the same stamp as Murdo, as Andy Bennett. He looked not unlike Orla. He looked, in fact, a lot like an older, harder version of Ciaran, with the anger worked through him and out the other side. He nodded as if she had said it aloud and said, 'Give her the gun. That will be enough. And give my apologies to Jamie Buchanan.'

She followed him down to the kitchen and watched from the back door as he shouldered his pack and walked down the first half of the lane. At the corner, he turned and waved. Hugh Carlaw made no effort to follow him. In fact, he made no effort to acknowledge his existence. He sat in his place by the newly laid fire drinking tea with the doctor, the pair of them mired in a discussion on the hand-tying of flies for the perfect luring of salmon. Morag McLeod walked back up the stairs to her bedroom and picked up her phone to call her daughter.

The clock at the bedside read ten fifteen.

Ten

Thursday, 27 March – Glasgow

The doorbell rang as Big Ben chimed nine. The technician waited, dressed to go out. The man standing on the doorstep was not the one she expected. He was taller than the other one and younger, with scruffy jeans and loose black hair that fell to his shoulders so that he looked like a sixties drop-out locked in the wrong millennium.

'Where's Jonathan?' she asked.

'Sorry.' The grin was disarmingly wide. 'His mother fell and broke her hip. He's sitting in casualty waiting to hear if they can find her a bed for after the surgery. I'm the fill-in' He bounced her car keys on the palm of his hand and glanced up at the sky. 'He said if it stopped raining, he thought you might like to go to the Fossil Grove. Or maybe Rouken Glen?'

'Did he, indeed? That boy makes it his life's work to tell me where to go and what to do with my time.' A pleasing thought struck her. 'Where would you like to go?'

'I'm easy. It's a nice day. We can go anywhere you like as long as we're back here for one o'clock.' His eyes were the colour of old sherry and warmed everything they touched. 'I make that a radius of about forty miles,' he said. 'Your choice.'

She smiled in a way she would not have smiled for Jonathan and spun the wheels of her chair. 'Forget the car. If it's that nice then it's five minutes from here to the Botanics. We can walk down and look through the gardens.'

231

It took less than five minutes. The chair was motorised and manoeuvrable but she liked it being pushed and he did it well. He was attentive and careful and knew how to ride the kerbs so that it didn't jar the compacted vertebrae in her spine that had been crushed in the fall. Better, he knew how to talk so that it sounded as if he cared about her. His voice was a dream. He had grown up in Pollok and spent his student days in Byres Road and, recently, he had stayed in the Highlands. Somewhere along the way he had spent time with someone of Irish descent and picked up the odd twist of the vowels and the strange reduction of subjunctives. She told him this and he acknowledged it with grace. In his turn, he told her about the gardens as they walked. He recited the botanical names and the history of the trees and shrubs and plants that they passed until she made him stop talking about plants and start talking about himself and discovered that he'd worked his student holidays as a groundsman. He knew the back ways down to the river that took her out of the bright sun and into the dappled shadows. The path down to the river was steep and she would have stopped him but he told her that he had pushed barrows up it without too much trouble and that if she were prepared to use the motor, it would be easy enough to get her back. She relaxed and let him go where he wanted.

The river was extraordinary, swollen with rain, brown with mud and silt, white-crested where it mounted the banks and surfed the mid-stream rocks. The rhododendrons at the side of it had been in early bud and caught the frost of a fortnight back. Someone, another student earning money on Easter vacation, had swept the blackened leaves into piles ready to be loaded on the barrows. At half past nine in the morning, there were no student groundsmen to be seen. In fact, it looked at first as if there was nobody at all prepared to make the effort to walk down into the dark when they could be making the most of the first good morning's sun of the spring. Then they crossed under a bridge and the pleasant solitude was broken. On the far side of it, a dark-haired young woman in a lilac ski jacket sat on a portable picnic stool with a laptop computer on her knees. She looked up and smiled and raised a thumb in greeting. The young man nodded and swung the chair round to face the river.

'Do we have to stop?' The technician smiled at him over her shoulder.

'Temporarily.' He leant on the square-cut stone of the bridge and let his jacket fall open. It was heavy sheepskin and he had kept it fastened all through the heat of the upper gardens. If it hadn't been for the eyes and the smile, she might have noticed that. The smile had gone, which was why she noticed now.

The technician was not stupid and she was not slow, but she would never be fast enough. He didn't need to draw the weapon, he simply let his jacket fall fully open so that she could see it. 'You could die here,' he said mildly, 'and no one would ever know.'

She gave a short, derisive snort. 'If you were going to kill me, I'd be dead in the water by now.' She twisted round to see him better. 'What will you do if I scream?'

'Gag you. If necessary, we *will* kill you.'

We, not *I*. The technician turned. The woman with the lilac jacket had picked up her stool and was standing beside the chair with the laptop held under her arm. To anyone passing, she was a friend and they were looking for a good place to work together.

The man carried the gun and had made the first contact. He was also, by far, the easier to deal with. The technician turned back towards him. 'What have you done with Jonathan?'

'I called him at home and told him that you have family visiting and don't need to be taken out today. He's fine. If you don't tell him anything different, he'll never know it wasn't true.'

She thought about that. It was plausible and easily checked. She nodded and let it past. 'So what do you want from me?'

Without the smile, he was older and more tired. 'You've done work for Tord Svensen,' he said. 'I need to know when it started, who recruited you, what you gave him and how each of you makes contact with the other.'

The name jolted through her, shocking the last vestiges of calm. 'I don't know anyone called Tord Svensen,' she said.

'Of course you don't. Nobody ever does.' The woman was behind her. 'Tell me then,' she said, 'does the name Luke Tyler mean anything instead?'

The technician closed her eyes. She had only moderate control of her bladder and she felt it beginning to fail. She said, 'No.'

'Really?' The woman knelt at the side of the chair. This close, one could see the white line of a scar running down from her eye, along the side of her nose to her upper lip. One could hear the background of Irish and west coast Scots in her voice, much stronger than the man's. One could remember a name that had been searched for and eventually found and the details that had been logged beside it. In doing so, one could make every effort to keep this new understanding from becoming apparent to the woman watching – and fail.

The woman smiled. 'Very good,' she said. 'We'll try that again, shall we? Do you remember Luke Tyler?'

'Yes.' It came out like the rasp of a crow.

'Do you remember how he died?'

'Not in detail.'

'No, well, we wouldn't want to disturb your sleep with the details. The basic principles will do.' The eyes were flat and densely grey, like sheet steel. Looking into them, one could see no real signs of life. 'My friend is going to ask you some questions. If you answer them accurately, concisely and fully, he will take you back to your flat and we will not trouble you again. If you waste time or prevaricate or attempt to lie, then we will not kill you, we will simply walk away and leave you here. By the time you have got yourself to the top where people will help you, Tord Svensen will have had word that you have been seen in conversation with Orla McLeod. I think you can imagine how he will respond to that.'

The technician didn't attempt to speak. She tried instead to swallow. It was taken as good as a word.

'Good. Well done.' The woman looked past her to the man beyond. 'All yours.'

Things moved very quickly after that. The picnic stool was placed in the middle of the path where the dark-haired woman could watch in both directions. The technician discovered that the computer and the mobile phone that went with it were her own. Later, sitting alone in her living room, she felt a great deal of disquiet at the fact that they had been taken when her alarm system had registered no intrusion. Now, she felt only relief at working with a system she knew well. The young man leaned over her shoulder as she opened it and logged on.

'Show me how you did it,' he said.

The technician said, 'It's working hours. I'll be seen.'

'I don't think so. You're better than that.' He said it as a statement of fact, not flattery. There was a possibility that he was right. Her fingers worked on of their own accord and the fire wall melted in front of her. She walked through the portals of someone else's server and felt like a thief working under a spotlight but she was not denied entry. 'I'm in,' she said. 'What do you want now?'

'I want a log of everything you've ever taken off this server – including the dates and times you took it – copied to the hard drive.'

'You're mad. That'll take too long. However good I am, they're bound to put on a trace.'

'Possibly.' He nodded. 'In which case you may want to think very carefully about who you choose to share your troubles with when the uniforms come knocking at the door. Does the name Donald Laidlaw ring any bells?'

It did. A dark morning darkened further.

'Fine. I thought it might.' His eyes were as warm as they had ever been. 'He put you inside,' he said. 'Did he help you set up again when you came out?'

Surprisingly, this amused her. She snorted, like a horse in hot weather. '*Laidlaw?* Are you crazy? That man would cross the street to spit in my face.'

'What about Gordon McRae?'

Some things are beyond contempt. She let it run through her voice. 'Give me a break.'

He nodded, thinking. 'So then who was it that recruited you this time?' He asked it casually, as an afterthought. Only the sudden tension in the dark-haired woman made it something else. The technician considered her answer with care.

'Svensen,' she said. 'He called me. He didn't say how he got my name but it won't have been difficult, I was all over the papers for a week or two while the trial was on.' The memory soured her mind. She shook her head. 'Fame – the wages of sin.'

'I think notoriety might not be quite the same thing. What did he say?'

'He made his offer. I said no. He made a better offer and then a better one after that and kept on until I agreed to do what he asked.'

'Which was what?'

'Break into your system whenever he had a question that needed an answer. He'd got the access codes, he needed someone who could walk in and walk out again without leaving the doors open behind them.'

She had been right to be careful. On the edge of her vision, the woman stood and walked away.

The tall man watched her go. Softly, he asked, 'How much did he offer you, when he made his best offer?'

'Enough.' She raised her eyes from her machine. 'Everyone has a price.'

'Possibly.' He might have argued with that but his eyes moved to the screen and the new things that were happening beyond her control. He leant over her shoulder and hit a key. 'I'd get a move on if I were you. This would not be a good time to be cut off.' There was a warning in that, however pleasantly phrased. She did what was needed. The hard drive chattered as the download began. On the screen, she saw the time when her presence was noted and the work begun to find out who she was and where, and she did nothing to stop it. The tall man looking over her shoulder saw it and nodded. 'They'll be round by tomorrow,' he said. 'If you decide you want to talk to somebody, ask for DCS Alec Strang. If anyone's talking to the opposition, it isn't him and he'll do what he can to keep you safe. I would suggest that, under the current fiscal system, if you had something to give him by way of barter, it would make it easier for him to justify the expense of a safe house. Think about that when you're at home again.'

'Thanks.'

She was closing down the final connection when a mobile phone rang, the noise muffled by the backdrop of the river. All three of them felt for their pockets. It was Orla McLeod who answered. She turned away with her hand to her head, blocking her free ear.

'Yes? What? No, there's no trouble. No, he hasn't phoned anyone since last night. Yes, I'm absolutely certain . . . Who? . . . When? Right. Yes, as soon as we can.'

She turned back. There was, after all, life in her eyes. She looked straight through the technician to the man beyond. 'That was the cottage,' she said. 'They've had a visitor. We need to get back.'

'How did he know we weren't at home?'

'Who knows? If they were searching for Faith Maguire on the computer then Maria Kilbride must have told him I was in Glasgow. He could have been watching the road out of the village and seen you leave. Or he could have had a watch on Gail Morgan's place with someone to call him as soon as we turned up there.'

'Or he could have been told.'

'There's only one man besides Andy who knew where we were.'

'I know. That's what I mean.'

'Murdo, we've been through this. You said at the start that it couldn't be him.'

'I could have been wrong.'

'Do you believe that?'

'No. But that doesn't mean it isn't true.'

They drove in relays, an hour each and then change. The road was clear and dry. Orla took the first stretch, Murdo the last. The one not driving at any given time used the mobile, liaising with base, giving directions to the forensic team, the motorbike courier, the faster ambulance with a discreet armed guard to replace the one that had not yet left the hospital to collect Andy Bennett. Later, when there was nothing left that could be done from a distance, they drove in silence.

At the crest of the mountain, Murdo stopped. Beneath them, the red scar on the scree showed where the Land Rover had gone over the edge, with a separate, deeper cut where the Connolly brothers had winched it back up to the road again. Murdo turned in his seat and lifted a set of binoculars from the floor behind the passenger seat.

'What's up?'

'Just checking.' The wind bent the grasses flat to the ground. He left his door open and stood in the shelter of it, using the roof as a prop to keep his elbows steady. The lenses scanned to the far horizon and back again and came to a stop. He lifted his head. 'Come and look.'

The view back inland was as spectacular in its way as the view to the coast. The road threaded between mountains that scraped the sky. A dozen different greens patched the slopes and the valleys, dusted with purple in places for the heather and, rarely, yellow for the early gorse. Orla stood in his place and lifted the glasses. 'What am I looking for?'

'Follow the road back. He was at the bridge. He'll be a bit beyond it by now.' She looked, pulling the focus and moving the lenses to make two blurred fields into one, sharp, tight circle bisected by the grey streak of the road. A motorcycle rider in black leather hunched over his tank, leaning hard into a bend so that the tyres streaked the white line up the centre. 'I have the bike,' she said.

'Not that. A mile or two behind him.' She edged sideways and found it; a blue Audi swept silently from left to right through the patchwork landscape. She pulled the focus tighter. The driver had a passenger. Even at this distance, the hair shone like burnished copper. She lifted her eyes from the lenses. 'He's with Art.'

'Yes.'

'He's the head of the Division. He has a right to be here.'

'Yes.'

She handed back the binoculars. The sun poked through a gap in the clouds. The wind keened round their shoulders. He reached for her hand and held it. Her fingers traced the edge of his broken knuckle and looped round it. He said, 'I want to be wrong.'

'Yes.'

They drove the last mile in silence.

*　　*　　*

'Jamie?'

The child heard the steps on both sets of stairs and recognised them. Before that, he had heard the two vehicles drive up and park at the barn; a car and a motorbike. The dog had clattered down and out to meet the incomers and he could tell from the length and style of the greeting that there were three individuals and one of them was a stranger. Now Orla, who was only occasionally a stranger, stood in his doorway with her hand on the latch, still with her jacket on from the journey, and said his name again. 'Jamie? May I come in?'

She was tired, he could hear it in her voice. That, and other things. He turned. She was leaning on the doorframe, her head lolling on the wooden post as if it took too much to keep it upright. Her face was more drawn than it had been. 'Andy's in hospital in Glasgow,' she said. 'He's had a scan. They think he'll wake up in a day or two. When his leg mends, he'll probably be able to walk. Maybe even to run.'

It had not occurred to him that it might be otherwise. He took that in and stored it, along with the fact that it mattered to her. His eyes moved back to the mountain. The day was bright and the sky was blue which was not good, but the snow was clear on the crest. It was the best he could do.

'Jamie?' She was sitting beside him now, on the edge of the bed. He heard her tugging at something and then she moved to sit cross-legged and he realised she had taken off her running shoes. He looked down. They had liquid mud splattered around the edges and the laces were damp, as if she had run through a puddle some time ago and they had not had time to dry. She laid them on the floor at the foot of the bed. 'Wrecked, aren't they? I should know better than to try and walk on water.' He thought she was making a joke. Squinting sideways to check, he was not so sure.

She had a plastic bag in her hand, which had been in her pocket. Laying it on her knee, she lifted out a gun and its holster, handling them only through the plastic. 'These are Andy's,' she said. 'There's a motorbike courier downstairs waiting to take them to Glasgow for fingerprinting but I wanted you to see them first. A man gave them to my mother along with some information which might be true. He also said to tell you that he was sorry but he didn't say what for. Do you know why he should be sorry, Jamie?'

The gun lay on her crossed knees. He looked from it to her face and back again. She was not smiling for him and she had positioned herself very carefully not to get in the way of the window. There was no sense of coercion. He was free to speak or not to speak; to think or not to think, to remember or to forget. Still, he felt pushed, as if he were at the top of a cliff and unseen hands were trying to push him off. Or perhaps to pull him. He remembered a man, coated in red, looming up from the depths of the earth and the giddy sense of falling overtook him. He looked back at the snow.

'The man said his name was Neil Jamieson.' She said it casually, as if all men carried his name within theirs. 'Did he scare you?'

A starling flew past the window. The feathers on its back glimmered with the muted iridescence of spilled diesel. He watched it until the sense of falling had gone and then he nodded.

'Neil Jamieson scared you?' Another nod. 'My mother thinks he was polite and intelligent and that, underneath, he was like Murdo and me. Do you think that?'

He did not. He turned his back on the snow and the starling to let her know that.

'No. I thought not. So what was he like?' She was sitting up very straight on his bed and there was something to her that wasn't simply tired or sad about Andy. She was taut, like a rubber band or a piece of string pulled to breaking, and when he looked beneath the quiet and the softness of her voice he saw that she was very, very angry. The boy swallowed convulsively and didn't know that he was not the first that morning to do so. He forgot the snow.

'Thank you.' She smiled for him, after a fashion, and he would have preferred her not to do it. 'The man thinks that Andy's car was shot at, to make it go over the edge. Do you believe him?' she asked.

He thought about that. He had no doubt that it was possible, even probable. He nodded.

'Yes. I do, too. Interesting, isn't it, that he should know?' She lifted a hand and ran it along the edge of the bed. They both watched her finger rise and fall over the carved whorls on the wood. She said, 'He had brown hair and grey eyes but my mother thinks he was wearing coloured contact lenses, which is a little ironic if you think about it.' The fingers lay still on the wood, held calm by a self-control he didn't want to think about. When she spoke, her voice was so soft that he had to lean forward to hear her. 'Did the man have brown hair and grey eyes when you saw him last time, Jamie?'

She knew. She knew and so he didn't have to speak it. Relief rushed into him, like air to a vacuum, lifting his eyes to hers. Still, the old memories surged up over the edge of the precipice and grabbed, shrieking at his feet and legs.

'Jamie?' She moved so he could see her face. 'It's my fault. I should never have gone away. I won't do it again. I won't let him touch you, I promise.'

The passion in that was enough to keep him safe from anything. He felt another wave of relief for the promise of protection and, more, for the understanding that her anger was not directed at him. A smaller, tighter tuck of sorrow followed as he understood that she was blaming herself for something that was not her fault. He touched his finger to her hand, to tell her that he didn't hold her responsible. She opened her palm to let his fingers slide across it and asked her question again, slightly differently. 'Was the man who called himself Neil Jamieson the same as the one you saw in the flat who called himself Tord Svensen? The one who hurt Luke?'

It was so much simpler than it might have been. Jamie Buchanan closed his fingers on her wrist as if grabbing a rope. His eyes stayed on hers. He nodded.

It was late by the time the front doorbell rang; the outer world was dark and foggy and the surveillance cameras that brought a constant digital image of her front doorstep to the top quadrant of the screen had gone into white-out without her noticing. The technician reviewed the last five minutes of useful data in fast forward and saw nothing. Her heart rate doubled and the pain in her guts that had been with her all day twisted into something more urgent.

'Who is it?' She called it from behind her desk, her hand hovering over her panic button.

'Police. Strathclyde CID.' The voice was guttural and Glaswegian and had the arrogance that goes with power. She took her hand off the button.

They'll be round by tomorrow. If you decide you want to talk to somebody, ask for DCS Alec Strang. He'll do what he can to keep you safe. I would suggest that, under the current fiscal system, if you had something to give him by way of barter, it would make it easier for him to justify the expense of a safe house. Think about that when you're at home again.

She had thought about it. She had, in fact, spent the afternoon and early evening compiling a digital gold mine for whomsoever might need it to offset a potentially dubious claim for expenses. Still, her heart tripped in her chest.

She wheeled towards the door. 'Have you identification?'

'I do.'

'Put it through the letterbox.'

There was a pause and a rattle and then a laminated card slid under the flap of her letterbox to hang, spinning, on the end of its chain. She sent the chair drifting forward to look. The card itself was worn and curved as if it had spent too many years in a hip pocket, squashed between buttock and chair. The photograph showed a younger man than the voice suggested. Neil Jamieson, Detective Sergeant in Strathclyde CID, had brown hair and grey eyes and was prone to wearing brown suits which was a mistake that would bar him forever from promotion. He didn't look as arrogant as he sounded. The technician let go of the card and held the flap of the letterbox open so that he could drag it back. She was raising a hand to the latch when a further doubt struck her.

'Why is there only one of you?' In her experience – admittedly all of it gleaned from the television – detectives never undertook an arrest in units of less than two.

'Why would there not be?' She could hear the frown in his voice, the loss of arrogance, the sudden reduction in power. This, too, would ensure that he never progressed beyond sergeant. Her heart rate slowed and her bowels ceased their threats. 'Never mind.' She opened the door.

He was, indeed, younger than he sounded and, although he was not wearing a brown suit, his clothing was similarly innocuous. For the first few seconds as she closed and locked the door behind him and followed him into the room, she believed him to be what he pretended to be. Then he sat down at her desk with his hand over her panic button and smiled at her across the room.

'No . . . !' It was a word shaped but not spoken. She didn't have the voice to make it real. Her hands flew off the controls and her chair lurched to a halt with a force that threw her forward. Falling, she scrabbled for the second button by the light switch on the skirting board.

The voice of her deepest nightmares said, 'I don't think so, Gail,' and light flickered briefly as a naked blade was placed flat on the top of her desk. She veered away from the wall as if pushed by unseen hands. Her heart slammed in her ears and hot bile hit the back of her throat. In returning to her chair, she lost control of her bladder.

'Good. We understand each other. That saves a lot of unnecessary discussion.'

The man who was not Neil Jamieson leant back in her chair and played idly with her keyboard. From her isolation in the centre of the carpet, the technician saw him open and examine the file she had spent all afternoon creating. It was not a short document and many of the concepts were of a technical nature. She sat in silence and watched him page down and frown and page back up again to read the sections he hadn't grasped first time. At length he closed the window and picked up the knife.

'Tell me,' he said, 'if I can pay you to find me the address of Orla McLeod's mother, what makes you think there is a safe house at which you can hide?'

She felt her jaw slacken and fought to bring it shut. Her breathing was coming shorter, whistling through her nose as it would after a run. It was a long time since she had thought about running. Her guts burned.

The man nodded. 'Quite. So I will tell you that you have been visited today by Murdo Cameron and Orla McLeod. There is no harm in that. If I hadn't wanted them to see you, they would not have left your home alive. Admittedly you might well have died in the crossfire but that's the price we all pay for fame and fortune.' He smiled again and she thought she might faint. He leant forward across the desk. The knife lay to one side, shining dully in the light of her desk lamp. For the space of a heartbeat, she wondered if she could move before he could. His eyes caught hers and held them. In the photograph, they had been unexceptional, a neutral grey to match the neutral hair. In life, they were crystalline green, the colour of sintered glass. 'Ms Morgan, do I seem to you the kind of man to take unnecessary risks?'

She sat still, paralysed by the eyes as much as the question. He angled his head, demanding an answer.

She said, 'No.'

'No.' He stood up. 'Unlike you. I would say you have spent a good part of your day taking some quite exceptional risks.' He moved back to stand with his shoulders to the wall, half a room away from his blade. There was no risk in that. If he had handed her a gun and put her finger on the trigger, she would not have had the strength of mind to pull it.

'What did she threaten you with,' he asked. 'Me?'

She nodded. It seemed enough.

'Excellent.' He smiled at the compliment. 'So then we know that it works.'

He moved like flowing water. He was beside her, his fingers drifting down her cheek. His other hand held the back of her head so that she couldn't move away. She sobbed aloud.

He knelt down by the chair, as the woman had done. She could see the fine, tight pores on the skin of his cheeks, the shadow of an old scar, very faint, across the bridge of his nose. His eyes had flecks of grey marbling the green. 'You're alive, Gail. Don't ever underestimate how wonderful that is.' His hand still gripped her head. The vibration of his words hummed down the length of her spine. 'And don't forget how truly appalling it can be if circumstances change.' The hand moved down to her neck and the touch of his fingertip burned her. 'Do you remember what you read of Luke Tyler?' he asked.

'Yes.'

'Good. He lived for six hours longer than he would have liked. When I leave, you will measure six hours and imagine it. And then you will remember that he died because I said that he could. If I have to come back for you, six hours will be the beginning. Do you understand me?'

Her eyes must have answered, she was beyond speech or movement. He nodded anyway, then stood up and backed away. 'So – I have something I want you to do for me before I go. There is a man I need to find. A dead man.' A slip of paper fluttered onto her keyboard. She watched it fall in the way she would watch a falling leaf, with detachment and little interest. She made no move to read it.

He sighed; a sound on the edge of patience. 'Gail, the sooner you do it, the sooner I will leave. I am sure that would suit us both.'

The tip of the knife tapped on the desk and it came to her in a sliding flow of terror that he wanted her to work, to think, to function, to be everything her reputation – her *notoriety* – said she could be. He had, indeed, moved round behind her chair and was pushing her to the desk. In the park, with the threat of him made but not near, she could do it. Here, in her own home, with the blade inches from her eye, and his hand on her neck, she was a child, facing the wrath of her father; too numb with terror to speak, to think, to act, to explain, to exculpate the nightmare. She opened her mouth and the noise she made was the incoherent babble of a child. She bent her head and tears splashed on her wrists.

He must have dealt with this before. It must, indeed, become increasingly common, the paralysing, incapacitating terror his presence induced. Like everything else, his way of dealing with it was direct. Before she realised he had gone, there was a coffee in her hand and she was drinking it. A cold cloth wiped her face. Her shower was turned on and she was assisted into it with a calm, impersonal efficiency. The clothes he found for her were clean and dry. In all of this, his presence shrank, the threat diminished so that by the time she was dry and dressed, she was coherent and no longer weeping and could talk through the hiccoughs and smile when he asked her to as she would have smiled for her father under similar circumstances. When he wheeled her back to her computer, she could remember how to place her hands on the keyboard and what to do. The slip of paper had been clipped to her copy arm and she could read the single name. It was not one with which she was familiar.

'Start in Glasgow,' he said. 'He lived here, he may well have died here. If we're lucky it will have been at one of the hospitals and there will be a pathology report. If that draws a blank, go through the major cities by size.'

Her fingers lay motionless on the keys. Her mind grasped the sheer size of the task. What he was asking was not difficult; any child could do it. But the scope . . . She said, 'This could take all night.'

He smiled thinly. 'If it takes only one night, I will be a very happy man indeed.'

He sat back in her armchair and picked a magazine from the pile at the side. 'Try not to waste more time than you have to.'

The clock on the monitor moved past midnight and into a new day. Outside, the fog gave way to rain and then to a cold clarity that could move to snow or to frost at the whim of the gods. Inside, he made her coffee hourly and listened to the radio, keeping the volume down so that it didn't break her concentration. Just after three, she found the thing he wanted.

'Aberdeen,' she said. 'He died last year in hospital in Aberdeen.'

'Really?' The radio snapped off. He was beside her, fingering the keys, reading the page and the one after that. If he needed sleep, it didn't show. When he had finished, he took back the sheet of paper, tore it up and replaced the fragments in his pocket. He raised a hand to his brow in salute. 'Thank you. You are as good as they say.' She made no attempt to reply.

He let himself out. At the doorway, he turned. 'An electrician will call round tomorrow morning to repair your cameras,' he said. 'Don't talk to him.'

'And the police?' She had been thinking as she worked. She needed orders that were clear. 'What do I tell the police?'

The knife was nowhere to be seen. He could have been a late-night guest taking his leave. 'If the police come, you know nothing. I suspect that Orla McLeod will shortly be too busy to bother you again; however if she or Murdo Cameron *does* comes back, let them threaten you and then show them everything you have found for me tonight. Don't tell them I told you to do it. I would prefer them to believe they have access to it against my will. Just bear in mind that I will know what she has asked and what you have said. If you are intelligent, you will be safe.'

Eleven

Jamie Buchanan lit the fire that Tord Svensen had laid. It flared brightly as the match touched the twists of paper and burned up through the kindling and small logs. Larger logs, lately split, lay to one side. He fed them to the flames, one at a time, balancing them at an angle over the core. It was an absorbing task and he was left to do it as he felt right while the adults sat in fractured silence around him, waiting for the phone to ring.

It had been a day of fractured silences, of awkward, uncomfortable moments and unfinished sentences, of shifting tensions and eyes sliding from contact, of tempers held tight, but not quite tight enough. Of the incomers, only the young man with the freckles and the copper hair had taken time to talk and make sense. Up at the mountain he had drawn a diagram in his notebook of the skid marks on the road and shown the child how you could tell the speed Andy was driving at and the order in which things had gone wrong. Later, at the Connollys' yard, where the Land Rover sat high on the hydraulic ramps over the inspection pit, he had lifted him up to see the scored marks on the wheel hubs where the bullets had hit and had explained, sketching with chalk on the concrete, how they could work out the angle of the shots and that this, together with the scored tyre marks, let them build a picture of the last few seconds of Andy Bennett's fight with the wheel before he lost control and the whole thing fell down the mountainside.

In between all of that was the change in Orla and Murdo. They were *together* again in the way they had been in the hotel before Andy came and it occurred to him slowly, over the course of the day, that this had nothing at all to do with the way they were dressed and everything to do with the way they behaved. There was a sharpness to them, a precision to the way they moved so that the child found that he became, with Morag, the centre of a web that wove and re-wove throughout the afternoon and evening. Watching, he saw the time when Morag became aware of it and, later, the man Strang who was, less definably, an outer thread in the weaving.

It was the same in the cottage. Unlike other nights, the child was not left alone with his fire. Murdo pulled the two fireside chairs together and sat with Morag to his left so that he guarded both her and Jamie from the rest of the room. His laptop lay open on the table in front of him and Morag leant inwards, her arm resting on his leg. Every once in a while she would point at something on the screen and say, 'A bit leaner beneath the eyes,' or 'Maybe not so fleshy under the cheekbones,' and the keys would tap or a thumb would move on the track pad and the wash of colours flickering across her face would change to reflect the new picture they were building.

Orla stayed at the edge of the circle. She sat on the window ledge at the far side of the living room, one knee clasped up to her chest and the other dangling down the wall. Outside, the evening had darkened so that, gradually, her hair became invisible against the backdrop of the night and her face, beneath it, dissolved in the shadows. The clock on the upper landing struck eight. As the last chimes fell into the silence, she turned away from the window and said, 'Why are we waiting? We know who it was.' Her voice was cool and measured. Her whole being was still.

'We need confirmation,' said Strang. 'I can't authorise anything without it.' He, too, was preserving the illusion of calm on the surface.

'How long are you going to wait?'

'As long as it takes.' He tipped his head right back over the top of his chair so that his glasses fell to his forehead and said, 'Art? How much longer?'

The young man with the copper hair was eating reheated pasta by the range. He took off his glasses and rubbed his wrist across his eyes. The light from the kitchen fired his hair red and bleached his freckles to nothing. The skin beneath them showed the patterned blue of exhaustion.

'I called Martha before I left the Connollys' yard,' he said. 'She got a complete set of prints from the gun and the mug and she's running them now. We'll have confirmation inside the hour.'

Of them all, he was the one most easily read. He was cold and tired and hungry and could have done with a bed now, not at the end of a long drive back to Glasgow. Still, he had given his report before he had eaten and it was as concise and ordered as his chalk drawing on the concrete: the skid marks at the corner of the road on the mountain confirmed three blow-outs, in the front right, rear right and rear left wheels respectively, probably in that order; there was a recently used vantage point in the woods above the road in which a putative sniper could have lain in wait but there remained no forensic evidence to prove any connection to the crash. Samples of grass and conifer loam had been taken from the area for microscopic analysis but it seemed likely that the individual concerned had used plastic sheeting and thus denied them access to any legally relevant evidence; there was, however, clear evidence on the Land Rover sitting in the Connollys' yard to confirm that each of the three wheels had been shot at. This last examination had been performed late and was not complete. The young forensics officer had removed the hubs for further investigation and was confident that, given time and the facilities available to him in Glasgow, he would be able to provide more detail on the ballistics, including the angle and distance of shot. In the absence of these, his initial assessment was, nevertheless, in accordance with the views of the man who had chosen to call himself Neil Jamieson; namely that Andrew Bennett's crash was neither an accident nor carelessness, that he had been targeted and taken out with professional efficiency and that the killer had left no useful clues to his identity. What he could not tell them, nor could anyone else when asked, was why Bennett was still alive when a single head shot would have killed him. Why, indeed, it was Bennett who had been called out and targeted when, a day or two earlier, the man could as easily have lain in the shadows of the pines on the hill and taken out the entire family, Murdo and Orla included, as they walked out of the back door in the morning.

They had been considering the possibility of that when the timer had gone for Art's pasta and, by the time he was settled in his seat by the range, the conversation lay dead in the water and no one felt moved to revive it. That was when Murdo had plugged in his computer and sat down with Morag to make a face that would fit, Alec Strang had pulled a chair away from the wall and folded his newspaper to a new page, and Jamie Buchanan had settled down at the hearth to light the fire.

Now, a while later, he was pleased with the result. The logs burned with all the ferocity of late winter wood. Hard frosts and slow thaws had opened the timber, drying it to a brittle lightness so that it burned fast, with a clear flame and little ash. The boy thought of the night ahead and the logs his fire could eat. He stood up, stretching the stiffness from his knees, and tapped the dog on the shoulder. Together, they wove a way through the chairs to the back door and out to the wood shed. It was dark outside. The wind blew warmly from the south, balancing the lack of cloud cover so that the ground was free of frost. The logs Morag had split in the morning lay to one side of the cutting block. He chose three, stacked them in a triangular heap and shovelled them onto his braced arms. The dog picked a fourth and carried it lopsided, banging on the ground at his side.

He had thought he might be allowed to do it alone but it was not so. As he turned, he found that Murdo had joined him; he stood on the far side of the log pile, looking up into the dark of the hillside. Orla was in the doorway, leaning sideways against the wooden doorpost, watching back into the house and forward into the night, keeping the web intact. Nothing was said. No one acknowledged that they had seen him go out or suggested that they might be concerned. When the dog clattered past Alec Strang, he banged his log on the side of his shin. No one said anything about that, either. The pressure might have been less if they had.

'Jamie?' Morag understood. Smiling, she beckoned him from her place by Murdo's chair. 'Sweetheart, we've made a picture of the man who was here this morning. Murdo wants to change his hair so that he looks more like he did before. It would help if you could show him what colour it should be. Could you do that for him?'

He could. He thought about it while he laid the logs in the basket by the hearth and retrieved the one from Bran before he could do any more damage. When he was happy with the way his fire was burning, he went over to her and stood at her left shoulder. Murdo came back to his chair. He had poured himself tea from the pot on the range but the milk was going off. Fatty lumps of it swirled in circles on the surface. Jamie noticed and considered telling him and decided it wasn't his business.

The tall man sat down and gestured to the computer creation. 'Is that him?' he asked.

The boy nodded. The face on the screen could have been a photograph. If he had done it, he would have made the hair wilder and the eyes less friendly but it was the same man, without question. Murdo said, 'He wasn't like that when you first saw him, though, was he?'

No. He was not like that. Jamie shook his head with emphasis.

'Was his hair lighter than that?'

It was. The boy pointed to his own head, to the hair at the side of his temple, where it was lightest. Murdo moved his pointer to a menu at the top and made the screen display a selection of blondes. 'Show me,' he said.

He leaned over and moved the pointer to the one that looked right but when Murdo hit another button and the new hair replaced the old, it was too strong, too yellow, too much like the sun. He shook his head and took control of the pointer and they went back and did it again and then again until he was happy with the overall shade. After that, Murdo moved the image so they could look down on the head from the top and they put the crown in at the back and to the left and shaded the hair round it slightly darker than the rest as it had looked from a tenement window in the strange light of a frozen evening.

When they came back to the front view, the man still had grey eyes. Jamie pointed to them and shook his head.

Murdo looked at him and frowned. 'The eyes are wrong, are they? How do you know that?'

Because he did. He pointed again. Murdo pulled down another menu. The palette this time showed the full range of all possible eyes. Jamie began to search through them. In doing so, he became aware that he had an audience. The man Strang had folded his newspaper in four and laid it on the table. Art Gould had finished his dinner and brought his coffee – without milk – to the hearthside. Orla had stopped watching the stars. Of them all, only Murdo hadn't changed. He sipped his tea. If he noticed the state of the milk, it didn't show. He said, 'If you know the colour of his eyes, then you must have seen him face on. Am I right?'

The boy nodded abstractedly. He was scanning through a hundred small pictures of irises, trying to find the right one. He had not wanted to be the centre of attention. It was easier, in many ways, when they ignored him.

'Jamie, was this before or after he did . . . what he did to Luke?' Orla's voice came from behind him. It would have been useful to see her face. He lifted his eyes from the screen. The biggest log had fallen into the centre of the fire and was burning faster than he had expected. He thought of putting on another and decided not. Behind him, Orla waited. 'Was it afterwards, Jamie? Did he look up at you from the snow?'

The snow. He remembered the snow. He remembered a man standing beneath his window, watching the car arrive, watching the strangers, who were no longer strange, run up the stairs. The man had looked up at him and waved before he walked out across the wasteland. That was when his hair was wild. The boy nodded.

Orla said, 'Did you really get a good look at his eyes when he was in the snow, Jamie?'

He had seen his eyes, but not the real colour of them. Not when the only light was orange. He shook his head.

'So you saw them before. Was it in the morning, when he came to talk to Luke?'

The morning had been cold, much more cold than the rest. He had worn his big socks and been laughed at. Before that, he had stood in the last warmth of the stairwell and looked out into the fresh snow of the morning. The man with the blond hair had stepped out of a car and walked past him, walking fast and smoothly, as if his joints were better oiled than those of the men in the flat. He had smiled then, too, and shown his two squint teeth, but not his eyes. The boy shook his head.

Silence fell again, which was good. He turned his attention back to the eyes on the screen. There was a colour of green that he wanted and which the machine did not have.

Alec Strang said, 'I thought you said he hadn't been to the flat before?' He was talking to Orla.

She said, 'I thought he hadn't,' and then, 'Jamie? Did you see the man another time, not in the morning or in the afternoon?'

Of course. He nodded for that.

'But it was that same day?'

Yes. A nod.

He found a shade that was almost right. He used the tracker pad to point to it and Murdo leant across to put the eyes in the picture. It was close. Not perfect, but close. He played with the pointer, trying to find a way to make the colour change.

'Was it at lunchtime that you saw him, Jamie?'

Orla was not so still now. He looked up at her. She was watching Murdo and they were trying to understand something complicated. He nodded.

'At lunchtime? You're sure about that?'

There was a time when he would have abandoned her for asking the same question twice. Now, he was a different person. He nodded a second time and pointed at her face, white as it was, and made a box of his fingers and held it to his eye like a camera and said 'Picture', very clearly. And then, with no idea how he had done it, he saw the floor fall out from under her.

In a while, when the quiet had lasted long enough, Murdo asked, 'Whose picture?' He was not asking Jamie. Orla had moved. She was kneeling now, at the edge of the hearth rug with the heel of one hand pressed to her forehead and her fingers clenching and unclenching in her hair. She said, 'Mine. Ours. Both of us. Jared and Trent were fucking about with a Polaroid. They burst in on Luke and me before we were up – just after Svensen left. I'd forgotten about it. It was horseplay. I thought it was horseplay. I wasn't even sure they'd got a picture.' She was watching the fire. She, too, could see the big log burning up in the

255

middle that would take the heart out of it. The boy slid away from the table and went to balance it up.

Alec Strang said, 'Did they have a camera before then?'

'No.' It was a whisper. A thin, white reed of a word. The man heard it and knew where she was and he pushed her anyway.

'He knew what Luke looked like,' he said. 'There was only you he hadn't seen. Not without the war paint, anyway.' He turned to the boy. 'Jamie, where did you see him? Was it near the school?'

The boy looked at him and said nothing.

'He doesn't go to school,' said Orla wearily. 'He hasn't been for years. How could he?'

She had reached some kind of base where the falling stopped. At least it was stable. Without moving her eyes from the flames, she asked, 'Was it at Rose's place, Jamie?'

Of course. Where else would it be? He made sure she knew that before he went back to his fire.

Strang said, 'Where?'

'There's a café round the corner next to the petrol station. The kids hang out there if they've not gone to school. It was where we used to buy . . .' And so she found the final piece of the jigsaw. 'It was Jared, wasn't it? When he went down to get fags? He brought the picture to Tord Svensen in Rose's café at lunchtime when Luke sent him out to stock up on cigarettes.'

Yes. He smiled it for her because she was hurt. Art Gould was still frowning, still trying to put together the pieces. But then he had not been at the flat and seen what she looked like. He hadn't seen the time she spent on the make-up every morning after she got out of bed – the effort she made to hide the scars, or the eyes that she put in to keep all attention away from the places where they showed. 'I don't see . . .' he began.

Quite gently, Murdo said, 'We have been running in circles looking for a leak, for someone who betrayed Orla and Luke to Svensen. Now it looks as if perhaps there isn't one.'

'I don't see how a photograph could make the difference.'

'No,' said Murdo. 'Neither do we.' And that was when the phone rang.

They had been waiting for it all evening and when it came, nobody moved. The thing purred into the silence and only the dog turned its head.

Morag, as lady of the house, took the call. She listened, nodded and handed it to Strang who took it through to the kitchen. He said one word and that wasn't distinctive.

Orla had not moved. She was hollow now, a shell with a voice. Whatever things she was watching in the hearth, they were not the flames and the logs.

The boy left his fire to its own devices. He would have done anything, then, to make her better, to fill in the hollow and make her whole. She looked at him and tried to smile. It didn't work. He sat on her knee and put an arm round her neck and pressed his lips close to her ear to make a whisper. '*Orla, we could—*'

'Orla.'

Her head turned away from him. Strang walked back from the kitchen and he looked as if he was about to be sick. He was not white, his skin was not the kind to go white when he was ill. He was pale yellow, like freshly cut wood. He stopped, stranded in the space behind the chairs. Five pairs of eyes met his.

'Orla, I . . .' He dried up and gathered himself and then tried again. 'Morag, I think you should . . . I think it might be better if you took the lad upstairs.'

'No.' It was Orla who spoke. Jamie felt the change in her, like electricity flowing through so that suddenly she was not hollow at all and it was Strang who had managed it, not him. He recognised the feel of her. She did not have need of him to make her whole again. He climbed down off her knee and went back to the fire.

'She's gone this far,' said Orla. 'They both have. They can stay a few minutes longer.'

'You don't know—'

'No. But waiting isn't helping.'

Strang still had the phone in his hands, the cord trailing behind him to the wall. He sat down on one of the hard chairs by the big table, holding it sideways between his knees. 'The prints from the gun and the mug match the partial print on the shell case,' he said. 'That means we can place the man who called himself Neil Jamieson at the site of Luke's death.'

Murdo said, 'So we can prove that Jamieson is Svensen?'

'Effectively, yes.'

'But?' asked Orla. Her eyes were very wide. Even in the dancing light of the fire, the pupils had dilated out all the way to the rim.

'Martha ran the prints through to Scotland Yard. We have another match from their data base. It gives us a name.' He was looking at Morag. 'I really think you should go.'

'No.' She had moved so she was standing behind her daughter, her hands on her shoulders, her fingers working at the muscles underneath. 'Just say it,' she said. 'Say the name.'

'Colm O'Neil. Colm Connaught O'Neil.'

'Right.'

As far as the child could see, Orla had stopped breathing. Her mother's fingers had stopped their work on her shoulders and lay very still. Both of them together could have been paintings on canvas.

Strang said, 'I'm sorry. I'm so very sorry. We didn't know he was out. They sent us the lists of names, twenty, thirty at a time. It went into a file and came no further. I don't know why—'

'But he shouldn't be out,' said Orla. Her brow had wrinkled, quizzically, as if she was studying an insect found with one too many legs and was having difficulty understanding how it could be so. 'It's not twenty-five years yet,' she said. 'They gave him twenty-five years minimum, no parole, no remission.'

'He was one of the early releases. Part of the Good Friday Agreement. They let him out in the summer. Two months later, we had the first hit by Tord Svensen in Glasgow.'

'You're saying Tord Svensen is Colm O'Neil?' It was Art who asked.

'It would seem so.'

'He's Irish. Why have we been looking for a Swede?'

'Or a Finn. Or a Dane. Or somewhere else far away from Ireland where the English sounds slightly odd but not enough to put your finger on.' Murdo had his fingers pressed on either side of his temples, circling slowly. 'Everyone notices his accent,' he said. 'It isn't right but it isn't easy to work out why not. People are lazy, they'll accept what they're told. They have a blond man with a Nordic name and they didn't look further. *We* didn't look further.'

'Then who is Colm O'Neil?'

Morag sat down in the spare chair by the fire. 'He was a Scots Catholic of Irish origin brought over from Glasgow by the loyalists to kill a visiting American senator with Republican sympathies.' She smiled tightly. 'Don't look at me like that, Art, you're not supposed to understand. Just believe it was normal for Ulster.'

'What has he got to do with you?'

Murdo said, 'He's the man Orla's father was prosecuting when he was shot.'

'They wanted him to drop the case,' said Orla tonelessly. 'My father never dropped a case in his life.'

Her eyes were on the fire again and she was watching the way it had collapsed in as they were talking. Jamie put his three new logs in a triangle over the big one in the middle, making a tepee. One of them had been cut on a bad angle and wouldn't sit properly. He played with the tongs, trying to get it steady. When he looked at Orla again, she was frowning into the fire in a way that suggested he had not got it right. Her mother was saying, 'O'Neil was convicted after the killings. Whatever they thought about him before, there wasn't a jury in the six counties would have found him innocent after he'd had those two kill one child and maim another. And then there was Orla's picture in the papers, they ran it time after time, the whole series of "before and after" from the moment she went into hospital to the day she came out. He will have seen those in his cell. The guards will have made sure of that.'

The dog was sitting with Morag, his head on her knee. Jamie slipped past them both, through the kitchen and out to the wood pile to collect some more logs. There was some cloud cover now, high and fast, and it covered the moon as he walked. At the chopping block he stood still, waiting for it to clear so there would be enough light to see by. It would have been easier with a torch but then he would have had one hand less for the wood. He watched the line of moonlight move across the wall towards him.

'Jamie?' It was a voice that he knew, even at a whisper. He stopped. A figure stepped forward out of the shadows by the shed. The cloud moved the last few paces so the moonlight bathed them both and he could see that the gun pointing at him was small and blunt-nosed, like the one Orla carried in the pocket of her jacket. He laid the logs down where they had come from. The gun followed the line of his heart down and back up again and then it twitched sideways towards the path. 'Good lad. This way and not too much noise. It's not far to the car.'

No one could say, afterwards, exactly when he had gone. Orla remembered the arm on her neck and the face pressed close to hers with its half started whisper of secrets into her ear. Her mother remembered him moving the logs. Murdo thought he might have gone out to get more and they checked but he wasn't there and there was no sign of him having been. They lost time searching the bedroom and turning over the rest of the house, calling and looking, in case it was simply that they had thrown too much at him in one night and he'd gone to find safety and peace somewhere else. The dog was no use at all. They said the boy's name, over and over so the beast spun in circles, but only once did it put its nose to the ground and follow a trail and that was in the pitch black of the night, down the lane behind the wood shed. They brought out torches and searched and found nothing but tyre tracks in the mud and even Art Gould couldn't say if they were new or had been made by his own car in arriving. Later, they called the Manse and the hotel, and Hugh Carlaw and Angus Shearer called other people and every able-bodied man and woman still out of bed brought their torches and their gas lamps and their dogs and searched the shoreline and the paths and the hillside. Later still, when the rest of the village had given up and gone back to their beds or their drinking, Orla and Murdo walked up through the woods in case he had decided to go and make tracks of his own in the melting remains of the snow. They didn't believe it. They were not expecting to find him. But they had to try.

Morag McLeod was a strong woman. Nevertheless, sitting alone in front of the dying fire at three o'clock in the morning, waiting for her daughter's voice and her footsteps on the path, she felt the threads of her courage slipping through her fingers. Earlier, when Alec Strang and his younger colleague had left, she had poured herself a glass of the dark Scotch that kept the voices of her past at bay. The sound of the men's departing was still echoing in her ears when she got up and poured it down the sink. It was not a night to be silencing voices, nor to escape from reality. For a while she tried to knit but that avenue, too, was closed. In the end, she simply sat with her fingers locked together and watched the logs burn to white ash in the hearth.

The dog lay at her side, subdued by the night and the chaos. He heard the sound of voices before she did and went to stand at the door in greeting. Morag filled the kettle that she had filled and refilled all through the day and set it on the hotplate on the range. In the last moments of waiting, she came as close to weeping as she had done since before the boy had been taken.

Murdo came in first. He did not have Jamie but then she knew that from the sound of their steps on the path. He stood in the doorway and looked round at the empty room. 'Where's Strang?' he asked. 'And Art?'

Morag said, 'They've gone back to Glasgow.' Her voice was level. She heard it and felt some relief.

Murdo looked over his shoulder and spoke to the shape behind him. 'He's left.'

'I know. His car has gone from the barn.' Her daughter spoke from the porch. It was too early to tell how she was. Murdo was leaning on the frame, levering the heel of one boot against the toe of the other. At first Morag thought he looked as the others had done before they left; exhausted and frustrated and angry and desperately trying to think too many moves ahead in a game of chess where the enemy has hijacked

261

the board and everything on it. With time to study him she realised she was looking at a man carrying one too many promises, deciding within himself which ones he will break. Even so, when he looked up and found her watching, he smiled and it brightened the night. 'Thank you for staying up,' he said.

'You're welcome but it's not entirely voluntary. I have a message for you.'

'From Strang?' Orla pushed past him to stand in her muddy boots on the bare wood of the floor. Her hair was wet from the forest and plastered tight to her head. Her face was pinched with cold and lack of sleep and the battering of the day but there was still time left to pretend that it was a simple homecoming from a hard night and that the world could be made whole by her presence.

Morag McLeod was a mother before she was anything else. She opened her arms. 'Orla.'

'Mum.' Because she was a daughter and it was her mother she faced, Orla McLeod made no effort to hide the things going on inside. Her mother's smile died on her lips.

'Orla, please. Don't go.' She said it without thinking, moved without planning to, did the things she had promised herself she would not. Her daughter was warm in her arms and her cheek burned against hers. Cool fingers wound tight in her hair and dry lips pressed to her forehead. 'I can't not, Mum. Don't ask.'

Orla sat down on the floor to take her boots off. The dog stood at her shoulder, pushing his nose in her ear. She made no effort to fend him off. 'Do you want to give us the message?' she said gently.

'Don't you know it?'

'Possibly.' She looked up at Murdo who had moved past them both to wash his hands at the sink.

He said, 'Strang wants us to stay here and look after you because the one thing worse than losing Jamie would be losing Jamie and Morag together. Is that it?'

'Yes. He said I was to remind you that you were off the case and of the reasons why. And if that didn't work, I was to ask about Jacob Turner and get one of you to tell me who he is.'

'Was,' said Murdo. 'Past tense. He was a pimp who challenged Svensen's ascendancy in Glasgow and paid for it with his life.'

Orla said, 'He was a man who let himself be goaded into making a mistake.'

'And are you not being goaded just the same?' asked her mother. 'O'Neil shot at Andy but he didn't kill him. Why else but to get you back here? He left you his fingerprints so you would find out who he was. He took Jamie because that's the one thing in the world that really matters to you. The man is playing games with you, Orla. Do you have to dance to his tune?'

'I'm not dancing to anyone's tune.' Orla still sat on the floor. The socks she had worn under the boots were her mother's and there was a darn at one heel with a thread loose. She twisted it, trying to push the long end back under the stitching. It was a thing Jamie would have done. She looked up and her smile was heavy with irony. 'If it makes you feel better, I can promise you now I am not going to die the way Jake Turner died.'

Behind her, Murdo poured coffee badly. Both of them heard the bash of the spout on the edge of a mug and a curse, cut off half done. He said, 'Orla, Jamie could be dead by now.'

'Possibly. I don't think he is.' Orla took off the socks, folded them and slid them into her boots. Every action now had the flavour of ritual, something to be savoured and stored against famine. Turning to her mother, she said, 'Does he think we'll do what he says?'

'Strang? No.' He hadn't said it in so many words but she had known it and the implications of that knowledge had been eating at her since he first explained what was happening. The certainty of it settled like cold lead in her abdomen.

Without expecting it to make a difference, Morag said, 'I am to make it clear that if you do go back to Glasgow then you are completely on your own. If he can, Strang will have you picked up and held until it's safe to let you go. He has given the description of Murdo's car to the traffic police with orders to pick it up and hold whoever's driving it. If you get past him, then clearly he can't guarantee to help if you get into trouble.' She paused. Her daughter was pulling on her running shoes. Dried mud crumbled under her fingers and dusted the floor. Murdo was searching for a fresh bottle of milk in the fridge. Each of them was lost in their own world. Strang's message passed them by, untouched. 'Why?' asked Morag. 'I don't understand why he is leaving you like this.'

Orla said, 'Because this is the way he always works. There are some things he can't be seen to condone.'

'And you going after Jamie now is one of them?'

'Yes. If I get him back, it will be because Colm O'Neil is dead. Strang can't be seen to give that kind of order.'

'And if you don't get him?'

'Then he has one more bit of evidence for the prosecution. I'll do what I can to make sure there's enough left lying around to make it stick.'

Morag pressed her hands to her eyes. It was not a brave or a useful gesture but it was necessary under the circumstances. Too many things made no sense on too many levels. Past, present and blood-stained future screamed to a collision she had no power to prevent. Something hard knocked on the table and a hand touched her arm. Murdo had brought a mug of coffee she didn't want. He placed it in front of her and sat down at the far side of the table. His eyes were angry and kind and held some of the things she was feeling. He took her hands and wrapped them round the mug and wouldn't let go until she had lifted and drunk.

When she spoke, Morag chose her words with great care. 'Your father spent the last years of his life speaking out against a security apparatus that thought it had the right to shoot dead the people who stood against it,' she said. 'He gave his life so that Colm O'Neil would go to prison. Do you really think he would want his daughter to take up her gun and shoot the man now?'

In the shocked silence that followed, Morag McLeod watched her daughter's head snap up and read the changing fire in her eyes. In all the rows, major and minor of adolescence and adulthood, neither of them had ever used the names of their dead against the other. Some things are sacrosanct, too precious to taint with the banalities of life. Knowing that she was breaking the last of her own taboos and that the damage to both of them might be irreparable, she said, 'Are you going after this man for your father and Ciaran? Or are you doing it for Luke?'

Orla McLeod stood slowly, pushing her back against the sink. The part of her that was thirteen years old yearned for peace and not to be so frightened. She knew from experience that, given time and space on her own, she could contain it sufficiently not to affect her actions. The part that was adult yearned not to create any more pain in the people she loved, which was quite different and she had no idea how to achieve it.

She crossed the room to her mother and took her hands between her palms. There was always a better connection when their hands touched. She crouched down so she could read the creasing of lines around the eyes, the fractional tensing of the jaw, the dozen other small things that made her mother who she was and made her readable. 'Neither,' she said, gently. 'This is not for any of the dead. This is because I have already broken two promises to a child.'

They moved quickly after that. It was clear that the discussion, the arguments, the pleas had all been made and countered on the walk back from the forest. There was nothing further Morag could say that Murdo had not said before her and she would not demean them both by asking again. So she found herself sitting at the table twisting empty fingers while Murdo checked her daughter's gun and Orla put through a phone call to Hugh Carlaw and asked, with the politeness required in asking a favour at half past three in the morning, whether she could borrow for a short while one of the three cars that he kept in his garage.

She took the stairs two at a time, lightly, and they heard her changing, as she had done once before although she was faster this time and did not bother to shower. When she reappeared at the foot of the stairs, she was wearing clean jeans and a nondescript shirt and a black leather jacket that would merge with the crowd anywhere she chose to go. Her hair was still black and still lay tight to her head and her eyes were the jackdaw grey she was born with.

Surprised, Morag said, 'Don't you need to look different?'

'I don't think so,' said her daughter. 'This time I want him to know who I am.'

Twelve

Friday, 28 March

'Are you awake?'

The rain was starting; small drops, like flecks of spit, hurled themselves in tightening spirals at the windscreen. The wipers moved intermittently, smearing them sideways to make a thin angled line that bisected his vision. The boy sat still and said nothing.

'She isn't coming for you now. Staring at the night won't make any difference.' The words spun in the vortex of the wind outside. The wind tore them apart and the fragments made no sense.

The man smiled and shrugged and drove on. They passed the service station where the boy had first seen the mountains and Murdo had bought him a burger. This time they didn't stop. Instead, the man drank from a hot flask and offered it sideways. The boy watched the swirling of rain in the headlights and made no move to acknowledge the offer. The flask was withdrawn and the cap replaced. The man said, 'What do you know about tiger traps, Jamie?'

Nothing. The boy looked out of the side window and counted trees.

'No. Never mind, I'll tell you. Tigers are immensely dangerous. There are two good ways to trap them. The first method uses a goat; the bleating of the goat attracts the tiger. Kipling wrote that. Do you know Kipling?'

The boy noted the different types of tree lining the road and the fact that the cloud layer was rising as they came down from the mountain.

The man said, 'I don't suppose they teach him at school any more, too English and colonial. Forget it. The point is that it only works if you have a goat that will bleat. If you don't, then you need to go for the second, more dangerous, option which is to wait by the water hole. Even tigers need to drink and if you can hide amongst the crowd of other animals at the edge of the forest near the water hole, you can shoot the beast before it realises you're there. The problem with that, obviously, is that if it sees you first, you're dead.'

The man paused in his story to unscrew the flask and drink again. He didn't offer it across. On the dashboard ahead of him, a green light blinked suddenly red and bleeped. The man watched it intently for a moment or two, frowning, and then reached into the back seat and brought forward a map. 'Hold this for me, can you?'

The boy held the map. The man switched on the overhead light and read it as he was driving. The thing on the dashboard bleeped again, more urgently. The blinking speeded to something like a flutter. The man smiled and said, 'Ah, now that *is* clever,' and started searching the road for somewhere to turn so that, very soon, they were going back the way they had come. At the next T-junction, they turned left. The blinking light settled from amber back to green. The man settled back in his seat, easing his shoulders. He drove with more care, keeping one eye on the dashboard and the other on the road and turned his mind again to his story.

'Where were we? Hunting tigers ... The problem we have, Jamie, is that the beast we're hunting is far more lethal than any tiger. Tigers are predictable, this is not. Tigers at least look like tigers and you can find them if you know where to look. This beast is like a chameleon, it changes all the time; it changes what it looks like, it changes its name, it changes the way it speaks. It changes everything, in fact, except what it does best – which is to kill the people it doesn't like. Sadly for all of us, I am one of the people it doesn't like.'

The man made a story of jungle beasts for a child who had watched threefold death spread out across the floor of his mother's living room. He tipped his head to the side to see the effect he was having. The boy looked straight ahead through the windscreen and watched the rain fall faster.

The man said, 'You should pay attention to this, Jamie. The key to understanding the world is to look at things from other people's points of view. In my case, I am not ready to die and yet, if I leave the beast alive, it will kill me. There are very few certainities in life but that is one of them. So, like Kipling and his tiger, we are setting the trap. In the beginning, without a goat, I had to find a water hole. Morag was my water hole – did you guess that? One of the few predictable elements of this particular tiger is its attachment to the things of its past. All I had to do was watch her and see when the beast appeared, which it did, right on cue although not quite in the way I had imagined. Then a miracle happened. They say that the gods help those who help themselves and it seems to be true. Just when I needed it most, they gave me a goat.'

They reached a crossroads. He turned left and the light on the dashboard blinked a steady green. He parked the car at the kerb.

'We'll wait here for a while. It may be that there is no need to go any further.' He turned in the seat to look at the child. 'We're not in the jungle, Jamie. We're in the real world, but nevertheless, you are not just a goat, you're a magical goat. In the normal way of things, you need the goat in the trap to catch the tiger. This trap is very remarkable because it works the other way round. Simply by *not* being where you should be, you are the thing that will spring the trap for me. You should be glad. It's a very powerful thing to be able to do.'

She could have wished the morning to be less ugly. Driving through the centre of Glasgow in the pre-light of dawn, the filth of it clung to the car, assaulting the senses. Rain drizzled half-heartedly onto the pavements. Early commuters choked the roads with noise and carbon monoxide. The overnight sleepers lay in shop doorways, wrapped in borrowed clothes and charity sleeping bags, sleeping off the drink. At Maria Kilbride's flat, the curtains were drawn and the milk bottles stood on the step; fresh marking posts for the neighbourhood dogs. She parked outside and sat watching the windows for signs of life. Somewhere beneath the cascading fear, she felt a measure of guilt for Hugh Carlaw that he would not see his smart car back again but it was not a feeling to last and other things counted for more: the feel of her mother's kiss, still sharp on her cheek after four hours of driving; the press of Murdo as he held her and the unspoken tremor of his anger, so much more tangible than her own; the rasp of her own clothes over skin that felt everything more sharply than it had ever done before. Without any conscious effort on her part, time had slowed and would not speed up which was, very clearly, how it must have been for Luke.

Nothing was happening in the flat. She wound down the window and listened to the sounds of the morning – the rising swell of traffic, the playground taunts of kids on their way to school, a screaming row in one of the upper flats. Nothing out of the ordinary. Nothing she hadn't heard every day for three months and yet it had an ugliness to it that she had chosen to ignore in all the mornings of wishing herself back in the action. The grass is ever greener.

She took out her gun, checked it and slid it back into place. Her palms were wet. She dried them on her thighs. Her guts were in constant spasm but there was nothing she could do about that. She pulled her jacket from the back seat and stepped out of the car.

Maria Kilbride had not survived into her fourth decade in Glasgow without knowing how to lock her doors at night. A five-lever lock and two bolts guarded the front door. All the windows were double glazed and had good locks. The hinges on the back door were the weakest point and the wood would have given way had she shot it but it was necessary not to attract police attention too early, so Orla walked round to the front and pushed the knuckle of her left thumb to the bell.

'Fuck off.' The voice was sleepy and female, which was good. She kept her thumb where it was.

'Fuck off, I'm telling you. Whatever you're selling, I don't want it.'

She pushed the letterbox open and put her mouth to the space and whispered, 'Maria? It's Faith. Faith Maguire. I need your help.'

She kept her voice low, but it carried enough. The fish-eye glass at the front flashed and dulled. The voice inside had lost its torpor. It said, 'Stand where I can see your face.'

She moved into the line of sight where the scars would not be distorted. The lens flickered again before the bolts were withdrawn and the door came back on a chain. Inside, the redhead was barefoot under a half-worn dressing gown. Her hair clung to one side of her face. Remnants of mascara ran at the corners of eyes that showed white all round the rims. The woman pushed her face close to the opening and whispered, 'Faith, you daft bitch, get the fuck away from here. Drew Doherty's upstairs.'

'I know. His car's outside. It's him I need to talk to.' She put one foot in the door. Her gun hung loosely from her hand, hidden behind her leg. You would have had to be looking hard to see it. 'Maria, let me in. They won't hurt you for this, I swear it.'

'Why are you talking weird?'

'Because I can't be bothered to fake a Gorbals accent. Now will you open the door or do I stand here and call for the bastard to come down?' He was awake anyway; he would come down soon if one or other of them didn't go up. She had heard the cough and the hawk and the spit that still damned what was left of her dreams. The smell of him drifted out through the crack in the door, bringing the bile to the back of her throat.

There was still no move from the woman in the doorway. Orla shrugged. 'Fine. If that's the way you want it.' She leant back to look up at the bedroom window and took breath for a shout.

'Fuck. You *are* mad.' Maria Kilbride blinked and retreated. 'Get your foot out. I can't open the door with it like that.'

She waited until the front the door was shut and bolted behind her, then she let the girl see the gun. 'Go into the kitchen and stay there,' she said. 'If I fuck up and he kills me, tell them I threatened you,' and when the woman hesitated, she brought the gun up to press against her forehead and said, 'So now it's true. Would you rather I killed you to save them the trouble?' As they passed the kitchen door, she said, 'Make yourself coffee. Sit still and don't get in the way. You'll be fine.'

Drew Doherty was in the bedroom she had left two days before. The sheets had not been changed on the bed. His clothes hung on the chair at the far side of the room. He lay face down on the bed, crooning to himself, with the duvet pulled up round his shoulders and his bare feet hooked over the end nearest the door. He levered himself up an inch or two and fell back down onto the bed.

'Maria? Bring us a fag.'

'On its way.' As she said it, she crouched down to brace her elbows on her knees and keep both hands steady on the grip of her gun. The muzzle faced squarely into the arch of his foot. It twitched in time to the rhythm of his breathing but no more than that. When it was at its stillest, she held her own breath and squeezed the trigger. The gun spat and jerked in her hands and there was a moment of total silence as blood and meat and bone sprayed out across the wooden board at the end of the bed. Then he screamed.

It is only on celluloid that a man can take a gunshot wound to the foot and still think and act and speak with any coherence. In the real world, Drew Doherty curled tight on the bed in a howling, cursing, foetal spasm. Both hands clutched at the injured limb, dragging it up to his groin, twisting himself in knots in the sheeting, spreading blood at random. If he recognised her, or even saw her, he gave no sign.

She gave him time for the first wave of it to pass then she raised her gun and put the second shot in the pillow beside his head. The shock of it punched the bed backwards and the shock of that stopped the screaming. He lay very still, staring wide-eyed at the hole that had grown in the bedding beside him.

She held the gun steady. When he looked at it, she said, 'I want to meet Svensen. Tell me how.'

It took longer than it might have done for him to find where she was and then recognise what he saw. He smiled through lips green with pressure. 'Cunt. You can kill me, but he'll still have you.'

'I don't think so.'

His mobile phone lay on top of his jacket. She turned it on and held it out. 'PIN number?'

'Fuck you.'

The wound was in the middle of his instep, close to the line of the artery. Blood pulsed between his fingers. He breathed through his nose in a high whine. She angled the gun at his other leg. 'I have spare rounds enough to break every other bone in your body. Look at me and say you don't think I'd enjoy it.'

Sweat ran down the side of his face onto the pillow. He spoke past clenched teeth. 'Three eight seven two.'

'So much hate in one so young?' She keyed it in with the thumb of her left hand. The phone caught a signal and beeped. 'Fine. Thank you.' She held it out to him. 'Call Svensen, tell him you want to see him.'

'*What?*' His eyes were like Maria's, stark white at the rims. She hadn't thought to ask what drugs they'd been doing. 'Get tae fuck—'

The gun spat twice more. He lay rigid on the bed, his head framed by a triangle of holes. He kept his gun under the pillow, both of them knew that. If she hit it, the shattering round would blow back through the padding and his face would dissolve in a spray of hot metal. Both of them knew that, too. 'Jesus Christ.' He reached for the phone.

'He's seeing him already.' Maria Kilbride spoke from the doorway. She was dressed to go out and the bag in her hand held more than her overnight clothes. 'Tord called last night. They're meeting in the back room of Rose's café at ten.' She stared at the man on the bed and her smile was not kind. 'Am I not right?' she said.

Maria Kilbride was a woman and she was taunting him and she was not holding a gun. Some things happen on reflex and are all the faster for not passing through the barriers of thought. Like the fat grunt before him, Drew Doherty favoured a revolver. The explosion of it matched the bright blood on the far side of the hallway and came less than a second before the three husked coughs of the silencer. His head, his throat and his chest blossomed red.

His gun smashed the glass of water on the bedside table as it fell. Orla heard the pieces of it hit the floor one at a time as she bent over the small, slight woman lying like a thrown doll against the far wall. She felt for a pulse and found it, lifted an eyelid and saw signs of life. Her other hand keyed in the three digits on the phone without her having to think about it. It rang twice and was answered. 'Ambulance,' she said, and gave the address. 'Thirty-two year old white female, point three eight calibre gunshot wound, right shoulder. Severe haemorrhage, probable punctured lung. Don't fuck about.' She hung up while they were asking for her name and relationship to the victim.

'Maria?' The woman was barely conscious. Her head tipped sideways at the sound of her name. 'They're coming. I don't want to move you in case I make anything worse. I'll leave the front door unlocked and a note to say where you are. I can't stay. I'm sorry.' The fallen head stayed where it was.

She wrote the note. On the reverse, she wrote Alec Strang's phone numbers, work, home and mobile, and labelled them 'next of kin'. Before leaving, she ran back upstairs and lifted the dead man's jacket, tie and shoes from the pile on the chair.

The street outside was empty. It was not the kind of place where anyone ever heard gunfire, however close.

The ambulance passed her as she turned out of the end of the road.

An ambulance screamed past and turned left at the next junction. The man watched it with interest. 'A woman with a mission. I'm impressed. Even for Orla, that was fast.' Very soon, the box blinked on the dashboard. The man started the car and turned round in his seat, looking for a gap in the traffic. As he pulled away, he smiled at the child. 'Shall we go? While the magic is with us?'

The car was worth serious money and it was parked in a place where you wouldn't see it unless you knew where to look, which meant that there were brains behind the chequebook. The driver was a woman, young and quite tall and dressed down in jeans and running shoes and a black leather jacket that had seen action in any number of street wars. She wore tinted glasses on a day when the cloud layer hung not far from the rooftops but then everyone wore shades of some sort and without them she would have been marked out from the start. As it was, Rose Tanner, watching from the till, saw the heads turn and turn away again as the lass wove her way between the chairs. Anyone who knows the way into Rose's is an old hand and has a reason to be there. Only Rose knew that the woman had never passed through the door before.

'Morning.' Rose folded her elbows on the counter and made it clear that all orders went through her.

'Marlboro, Swan and tea. Thanks.' The money was already on the counter, right to the nearest penny. Her eyes skated past Rose and took in the wolf pack ranged along the back wall, the bitches on heat showing off in the window and the gap in the middle waiting to be filled.

'Anything to eat?'

'No.' Closer, the woman was more wiry than thin and there was a tension to her that you might get from a bad period or a hangover or coming down off the crack. Closer still, there were scars on her face and her temples that stretched her eye on one side and turned her smile to something you might want to avoid.

'Fine, if you're sure.' Rose smiled back, more for its effect on the audience than the woman. Rose Tanner smiled only for her friends and her friends were not to be fucked with. This much, she could do. 'Milk and sugar are on the side,' she said.

'Thank you.' The woman took milk, but not sugar which was what you would expect and then she stopped and picked up a copy of the *Sun* from the counter which went with some bits of her and not with others. She went to sit at the table with her back to the far wall, midway between the wolves and the window. The newspaper absorbed her. She read the front page more than once but that was not difficult; all but one column of the space was taken up with the picture of the wee boy who'd gone missing and the single column told his story. In between serving the kids on their way to school, Rose watched the woman tear off the front page and fold it in eight and slip it into the back pocket of her jeans. After that, she read the rest of it like everybody else so that her eyes looked at the pictures and her brain skipped over the words.

The front page was a tribute to Strang's ability to call in favours. The planned leader, whatever it had been, was gone. In its place, Jamie stared out at her in the best range of colour newsprint can provide. The shot had been taken as he lay in the hospital. He looked sullen and sore. If you knew him well, you would know that he was incandescently angry, particularly with the one taking the photograph. She would have liked to have been asked about that, or at least informed that it had happened. Beneath the print, a banner headline read simply HAVE YOU SEEN THIS BOY? Alongside it, three paragraphs explained the tragic story of young Jamie Buchanan who had disappeared, whereabouts unknown, believed to be in Glasgow. A further three pages inside were devoted to similar disappearances countrywide and the possibility of an organised paedophile ring. She tore the front page from the paper simply to see who noticed and how they reacted. Rose saw her but did nothing which was what she expected from Rose. The wolf pack and the window were too absorbed in the internal narcissism and convoluted pack dynamics to take any notice of a woman who was neither victim nor competition. Nobody else knew she existed.

She turned the pages of the paper and watched the rest of the room. Rose made her usual morning trade. Kids flowed in and out buying cigarettes and comics and roll-up and chocolate. Men on their way to work came in for their morning papers, those on the dole came in for tea to wash down the hangover out of hearing of the weans and the wife. Women came in for the same as the kids. At two minutes to ten, the man Orla had found and bought walked in wearing Drew Doherty's jacket, tie and shoes. He was not the same height but the build and the hair were right. He bought a coffee and, without asking permission, took it through the unmarked door between the ladies and the emergency exit. He didn't come back out.

Five minutes later, the door opened and a single man came in. It was the change in the wolf pack that made her look twice, a nameless shifting of status. One of the lower orders grinned and gave a poorly hidden nod that was pointedly not returned. For that alone, the subordinate was elevated to alpha male. She lifted her newspaper and studied the newcomer. He was not a tall man, but there was an athleticism to him that stood him apart from the rest and he was well dressed for Rose's place. He had dreadlocks that hung down on either side of a pale face. His eyebrows were dark. He stood in the queue and half turned to scan the room and his eyes were hidden behind shades that made hers look bland. When he smiled up the queue to Rose – who beamed back – his eyeteeth in the upper arcade angled inwards at five degrees.

The woman in the black leather jacket tried to light a fresh cigarette and discovered that her lighter would not produce a flame. In irritation, she dropped the newspaper on the table and joined the queue to buy another. The man ahead of her had picked up a copy of the same paper and was studying the front page.

'Not very flattering, is it?'

It took him a moment to realise that he was being addressed. In that moment, the gun, which had been in her pocket, came out of it and was shielded from the rest of the room by her body and his. Ahead of them, a school group of five argued over the choice between processed cheese or ham-in-a-tube for their sandwiches. The woman smiled her tight, taut smile. With her free hand, she removed her glasses. She said nothing but the barrel of the gun twitched sideways. The man laid his newspaper back on the counter. The knife thus revealed in his right hand gleamed dully. She held her left palm flat. Slowly and with exaggerated care, the knife was reversed and placed into it, hilt first. With very few additional gestures, a .38 revolver followed the same route. The woman's smile tightened. 'The emergency exit is open,' she said. 'I'm sure you know the way to the flat.'

Rose Tanner watched the man to whom she paid the bulk of her protection money walk through the wrong door with the young woman after him. She had two phone numbers printed on a slip of paper Sellotaped inside the front of her till drawer. The next time she opened the till, she picked up the phone and dialled six digits. On sober reflection, she replaced the handset without completing the number. This man gave orders and expected them to be followed to the letter. Her orders in this case stated that the numbers were only to be used in cases of extreme urgency and she had been strongly advised to clear the café of clients and leave after dialling either one of them. The man had walked through the door freely ahead of the woman. If he had wanted Rose to act, he would have let her know. In the absence of orders to the contrary, Rose continued with business as usual.

Luke was there. Sometime in the space between leaving the café and crossing the wasteland behind it, he had joined her. He hadn't spoken, but then perhaps he had no need. She stood with him in the place of his death, a basement room that had become a cross between a morgue and a forensics laboratory, a place of no light with an infestation of rats that smelled equally of old blood and fresh cat urine and fingerprint powder. In the absence of light, she had brought down the torch from the cupboard under the sink in the flat. Amongst all the useless junk in that place, it was one of the few things of worth, good and bright with batteries that worked. She swung it sideways and played the light along the wall until it caught and held a small pocked crater high up to her left. With her other hand, she lifted her gun from her pocket.

Colm O'Neil sat in Luke's chair. It was solid, unvarnished wood and Laidlaw's team had made no effort to remove the bolts that fixed it to the floor. They had left the roll of gaffer tape, too, on the seat. O'Neil held it now in his hand.

She brought the torch round to his face. 'Two choices,' she said. 'I can put a round now through each of your hands and your feet or you can tape yourself to the chair the way you did Luke.'

He watched her for a moment, considering. She was ten feet away, leaning up against the boiler. The hum of its working shook through her shoulders. The thermostat ticked in her ear. However good his reflexes, however fast his start from the blocks, she was too far for him to reach her and live. The door was too far back and she had closed it to keep in the light of her torch, locked it, to keep out passing strangers, and plugged the keyhole with the foil from her cigarette packet. To reach it would be to make a target of his back.

He raised his hands to the top of his head and swept them back, lifting the dreadlock wig like a cap. The hair underneath was the blond that Jamie had picked from the palette, stuck down with sweat. A fine red mark still showed along the brow line where the hairpiece had been.

It moved now, rising up in a frown as he dropped the wig on the floor behind the chair. He said, 'Orla, this is not going to work. I don't have the boy.' His eyes were steady and held hers without effort. She looked for fear and didn't find it.

Her thumb moved on the gun so that the safety flicked off. 'Drew Doherty's dead,' she said. 'He woke up with a hole through his foot.' She brought her hand up and sighted. 'Of course the range was less. There's always a chance I might miss at this distance.'

'Like you missed with Jared and Cas and Trent? I think not.'

She put the torch on the pipes and brought her second hand up to steady the grip, but he was already bending, folding the leg of his jeans against his shin to tape his ankles, left and then right, to the legs of the chair. He did it deftly as one would if well practised although, in honesty, it is not a thing that could be done badly; gaffer tape is not string and there is no man alive who could tear out of three turns by brute force alone. When he finished the second leg, he looked up.

'Take off your shirt,'

He considered that, too, for a moment and then shrugged and drew it off and folded it neatly and laid it at the side. Beneath it, his skin was the fish-belly white of long-term incarceration. The puckered seam of a surgical scar made a brighter line below his rib cage. As her eye touched it, moved over and came back, he ran his thumb along the full length. 'I had a misunderstanding with a fellow inmate when I first went inside,' he said. 'He ruptured my spleen. The medics took it out the next day in hospital.'

'And the other man?'

'He's dead.' He shrugged, wryly. 'Self defence.'

Without asking, he used his left hand to fix his right then took off his watch and laid it on the pile of his clothing and tossed her the roll. His eyes mocked. 'Your turn.'

She wound it more tightly than he had done and the skin on either side blanched with the pressure. He flexed his fingers, testing, and let them rest. She lifted the torch up on top of the boiler, shining it onto the wall at the side of his head so that the light spilled inward, flooding the right half of his face. His knife and her gun, his watch and her car keys lined up along the pipe beside her. Her cigarettes and the lighter went up on the boiler with the torch. Her father had joined Luke. They stood together near the opposite wall, far away from the light. Ciaran was not there yet.

She sat down on the single horizontal pipe that ran along in front of the chair. A black stain spread across the floor from his feet to hers; dry and already fading. She rubbed across it with her toe.

'How long did it take for him to let go of his cover?' she asked.

He tipped his head on one side. His tongue ran across one of the crooked eyeteeth. A small string of saliva stretched from the tip of it to his lower lip until the tongue swept back and smoothed it away. He said, 'Orla, why are you doing this? Your priority is the child and I don't know where he is. If I did I would be using him now to buy my way out. I am not doing that because I don't have him. You don't have time to play games.'

'I haven't played games since I was thirteen.' She stood up without meaning to. She was close to him now, close enough to feel the rhythm of his breath, to see the first wash of sweat on his shoulders and the gooseflesh on his arms. The knife had come to hand more readily than the gun which was, perhaps, why Ciaran was not there yet. She held it to his right eye so that the tip slid in between the lashes of the lower lid. A puddle of iced green reflected in the sheen of the metal. A single bead of crimson grew at the tip. 'Jamie's dead,' she said.

'Ah.' He closed both eyes. His breathing was tighter than it had been. 'Have you seen him?'

'No. But, as you said, if he was still alive, you would have started the barter on the way across from the café.' The bead became a welling line. 'At some point, no doubt, you will choose to tell me where to find the body. In the meantime, there are other questions that matter.' The knife was exceptionally sharp. The eyelid parted along half its length, showing the white of the eye beneath it. His breathing stopped altogether. She took a half step back and made herself think of things other than the child. 'Why did you go and take tea with my mother?' she asked.

'Because I wanted to see her. Because I wanted her to see me. I have spent the past twenty-four years believing that, of all of us, she was the most damaged by what happened the day your father died.' He shrugged, very slightly, not moving his head. 'We all make mistakes.'

'I don't think so.'

'You wouldn't.' He opened both eyes and made them rest on her face. Blood pooled in the shelf above his cheekbone. The knife hung steady in the space between them. He said, 'I can't tell you where the child is. I don't know. I can tell you who else might have taken him.'

'You're welcome to try.' She reached back for the lighter. 'Luke had three fall-back cover stories, did you believe any of them?'

'This isn't a—' He stopped himself before she did. He could think on his feet, which was good in its way. It was, no doubt, what had kept him alive for two decades as an outsider in the Maze. He said, 'He didn't use any cover stories, there was no point. I had a copy of the last tape he made for Strang and photographs of the drop and the pick-up.' There was a scar along the other cheekbone. It caught the light as he moved his head towards her. 'Orla, listen. Luke fucked up. I followed him to a drop and he didn't see me. From that moment on, he was dead. It was one of the risks of the job. He knew that when he started. I don't believe you didn't.'

'Nobody told you about us?'

'No. Who could do that? The pond life I was working with don't have access to that calibre of information.' He smiled, very slightly, tilting his head. 'You're not so paranoid as to think I'd turned Strang?'

'No. But I'd be curious to know who told you about Maria Kilbride.'

'She did. I only kill the ones who try to hide things. The ones who come to me of their own volition are different.' His eyes searched hers. 'You *are* paranoid. Who am I supposed to have turned? Billie Reid? Is there enough gold in Scotland to do that? Laidlaw? The man with the mission to clear filth from the streets of Glasgow. McRae? Now *there's* a—'

'Forget it, O'Neil. You're doing yourself no favours.'

She lit herself a cigarette. He watched the glowing end of it circle in the air. She blew the smoke upwards. 'Luke made the last drop ten days before you took him,' she said. 'Why did you wait?'

He sobered with commendable speed. 'Because he was more useful to me alive than dead. He was bringing me the biggest shipment this country has seen in years and he was sacrosanct. He could do whatever we asked of him and not a single member of the security forces was going to touch him. That kind of gift is worth waiting for.'

'Then why didn't you let him go on through to the end?'

'Because the shipment was the end. Half of Scotland would have been waiting for us at the pick-up. At best, we'd have got out alive. At worst, we'd have been inside again or dead. Instead, by taking him when we did, everyone who mattered was here. Half of them were taking pictures of Luke, the other half were watching you and the child in the hospital. The big men took their eyes off the ball and we got what we would otherwise not have got. It's called strategy. You win some, you lose some. That's the way it goes.'

'Is that right?' The cigarette died under her heel. The lighter flickered again in her hand and the knife-tip blackened above it. She played the flame along the length of the blade. 'What about the photographs Jared took of me? Were you waiting for them?'

'How do you—?' His eyes narrowed and cleared. 'Jamie?' He shook his head. 'Jared did that on his own initiative. He knew we were after Luke. It hadn't occurred to me that you were part of it.'

'But you recognised me?'

'Of course. I had your pictures on the wall of my cell for over two decades.'

'Then why did you take Luke and not me?'

'Why would I want you? He was the one who knew the details of the drop.' The knife shimmered in the heat. His nostrils flared wide. 'I would have killed you for who you are now, not what you were as a thirteen-year-old child. The past is over, Orla. I lost twenty-three years of my life, you lost your father and your brother, your mother lost her family and her career. None of it is good but it doesn't have to change everything we do in the present.'

'Oh, I think it does.' Ciaran was there at last, on his own and cheerful. She nodded to him over the top of the pale head in front of her.

The lighter snapped off. The blade came close to the gap in his eyelid. The man in the chair looked past it to her and said, very clearly, 'I am not responsible for the death of your father.'

He made the kind of noise Luke had made at the start; a choked, bitten grunt that came out through fixed teeth. And he wrenched his head to the side which was how he came to lose half of his ear. The heat singed the hair at his temple. The blade sliced down the side of his face, cutting into the cartilage and only stopped when she pulled it free. She moved it down to his throat and pressed the flat of it into the skin over his jugular and it was still hot enough to burn. In a voice without tone she said, 'Be very, very careful how you talk about my father.'

His eyes had closed again. He forced them open. His lips were white. His fingers pressed flat on the wood of the chair. If there was no fear, at least there was anger. He said, '*Colm Connaught O'Neil is innocent.* Do you remember when you last heard that, Orla? Do you? In your home, in the living room, from the mouth of a man with a mask on his face and a Sterling sub-machine-gun in his hand who was about to kill your father. How do I know that? How could I possibly know?'

She stepped back. The burn of the blade showed red on his neck. Blood flooded from his ear, washing down to his shoulder and onto the chair. None of it had yet reached the walls or the floor. The knife sang as a thing alive in her hand and the music called in every ghost there had ever been. If her mother had asked her the question now and she had given the same answer, it would not have been truthful. She took a deep breath and smiled and watched what it did to him. 'You should have stayed with the present, O'Neil, it was safer ground.'

'No. Not now.' His eyes were wide and there was grey at the edge of the green. 'Think, woman. Gaskill and Mayhew were dead in a ditch within eight hours of the shootings. You and your mother took the full blast of a Coke bottle full of petrol and I don't believe either one of you was telling stories to the neighbours before the stretchers came to pick you up. Still, it was on the front page of every daily in Ireland the next morning. '*"Colm Connaught O'Neil is innocent," say gunmen* and full colour pictures of you and your family, before and after. Who told them what Colin Gaskill had said?'

'You?'

'Christ.' He laughed and it was remarkably like the noise he had made before; bitter and harsh and bitten off before it finished. 'How would I do that? No, no, forget that.' He tipped his head back on the chair and she watched him fight for clear thought. 'Why? Why would I do something so spectacularly, so fundamentally stupid? I was a twenty-four year old postgraduate and I had never been out of Scotland. I had no paramilitary connections besides the one man who had given me the contract. I had three professors of law queuing up to give me a character reference and I had an alibi that even your father couldn't impugn. Until the hit on your family, I was sitting in the cells counting the days until I could go home and get out the chequebook.'

'You killed Patrick Colquhoun. My father knew that.'

'Of course I did. The money was extraordinary and I was promised a clean run. That's not the issue. We're talking points of law and that, as you are well aware, has nothing to do with the truth. Your father was building a case full of holes and he knew that, too. He couldn't prove that I had even held the gun that killed Colquhoun, still less that I used it in that place at that time with intent to inflict injury. Even in Scotland, all they need is reasonable doubt. In Ulster, he was a lapsed Catholic prosecuting another Catholic and we had a hand-picked jury. There wasn't a cat's chance in hell of them sending me down.'

The Irish came out in his voice at last, displacing the veneer of other countries. She listened to the flow of it and let the words go past.

'Then your father died and your brother with him and Morag and Orla McLeod were daily on the front page of the papers and I was the Catholic who'd killed for the Protestants, going down for life in Long Kesh.' He looked down at the scar on his abdomen. 'I was lucky. I made friends. Had I not, I would have died inside the first month which was, without doubt, the intention.'

He looked up. He was shaking in ways he had not been shaking before.

'*Think,*' he said again. 'This was never about me. I was an expendable nobody. It was never even about Pat Colquhoun, there are a dozen more where he came from, all desperate to prove their Irish roots. This was about killing your father in ways that could be attributed to nobody.'

Cold lodged at the base of her spine. Her father was leaning forward to listen. She said, 'Why would anybody want to kill my father?'

'Christ, woman, it was Ulster, is that not enough? Because he was an honourable man in a time of no honour, because he expected truth when the world dealt in lies, because he was accountable to neither side and he was wading through the deniable zone asking questions of men who didn't want those questions answered. I was offered silly money and told I would walk and I didn't see it coming. Gaskill and Mayhew were wound up and pointed in the right direction and they were dead meat from the time they walked in through your front door. The public had a nice chain of events that led back to no one. Obvious cause and expected effect and the bad guys dead or in prison. Clean. Finished. Over. No loose ends.'

He took a breath and slowed down. The shuddering stopped. More calmly, he said, 'The man who set me up was called Robert Christie. If he was happy to see me dead all that time ago, he's desperate for it now. I would have killed him already if I had known where to find him, but there's a death certificate in his name and, until very recently, I had no idea where he was. Now that I know exactly where he is and who he is pretending to be, he can't afford to let me live. His only problem is that he's never done his killing directly. The closest he got was yesterday when he tried to knock Andy Bennett off a mountain and failed. Then he took the boy and if you go on to the end of this – if you do what he's pushing you to do – he'll have got exactly what he wants without having to lift a finger to risk his precious new identity – and you will have lost Jamie Buchanan.'

She stood very still. The white noise in her head was giving way to the quiet rush of her pulse, like listening to the sea in a shell. The flickering presences faded back into the walls, all except Ciaran who wanted her to go on and her father who wanted her to stop. That was ever the way of things. She looked for Luke to give a third opinion and couldn't find him. In his absence, there was always his blood staining the floor at her feet.

The man in the chair stopped talking, suddenly, like a clockwork toy that has run out of time. She picked up his shirt from the floor and wiped the blade free of blood. Clarity flooded the places where there had been none before.

'That's very good.' She flipped the knife up so that it spun in the torchlight and came back to her hand. She lifted the gun and reversed it, holding the barrel and testing the weight of the grip. She felt something very close to peace. 'We'll call that cover story number one. Let me know when you want to change it. If you feel like moving to something new, you can tell me what you did with Jamie. If you don't feel up to that, you can tell me – since you brought it up – why you tried to kill Andy Bennett.'

The knife had two edges which was not ideal, but she didn't need them both to stay sharp. She moved the blade down to his left hand. When he saw what she was doing, he clenched his fist.

'Curious.' She frowned. 'How did you get Luke to—'

'Orla. If I wanted Andy Bennett dead, he would be dead.'

'You had more people, I suppose. You could get one of them to hold him still.' She reversed the gun again and pressed the muzzle into the back of his hand. 'You can lose a finger or you can lose the whole hand. It doesn't matter to me.' With something bordering on regret, she watched his fingers begin to unfold. 'You got very close with Andy,' she said. 'He's unconscious. They're not sure if he'll be a vegetable when he opens his eyes. And forensics are seriously upset at the lack of tangible evidence.'

His fingers lay flat on the arm of the chair. His whole arm was rigid. She balanced the tip of the knife on the far side of the small finger and rested the butt of the gun on the back edge of the blade.

His eyes fought to hold hers. He spoke fast and flat, to deliver the most information in the least time. 'I don't use a rifle,' he said. 'I never have. I use a handgun if I have to and I can use a knife like it was an extension of my own hand, but—'

The scream soared and stopped, as Luke's had done; as a great many of Luke's had done. The pattern of blood on the central heating pipes was a repeat of what was already there, but thinner and less widely spread. A long time passed before he came back to her from where he'd gone. In the space between, she tore a strip from his shirt and made a tourniquet at the base of his wrist, winding it tight with a pressure point over the artery. The bleeding had slowed almost to nothing by the time he opened his eyes.

'You were saying?' she said helpfully. 'You can use a knife like an extension of your own hand but – what? You can't use a rifle?'

'I can't.' It came out as a whisper. His breathing was ragged and got in the way of the words. His eyes were the black of oblivion with a thin rim of green. He said, 'Christie hit a moving tyre on the angle at three hundred yards and then two more in a hurry after it. How many men do you know who could do that?'

'I don't know any but I'm sure Alec Strang knows a couple. Equally, I'm sure you could hire one or two if you were desperate. I'm not really bothered about who or how, we can work that out later. What I was asking is why.'

She picked up the gun and the knife and moved round to his other hand. The fingers clenched tight far faster than they had done before. His whole body jerked on the end of a need to stand. 'No! For God's sake—'

'Luke had six hours, O'Neil. We've barely started.'

'You don't *have* six hours. You probably don't even have one. Jesus Christ, will you listen?'

'What for? The seventh cavalry is not on its way, I promise you. Strang will take the rest of Glasgow apart brick by brick and stone by stone before he ever thinks of coming here. He's a good man, but he's still a man. He thinks women are delicate and don't like to go back to the scenes of past traumas.'

'It's not Strang. It *isn't* Strang—'

'No, of course not. It's some mythical individual who is, as we speak, murdering Jamie.' She balanced the point of the knife on the back of his fist and raised the grip of the gun above it, as a hammer over a nail. 'Maybe next time you come round you might like to think up a name.'

'*Orla . . . ?*'

He had opened his mouth, to answer, or to argue, or neither, but it wasn't his voice that came out. A child whispered instead, a boy of nine who knew her best and who knew where she might be. She heard him moving on the far side of the locked door and then he did it again; an urgent stage whisper pushed through the blocked gap of the keyhole. '*Orlaaaa.*'

The world imploded around her. The light of the torch danced before her eyes. The knife came away from the back of his hand. She drew breath to shout back.

'*NO!*'

It was a word without sound; a tight, compressed pulse that hit her harder than when he had screamed. She let out the breath and lifted the knife, and the need to kill very nearly balanced the need to be with the child.

'Orla. No.' He said it again, urgently, in a voice so low it merged with the hum of the heating. 'That man can hit a moving six-inch square at three hundred yards. How difficult is a standing child? From the moment you let him know you're in here and alive, Jamie is dead and you with him.'

She hovered, frozen, on the balls of her feet. Outside, the child rattled the door handle.

'Orla, please, please listen to me.' The words tumbled over themselves. 'Hugh Carlaw is dead. He died eighteen months ago in the Aberdeen Royal Infirmary, ten years after his son, three years after his wife. He was five foot ten with grey eyes. Robert Christie is six one with brown eyes, he has never married and he has no children. He captained the Glasgow University rifle team for three years. He ran a business for all of his working life with offices in Edinburgh and Belfast. His father and brother were in the RUC. He faked his own death three weeks after Hugh Carlaw died. All these things are on record, they can be proved.'

She sank her heels back to the floor. The knife stayed at his chest. The noises at the door died away. She shook her head. 'Hugh Carlaw is one of the most reasonable, gracious, intelligent men I have ever met. He is a friend of my mother's. I don't believe you.'

'Yes you do. Reasonable men will kill if they think they have good cause. Look at the people you work with. And while you're at it, ask yourself why Andy Bennett had to go if it wasn't because he could identify him? Bennett was in Edinburgh at the time the real Hugh Carlaw's son died. Has he met Carlaw? Could he have said something to Christie? Has he? Look at me, Orla. *Think.*'

She didn't want to look at him. Instead she said, 'I am thinking. We checked Hugh Carlaw when we first went to the cottage. His record is clean.'

'*So?* Tell that to Murdo. Or Gail Morgan. If you look at the same records, you're married to Luke Tyler and he isn't dead yet.' He fought to catch and hold her eyes. She swallowed on nothing. Bizarrely, the shaking started as it had a lifetime ago in the flat. He said, 'We haven't got time for games, Orla. The man outside has Jamie. If he has the slightest reason, he will kill him. Does it matter what his name is?'

'Probably not.' A pleasing thought struck her. 'What will he do to you if he finds you in here?'

His eyes slid away from hers. For the first time, she saw fear she could believe in. He said nothing.

'Fine. So maybe there is a God.' She could breathe again, which was good. She slid the knife through her belt. The gun hung loose in her hand. She checked the magazine, because it was a reflex to do so and found it full. Her eyes searched the room, looking for other exits.

'Orla, how did he know you were here?' His voice was different. The despair ran deeper than it had done. She heard it and felt a small surge of elation.

'I don't know. I was just thinking about that. I borrowed his car. If he has police connections, maybe he has access to the right electronics to put on a tail.'

'Or maybe he has friends in high places. Maybe there's more than one of them out there.'

'Maybe.' There was no door she could see in the walls. She swung the torch in a high arc, looking upwards for ventilation holes.

'It's in the wall behind the boiler.'

'What?'

'The back way out. There's a door behind the boiler. It brings you out beside the fire escape to the flat.'

She looked for it and found he was right. The door swung open under her hand. His voice followed her. 'He'll use the boy as a shield. Even if you live, Jamie won't.'

'O'Neil?' She turned back and snapped the torch to his face. Her gun rose of its own volition. She eyed him curiously. 'Are you trying to get me to kill you?'

'No.' He had control of himself again. His eyes made a circuit that took in the tape at his wrists and the knife at her belt and came back to her face. 'I want Robert Christie dead as much as you do, possibly more so. You can't do it alone, not while your attention is split with the child. You need somebody else.' He smiled. The angled teeth shone briefly amber in the light. 'I am offering help.'

She was there. He could feel the closeness of her, smell the scent of her in the air. All the time they were driving across town, following the blinking light on the dashboard, coming closer to the places he knew, he had felt the proximity of her tugging at the core of him, like a distant shout. For in the car three blocks away from the flat waiting for something to happen, he had thought it but said nothing. Only when the man had started the car again and followed the blinking light to the alley at the side of Rose's café had he known for certain and chosen to speak.

They overshot the end of the road and pulled into the garage beside it to fill up with petrol. Jamie waited until the man had run his credit card through the slot and was holding the nozzle into the tank then he poked his head out of the window and pointed to the café and said carefully, 'Luke.'

It was the first time he had opened his mouth since they left the cottage. His voice was a little hoarse and perhaps not so easily heard.

The man frowned at him. The white brows twisted like string. 'Luke's dead,' he said.

Some things are too obvious for words. The boy nodded and pointed and said it again, more clearly, 'Luke'.

The man fitted the nozzle back in the pump. He leant over with his hands on the roof of the car. 'Let me get this straight,' he said. 'Luke used to spend time in there? Or you think Orla might have gone in there because of Luke?'

'Yes.' The child smiled brilliantly and said nothing more. His mother had taught him that.

'Right.' There was a queue behind them, waiting for the pump. The man got back in the car and drove it down the side between the garage and the café. He parked it behind a pair of tall, rectangular rubbish bins where it would not readily be seen from the road. He had switched off the box on the dashboard as soon as they found Orla's car. Now he took it round to the boot and found a space for it beside the longer of the two guns. He took off his coat and hung it over his arm. Coming back, he crouched by the door. 'OK, Jamie, I'm going to go inside and see if they know where Orla might be.' He reached in through the window and ruffled the child's hair. The boy didn't jerk his head from the touch. 'I think she's in trouble or she would have come back to the car by now. You and I are the only ones who can help her but we have to find her first. Do you understand that?'

The child who had, less than twelve hours before, been the bleating goat in the trap listened as his role was transformed to that of saviour. He nodded for that, too, because it was expected.

'Good lad. We'll make a hero of you yet.' The man patted him one more time and left, locking the car from the outside. At the door to the café, he turned and waved. The boy waved back. He knew Rose Tanner. Even at the age of nine, there are some things that are cast in stone. Her complete inability to answer the questions of strangers was one of them. Not that she wouldn't do her best to seem helpful. She could take half an hour seeming to be helpful. At the very least, she would buy him five minutes.

Jamie Buchanan watched through the window as the big, square-edged shape worked its way between the chairs towards the counter. When he could no longer see or be seen, he slid over to the driver's side door – which was the one without the child locks – undid it from the inside and let himself out. From there, it was a two minute run down the alley, out onto the wasteland and across to the flat. Because Orla had trained him and he knew that the man could track him across the mud of the wasteland, he turned sharply at the corner and took the longer route down the side by the wall where all the people walked and where his footprints were lost in the general mess.

She had gone to be with Luke. The certainty of it drove him. At the side door of the flat – the one leading down to the basement – he lifted his feet and dried the sole of each shoe on the leg of his jeans and then stepped far in over the threshold so that his wet footprints wouldn't be seen. Looking back, he was pleased with the way it had worked. There were other prints here, the zigzag tread lines of three men's boots in fading brown that led to the foot of the stairs. He tracked them down the short flight of steps towards the boiler room. The door, which was never normally shut, was closed to him now. He caught the handle and turned it. When that didn't work, he knelt low and put his mouth to the keyhole and whispered her name. The noise of it echoed about him and something else shifted in the wind. He looked round, sharply, expecting to see a man standing at the top of the steps but there was nobody there.

He turned back to the door. She had been there. He could feel her. He tried again, whispering her name in through the keyhole as loud as he could without raising a shout. For a long moment afterwards, he held his breath, waiting, but nothing happened. Frustrated, he gave the handle one last turn and then backed away.

The door to the flat was round at the front of the building. Of all the places in the world Jamie Buchanan very badly did not want to be, the flat came top of the list. Still, it was the next most obvious place to look. He was sitting on the steps thinking about this when the sound he had heard before happened again. He spun round, sharply. The man *was* there, standing in the doorway, carrying his small gun in one hand and the sight from the long one in the other. His smile was sharp, like a cat's. He nodded. 'Good lad, I knew you could do it.' He jerked his head over his left shoulder, in the direction of the front door. The gun made the same swing, turning a suggestion into an order. 'Onwards and upwards?'

The fire escape door was closed but not locked. She pushed it, praying for silence and was given, if not total quiet, at least not the expected scream of unoiled metal. It occurred to her that this way had been known about and prepared in advance as an exit or entrance and that neither she nor Luke had been informed. The small part of her mind that expected to survive took that in, matched it to what she had been told and stored the result for later.

She stepped out into the upstairs landing. The flat was cleaner than it had been. It smelled of dust and the technology of forensics and not of cheap perfume and sour food. Fine white powder covered the surfaces. In the bedrooms, the doors to the cupboards hung open and the contents had been removed. Everywhere showed signs of extraordinary activity, none of it recent.

'Downstairs?' The word came as a thought. Colm O'Neil was beside her. His gun hung from his right hand. His knife was in his belt, not hers. He wore no shirt. She nodded and put her mouth to his ear. 'One at a time. The edges make least noise. Fourth, seventh and ninth steps are loose.'

He went first. In the time it had taken to cut him free, they had framed the only set of tactics that made sense: the man she knew as Hugh Carlaw would not use the child as a shield if he saw Colm O'Neil, for the simple reason that it wouldn't work. He had made no pretence about that. 'He knows that I want him dead. Whether the child lives or not is irrelevant. For you it is the other way round.' Which was why she needed him. Which was why he was here.

He moved like a ghost and the stairs made no noise. At the foot, he stationed himself at the door to the living room and signalled. She wiped her palms on her jeans, took a fresh grip on her gun and stepped down.

For three months she had practised the route down the stairs and the rhythm of it came back without effort: one, two, three – miss one – five, six – miss one . . . and on to one of the only two floorboards that didn't move, the one running closest to the kitchen. Her head was empty of others' advice. Her head, in fact, was empty of anything but the whisper of a child, saying her name. She looked across the hallway and her eyes asked a question. In mime, it was answered. Her fingers tapped out a sequence on her arm. One, two, three.

Go.

It was easier than before, as if, having killed already in this place, the prospect came more easily a second time. Silently, she spun round the edge of the door into the kitchen Her gun led, an extension of her hand. Her left foot held the door to the wall, trapping anything or anyone behind it. It was broad daylight and the cloud was lifting and light from the window scoured the room as nothing else could do. The kitchen was empty.

Things sang in her head; disappointment and an echo of doubt. She was spinning back to check behind the door when a silencer coughed in the living room and a falling body hit wood.

Colm O'Neil had no silencer.

She stepped out onto the landing and stopped. O'Neil was ahead of her, clearly visible through the doorway, crouching down behind the sofa, pushing himself tight into the alcove at the far end. His focus was on the far corner of the room, the one closest to the door and furthest from the window. He raised his head, the better to be heard and said, 'Forget it, Christie. You've never killed with your own hand yet.' He spoke too clearly to have been hit.

'You'd be surprised what I've done in the past twenty-four years, Colm.' The voice was mannered and even and it grated like a boat over sand. She thought of how she could tell her mother and thought it might be better to be dead. 'Where's McLeod?'

'In the basement, where else? Were you wanting to take a look at the body?' He knew where she was. His free hand came up, palm out and flat. He pointed in the direction of the corner she had already identified. She nodded and pressed tight to the wood of the doorframe and waited.

'Later, maybe. When we've finished up here.' The gun spat again. The back of the sofa jerked and parted. A spent round hit plaster and tumbled across the floor. Colm O'Neil ducked further back in his alcove. In the flurry of silent movement, Orla switched to the other side of the door.

'You're a dead man, Christie. You should have killed me on the mountain with Bennett.'

'So it would seem. I thought you were a civilian or I would have done.'

'And you always so careful.' O'Neil rose on one knee. He had sworn he wouldn't shoot blind while there was a risk of hitting the child. On the strength of this, she had let him go. He raised his head and spoke again. 'How did you know McLeod would be here? I can't believe Jamie Buchanan would want to see Orla dead. Not when she brought him out of here and gave him a new life in the cottage.' That was said for the child. The words flowed and teased.

'She's not dead!' And so he was there. It was the first time she had heard him speak his anger out loud. She bit her lip and tasted blood. In the unseen half of the room, someone small struggled with someone large. It is difficult to fire a gun with any accuracy while one hand is holding a struggling child. She had caught O'Neil's eye and begun the final step forward, raising her gun, when the child choked and cried out and the pleasant, gravelled voice said, 'You know, Jamie, I think you might just be right.'

She stopped then, holding her breath. Colm O'Neil jerked down and was still.

'Orla?' He was moving. The voice came from somewhere new in the room. 'I have the boy. I'm sure if you look, you'll find you can see your nemesis from the door. Why you haven't killed him already is beyond me, given what he has done to you. That notwithstanding, if you kill him in the next thirty seconds, I will let Jamie go. If not, he will die.'

She could, indeed, see O'Neil from the door. He made a small, compact shape at the far side of the room, shielded between the sofa and the wall.

He sat very still with his gun raised in his right hand. The shirt bandage on his left was beginning to leak blood. With his eyes on hers, he said clearly, 'You're wasting your breath, Christie. The dead don't kill.'

'Is that right?' She could hear the smile. 'Well then, the child will die anyway and leave the rest down to you and me. Myself I think it would be a terrible waste of a young life but others might not see it like that.' The smile vanished. 'Twenty seconds and counting, McLeod.'

Time slowed to a stop. Green eyes filled all of her vision. The voice of a child held her mind. Her father and Luke stood together, watching. Neither of them offered advice.

Some decisions are simpler than others. Her gun rose to the horizontal and she fired. The man she had spent all but ten years of her life wanting to kill made less noise than he had done in the basement but then death can be a quiet thing. The bullet flattened itself in the plaster behind him. She fired twice more. The cough of the gun covered the noises of impact. In the silence of afterwards, his gun hit the floor.

'Thank you, Orla. It's very refreshing to meet someone so utterly reliable.'

Hugh Carlaw stepped sideways into view. The child came after him, unwillingly, fighting to stay clear of the gun at his throat. The door no longer blocked either field of view. She had swivelled sideways, aiming for his head when he moved. The mouth of his gun scored the cheek of the child and drew a gasp that was no longer angry, just afraid.

'Drop it.'

'Hugh—'

He grinned much as he had done in the forest, in the Manse over coffee, in the hotel when they met him for lunch; wide and in a way that showed the horse's gap in his teeth. 'Not Hugh,' he said. 'Hugh, regrettably, is no longer with us. I'm sure O'Neil did his best to explain. You might like to consider he was telling the truth, it will make more sense of the things that have to happen now. Please drop the gun.'

She did. It fell further and so landed more heavily than O'Neil's had done.

'Kick it forwards.' She did that, too. It skittered across the floor and lodged at the leg of the sofa. The child looked on. The meltwater eyes blazed fear and fury and a wavering hope. She smiled her best smile and stepped forward with one arm stretched out. 'Come on, Jamie, let's go home.'

Above his head, the adult smile was perfect. 'Sorry, Orla, nothing personal.' The gun left the neck of the child and began the brief journey upwards.

'Jamie, get *down*.'

She was going in and down, aiming for the boy and for the only space on the floor where there was room to roll and take him free. Beside her and in front of her, two weapons fired together, the one soft and sibilant, the other with a noise that shattered the world. In the moments of falling, she saw the child wrench free and throw himself to his knees, then something reached from the air and punched her round and she fell on her side which was not right at all for the roll and Jamie screamed her name in a way he had never done before. She reached out to hold him but her father was in the way and Luke was there at her other side and between them they gathered her up in their arms and held her tight and there was another crack of thunder that came from too close to be good and the black veil of night came in early and pushed her to sleep.

The phone rang twice before she picked it up.

'Yes?'

'Morag McLeod?' It was a voice she knew but did not expect.

'Yes.'

'You know who I am. I have just left your daughter. She's hurt.'

Too many questions. Her voice said, 'How?'

'Gunshot. Not mine, I promise you. If she lives, she can explain. If she doesn't, ask Jamie, he saw enough.'

'Is she—'

'She was alive when I left. I have called an ambulance and I believe they have grasped the urgency but you will understand that I had to leave before they arrived. Jamie is with her. He knows to tell them that

Orla is his mother and that you are the next of kin but he will need you very soon.'

In all the rest, that got through. 'Where is he?'

'In the place where it started. Ask Murdo. And Morag?'

'Yes?'

'When you speak to her, tell her thank you from me.'

'Why? For failing to kill you?'

'No. For choosing not to, twice.'

Epilogue

———•———

The waitress working alone in the upstairs luncheon bar of Bewley's was in her late fifties and served with the delicacy of another century and another country. Her accent was a variant of English found in those parts of the former empire abandoned by colonists at an earlier era of linguistic development. The man sitting in the corner ordered coffee for two with a grace that matched the service and the surroundings. It was the second day on which he had done so which made him, if not a regular, at least a man of good taste and admirable tenacity. Yesterday, he had allowed the waitress to remove the second cup when it was cold and his expected companion had not arrived. Today, he had asked her to leave it but had ordered a second for himself. On returning, the waitress found that the man had changed places and was sitting with his back to the room while the seat he had formerly occupied, the one with its back to the corner and the view from the window down the length of Grafton Street, was occupied by a dark-haired woman with pale, tired skin and a scar on her face and an accent that came from the north.

'Thank you.' The man's smile was less formal than it had been. He was glad that the woman had come. 'Orla, yours is cold. We could order another?'

'No. Thank you. Cold is fine.'

'We have a selection of cakes and pies,' offered the waitress. 'Luncheon will be served after twelve.'

299

'No. Thank you. This is fine.' The woman was tense and not happy with company. The waitress left.

'Thank you for coming. I wasn't sure that you would.'

'I'm not in the habit of breaking my word.'

'No. But you couldn't be sure I would keep mine.'

'You kept it yesterday.'

'You were here?'

'No. Murdo and Andy were here. They say you were alone. I believe them.'

'You should. I have no reason to lie to you.' He had made no effort to disguise his identity. She would have known him from his teeth alone, but his hair and his eyes were as she had last seen them and if he took care to hide his left hand, he did it in a way that made it seem natural. Only when he saw her looking did he bring it up into view. The tip of the smallest finger was missing. The cut end had healed cleanly.

'What do you tell people?' she asked.

'The truth. That I had a misunderstanding with a woman and she cut it off.'

'Do they believe you?'

'Of course not.'

The coffee was strong and bitter and entirely cold. She spun cream in the top of it and watched the tornado swirls smear into emulsion. 'Why are you here?' she asked. 'I could have had you arrested yesterday as you walked down the street.'

'I don't think so.' He was relaxed and very sure of himself. 'Ireland is a sovereign nation. You have no jurisdiction here. I am attached to the Canadian delegation working in the North which gives me at least nominal diplomatic immunity and I have well-placed friends – one very well-placed friend – in the consulate who would make it very difficult indeed for you to do anything that would destabilise the negotiations.'

'We could still kill you.'

'Not here. Not even Strang would push so far as to send armed

British agents into the Republic to shoot a man now. The political fallout would set the peace back decades.'

'You think they would notice?'

'I'm sure of it. There is one man who knows where I am and why I have come. The rest will want me back by tomorrow and will be visibly upset if I am not there. I have a certain unique insight into both sides of the sectarian divide. Twenty years of my life were spent living in close quarters with the key players without ever having been attached specifically to one side or the other. Odd though this may sound, they trust me not to lie to them. It makes me useful.'

'And in the meantime, you're selling smack to both sides so they have a decent income when all the shooting is finished? You do, of course, have a great deal to dispose of.'

He flushed. It was a new experience, to see him irate. 'And I am, of course, stupid enough to take an entire shipload across the Atlantic and back while being actively hunted for murder. Use your head, Orla. Money is manoeuvrable by electronic means, several hundred kilos of white powder is not. It's all in Glasgow where I left it. If Strang had bothered to look for it, he would have found it by now and no, I'm not going to tell you where it is. If the man hasn't the sense to go looking, it can rot where it sits.'

'So then why are you here?'

He was still angry and trying to control it. Salt had spilled on the table. He swept it together with the edge of his hand, making a neat, clean-edged square. When his breathing was less tight, he said, 'I'm in the North because I can provide a genuine service, because I care about the outcome.'

'How very noble. Why take the risk to come here?'

'Because I wanted to see if you were all right.'

'Don't give me that. The medical report is on the computer. You can look it up as easily as Murdo.'

'I can't, actually. I missed the computer revolution while I was staring at walls in Long Kesh. Without Gail Morgan, I couldn't have done half of what I did in Glasgow. But you're right, I can find someone else to do it for me, albeit without her flair for dramatics.' He swept the salt to the edge of the table, brushing it into the palm of one hand. The grains caught in the sweat of the creases, etching it white. 'So, for what it's worth, I know that you lost twelve units of blood in the first twenty-four hours and they operated twice to find the bleeders. On the second occasion, they removed a lobe of your right lung but that appears not to have diminished your respiratory capacity. It is estimated that you will be fit for return to work by the new year although on current evidence it would appear that you are already working.' He raised his head. 'You look better than I expected.'

'Thank you. Is that it?'

'Not quite.' He scooped the salt onto his palm. Without looking up, he said, 'Are you still married to Murdo?'

She stared at him flatly. 'The devil is over your left shoulder,' she said, 'if you were planning to throw the salt.'

He considered it for a moment then dusted his palms and the salt was lost on the floor. He watched it settle. 'Seven years' bad luck?'

'No. I think you have to break a mirror for that.'

'I'm sure it could be arranged.' They sat in silence. Around them, the tables filled with soft-voiced shoppers and loud, late-season tourists. The waitress flitted from one to the other, taking orders for soup and pasta and Irish stew.

Orla leant forward with her elbows on the table. 'I could leave now. Or you could tell me the real reason we're both here.'

'I really wanted to see you, to know you were well.' His eyes held hers without flinching and she didn't trust them at all. 'However, since we're on the subject, it would also be useful to know if I am going to spend the rest of my life looking back over my left shoulder for a woman with a knife in her hand.'

He said it as an afterthought, lightly, with no real weight but it was what he had come to find out, what he had taken insane risks to ask her in person. She smiled, knowing exactly what it did to the planes on her face. 'You mean you don't want to spend your life waiting for me the way Robert Christie spent his life waiting for you?'

'Correct.'

With impeccable timing, the waitress passed. Orla ordered more coffee. It arrived almost immediately and the cream, which she had barely touched, was replaced with a fresh jug. The coffee was hot. She drank it black. He watched her and said nothing. In a while, as she continued to drink and continued not to speak, he took his eyes from her face and leaned, instead, on the table with his left hand supporting his brow and his eyes on the window. The stump of his small finger curled into his hand so that it could have been whole.

She put her mug back on the table. 'If there was nothing else, perhaps I could leave?'

He let his hand drop away from his face. The pressure of it had left a mark on the skin below the hairline. 'In a moment. I have something to give you.' His left arm lay flat on the table between them. He pushed back his sleeve. The watch strapped to his wrist was one that she recognised.

'*Christ.*' Something rigid broke open in her chest. Flying fragments nailed her breathing to the back of her ribs. She stared and her eyes burned with the pressure. 'You sick, arrogant, mindless *bastard.*'

'Orla—'

'Fuck *off.*' She had no power to stand and run. Because he would not go away, she pressed her face in her hands.

'I'm sorry. I'm not doing this very well, am I?' The man who had once been Tord Svensen reached across and touched her hand. She shrugged him off. The energy of that allowed her to shove back her chair and reach for her bag. 'Don't touch me. I'm leaving.'

'No.' He stood before she did, gathering his jacket from the back of the chair. 'I'm sorry. I hadn't thought this through properly. I'll go. You stay and finish your coffee. Forget I ever came.'

She considered it. She very nearly let him do it. As he passed her chair she caught his sleeve. 'Stop. Don't go down. I have to go out first.'

He stopped. His brows arced. 'Or we will be the cause of an international incident?'

'No. They're better than that. Nobody would know you'd ever been.

But if you were telling the truth, we may be responsible for slowing the negotiations in Stormont. I wouldn't want that.'

'No. Of course not.' He turned so they were not making a scene that would upset the waitress. 'I have seen three.' He nodded down to the street below. 'I was assuming the fourth was at the rear entrance.'

She said, 'You have seen the ones you were supposed to see. There are four full units out there, plus Murdo and Andy and Strang.'

'The entire Division?'

'All of it.'

He sat down. His tongue traced the angled line of his teeth. A number of diverse expressions crossed his face, very few of them ones she expected. 'I could have let you die,' he said mildly. 'I didn't have to call the ambulance.'

'I didn't ask you to.'

'True.' They sat in silence. He scanned the street more carefully than he had done. 'No good deed goes unpunished.'

'Something like that.'

'Orla . . .' His eyes came away from the window. He stared at her, frowning.

She took a breath and reached for his wrist. The watch dug into her palm. 'Luke was wearing this when he . . . when you . . . in the flat.'

'Yes. I *am* sorry. I hadn't thought what it would do.' He drew up his sleeve for a second time. The strap came free without fuss. 'The glass was broken,' he said. 'I have had it repaired. I thought Jamie should have it. Or if not him, then Andy Bennett.' He turned the watch over. On the back was Luke's name as she remembered it, the engraving rubbed flat with two decades of wear. Beneath it, more recently cut, was a four digit number.

'What's this?'

He let out a breath through tight lips. His eyes caught hers and slid away. 'This, too, may be a mistake. It's a box number in Edinburgh in the name of Luke Tyler. If you write to me there, I will answer it within a month. I have set up a trust fund for Jamie. The seed money was one hundred thousand pounds sterling. Most of it has been invested in the emerging technologies. I would estimate a tenfold increase over the next decade. He can have access to it as soon as he's eighteen. Whatever the insanities of our politicians, it should be enough at least to see him through university and out the other side.'

She stared at him. Surprise curdled inside her. She stood, hooking her bag over her shoulder. 'I can't. You must know that.'

'At least take the watch.'

'No.'

'Please?'

It had been a mistake to ask for the corner seat. She had to squeeze past him to get out. He dropped the watch into her pocket as she passed. To give it back to him, she had to lift it, to hold it and that, too, was not good. It was heavier than she had imagined it to be but then it had been his grandfather's, made in the days when weight was synonymous with quality. For three months in the flat, the tick had counted their minutes through the days. At night, the solid, metal sound of it reached up through the weight of the pillows and rocked them to sleep. Every morning, on waking, he had wound the spring tight for the next day. Now, she checked the time against her own watch. It was out by three seconds. She curled her fingers round it and moved to give it back. To do that, she had to look at him which she did not want to do. She raised her eyes and stopped.

'Luke?' He was there, as solid and real as he had ever been. She held out her hand. By chance, it held the watch. He laid his palm flat on hers. *It's mine, kiddo. Do you want him to keep it?*

All summer, she had waited for him. It should not happen here. She wanted to hold him, to talk, to ask questions, to revel in the joy of his presence.

He put a finger to his lips. *Not now.* The breath of his passing brought her closer to weeping than she had been since her father died.

'Orla?'

'Don't speak. Just . . . don't speak.' She tipped her hand and let the watch slide back to her pocket. At length she said, 'I'll give it to Andy. If he wants to give it to Jamie, that's up to him.'

'Thank you.'

Like Murdo, he watched her too closely. She stepped past him. Outside in the street, members of other units saw her and moved their positions accordingly. He counted them with her.

She said, 'I came in here alone. That was all you asked. If I go out alone, nothing further will happen.'

'Really?' He didn't believe her.

'Yes, really. Like you said, this is not our jurisdiction. They're here for my protection, nothing more. When I leave, they will follow me back to the airport. If you give it half an hour, they'll all be gone.'

'And afterwards?' His hand was on her arm. The nub of the ruined finger pressed on her skin. 'Life doesn't end at the airport, Orla.'

The waitress was becoming restless. The queue stretched from the silk rope that had been pulled across the entrance, back down the stairs to the confectionery hall below. Orla broke out of his grasp and moved past him, charting a course towards the till. Before she reached the next table, she turned. He was watching her, not the others in the street, as she would have been. He had more sense than to ask his question again.

She said, 'I have a life to lead, O'Neil. I have a child to raise and a career to put back together. I don't have time to run in circles trying to find out what name you're using this month, what colour your hair is, what country you're living in.'

'So?'

Murdo and Andy were at the back of the queue. Neither of them had bothered to change their appearance. They, too, were growing restless. He saw them the same time she did. She signalled them to wait and took a step back towards him. 'So, as far as I'm concerned, you died in the flat with Robert Christie. I am not going to waste my life chasing a dead man.'

'Thank you.'

He sat very still. Some time later, he lifted his left hand, showing all of the fingers. She had already gone.